Kaleidoscope

Danielle Steel

SPHERE BOOKS LIMITED

SPHERE BOOKS LTD

Published by the Penguin Group
27 Wrights Lane, London W8 5TZ, England
Viking Penguin Inc., 40 West 23rd Street, New York, New York 10010, USA
Penguin Books Australia Ltd, Ringwood, Victoria, Australia
Penguin Books Canada Ltd, 2801 John Street, Markham, Ontario, Canada L3R 1B4
Penguin Books (NZ) Ltd, 182–190 Wairau Road, Auckland 10, New Zealand

Penguin Books Ltd, Registered Offices: Harmondsworth, Middlesex, England

First published in Great Britain by Michael Joseph Ltd 1987
Published by Sphere Books Ltd 1988
Reprinted 1988

Printed and bound in Great Britain by
Richard Clay Ltd, Bungay, Suffolk
Filmset in Monophoto 10 on 12pt Bembo

To three very special little sisters:
Samantha, Victoria, and Vanessa,
precious little ladies,

and their very big sister, Beatrix,
who is so lovely,

and their three big brothers,
Trevor, Todd, and Nicky,
who are very special too.

May each of you be blessed
with good lives, and good fortune,
good hearts, and good people to love you
and who you love well.
May you always be safe, and strong,
and happy . . . and together!

And may each turn of the kaleidoscope
bring you joy!
The first turn, which was our turn
brought you to us, one by one,
special gifts, greatly loved, precious people.
And may your own turns bring you love,
and flowers . . . never demons . . .
Hold fast to each other, beloved ones,
bring each other strength, and laughter
and good times and love . . . just as once
we brought them to you.

With my love, for you and your Daddy,
and with ours, for each other,
and you.
With all my heart.

ds.

kaleidoscope

the first,
   shimmering moment
      of life,
like a diamond
      in the sea,
   glittering
      in the noonday
         sun,
brightly lit
   and glowing
         flame,
a brand new name,
   a shining light,
then gentle twist
   and darkest night
         comes
            for the first
               time,
   then happy rhymes
      and gentle songs,
         hearts that belong
until one stands
         alone,
   from brightest
            dawn
   to deepest dusk,
from morning sun
to twilight dreams,
   fantastic schemes,

and lives
that sometimes
go awry,
such shining
hopes,
such sudden turns,
from bright
to dark
from grim
to grand
from joy
to sorrow,
always waiting
for tomorrow
and a twist
of fate,
a ray of hope . . .
with the faintest
sleight of hand,
the alteration
of all life's
schemes
and all its scope . . .
all with one tiny turn
of life's kaleidoscope.

Part I

SOLANGE

Chapter 1

The rains were torrential north-east of Naples on the twenty-fourth of December 1943, and Sam Walker huddled in his foxhole with his rain-gear pulled tightly around him. He was twenty-one years old and had never been in Europe before the war. It was a hell of a way to see the world, and he had seen more than he'd ever wanted. He had been overseas since November of '42, fighting in North Africa, and taking part in Operation Torch until May of '43. He had thought Africa was bad with the deadly heat and desert winds and the sandstorms that left you half blind with red eyes that burned for days and tears constantly pouring down your cheeks, but this was worse. His hands were so numb he could hardly hold the cigarette butt his buddy had given him as a Christmas gift, let alone light it.

The wind from the mountains went right through your bones, it was the worst winter Italy had ever seen, or so they said, and he suddenly longed for the torrid heat of the desert. He had reached Sicily in July, with the 45th Infantry, attached to Clark's Fifth Army, and after Sicily they had been in the battle of Naples in October. And the battle of Termoli after that, but for two months now they had crawled over rocks and through ditches towards Rome, hiding in barns when they found them, stealing what food they could, fighting the Germans

3

every inch of the way, and bleeding over every step they covered.

'Shit . . .' His last match was drenched, and by then so was the butt that had been his only Christmas present. He was twenty-one years old, and when the Japanese struck Pearl Harbor he had been at Harvard. Harvard – the thought of it would have made him laugh if he hadn't been so bone-tired.

Harvard . . . With its perfect life and its pristine Quad and its bright young faces so sure they would one day run the world. If they only knew . . . It was difficult to believe now that he had ever been a part of all that. He had worked so damn hard to get there. He was a 'townie' from Somerville, and all his life he had dreamed of going to Harvard. His sister had laughed at him; all she had wanted was to marry one of the boys in her high school senior class – any of them would do – and she had certainly slept with enough of them to audition for the part. She was three years older than Sam and she had already been married and divorced by the time Sam finally got into Harvard, after working at every odd job he could for a year after finishing high school. Their parents had died when he was fifteen, in a car accident on a trip to Cape Cod, and he had wound up living with Eileen and her eighteen-year-old 'husband'. Sam had walked out four months before Eileen's erstwhile spouse, and they had hardly seen each other after that. He had gone to see her once, to say goodbye, three days after he'd been drafted. She'd been working in a bar, had dyed her hair blond, and he had hardly recognized her in the dim light when he'd first seen her. She'd looked embarrassed at first, and there was the same cunning light in her eyes he had re-membered and always hated. Eileen looked out for number one, and her little brother had never meant much to her.

'Well, good luck . . .' She'd stood awkwardly staring at him in a dark corner of the bar, as he wondered if he should kiss her goodbye, but she'd seemed anxious to get back to work, and didn't seem to have anything more to say to him. 'Let me know where you are . . .'

'Yeah . . . sure . . . take care of yourself . . .' He had felt twelve years old again, saying goodbye to her, and he remembered all of the things he had never liked about his sister. It was hard to remember anything he had liked. They had always seemed like two people from different worlds, different lives, almost different planets. She had tortured him as a child, by telling him he was adopted, and he had believed her until their mother had whipped her one day and told Sam in her pathetic boozy way that Eileen was lying. Eileen always lied, she lied about everything, and whenever possible she had blamed Sam for whatever she'd done, and most of the time their father believed her. Sam had felt foreign to all of them, the big, burly father who had worked on a fishing boat all his life, the mother who drank too much, and the sister who partied all night. He had lain in his bed at times, imagining what it would be like to be part of a 'real' family, the kind with hot meals on the table, and clean sheets on the bed . . . a family from Beacon Hill perhaps . . . who summered on Cape Cod . . . a family with little children and dogs, and parents who laughed a lot. He couldn't remember ever seeing his parents laugh or smile or hold hands, and sometimes he wondered if they ever had. Secretly, he hated them for the tawdry lives they led, and the life they had condemned him to. He wanted so much more than that. And they hated him in return for his good grades, his bright mind, his starring roles in his high school plays, and the things he said to them, about other lives, other worlds, other people. He had once confided in his father that he wanted to go to Harvard one day, and his father had stared at him as though he were a stranger. And he was, to all of them. When he finally went to Harvard, it was a dream come true, and the scholarship he had won had been the gift of a lifetime . . . the gift of a lifetime . . . and then that magical first day, after working so hard for so long, and then suddenly three months later it was over.

The rain beat on his frozen hands and he heard a voice next to him for the first time, as he glanced over his shoulder.

'Need a light?'

He nodded, startled out of his memories, and looked up to see a tall blond man with blue eyes and rivers of rain pouring down his thin cheeks. They all looked like they were crying.

'Yeah . . . thanks . . .' Sam smiled, and for a moment his eyes danced as they had years before. He had been full of mischief once, aeons before. He had dreamt of being the life and soul of the drama club at Harvard. 'Nice Christmas, huh?'

The other man smiled. He looked older than Sam, but even Sam looked older than his years now. After North Africa and the Italian Campaign, they all felt like old men, and some of them looked it. 'Arthur Patterson.' He introduced himself formally and Sam laughed out loud as a gust of wind swept them both against the side of the foxhole.

'Charming place, Italy, isn't it? I've always wanted to come here. A truly marvellous vacation.' He looked around him as though seeing beautiful girls in bathing suits and beaches with endless lovely bodies, as Patterson grinned and chuckled in spite of himself.

'Been here long?'

'Oh, about a thousand years. I was in North Africa last

Christmas. Terrific place. We were invited by Rommel.'
He gratefully took the light from the tall blond man, lit
the butt and got two good drags before burning his fingers.
He'd have offered it to his new friend but there wasn't
time before the rain put out the mere half inch that
remained, and he looked apologetically at his benefactor.
'I'm Sam Walker, by the way.'

'Where you from?'

He wanted to say Harvard, just for old times' sake, but
that would have sounded crazy. 'Boston.'

'New York.' As though it mattered now. Nothing
mattered now, they were all names of places that didn't
exist. All that existed were Palermo, Sicily, and Salerno,
and Naples, and Rome, their ultimate goal, if they ever
got there.

The tall blond man looked around him, squinting in the
wind and rain. 'I was a lawyer before all this.'

Sam would have been impressed, but like the places
they were from, the people they had been no longer
mattered. 'I wanted to be an actor.' It was something he
had told hardly anyone, certainly not his parents before
they died, or his sister after that, and only a few friends,
but even they had laughed at him. And his teachers had
told him that he needed to study something more
worthwhile. But none of them understood just what acting
meant to him, what happened when he stepped on stage.
It was like magic reaching from his soul, transforming
him into the character he was playing. Gone were the
parents he had hated, the sister he had loathed and all his
own fears and insecurities with them. But no one seemed
to understand that. Not even at Harvard. Harvard men
weren't actors, they were doctors and lawyers and busi-
nessmen, heads of corporations and foundations, and
ambassadors . . . He laughed softly to himself again. He

7

sure as hell was an ambassador now, with a gun in his hand, and his bayonet fixed all the time so that he could run it through the guts of his enemies as he had time and time again in the past year. He wondered how many men Patterson had killed, and how he felt about it now, but it was a question you didn't ask anyone, you just lived with your own thoughts and the memories of the twisted faces and staring eyes as you pulled your bayonet out again and wiped it on the ground. He looked up at Arthur Patterson with the eyes of an old man and wondered briefly if either of them would be alive to see another Christmas.

'What made you want to be an actor?'

'Hmm?' He was startled by the serious look in the other man's eyes, as they both sank to a sitting position on a rock planted in the mud near their feet as the water in the foxhole swirled around them. 'Oh, that . . . Christ, I don't know . . . it seemed like an interesting thing to do.' But it was more than that, much more than that, it was the only time he felt whole, that he felt powerful and sure of himself. But he couldn't tell this guy that. It was ridiculous to talk about dreams sitting in a foxhole on Christmas Eve.

'I was in the glee club at Princeton.' It was an absurd exchange, and suddenly Sam Walker gave a crack of laughter.

'Do you realise how crazy we are? Talking about glee clubs and drama clubs and Princeton, sitting in this goddam foxhole? Do you realise we probably won't even be alive by next week, and I'm telling you I wanted to be an actor . . .' He suddenly wanted to cry through his own laughter. It was all so goddam awful, but it was real, it was so real they could taste it and feel it and smell it. He had smelled nothing but death for a year, and he was sick of it. They all were, while the generals planned their attack on

8

Rome. Who gave a damn about Rome anyway? Or Naples or Palermo? What were they fighting for? Freedom in Boston and New York and San Francisco? They already were free, and at home people were driving to work, and dancing at the USO and going to the movies. What the hell did they know about all this? Nothing. Absolutely goddam nothing. Sam looked up at the tall blond man and shook his head, his eyes full of wisdom and sadness, the sudden laughter gone. He wanted to go home . . . to anyone . . . even his sister, who had not written to him once since he'd left Boston. He'd written to her twice and then decided it wasn't worth the trouble. The thought of her always made him angry. She had embarrassed him for all of his teenage years, and several before that, just as his mother had . . . and his stolid, taciturn father. He hated all of them, and now he was here, alone, with a stranger who had been in the glee club at Princeton, but he already liked him.

'Where'd you go to school? Patterson seemed desperate to hold on to the past, to remember old times, as though thinking about it would take them back there, but Sam knew better than that. The present was right here, in the filth and frozen rain of the foxhole.

Sam looked at him with a lopsided grin, wishing he had another cigarette, a real one, not just half an inch of someone else's. 'Harvard.' At Harvard he had had real cigarettes, any time he wanted – Lucky Strikes. The thought of them almost made him weep with longing.

Patterson looked impressed. 'And you wanted to be an actor?'

Sam shrugged. 'I guess . . . I was majoring in English lit. I probably would have ended up teaching somewhere, and running the school plays for snotty freshmen.'

'That's not a bad life. I went to St Paul's, we had a hell

of a drama club there.' Sam stared at him, wondering if he was for real . . . Princeton, St Paul's . . . what were they all doing here? What were any of them doing here? . . . especially the boys who had died here.

'You married?' Sam was curious about him now, like a Christmas angel who had been visited on him, he appeared different in every possible way, and yet they seemed to have some things in common.

Arthur shook his head. 'I was too busy starting my career. I worked for a law firm in New York. I'd been there for eight months when I signed up.' He was twenty-seven and his eyes were serious and sad where Sam's were full of mischief. Sam's hair was as black as Arthur's was fair, and he had a medium build with powerful shoulders, long legs for his size, and a kind of energy about him which Arthur seemed to lack. Everything about Arthur Patterson was more restrained, more tentative, quieter, but then Sam was also younger.

'I have a sister in Boston – if she hasn't got herself killed by some guy in a bar by now.' It seemed important to share information about themselves, as though they might not have another chance, and they each wanted someone to know them. They wanted to be known before they died, to make friends, to be remembered. 'We never got along. I went to see her before I left, but she hasn't written since I've been gone. You? Sisters? Brothers?'

Arthur smiled for the first time in a while. 'I'm an only child, of only children. My father died when I was away at school, and my mother never remarried. This is pretty hard on her. I can tell in her letters.'

'I'll bet.' Sam nodded, trying to think of what Arthur's mother would be like, trying to envisage her: a tall, spare woman with white hair that had once been blond, probably from New England. 'My parents died in a car accident when I was fifteen.' He didn't tell Arthur that it was no loss, that he had hated them, and they had never understood him. It would have been too maudlin now, and it was no longer important. 'Have you heard anything about where we go from here?' It was time to think about the war again, there was no point dwelling too much in the past. It would get them nowhere. Reality was here, north-east of Naples. 'I heard something about Cassino yesterday, that's over the mountains. It ought to be fun getting there.' Then they could worry about snow instead of rain. Sam wondered what other tortures they had in store for them at the hands of the generals who owned their lives now.

'The sergeant said something about Anzio last night, on the coast.'

'Great.' Sam smiled wickedly. 'Maybe we can go swimming.'

Arthur Patterson smiled, he liked this outspoken boy from Boston. One sensed that beneath the bitterness born of war there was a light heart and a bright mind, and at least it was someone he could talk to. The war had been hard on Arthur in a lot of ways. Spoiled as a boy, over-protected as a young man, particularly after his father died, and brought up by a doting mother in a highly civilized world, war had come as a brutal shock to him. He had never been uncomfortable in his life, or endangered, or frightened, and he had been all of those endlessly since arriving in Europe. He admired Sam for surviving it as well as he had.

Sam pulled out the K-rations he had been saving as his Christmas treat, and opened them with a wry face. He had already given away the candy to some local children. 'Care for a little Christmas turkey? The dressing's a little rich, but the chestnuts are marvellous.' He offered the pathetic tin with a flourish and Arthur laughed. He liked Sam a lot. He liked everything about him, and instinctively sensed that he had the kind of courage he himself didn't have. He just wanted to survive and get home again to a warm bed, and clean sheets, and women with blonde hair and good legs who had gone to Wellesley or Vassar.

'Thanks, I've already eaten.'

'Mmm . . .' Sam murmured convincingly, as though eating pheasant under glass, 'fabulous cuisine, isn't it? I never realised the food was this good in Italy.'

'What's that, Walker?' The sergeant had just crawled past them, and stopped to stare at them both. He had no problems with Sam, but he kept an eye on him, the boy had too much fire for his own good, and had already risked his life foolishly more than once. Patterson was another story, no guts, and too goddam much education. 'You got a problem?'

'No, Sergeant. I was just saying how great the food is here. Care for a hot biscuit?' He held out the half-empty tin as the sergeant growled.

'Cut it out, Walker. No one invited you over here for a party.'

'Damn . . . I must have misread the invitation.' Undaunted by the sergeant's stripes or the scowl, he laughed and finished his rations as the sergeant crawled past them in the driving rain, and then glanced over his shoulder.

'We're moving on tomorrow, gentlemen, if you can take time out from your busy social schedules.'

'We'll do our best, Sergeant . . . our very best . . .' With a grin in spite of himself, he moved on, and Arthur Patterson shuddered. The sergeant admired Sam's ability to laugh, and make the other men laugh too. It was something they all needed desperately, particularly now. And he knew they were in for tougher times ahead. Maybe even Walker wouldn't be laughing.

'That guy's been riding my ass since I got here,' Arthur complained to Sam.

'It's part of his charm,' Sam muttered as he felt in his pockets for another butt, in case he'd forgotten one, and then like the gift of the Magi, Arthur pulled out an almost whole cigarette. 'My God, man, where did you get that?' His eyes grew wide with desire as Arthur lit it and handed it to him. 'I haven't seen that much tobacco since the one I took off a dead German last week.' Arthur shuddered at the thought, but he imagined Sam was capable of it. It was partially the callousness of youth, and partially the fact that Sam Walker had courage. Even sitting quietly in the foxhole, cracking bad jokes, and talking about Harvard, one sensed that.

They slept huddled side by side that night and the rain abated the next morning. The following night they slept in a barn they'd taken over in a minor skirmish, and two days later they headed for the Volturno River. It was a brutal march that cost them more than a dozen men, but by then Sam and Arthur were fast friends. It was Sam who literally dragged Arthur and finally half carried him when he swore he could no longer walk, and it was Sam who saved him from a sniper who would have killed them all.

When the invasions at Nettuno and Anzio failed, the brunt of breaking through the German line at Cassino fell to Sam and Arthur's division. And this time Arthur was wounded. He took a bullet in the arm, and at first Sam thought he was dead when he turned to him as the shot whizzed past him. Arthur lay with blood all over his chest, and his eyes glazed, as Sam ripped his shirt open, and then discovered that he had been hit in the arm. He carried him behind the lines to the medics and stayed with him until he was sure he was all right, and then he went back and fought until the last retreat, but it was a depressing ordeal for all of them.

The next four months were a nightmare. In total, 59,000 men died at Anzio. And Sam and Arthur felt as though they had crawled through every inch of mud and snow in Italy as the rains continued, and they made their way north to Rome. Arthur was restored to duty rapidly, and Sam was thrilled to have him near at hand again. In the weeks before Arthur was shot, they had developed a bond which neither of them spoke of, but both felt deeply. They both knew it was a friendship that would stand the test of time, they were living through hell together and it was something neither of them would ever forget. It meant a lot more than anything in their past, and for the moment even anything in their future.

'Come on, Patterson, get off your dead ass.' They had been resting in a valley south of Rome, in the steady march to defeat Mussolini. 'The sergeant says we move out in half an hour.' Patterson groaned, without moving. 'Lazy fart, you didn't even have to fight in Cassino.' In the weeks after Arthur had been hit, they had struggled for Cassino, and fought until the entire town was reduced to rubble. The smoke had been so thick that it had actually taken several hours to see that the huge monastery had been totally destroyed and had virtually disappeared from the shelling. There had been no major battles since then, but constant skirmishes with the Italians and the Germans. But since 14th May, their efforts had been stepped up, as they joined the Eighth Army to cross the Garigliano and Rapido rivers, and by the following week all of the men were exhausted. Arthur looked as though he could have slept for a week, if only Sam would let him. 'Up, man, up!' Sam nudged him with his boot. 'Or are you waiting for an invitation from the Germans?'

Arthur squinted up at him through one eye, wishing he could doze for another moment. The wound still bothered him from time to time, and he tired more easily than Sam, but he had before the wound too. Sam was tireless, but Arthur told himself that he was also younger. 'You better watch it, Walker . . . you're beginning to sound just like the sergeant.'

'You gentlemen have a problem?' He always seemed to appear at the least opportune moments, and to have a sixth sense about when his men were talking about him, and in less than flattering terms. As usual, he had materialized behind Sam, and Arthur scrambled quickly to his feet with a guilty look. The man had an uncanny knack for finding him at his least prepossessing. 'Resting again, Patterson?' Shit. There was no pleasing the man. They had been marching for weeks, but like Sam, the sergeant never seemed to get tired. 'The war's almost over, if you can just stay awake long enough to watch us win it.' Sam grinned, and the crusty sergeant stared at him, but there was an *entente* between the two men, a mutual respect which totally eluded Arthur. He thought he was a sonofabitch to his very core, but he knew that secretly Sam liked him.

'You planning to get your beauty sleep too, Walker, or can we get you two on your feet long enough to join us in Rome?'

'We'll try, Sergeant . . . we'll try.' Sam smiled sweetly, as the sergeant roared over his head to the others.

'Move 'em outtttt!!!! . . .' He hurried on ahead to roust them and ten minutes later they were heading north again, and it felt to Arthur as though they never stopped until 4th June, when, exhausted beyond words, he found himself literally staggering through the Piazza Venezia in Rome, being pelted with flowers, and kissed by shrieking Italians. Everywhere around them was noise and laughter and singing and the shouts of his own men, and Sam with a week-old beard shouting in delight at him and everyone in sight.

'We made it! We made it! *We made it!*' There were tears of joy in Sam's eyes, matched by those in the eyes of the women who kissed him, fat ones, thin ones, old ones, young ones, women in black and in rags and in aprons and cardboard shoes, women who might have, at another time, been beautiful but no longer were after the ravages of war, except to Sam they all looked beautiful. One of them put a huge yellow flower into the mouth of his gun and Sam held her in his arms so long and hard that Arthur grew embarrassed watching.

They dined that night in one of the little trattorias that had been thrown open for them, along with a hundred other soldiers and Italian women. It was a festival of excitement and food and song, and for a few hours it seemed like ample reward for the agonies they'd been through. The mud and the filth and the rain and the snows were almost forgotten. But not for long. They had three weeks of revelry in Rome and then the sergeant gave them the word that they were moving out. Some of the men were staying in Rome, but Sam and Arthur were not among them. Instead, they would be joining Bradley's First Army near Coutances in France, and for a while, they told themselves it couldn't be a very difficult assignment. It was early summer, and in Italy and France the countryside was beautiful, the air was warm, and the women welcomed them, along with a few German snipers.

The sergeant saved Sam's hide this time, and in return two days later Sam kept the entire platoon from being caught in an ambush. But on the whole, it was an easy move with the German army in full retreat by mid-August. They were to press through France, join General LeClerc's French division and march on Paris. As the word filtered through the ranks, Sam quietly celebrated with Arthur.

'Paris, Arthur . . . sonofabitch! I've always wanted to go there!' It was as though he'd been invited to stay at the Ritz and go to the Opera and the *Folies-Bergère*.

'Don't get your hopes up, Walker. You may not have noticed, but there's a war on. We may not live long enough to see Paris.'

'That's what I love about you, Arthur. You're always so optimistic and cheerful.' But nothing could dampen Sam's spirits. All he could think of was the Paris he had read about and dreamed about for years. In his mind, nothing had changed, and it would all be there, waiting for him, and for Arthur. He could talk of nothing else as they marched through towns and villages filled with excitement and the end of four years of bitter occupation. Sam was obsessed by the dream of a lifetime, and even the thrill of Rome was forgotten now as they fought their way to Chartres in the next two days, and the Germans were retreating methodically toward Paris, as though leading them to their goal, and what Arthur was sure would be total destruction.

'You're crazy. Has anyone told you that, Walker? Crazy. Totally insane. You act as though you're going on a vacation.' Arthur stared at him in total disbelief as Sam rattled on between killing Germans. He even forgot to raid their pockets for cigarettes, he was so excited.

In the early hours of 25th August Sam's dream came true. And in an eerie hush, with eyes watching them from every window, they marched into Paris. It was totally unlike their victorious march on Rome. Here, the people were frightened, cautious, slow to come out of their houses and hiding places, and then little by little, they emerged, and suddenly there were shouts and embraces and tears, not unlike Rome, but it all took a little longer.

By two-thirty that afternoon, General von Choltitz surrendered and Paris had been officially liberated by the Allies, and when they marched down the Champs-Elysées in the victory parade four days later on 29th August Sam unashamedly cried as he marched with his comrades. The thought of how far they had come and how much they had accomplished, and that they had freed the Paris of his dreams left him breathless. And the shouts from the people who lined the streets only made him cry more, as the troops marched from the Arc de Triomphe to Notre Dame for a service of thanksgiving. Sam realized he had never been as grateful for anything in his life as he was for having survived the war this far, and having come to this remarkable city to bring freedom to its people.

After the services at Notre Dame, Arthur and Sam were deeply moved as they left the Cathedral and they walked slowly down the rue d'Arcole. They were free for the rest of the afternoon, and for a moment Sam couldn't even think of what he wanted to do, he just wanted to walk and drink it all in and smile at the people. They stopped for a cup of coffee at a tiny bistro on a corner, and were given a small steaming cup of the chicory everyone drank, and a plate of tiny biscuits by the owner's wife as she kissed them on both cheeks. When it came time to leave she wouldn't let them pay, no matter how much they insisted. Arthur spoke a little French, and Sam could only gesture his thanks and kiss the woman again. They knew only too well how short of food everyone was, and the gift of biscuits was like bars of gold, offered to a stranger.

Sam was speechless with awe as they left the bistro.

Maybe the war hadn't been so bad after all. Maybe it was all worth it. He was twenty-two years old, and he felt as though he had conquered the world, or at least the only part that mattered. Arthur smiled down at him as they walked. For some reason, Rome had moved him more. Perhaps because he had also spent time there before the war, and Rome had always been a special place for him, the way Paris seemed to be for Sam, even though he had never been there.

'I don't ever want to go home, you know that, Patterson? Sounds nuts, doesn't it?' As he said it, he noticed a young woman walking ahead of them, and he was distracted when Arthur answered. She had flaming red hair pulled back in a knot at the nape of her neck, and a navy-blue crepe dress that was so old it was shiny, but which showed all the rich curves of her figure. There was a proud tilt to her head, as though she had nothing to thank anyone for – she had survived the Germans, and she owed nothing to anyone now, not even the Americans or the Allies who had freed Paris. Everything she felt was spoken by the way she carried herself, and Sam stared at her shapely legs and the sway of her hips as they followed her down the street, all conversation with Arthur halted.

'. . . Don't you think?' Arthur asked him.

'What?' Sam couldn't concentrate on what he was saying. All he could see was the red hair and the slim shoulders, and the proud way she moved. She stopped at the corner, and then crossed the bridge over the Seine and turned down the Quai de Montebello as Sam unconsciously followed her.

'Where are you going?'

'I don't know yet.' His voice was intense, his blue eyes serious, as though if he lost her from sight for a moment, something terrible would happen.

'What are you doing?'

'Hmm? . ' He looked at Arthur for the merest instant and then quickened his pace, as though terrified to lose the girl. And then suddenly, Arthur saw her too. He looked at her just in time to see her face turned toward them, as though she suddenly sensed them behind her. She had a face like a cameo, with creamy white skin, delicate features and huge green eyes that bore right into them, one by one, and her gaze seemed to stop on Sam, as though warning him to keep his distance.

He was paralysed by his lack of French and the crushing look she gave him, but when she began to walk again, he followed her with even greater determination. 'Have you ever seen a face like that?' he asked Arthur without glancing at him. 'She's the most beautiful woman I've ever seen.' There was an aura about her that easily captivated the attention, and a strength one could sense even at a distance. This was not a girl throwing flowers at the Allied troops, or ready to throw her arms around the nearest soldier. This was a woman who had survived the war, and was ready to thank no one for it.

'She's a pretty girl,' Arthur agreed, sensing the inadequacy of his own words, but feeling somewhat embarrassed, too, by Sam's dogged pursuit of her every step. 'I don't think she's too pleased at having us follow her, though.' That was clearly an understatement.

'Say something to her.' Sam was totally mesmerized by her as the distance between them narrowed.

'Are you crazy? That wasn't exactly a friendly look she threw us a minute ago.' And they both watched her disappear into a shop, while they stood helplessly outside on the pavement.

'Now what?' Arthur looked embarrassed to be pursuing this woman on a Paris street. Liberation or no, it seemed an awkward thing to be doing, and he didn't like it.

'We'll wait for her. Let's invite her out for a cup of coffee.' He suddenly wished he had saved the plate of tiny biscuits. She was awfully thin; she probably hadn't seen anything like that in years, and she deserved them. All he'd done was crawl his way across North Africa and Italy on his belly, and march through France on his knees. Hell, what was that in comparison to surviving occupation by the Germans, particularly as a woman. Suddenly, he wanted to save her from everything that had ever happened to her, and anything that could happen now with thousands of Allied troops running crazed all over Paris.

She emerged from the shop carrying two eggs in a basket and a loaf of bread, and she glanced at them with obvious annoyance when she saw them waiting outside for her. Her eyes blazed as she said something directly to Sam which he didn't understand and he quickly turned to Arthur for a translation.

'What did she say?' It was obviously not anything endearing, but even that didn't seem to matter now. At least she had spoken to them, and there was a faint blush on Arthur's cheeks as he glanced at Sam in annoyance. This was most unlike him. He had behaved himself on the whole in Rome and every place else they went, with the exception of a few pinches and hugs and kisses, but this was something new, and Arthur was not at all sure he liked it.

'She said that if we take one step near her, she's going to go to our commanding officer and have us arrested. And frankly, Walker, I think she means it.'

'Tell her you're a general.' Sam grinned, seeming to regain some of his aplomb and good humour, as his desperation left him. 'Christ . . . tell her I'm in love with her.'

'Shall I offer her a candy bar and silk stockings too, while I'm at it? For heaven's sake, Sam, come to your senses and leave the girl alone.' She stopped in another shop just then, and it was obvious that Sam had no intention of leaving. 'Come on . . .' Arthur tried to induce him to leave, but to no avail, she came out of the shop as they were still arguing about it, and this time she walked right up to both of them, and stood so close to them that Sam thought he was going to faint from the sheer impact of being so near to her body. Her skin was so creamy-looking that he wanted to reach out and touch her arm, as she blazed at them in her very limited English.

'Go out! Go back! Go away!' she said, but despite the odd choice of words, they both got the message. She looked as though she were going to slap them, particularly Arthur, as though she expected him to be the sensible one and do something about Sam. '*C'est compris?*'

'No . . .' Sam immediately launched into frantic conversation with her. 'No *compris* . . . I don't speak French . . . I'm American . . . My name is Sam Walker, and this is Arthur Patterson. We just wanted to say hello and . . .' He gave her his most winning smile, and something in her eyes was angry and hurt beyond anything Sam could have understood, anything he had ever felt or experienced, and he felt desperately sorry for her.

'*Non!*' She waved her arms at them. '*Merde! Voilà! C'est compris?*'

'*Merde?*' Sam looked blank and turned to Arthur for translation. 'What's "*merde*"?'

'It means shit.'

'Very nice.' Sam smiled as though she had invited them

to tea. 'Would you like to join us for a cup of coffee ... *café*?' He was still smiling at her as he spoke to Arthur, 'Christ, Patterson, how do I invite her for a cup of coffee? Say something will you, please?'

'*Je m'excuse ...*' he said apologetically, trying to remember his schoolboy French, most of which seemed to have escaped him in the face of this incredible-looking French woman. Sam was right. She was the most beautiful girl he'd ever seen. '*Je regrette ... mon ami est très excité ... voulez-vous un café*?' he said lamely at the end, suddenly not wanting to let go of her either. Her response was one of immediate outrage.

'*Quel sacré culot ... bande de salopards ... allez-vous faire ...*' And then, with tears in her eyes, she suddenly shook her head and hurried past them, going back the way she had come, with her head down now, but her shoulders still as proud as ever, walking faster in shoes they could see were well worn and too big for her, like the dark blue dress that looked as though it might have been her mother's.

'What did she say, Arthur?' Sam was already hurrying after her, and had to scurry through a crowd of soldiers who seemed to have sprung up from nowhere.

'I think she was about to tell us to go to hell, I didn't quite catch the rest. I think it was argot.'

'What's that? A dialect?' Sam looked instantly worried, French was complicated enough without worrying about dialects, but he was more concerned about losing her in the press of people on the street.

'It's Paris slang.' She had darted into a short street, the rue des Grands-Degrés, stopped suddenly in a doorway, and then disappeared, loudly banging the door behind her, as Sam stopped and sighed with a victorious grin. 'What are you looking so pleased about?' Arthur asked.

'We know where she lives now.' The rest would be easy.

'How do you know she's not visiting someone?' Arthur was fascinated by the intensity of his passion. He had never felt anything like it himself, but he had also never seen anyone like her. She was truly lovely.

'She'll come out sooner or later. She has to.'

'And you plan to stand here and wait for her all day? Walker, you *are* crazy!' Arthur shook his head in dismay. He didn't intend to spend all his time in Paris loitering outside some girl's doorway ... a girl who obviously didn't want to speak to him, when there were a thousand others who would have been thrilled to show them all sorts of gratitude and passion. 'I am *not* going to stand here all day for chrissake ... if you think ...'

Sam looked nonplussed. 'So go. I'll meet you later. Back at the café where we had coffee.'

'And you're just going to wait here?'

'You got it.' He lit a cigarette, and lounged happily against the wall of what he assumed was her building. He was thinking of going inside, but that could wait. Presumably, she'd come out again ... eventually ... and he had every intention of waiting.

Arthur stood on the pavement fuming and trying to convince him to do something more constructive with his time, but to no avail. Sam had no intention of leaving. And in total irritation, Arthur gave up, and decided to hang around with him, partially because he didn't want to leave Sam and partially because he found her intriguing too. It was less than an hour before she emerged, carrying some books in a string bag. Her hair was combed loose now, and she looked even more beautiful than she had an hour before. She saw them immediately as she stepped out of her house, started to back inside for a moment, and then decided against it. With her head held high, she walked past them, and Sam ever so gently touched her arm to catch her attention. At first she looked as though she were going to brush past, and then she stopped, the green eyes blazing, and looked at him. The look she gave him spoke volumes, but she also looked as though she understood there was no point in trying to say anything because he wouldn't understand, and what's more he didn't want to.

'Would you like to go have something to eat with us, mademoiselle?' He made the gesture of eating and his eyes never left hers. There was something very compelling about the way he looked at her, as though he wanted her to understand that he wasn't going to hurt her or take advantage of her. He just wanted to look at her . . . to see her . . . and maybe even to reach out and touch her. '*Oui?*' He looked boyishly hopeful and she shook her head.

'*Non*. Okay?' Her French accent on the single word sounded endearing and he smiled as Arthur watched the exchange, unable to speak up in his limited French. Something about the girl left him speechless. 'No . . .' She repeated the gesture Sam had made to indicate eating and shook her head.

'Why?' He struggled to find the word in French. '*Pourquoi?*' He suddenly glanced at her hand in panic. Maybe she was married. Maybe her husband was going to kill him. But there was no ring there. She seemed awfully young, but maybe she was a widow.

'*Parce que,*' she spoke slowly, wondering if he would understand, but almost certain he wouldn't, '*je ne veux pas.*' Arthur spoke up then in a whisper.

'She says she doesn't want to.'

'Why?' Sam looked hurt. 'We're nice guys. Only lunch – food . . .' He made the eating gesture again, '. . . *café* . . . okay? . . . five minutes?' He held up five fingers on one hand. 'Okay?' He held out both hands, palms up, in a gesture of helplessness and peace, and she looked suddenly weary as she shook her head. She looked as though she had had years of this, years of soldiers harassing her, of strangers in her homeland.

'No German . . . no American . . . no . . . no *café* . . . no . . .' She did the now familiar eating gesture again.

Sam folded his hands in supplication and for a minute he looked as though he might burst into tears. But at least she was still standing there, listening to him. He pointed to himself and then to Arthur. 'North Africa . . . Italy . . . now France . . .' He pretended to shoot, he pantomimed Arthur's wounded arm, and looked at her imploringly, 'One *café* . . . five minutes . . . please . . .'

She seemed almost sorry this time when she shook her head and then started to turn away. '*Non . . . je regrette . . .*' And then she walked away quickly as they stared after her. Even Sam didn't follow her this time. There was no point. But when Arthur started to walk away, Sam wouldn't follow.

'Come on, man, she's gone, and she doesn't want to see us.'

'I don't care.' He sounded like a disappointed schoolboy. 'Maybe she'll change her mind when she comes back.'

'The only thing that'll be different is that maybe this time she'll have her father and seven brothers come and knock our teeth out. She told us no, and she meant it, now let's not waste all day standing here. There are a million other women in Paris, dying to show their gratitude to the liberating heroes.'

'I don't give a damn.' Sam wasn't moving. 'This girl's different.'

'You're damn right she is.' Arthur was finally getting angry. Very angry. 'She told us to take a hike. And personally, I intend to follow her advice, no matter how good her legs are. Are you coming, or not?'

Sam hesitated for a moment and then followed him, but with obvious regret. And wherever they went that day, all he could think of was the beautiful girl with red hair on the rue d'Arcole with the green eyes that blazed fire and sadness. There was something about her that haunted him, and after dinner that night, he left Arthur at the table with three girls, and quietly slipped away to walk slowly down her street, just to be near her. It was a crazy thing to do, and even he knew it, but he couldn't help himself. He wanted to see her one more time, even if only from a distance. It wasn't just her looks, there was something more about her. Something he couldn't define or understand, but he wanted to know her . . . or at least see her. He had to.

He stopped at a little café across the street, and ordered a cup of the bitter coffee that everyone drank black and without sugar, and sat staring at her doorway, and then watched in amazement as he saw her walking down the street with her string bag still full of books, and walk slowly up the steps to her house and stop there for a moment, looking for a key in her purse and glancing over her shoulder, as though to be sure no one was following her. Sam leapt to his feet, dropped a handful of coins on the table, and ran across the street, and she glanced up, startled. She looked as though she were going to bolt, but then held her ground with defiance. In occupied Paris, she had faced more ominous men than Sam, and she looked as though she were ready to face one more. But her eyes were more tired than angry this time when she faced him.

'*Bonjour*, mademoiselle.' He looked more sheepish now than he had before, and she shook her head, like a mother scolding a schoolboy.

'*Pourquoi vous me poursuivez?*'

He had no idea what she had said, and this time he didn't have Arthur to rely on, but she spoke more English than he had originally thought. She repeated her question to him in her gentle husky voice. 'Why you do that?'

'I want to talk to you.' He spoke softly, as though caressing the graceful arms that shivered slightly in the cool night air. She had no sweater, only the ugly old blue dress.

She waved vaguely toward the people in the streets, as though offering them up instead. 'Many girls in Paris . . . happy talking Americans.' Her eyes grew hard then. 'Happy talking Germans, happy talking Americans . . .' He understood her.

'And you only speak to Frenchmen?'

She smiled and shrugged. 'French people talk Germans too . . . Americans . . .' She wanted to tell him how France had betrayed itself, how ugly it had been, but there was no way to say all that with the little English she knew, and after all he was a stranger.

'What is your name? Mine is Sam.'

She hesitated for a long time, thinking he didn't need to know it, and then shrugged, as though talking to herself. 'Solange Bertrand.' But she did not hold out her hand in introduction. 'You go?' She looked at him hopefully and he gestured toward the café across the street.

'One cup of coffee, then I go? Please?'

For an instant, he thought she would get angry again, and then, her shoulders drooping for the first time, she seemed to hesitate.

'*Je suis très fatiguée.*' She pointed to the books. He knew she couldn't be going to school at the moment. Everything was disrupted.

'Do you go to school usually?'

'Teaching . . . little boy at home . . . very sick . . . *tuber-culose*.'

He nodded. Everything about her seemed noble. 'Aren't you hungry?' She didn't seem to understand and he made the eating gesture again, and this time she laughed, showing beautiful teeth and a smile that made his heart do cartwheels.

'*D'accord . . . d'accord . . .*' She held up one hand, fingers splayed. '*Cinq minutes . . .* five minute!'

'You'll have to drink fast and their coffee is pretty hot . . .' He felt as though he were flying as he took the string bag from her and led her across the street to the café. The owner greeted her as though he knew her, and seemed interested by the fact that she was there with an American soldier. She called him Julien and they chatted for a moment before she ordered a cup of tea, but she refused to order anything to eat until Sam ordered for her. He ordered some cheese and bread, and in spite of herself, she devoured it. He noticed then for the first time, how thin she was when he looked at her closely. The proud shoulders were mostly bones, and she had long graceful fingers. She sipped the hot tea carefully and seemed grateful for the steaming liquid.

'Why you do this?' she asked him after she had sipped the tea. She shook her head slowly. '*Je ne comprends pas.*'

He was unable to explain even to her why he felt so compelled to speak to her, but the moment he had laid eyes on her, he knew he had to.

'I'm not sure.' He looked pensive, and she seemed not to understand. He threw up his hands to show her he didn't know himself. And then he tried to explain it, touching his heart, and then his eyes. 'I felt something different the first time I saw you.'

She seemed to disapprove and glanced at the other girls

in the café, with American soldiers, but he was quick to shake his head. 'No, no . . . not like that . . . more . . .' He indicated 'bigger' with his hands, and she looked sadly at him as though she knew better.

'*Ça n'existe pas* . . . it do not exist.'

'What doesn't?'

She touched her heart and indicated 'bigger', as he had.

'Have you lost someone in the war? . . .' He hated to ask, 'Your husband?'

Slowly she shook her head, and then not knowing why, she told him. 'My father . . . my brother . . . the Germans kill them . . . my mother die of *tuberculose* . . . My father, my brother, *dans la Résistance.*'

'And you?'

'*J'ai soigné ma mère* . . . I . . . take sick my mother . . .'

'You took care of your mother?' She nodded.

'*J'ai eu peur* . . .' She waved her hand in annoyance at herself, and then indicated fright, '*de la Résistance* . . . because my mother she need me very much . . . My brother was sixteen . . .' Her eyes filled with tears then, and without thinking he reached out and touched Solange's hand, and miraculously she let him, for an instant at least, before drawing it away to take another sip of tea, which gave her the breather she needed from the emotions of the moment.

'Do you have other family?' She looked blank. 'More brothers? Sisters? Aunts and uncles?'

She shook her head, her eyes serious. She had been alone for two years now. Alone against the Germans. Tutoring to make enough money to survive. She had often thought of the Resistance after her mother died, but she was too frightened, and her brother had died such a pointless death. He hadn't died for glory, he had died, betrayed by one of their French neighbours. Everyone seemed to be collaborating, and a traitor. Except for a handful of loyal Frenchmen, and they were being hunted down and slaughtered. Everything had changed. And Solange along with it. The laughing, ebullient girl she had once been, had become a smouldering, angry, distant woman. And yet this boy had somehow reached out and touched her and she knew it. Worse yet, she liked it. It made her feel human again.

'How old are you, Solange?'

'*Dix-neuf . . .*' She thought about it for a minute, trying to find the right numbers in English. 'Ninety,' she said quietly and then he laughed at her, and shook his head.

'No, I don't think so. Nineteen?' Suddenly, she realized what she had said, and she laughed too, looking suddenly young again and more beautiful than ever. 'You look terrific for ninety.'

'*Et vous?*' She asked the same question of him.

'Twenty-two.' It was suddenly like boy-and-girl exchanges anywhere except that they had both seen so much of life. She in Paris, and he with his bayonet, killing Germans.

'*Vous étiez étudiant?* . . . student?'

He nodded. 'At a place called Harvard, in Boston.' He was still proud of it, even now, oddly enough with her it still seemed to matter, and he was doubly proud when he saw a light of recognition in her eyes.

''Arvard?'

'You've heard of it?'

'*Bien sûr* . . . of course! . . . like la Sorbonne, no?'

'Probably.' He was pleased that she knew it, and they exchanged a smile. The tea and bread and cheese were long gone, but she didn't seem so anxious to leave now. 'Could I see you tomorrow, Solange? To go for a walk maybe? Or lunch? . . . dinner?' He realized how hungry

31

she was now, how little food she probably had, and he felt it his duty to feed her.

She started to shake her head and indicated the books in the string bag.

'After? ... or before? ... please ... I don't know how long I will be here.' There was already talk of their leaving Paris and moving on to Germany, and he couldn't bear the thought of leaving her. Not now ... not yet ... and maybe not ever. It was his first taste of puppy love, and he was totally in her thrall as he gazed into the green eyes that seemed so much gentler now, and so full of wisdom.

She sighed. He was so persistent. And in spite of herself, she liked him. During the entire Occupation, she had not made friends with a single German, and certainly no soldier, and she didn't see why the Liberation should be any different, and yet ... and yet, this boy was different. And she knew it.

'*D'accord*,' she said reluctantly.

'Don't look so excited,' he teased and she looked confused as he smiled, and took her hand again. 'Thank you.'

They stood up slowly then and he walked her to her door across the street. She gave him a formal little handshake and thanked him for dinner, and then with a resolute sound, the heavy door closed behind her. As Sam made his way slowly through the streets of Paris, he felt as though his whole life had changed in only a few hours. He wasn't sure how, but he knew that this woman ... this girl ... this extraordinary creature ... had come into his life for a reason.

Chapter 2

'Where were you last night?' Arthur yawned as they had
breakfast together in the dining room of the hotel where
they were quartered. It was the Hôtel Idéal on the rue
Saint-Sebastien, and troops were being billeted in similar
quarters all over Paris. Arthur himself had had a particularly pleasant evening, which ended with too much
wine, but not too many women.

'I had dinner with Solange,' Sam said casually as he
finished his coffee, trying to make it sound like any
ordinary date, which they both knew it wasn't.

'Who's that? Someone you picked up after you left
me?'

'Nope.' Sam looked him right in the eye, with the
famous grin full of mischief. 'You remember her . . . we
met her yesterday on the rue d'Arcole . . . red hair, green
eyes . . . nice legs . . . great walk . . .'

'Are you serious?' He looked stunned, and then he
laughed, it was obvious that Sam was teasing. 'For a
minute, I believed you. Seriously, where were you?'

'I told you. With Solange.' And this time he looked as
though he meant it.

'Walker, do you mean it? *That girl*? Where in hell did
you find her?'

'Outside her house. I went back, just in case, and she
was coming home. She tutors a kid with tuberculosis.'

'How the hell do you know? As I recall, she only spoke French to us, argot at that.' Arthur looked stunned.

'She speaks a little English. Not a lot, but enough. Other than the fact she told me she was ninety years old, we got along great.' He smiled a proprietary smile at Arthur. It was clear that Solange was already his woman, and looking at him, Arthur felt a pang of regret for not having persisted. There was something about Sam, and people like him. Invariably in life, they won all the prizes.

'How old is she?' He was curious now. Like Sam, he wanted to know everything about her.

'Nineteen.'

'And her father didn't come after you with a butcher's knife?'

Sam shook his head quietly. 'Her father and brother were killed by the Germans. Her mother died of tuberculosis. She's alone.'

Arthur look impressed. They really had had a conversation. 'Are you seeing her again?'

Sam nodded, and then smiled knowingly at his friend. 'Yes, I am, and she doesn't know it yet, Patterson, but after the war, we're going to get married.'

Arthur's jaw almost dropped as he stared at his friend, but this time he didn't even bother to tell him he was crazy, because he suddenly sensed that Sam meant it.

Sam and Solange met again for dinner that night, and this time, she told him what it was like living in Paris with the Germans. In a subtler way, it was worse than what he'd been through, and she had been defenceless. She'd had to live by her wits, avoiding being arrested or tortured or merely raped by the Germans who felt they owned Paris and all the women in it. And after her father had died, she had had to support her mother. They had had hardly any food, and she had given almost everything to

34

her mother. They had lost their apartment eventually, and her mother had died in her arms in a rented room – the room she still lived in now. It was filled with ugly memories and sad ghosts, but she had nowhere else to go now. And after what she'd seen during the war, there was no one left that she trusted. Her brother's betrayal had been the final blow to any feeling she had once had for France or her fellow Frenchmen.

'I'd like you to come to America one day,' he said as though testing the waters, watching her eat. He kept ordering food, and was gratified that she ate it.

She shrugged in answer to his invitation, as though it were an impossible dream, not even worth thinking about. 'Very far . . .' She gestured and then explained in French, '*C'est très loin.*' In every possible way, was what she was thinking.

'Not so far.'

'And you? 'Arvard again after the war?'

'Maybe.' If it even mattered anymore. It was hard to imagine going back to school again. Maybe he would try acting after all. He and Arthur had talked about it a lot, at night, in the foxhole. It made sense there. But it was hard to know what would make sense once they got home. Things would be very different. 'I want to be an actor.' He tried it out on her, to see what she would say, and she looked intrigued by it.

'An actor?' And then she nodded, as though it made sense to her and he wanted to kiss her. He smiled at her and she wasn't quite sure why, and then he ordered a bowl of fruit for her, which was the first she'd had in months, or even dreamt of. His generosity embarrassed her, yet in another way it seemed very natural, as though they were old friends. It was difficult to imagine that this was only their second dinner together.

Their friendship seemed to flourish as they took walks along the Seine, and stopped in little bistros and cafés to talk and eat and finally hold hands. Sam had hardly seen Arthur in days, and when they met over breakfast, Sam didn't like what he had to say. Patton crossed the Meuse two days after their victory parade down the Champs-Elysées, and the day after was at Metz on the Moselle on the way to Belgium. It was unlikely that they would be allowed to languish in Paris for much longer. And on 3rd September Brussels was liberated by the British, and the following day Antwerp as well.

'They're going to have our asses back out there any day, Sam, mark my words,' Patterson said gloomily over coffee, and Sam knew he was right, but he was desperate to stay with Solange now. And on the day Brussels had fallen to the British, he had gone to her room, and he had gently pulled away the old blue dress that had been her mother's and made love to her for the first time. And to his amazement, and delight, he had discovered that she was a virgin. She had lain in his arms afterwards with tears of happiness washing her cheeks as he kissed her. And Sam had fallen more desperately in love with her than ever.

'I love you so much Sam.' Her voice was husky and gentle as she carefully pronounced the words.

'So do I, Solange . . . so do I . . .' He couldn't bear the thought of leaving her, and he knew she hated the thought too. She seemed so much more dependent on him now, more trusting and open. But two weeks later, he got his orders. They were moving on to the German Front, there was a war to fight after all, and at least the end was in sight now. Everyone was certain that with the rest of Europe liberated, Germany would fall quickly . . . maybe even by Christmas, he promised her late one night, as he sculpted her exquisite body with hungry fingers. She had flesh of a

36

satin he had never touched before, and hair that fell past her shoulders and over her breasts like benign fire as he kissed her.

'I love you, Solange . . . oh God, how I love you.' He had never known anyone like her. Surely not in Boston, or anywhere since then. 'Will you marry me when the war is over?' Her eyes were full of tears when he asked her, and she didn't answer. He forced her to look at him, and the tears spilled slowly down her cheeks as though she knew something he didn't. 'What's the matter, sweetheart?'

She could hardly force herself to say the words, and it was even harder for her in English. 'Many things change in war, Sam . . .' He loved the way she said his name, he loved the way she breathed and spoke and smelled. He loved everything about her with a passion that seemed to sweep him right into the heavens. He had never before felt any of the emotions she brought him. 'You go to 'Arvard again . . . après . . . and . . .' she shrugged helplessly, 'you will forget Paris.' What she really meant was that he would forget her, and he stared at her in amazement.

'Do you really think I could forget this? Do you really think this is some kind of soldier's sport? Dammit, I *love* you!' For the first time, she saw him angry, and he made love to her this time with a vengeance. 'I love you. Do you understand that? *This* is what's important! And when the war is over, I'm taking you home with me. Will you come?'

She nodded slowly, still unable to believe that he would really want her when the war was over . . . if he even lived through it. She could not bear the thought of that. She had lost everyone in the war, and perhaps now she would lose him too. It was enough to make her fearful of loving him, and yet, like him, she was unable to stop it. It was a passion greater than both of them.

Sam felt as though his soul was being torn from hers. On the day he left Paris she had come to say goodbye, and she and Sam were both speechless with tears when he finally left her. Arthur had never seen him like that as the troops marched out of the Porte Saint-Cloud. Sam had to force himself not to look back again, or he might have deserted. He couldn't bear seeing her standing there as he marched away. She was sobbing the last time he saw her.

When they reached the Ardennes, Sam fought with an even greater vengeance than he had before. It was as though the harder he fought the quicker he could get back to Solange and take her home with him. But by the end of September, the dream was beginning to fade, not the dream of Solange, but the dream of seeing the war end by Christmas. The Germans were not as weakened as everyone had thought, and they fought ruthlessly. It was only at the end of October that Aachen fell, restoring some hope to Sam and Arthur and their comrades. In Arnhem, they weren't as lucky, and by then winter had set in, and the bitter winds and freezing cold began to remind Sam and Arthur of the previous winter they had spent in the Italian trenches.

From November to December they fought in the bitter cold and snows and felt as though they were getting nowhere. Hitler had added new Panzer brigades, and the tanks just seemed to keep on coming forever.

'Christ, do you believe this shit?' Sam looked exhausted as he and Arthur sat in the dark one night, their hands frozen, their feet numb, their faces tingling in the cold, and it was the first time Arthur had seen him so discouraged. All he talked about was spending Christmas with Solange, and it was long since obvious to all of them now that that was not going to happen.

On 16th December, the Battle of the Bulge began and

for a solid week, the Germans pounded the Allies. It wasn't until the skies cleared on the 23rd, that the Allies were able to begin pushing them back, and even then victory for the Allies was uncertain. It was even more disheartening to learn that on 17th December, ninety prisoners of war had been killed by the Germans at Mamedy, in a singularly heartless gesture that violated all of the ethics of war, if any such thing still existed.

And on Christmas Eve, Arthur and Sam sat side by side in a snow-filled trench, trying to keep warm and sharing their rations.

'I don't know, Patterson ... I think the turkey was better last year. Think we should look for a new chef?' But despite the words so typical of Sam, his eyes were glazed with exhaustion and he wore a week's beard on his thin cheeks. He seemed to have aged ten years since he had left Paris, perhaps because he had so much at stake now.

Their sergeant had been killed crossing the Ardennes, and suddenly Sam found himself missing him ... Solange ... even his sister in Boston, from whom he had still heard nothing.

'I wonder what she's doing in Paris?' Sam said the words almost to himself, thinking of Solange, and if Arthur hadn't been so bitter cold to the bone, he would have smiled at him.

'Thinking about you probably. Lucky bastard.' He still remembered how beautiful she was, and wished he had been as persistent as Sam in speaking to her. He spoke French after all, but ... that was silly. She was Sam's girl now.

'Care for some chocolate cake?' Sam held out a piece of rock-hard biscuit he'd been carrying around in his jacket for a week and Arthur declined with a wry face. 'Waiting for the soufflé? I don't blame you.'

'Cut it out, you're making me hungry.' But in truth, they were too cold to eat, too cold, and too tired, and too frightened.

The Germans didn't begin to fall back until two days afterwards, and the Battle of the Bulge was finally over. In March, they took the Bridge at Remagen near Bonn, and in April they met the Ninth Army at Lippstadt and then went on to take 325,000 German prisoners near the Ruhr, and it finally looked as though the end was approaching. And on 25th April at Torgau, they joined forces with the Russians. Roosevelt had died two weeks before, and the news had saddened everyone, but the men on the front were intent on winning and getting home. The Battle of Berlin had begun, and on 2nd May, Berlin was silent at last. On 7th May, Germany surrendered, and Arthur and Sam stood looking at each other, with tears running down their faces. Was it over? Could it be? From North Africa to Italy to France, and now Germany, it felt as though they had crossed half the world, and they had. They had freed it.

'My God, Sam . . .' Arthur whispered to him as they heard the news . . . 'It's over . . . I don't believe it.' They embraced like the brothers they had become, and Sam had an odd feeling of nostalgia that that moment would never come again, and then a moment later he was grateful that it wouldn't. He threw his helmet in the air, and gave a tremendous whoop, but it wasn't Arthur he was thinking of now. It was Solange . . . he was going *home*! And just as he had promised her eight months before, he was going to take her with him.

Chapter 3

The Army had given him three days leave before shipping him back to the States in May 1945, and Sam had headed straight for Paris, where he had found Solange just as he had left her. There was such relief on her face when she saw him that it was easy to read what her feelings were, and the three days flew by faster than either of them could have dreamed.

And she cried copiously this time when he left her at the station to return to Berlin, and from there back to the States for his discharge. He had thought of marrying her before he left Paris, but there was too much red tape, and it would be easier to marry her in the States. He had promised to send for her by the end of the summer. But he had to make some money first. He had already decided not to go back to Harvard, and he wanted to try his luck as an actor. But he was willing to do anything to make the money he needed to pay Solange's passage. He was going to have her come to the States on a tourist visa, and marry her the minute she arrived. He could hardly stand the thought of the months ahead without her.

In New York Arthur had talked him into moving in with him until Sam found an apartment, and all Sam could think of was getting settled.

'Don't cry, sweetheart. I promise ... no later than September.' That gave him four months to get everything organized and have enough money to support her. He was twenty-three years old, he had survived the war, and he had the world by the tail now.

'I love you, Sam!' she shouted as the train pulled away, and she waved for as long as he could see her.

'Cute girl you got, Private,' an admiring sergeant said as they settled down on the train, and Sam only nodded. He wasn't anxious to discuss Solange with anyone, and he wasn't particularly keen on the other soldiers' constantly admiring glances. She was a beautiful young woman, but she was more than that. She was his now.

The train pulled into the Berlin Station at midnight, and Sam made his way back to his quarters to look for Arthur. Arthur had been keeping himself busy with the German girls, and he seemed to have a decided preference for tall blondes. He was in seventh heaven in Germany, and Sam teased him about it constantly, but when he came in that night, Arthur wasn't there, and Sam went to bed, his head filled with thoughts of his bride to be, and the life they would share in New York. And before he knew it, it was eight o'clock the next morning. He left Germany two days after that with Arthur scheduled to come home two weeks later.

Sam was flown to Fort Dix, New Jersey, to muster out, and he took the train to New York from there, and as he stepped off the train in Penn Station, he felt as though he had landed on the moon. After three years in Europe, fighting in the filth and the mud and the rain and the snow, it seemed incredible to be home and see people going about their normal lives. He could hardly adjust to any of it, not even the little hotel where he stayed on the West Side, and he was desperately lonely for Arthur and Solange as he pounded the pavement, going to agents and acting schools, and looking for jobs that would help him keep body and soul together in the meantime.

The army had given him one hundred and fifty-four dollars when he was discharged and his funds were dwindling rapidly. It was a huge relief when Arthur came home two weeks later and Sam could move in with him and his mother. He hadn't wanted to impose on her before that. But it was a joy to be with him again, not just because of the money he was saving but because at last he had someone to talk to. They talked for hours in the bedroom they shared, like two kids. Although Arthur's mother often complained that she could hear them, and she wore a disapproving look whenever she spoke to Sam, which was not often. It was as though the war had somehow been Sam's fault, and their laughter and re-membered tales only helped to prove that they'd been having a good time, and had stayed away just to cause her anguish. She seemed to view Sam as a constant, unhappy reminder of a difficult time and it was a relief when Arthur found a place of his own, and let Sam stay with him there. By then, Sam had a job as a waiter at P. J. Clarke's on Third Avenue, and had enrolled in an acting school on West Thirty-ninth, but he hadn't been offered any parts. He was beginning to wonder if it was all a hopeless dream, when someone finally auditioned him for an off-Broadway show. He didn't get the part, but he felt a little closer than he had before, and he knew where he had gone wrong. He discussed it at length with his acting coach, and when he auditioned a second time in late July, this time he got a walk-on part in another off-Broadway show, and he wrote about it to Solange as a major victory. But it was far more exciting to both of them when in September, he finally sent her enough money to come over. It was just enough for her fare, and a few extra dollars to buy some clothes, and he had explained at length to her that they would be living on his waiter's salary and tips, and the going would be rough for a long time. But there was no doubt in his mind that he wanted her with him.

She arrived on 26th September, tourist class, on the *De Grasse*, which was still the only ship sailing out of Le Havre since the war had ended. And Sam stood staring at the decks with a pair of binoculars Arthur had given him. He searched every face he could see, and for a moment he panicked, fearing she hadn't made the journey . . . and then . . . on a lower deck, he saw a white dress, and a small white hat, and beneath it the red hair he loved so much and the face he had longed for. He waved frantically, but there were too many people on the dock and he knew she hadn't seen him.

It took hours for Solange to clear customs as he waited impatiently. It was a brilliantly sunny day, and it was warm on the docks, with a gentle breeze. It was a perfect day for her to come home to him. Then suddenly she was free and flew into his arms, her hat askew and tears pouring down her cheeks as he kissed her and held her in his powerful arms as he cried too. It was the moment he had wanted so desperately, and he laughed with relief and joy and kissed her.

'Oh God, Solange, how I love you.' It was a passion almost beyond reason or measure. He couldn't bear to tear himself away from her, he missed most of his acting classes after she first arrived, and he could hardly stand going to work every night at five o'clock. He had found a tiny studio apartment for them in the East Forties, under the elevated train, and every night, no matter how cold it was, she would walk him to work. And at two-thirty, when he came home, he would bring her food, and she was always waiting up for him. They would eat after they had made love, sometimes at four o'clock in the morning. And then finally at Christmas, she insisted that he had to get serious about his career, and start thinking seriously about his acting. It still seemed like a remote dream to him, and she was far more real, but he knew she was right. Sometimes she would go to acting classes with him, and she was struck by how talented he was, as was everyone in the class. But his teacher was merciless, and demanded more and more from him. In the mornings, he would read plays, and scan the papers for auditions.

They saw Arthur from time to time too, but less than Sam would have liked. It was difficult because Sam worked at night, and Arthur now had a steady girlfriend. A girl who had graduated from Vassar before the war, with a nasal voice, and smooth blond hair which she wore in a page-boy. She did not seem particularly amused by Sam, and always seemed to find an opportunity to mention that Sam was a 'waiter'. What's more, she made it obvious to everyone that she hated Solange, much to Arthur's embarrassment. And when they were alone, she always referred to Sam and Solange as 'the gypsies'. Her name was Marjorie and she was not touched by Arthur's tales of the war, or by the fact that Solange had survived the occupation of France and lost her entire family. She had spent the war doing volunteer work for the Red Cross and the Junior League, which she felt sure was far more noble. And it was obvious that at twenty-eight, she was terrified of never getting married. There were a lot of girls like her after the war, girls who would have got married years before, if all the best men hadn't been overseas, as they claimed. And she was working hard on Arthur to change her status. But Arthur had problems of his own. His mother hadn't been well, he told Sam, and it worried her to think of him getting married to Marjorie.

He was back at his old law firm, and doing well, but he was afraid to upset his mother who thought he should find someone a little younger . . . or different . . . or never. Sam had seen her for what she was when he stayed with them, and he felt sorry for Arthur and the pressures he let everyone put him under. His mother wanted to keep a grip on him and live vicariously through him. And she saw all the women in his life, and even his male friends as competition. She wanted her son to herself, and she tried to make him feel guilty for every moment he didn't spend with her.

'*Il manque de courage*,' Solange had said bluntly about Arthur after she came to the States, waving her hands as they chatted one night, over one of their three am dinners. 'He has . . . no . . . guts . . .' She looked victorious over finding the right word. 'No heart . . . no . . . courage.'

'He has a lot of heart, Solange. He's just not as forceful as he could be.' And his mother had a hold on him like a vice, but Sam didn't say that.

'*Voilà*.' She agreed. 'No courage. He should marry Marjorie if he wants to or say *au revoir*, or perhaps,' she said mischievously, 'he should beat her.' Sam had laughed at the thought but he couldn't disagree with her. 'And he should say to his mother . . . *merde*!' Sam laughed even harder at that one. They got on famously, in bed and out. They shared most of the same views, she had a heart of gold, and she was fiercely devoted to him, and she was even very fond of Arthur, which meant a lot to Sam. He had been the best man at their wedding at City Hall three days after she arrived on the *De Grasse*, and he had taken care of all of Solange's papers. She called him her '*grand frère*', her big brother, and looked at him lovingly with her huge green eyes, and he always looked as though he would gladly die for her.

But in the end, Marjorie got her way, and in the spring of 1946, they had a small wedding in Philadelphia, where she came from. In Sam's eyes, Arthur had traded one difficult woman for another, but he didn't say so. Arthur's mother was too ill to go, she said her heart was simply not strong enough to allow her to travel, and she had stayed home on the advice of her doctor. Solange and Sam hadn't gone either, but in their case it was because they were not invited. Arthur had explained endlessly that it was a tiny wedding, only family, only Marjorie's very closest friends, too far . . . too complicated . . . sure they wouldn't have liked . . . he had agonized over it every time he saw Sam, but Solange saw the announcement in the papers. It was a wedding for five hundred guests in St Peter's Episcopal Church in Philadelphia, with a reception at the Philadelphia Club. Arthur had seen the notice too and prayed that the Walkers hadn't seen it.

'That was not nice of him, Sam.' Solange was hurt, and disappointed for Sam, but Sam seemed surprisingly understanding.

'It's Marjorie's fault, not his.'

'*Quand même* . . .' Still . . . it only confirmed what she had previously said. Arthur had no guts, and Sam suspected that Marjorie was going to seriously hamper their friendship.

Time did not prove him wrong, and he and Arthur met for lunch, sometimes with Solange, but their meetings did not include Arthur's wife, who had announced, now that she had his ring firmly on her left hand, that she wanted to go to law school, and did not intend to have any children until much later. Arthur was still reeling from the blow. He had hoped to have children as soon as possible, and she had nurtured that hope during their entire courtship.

But Sam and Solange had enough to fill their own lives,

without worrying about Arthur and his bride. Solange was totally involved in Sam, night and day, and encouraging him constantly now to get serious about his acting. By the autumn of 1947, she knew every play on Broadway, had wormed her way into rehearsals whenever possible, and read every trade paper and notice available, while Sam went to acting school every day and went to all the auditions she directed him to. It was a joint effort which bore fruit, sooner than they expected.

His big break came just after Christmas. He got a leading role in an off-Broadway play, and got extraordinarily good reviews which won him the respect of the critics. The play closed in four and a half months, but the experience had been invaluable. And that summer he did summer stock at Stockbridge, Massachusetts, and while they were there, he decided to look up his sister. It was embarrassing to realize that in the three years since he'd been home from the war, he had never tried to find her, and Solange scolded him for his lack of family devotion. Until she met Eileen and Jack Jones, and then she understood a little better why he had preferred to ignore her. He tracked her down from the old neighbourhood and found her married to an ex-Marine, who grected them with a constant flood of lewd jokes. Eileen said very little and she was probably more than a little drunk as they sat in her living room on an ugly street, in an ugly suburb of Boston. Her hair was still bleached blond, with dark roots, and her dress was so tight she might as well have worn nothing, which would obviously have pleased her husband. It was difficult to believe that she and Sam were even remotely related and it was a relief when Sam and Solange finally left their home, and Sam took a deep breath of fresh air and looked at his wife with a rueful grin mixed with disappointment.

'Well, darling, that's my sister.'

'I don't understand . . . what happened to her?' It still amazed Solange, who had grown more beautiful as she grew older, and dressed beautifully in spite of their limited funds. She looked like an actress herself, or a very successful model.

'She was always like that,' Sam explained. 'We never got along.' He sighed. 'To be honest with you, I never liked her.'

'It's too bad.' It was a relief to get away from them. And they both knew she was no loss in their lives. But the loss of more frequent contact with Arthur was one they both regretted. He came up to see Sam in summer stock once that summer, and was greatly impressed by his performance. And of course he made all the appropriate apologies for Marjorie, who felt terrible not to be able to join them, but she had supposedly gone to visit her parents at their summer home near Philadelphia. She was entering Columbia Law School in the autumn, and was anxious to get a holiday before beginning the school year. And of course Solange and Sam didn't question him any further.

But in September, Arthur and Marjorie became a great deal less important. Sam got an offer for his first big part and Solange was so excited she went out and bought a magnum of champagne which they drank in total abandon together. It was for the leading role in *Wilderness*, and promised to be one of the most important plays on Broadway. It was a fabulous part for Sam, and both of them were hysterical with excitement. Arthur handled the contracts, Sam told P. J. Clarke's he wouldn't be coming back that autumn, and they went into rehearsal almost immediately. The play was handsomely backed, and produced by one of Broadway's most successful producers. Sam Walker's career was launched, and he was going to

49

be in good company that winter. Rex Harrison was going to be appearing in *Anne of the Thousand Days* at the Schubert, with Joyce Redman. Henry Fonda and David Wayne were already in *Mister Roberts* at the Alvin, and Anne Jackson was opening on 6th October in Tennessee Williams's *Summer and Smoke* at the Music Box Theater. This was going to be a year they would always remember.

Arthur took them both to lunch at '21' to celebrate. He explained that Marjorie was already busy with law school and couldn't join them, and Solange had an announcement of her own. She had already told Sam the night before, and he was flying high. Suddenly, they had everything they wanted. He and Solange were going to have a baby. It was due in April, and by then Sam would have settled into the play. Everything was just perfect, and Arthur looked at them wistfully over lunch. He was only thirty-two years old, but lately he seemed much older. He had wanted children too, but by the time Marjorie finished law school she'd be thirty-three years old and anxious to start on her career. Realistically, he knew he would never have a child now, and for some reason it made Solange and Sam's baby seem even more important.

'I envy you both.' Not only the baby, but everything they had, the love that was so obvious, the excitement over Sam's career. Everything seemed to be beginning for them. Sam was twenty-six years old, and Solange was twenty-three. It seemed light-years from the day they had first seen her, after the liberation of Paris. She was so elegant and sleek, she was even more beautiful now, and she seemed so constantly full of life and excitement.

And the excitement didn't dim that autumn, as Sam rehearsed the play night and day, and honed it to perfection. He came home exhausted at night, but never too exhausted to make love to Solange, or tell her about the cast, or the changes in the play. His leading lady was Barbara George, a major star of Broadway, and she was teaching him a great deal, all of which he told Solange with fire in his eyes and the laughter that made her love him.

They opened on 9th December, the day after Rex Harrison in Anderson's play, and Sam's reviews were even better than those he'd had before. It was difficult to believe ... more than that ... incredible ... He had made it!

Chapter 4

The baby was born while they were still riding high on his enormous success on Broadway. Solange timed it perfectly, she went into labour after the curtain call on Saturday night, and the baby was born at ten o'clock the next morning at Doctors Hospital on East End Avenue. It was a natural birth, and they had a little girl, she nestled in her mother's arms, with her father's dark hair and her mother's green eyes the first time that Sam saw her. He was overwhelmed by how pretty she was, and how beautiful Solange looked, tired but proud, as though she knew an important secret now, and had worked hard to learn it.

Arthur was their first visitor the next day, and his eyes grew damp as he looked through the window at the baby. They had named her Hilary, and Solange loved the name even though it was difficult for her to say it. She had never mastered the American '*H*', and she called her 'Ilary', and whispered to her in French when they brought the baby to her for her to nurse. They had asked Arthur to be her godfather, and he was deeply touched, but instead of Marjorie, Sam had asked his leading lady, Barbara George, to be the baby's godmother.

The christening was at St Patrick's Cathedral with full pomp and circumstance. The baby wore a beautiful lace gown that her godmother had bought her at Bergdorf Goodman. And Solange was wearing a new mink coat and a diamond ring that Sam had bought her for having the baby. Their circumstances had greatly improved since his role in *Wilderness*, and they moved to a larger apartment on Lexington Avenue, which wasn't luxurious, but it was a great deal nicer than the one they'd had under the Third Avenue elevated train. The baby had come home to her new room, overlooking a little back garden, and Sam and Solange had a cosy room of their own, and a spacious living-room to entertain their friends. There seemed to be a constant flow of people in their apartment now, new friends, actors mostly, and people in Sam's play. Solange didn't mind having them around, on the contrary, she liked it.

The play ran for a full year, and closed after the Christmas of 1949. Sam had many offers within a month, and when he finally chose one he liked he barely had time to catch his breath with Solange and Hilary before he went to rehearsals. Hilary was nine months old by then, and crawling everywhere. She turned up at his feet in his bathroom, when he was shaving, and under the breakfast table in the morning as he drank his coffee, with a constant chorus of 'Da Da Da's' which delighted him. He wanted to have another child soon, hopefully a boy, but Solange wanted to wait. She was content with little Hilary and wanted to give her her full attention. She was a devoted mother, and she seemed even more loving with Sam now since the baby had been born. It was as though it had increased her supply of love for him tenfold.

And motherhood certainly hadn't harmed her looks. She was an incredibly beautiful girl, even more so now, and the press had begun to talk about her increasingly as Sam Walker's fabulous-looking wife. She had been interviewed more than once, but she always directed the attention back to Sam, and talked about what an important

53

actor he was. And the critics agreed with her more than ever after the opening of his new play. It ran for two years, and when it finally closed, Sam decided to take some time off, and Solange almost immediately got pregnant. And nine months later, another daughter, redheaded this time, like her mother, was born on the opening night of Sam's new play. Solange had to rush to the hospital with Arthur just after the curtain went up. She felt terrible not to see Sam's opening night, but she barely made it to the hospital, squeezing Arthur's hand, while he begged the driver to go faster. Alexandra was born ten minutes after they arrived, on a stretcher just outside the delivery room. The baby gave a lusty cry, and Solange lay back with a soft moan, spent with the effort. Arthur came to see her as soon as she was put in a room, and teased her about their going back in time for the final curtain with the baby. Solange loved the idea and wished she could actually do it. Instead, she made him promise to bring Sam back with him afterwards, and Arthur left promising to see her the next day.

Sam didn't get to the hospital till the next morning. He explained that he'd been tied up with endless cast parties, and he pretended not to see the hurt look in her eyes. She had waited for him all night and he hadn't even called her. He brought her a spectacular emerald bracelet, but still, she had silent questions about where he had been, and she was desperately hurt that he hadn't come to see her. He was so much less attentive these days, because the play was a demanding one, he said, and she knew this part was the most difficult of all, but still . . . to her, their baby was more important. But all he could talk about was his leading lady. He seemed obsessed with her. And it was Arthur who took Solange and Alexandra home from the hospital while Sam was at rehearsal. He seemed to be out constantly and she didn't say anything to Sam when he came home late at night, but she always noticed. She particularly noticed the heady scent of another woman's perfume, and although she didn't say it to him, she knew that lately their marriage was different. She felt a void in her own life as a result, an emptiness that was a constant pain, and only Arthur seemed to understand it. He was the only one she could talk to. He had his own problems as well. He still wanted children, and Marjorie wouldn't hear of it. And for his own part, Arthur thought Sam was a damn fool, but he never said so. He only did his best to bolster Solange's spirits during their frequent lunches. It wasn't fair to hurt a woman who was so much in love with her husband. And he often found himself wishing that he had won over Sam, years before, but it was too late now. Solange was married to Sam, and she adored him.

'And you, Arthur, what about you, are you happy? No, of course not,' she answered for him and he didn't disagree. How could one be happy, with a woman like Marjorie? She was a selfish, ambitious iceberg. 'You should force her to have babies if you want them.' She looked serious and he laughed. It was impossible to force Marjorie to do anything she didn't want to do. Impossible for him anyway. He wasn't that kind of person.

'You can't force a woman to have a baby.' He smiled ruefully. 'You'd only have an unhappy mother and eventually an unhappy child. Not like yours.' They were perfect little cherubs, her children Hilary and Alexandra, and he adored them. Hilary was still as dark as Sam, while Alexandra had bright red hair and big green eyes. He smiled at Solange then, and saw the sadness in her face. She knew what Sam was up to, just as everyone else in New York did, she had heard the rumours, and there were constant items about him in the papers.

'He's a damn fool. He's thirty-one years old and he's got the world by the tail . . . and a wife most men would give their right arm for.'

'What would I do with a right arm?' She smiled at him philosophically, looking very Gallic. 'I want his heart, not his arm . . . or all that expensive jewellery. I always know when something is wrong – he comes home with boxes full of diamonds.'

'I know.' Arthur frowned. He still advised Sam on his business affairs, and for some time now had been urging Sam to save money. But Sam was still playing, and enjoying the initial impact of his success. He was buying and buying and buying: toys for the girls, furs and jewels for his wife, clothes for himself, and expensive presents for the women he got involved with. There had been several Arthur knew about, and he disapproved of them all, and he always hoped that Solange knew nothing about them. But he sensed that this time was different. This was the first time he'd had the feeling she was really unhappy.

'I don't know what to do, Arthur. I don't know if I should make a scene, tell him I know what's going on, or sit back quietly and wait for it to be over. Because it will be over soon. It always is with Sam . . . and then he comes home to me.' She smiled a smile that would have brought Arthur to his knees, if he'd been standing, and if it had been meant for him, but it wasn't.

'You're a very sensible woman, Solange. Most Americans aren't. Most women in this country go crazy if they think their husband is having an affair. They hire detectives, sue for divorce, take him for everything he's worth . . .' She was amazing.

But she only smiled at him again, that wise little smile that said she was a thousand years old, even if she only looked twenty. 'I don't want "things", Arthur. I only want my husband.' It was obvious that she adored him. And Arthur envied his friend, though not for the first time. He had always wondered what would have happened if he had pursued Solange, if he had spoken to her that day on the rue d'Arcole. What if . . . it was something he would foolishly ask himself for a lifetime. And it didn't matter now. Sam was the lucky one. Luckier than he knew. The bastard.

'I suppose he'll quiet down again.' Solange sighed and finished her wine. 'With each leading lady now we have a little problem, and then eventually he gets tired of them. It's hard for him, he becomes so involved in the play . . . the theatre is a hard life for him. It's so extremely demanding.' She looked as though she genuinely believed what she said, but Arthur shook his head.

'It's not that demanding. He's spoiled. Spoiled by success, by the women he meets . . . and by you, Solange. You treat him like a god, for heaven's sake.'

'He is – to me. He means everything to me.' Her huge eyes reached out to Arthur and her words cut him to the quick.

'Then sit tight. He'll come home again. He's just playing, Solange. As long as you understand that, perhaps it isn't so important.'

She nodded. It was good advice. And she was always prepared to sit it out. She would rather have died than lose him.

The affair went on for six months finally, and then ended brutally, with the attempted suicide of his leading lady. After which she left the play, for reasons of 'ill health', and Sam's life returned to normal. It was callous of him in some ways, but Solange was relieved to see it. For now, the threat was over. It was 1954 by then, and he stayed with the play for another year and as usual returned to his wife and children. It was the longest run he had ever had in any play, and they were both sad when it was over. He took her and the girls to Europe after that for a summer in Saint-Tropez. It was something he had always talked about. He had been there during the war, though only for a day, and he had always wanted to go back there.

They sent Arthur a postcard from Saint-Tropez and another from Cannes, and then they went on a little pilgrimage to Paris, and Solange showed the children where she had lived as a child. It was emotional for her going back. It was ten years since she had left, and there were painful memories for her there, but happy ones too. Hilary was only six years old, but Solange hoped she would enjoy the trip, and Alexandra was still only a baby. They had brought along a nurse to help them with the children. It was a far cry from the way Solange had left France, with her steamship ticket in her pocket and barely enough money to eat. She had left owning three dresses and two pairs of shoes, and the hat on her head, and an old worn-out coat that had been her mother's. And now here she was with trunks of clothes. They had arrived travelling first class on the *Liberté*, and they stayed at the Ritz in Paris. Sam took her to Givenchy and Chanel and Dior to buy her clothes, and to Cartier where he insisted on buying her a new diamond bracelet.

'But I don't need it, Sam!' she protested laughingly as he forced it on her arm. He was as loving as he had always been, and he had been spoiling her as though she were a new mistress. He had acquired some expensive habits in recent years, and sometimes it frightened Solange. Like Arthur, she wanted him to start saving money for their children.

'Every girl needs a diamond bracelet, Solange.'

'But I have three!' She pulled her arm away with a grin

and shook her head. '*Non, chéri! Je ne veux pas!* I want you to save our money.' He looked momentarily annoyed as he glanced at her.

'You sound just like Arthur.'

'Well, he's right. We have to start thinking of the children.'

'Fine.' He pointed to another bracelet in the case, indicating for the salesgirl to take it out. 'We'll take two of them.'

'*Ah non*, Sam! *Quand même voyons!*' Since returning to Paris, she had slipped back into French again, and it pleased her to hear Hilary speaking to people easily. She spoke only French with the two girls, and Hilary was completely bilingual. Alexandra didn't speak yet at all, but when she would, she would speak French too. In some ways, Solange had not totally renounced her homeland. And it felt good to be back again. There were places and memories that still warmed her heart and as they walked into the Place Vendôme at night, with the lights and the statue of Napoleon, she felt her heart soar in a way that it hadn't since she'd left Paris.

They had dinner at Maxim's that night, and at La Tour d'Argent the following day, and the day they left Paris, Sam gave her both diamond bracelets, and a new ring. Solange tried to discourage him, but she knew it was hopeless, and as they sailed back to the States, she thought about what a lovely trip it had been. It had felt good to go back, and good to go home again as they returned. New York was home now. She had lived there for ten years and it meant a great deal to her. They had an apartment on Sutton Place now, with a spectacular view of the river, and lovely rooms for the girls. It was a split-level flat which allowed them to entertain lavishly, and Marilyn Monroe had an apartment nearby. She was a good friend of Sam's, and always spent time with him when she was in New York, but Solange knew they had never had an affair. And she liked Marilyn very much, she was an amusing girl, and she kept telling Solange she should be in movies, which only made Solange laugh.

'One star in the family is enough!' she always said, with her still noticeable French accent.

Sam was offered a part in a new play that autumn but he turned it down. He didn't think it was challenging enough for him. And he surprised everyone by agreeing to make a movie. They went to Hollywood for the film, and Solange found it a completely amazing place, filled with remarkable people who couldn't tell the difference between fantasy and real life. They lived in a 'bungalow' at the Beverly Hills Hotel, with another smaller one for the children and the nurse, and for a year it was a totally unreal existence. Solange thought the movie was very good, but Sam was not pleased and he was relieved to get back to New York and start rehearsals for a new play in January of 1956. He became totally involved in his craft again, and within two months he was also involved with his leading lady. And this time, Solange was seriously annoyed. She had lunch with Arthur regularly, and more often than she liked, she found herself crying on his shoulder. Arthur's marriage was in form only. Marjorie was always occupied elsewhere, and his mother had died while they were in California the year before. He seemed terribly alone suddenly, just as alone as Solange felt, despite Sam's denials and constant gifts, and he was always especially nice to his daughters when he felt guilty.

'Why? Why do you do this to me?' She waved the gossip column at him one morning at breakfast.

'You're imagining things again, Solange. You do this every time I start work on a new play.'

'Ah . . .' She threw the paper in the sink, 'It's because you sleep with your leading lady *every* time you start work on a new play. Do you have to work on the leading lady too? Couldn't one of the other actors do that? Your understudy perhaps. Couldn't that be one of his duties?'

Sam laughed at her and pulled her close to him, pulling her down on his lap and nuzzling the mane of resplendent red hair that was more beautiful than ever. 'I love you, crazy one.'

'Don't call me crazy. I only know you too well, Mr Walker. You cannot fool me. Not at all!' She wagged a finger at him, but somehow she always forgave him. He drank too much, and when he did was sometimes hostile and threatening when he came home. It was impossible for her to stay angry at him. She loved him too much. Too much for her own good, Arthur said, and maybe he was right. But it was the only thing about Sam she would have changed. His other women. The rest she loved just as it was. That spring she got pregnant again, and the baby was born just after Christmas when Sam was in California. It was another little girl and they named her Megan. Once again Arthur took her to the hospital and it took Solange two days to track Sam down in California. She had heard the rumours again, and she knew what he was doing in Hollywood. And this time she was fed up and she told him so when he came back to New York, when the baby was three weeks old. She even threatened to divorce him, which was totally unlike her.

'You humiliate me to the entire world . . . you make a fool out of me, and you expect me to sit here and take it. I want a divorce, Sam.'

'You're out of your mind. You're imagining things. Who've you been talking to again? Arthur?' But he looked worried.

'Arthur has nothing to do with this. And all you have to do is read the newspapers. It's in every column from here to L A, Sam. Every year, every month, every movie, every play, it's a new showgirl, a new leading lady, a new woman. You've done it for too long. You've done nothing but play, and you're so impressed with yourself that you think you owe it to yourself. Then fine, okay, but I owe myself something too. I owe myself a husband who loves me and is willing to be faithful too.'

'And you?' He tried to turn the tables on her, even though he knew how desperately devoted she had been. 'What about all your goddam lunches with Arthur?'

'I have no one else to talk to, Sam. At least he won't call the papers and tell them what I say.' They both knew that everyone else would. She wasn't wrong. She was Sam Walker's wife after all. And he was a star now. 'At least I can cry on his shoulder.'

'While he cries in your soup. You're the most pathetic pair I've ever heard of. And remember what I told you, Solange. I will not give you a divorce. Period. Amen. So don't ask me again.'

'I don't have to ask you.' It was the first time she had openly threatened him.

'Oh no?' There was a thin trace of fear in his voice, carefully masked, but she knew it.

'All I have to do is have you followed. I could have divorced you fifty times by now.'

He had slammed out of the house without saying another word, and he had left for California again the next day. It had delayed rehearsals of his play by a month, but they always forgave Sam Walker.

When he returned things were just as stormy with Solange. She knew whom he had taken to the West Coast and she was finally fed up with him. One night he came back to find her waiting for him, and when she confronted him, their fighting was so loud that it woke Hilary. Alexandra's room was further down the hall, and Megan was only eleven months old then. But Hilary was eight years old. And she remembered everything. The ambulances and the police ... the sirens ... and her mother being taken out in a sheet ... she remembered what they had said ... and her father crying as they led him away. He hadn't even seen her standing near the door, watching. And then she remembered the nurse calling Uncle Arthur.

He had come almost at once, his face grey. He couldn't believe what they had told him. There had to be some mistake ... had to be ... it wasn't possible. He knew they had been having problems for a while, but Sam adored her, just as she loved him. It was a love that had often gone well beyond reason, a love that forgave him everything, a love that had led him to follow her doggedly down the rue d'Arcole right from the beginning. It was a love that touched everyone who came near them ... a love that ... he just couldn't understand it as he sat in their apartment as the dawn came and the doorman brought the paper upstairs and knocked discreetly on their front door. But it was all there, as Arthur held out a trembling hand and took the paper. It was all there ... the end of a dream ... the end of a life ... Sam had killed her.

Part II

ARTHUR

Chapter 5

The door to the holding cell slammed hard behind Arthur as he waited to see him. Sam was being held at the 17th Precinct on East Fifty-first Street and it was after noon before they let Arthur in to see him. They had interrogated him until then, for hours and hours, although they had no need to. He had admitted everything. He had sobbed. He had stared glassy-eyed . . . he had remembered every minute of those first hours in Paris. He didn't understand why he had done it . . . he knew he'd been drunk . . . she had frightened him by saying she was leaving. But still . . . he couldn't understand why he'd done it except that he didn't want to lose her and she had said . . . she had said . . . With a look of despair he stared up at Arthur when they led him in. And Sam seemed almost not to see him.

'Sam . . .' Arthur's voice was hoarse. He had been crying all morning. And he reached out to touch Sam's arm, as though to bring him back from the edge of the abyss. Sam looked as though he wanted to die himself. He stood in the centre of the room after they left him there and just stared at Arthur.

'I killed her, Arthur . . . I killed her.' He seemed almost not to see him . . . only her face when he strangled her . . . the red hair he loved so much . . . why? . . . why had he done it? . . . why had she said all those terrible things to him? He looked blindly at his friend as the tears began to roll down his cheeks again.

'Sit down, Sam ... come on.' He gently helped him into one of the room's two straight-backed chairs, facing each other over a narrow, battered table. 'We have to talk.' Sam seemed barely coherent, but they had to talk. 'Do you want to talk about what happened?'

Sam only stared at him. It was all much too simple. 'I killed her.'

'I know that, Sam. But what happened before that? Did she provoke you?' He had to find him a good defence attorney, and before he did, he had to know what they were up against. Now Sam was not just his best friend, he was indirectly a client. 'Did she strike you?'

Sam shook his head, his eyes distant and vague. 'She said a lot of terrible things ... she was very angry.'

Arthur suspected why, but he asked anyway. 'Why was she angry?'

Sam stared at the floor, remembering Solange's fury. He had never seen her like that. He knew he had pushed her too far this time. And he was desperate not to lose her. But he had anyway ... the only woman he loved ... He looked up at Arthur in despair. 'She knew I was having an affair again ... it didn't mean anything ... it never did ...'

'Except to Solange, Sam.' His voice was quiet, and he had to remind himself that it was Sam he was defending, not Solange now.

Sam looked at him strangely in answer, and he was silent for a long time.

'Did she threaten to divorce you?'

He nodded, and then he had to clear the air. He had to ask him. He had to know. It was, in a sense, why he had killed her. Except that he was also drunk and had lost control and the things she said were so terrible, and he was terrified that she meant it and he would lose her. 'She said you and she were having an affair. Is that true?' His eyes pierced his friend's, and Arthur looked back at him with sorrow.

'What do you think?'

'I've never thought about it before. I know you were close to her . . . you two used to go to lunch a lot . . .'

'But did she ever hide it?' Like all good lawyers, he knew the answer before he asked the question.

'No . . . she always told me . . . at least I think so . . .'

'Don't you think she was just trying to get back at you by saying that, for all the pain you'd caused her, and how else could she?'

Now, in the clear light of day, he knew that. But the night before, in the heat of passion, Sam had believed her . . . he had gone crazy . . . and he had actually killed her. The thought of it made the panic rise in his throat like a hand reaching up from his guts to strangle him, and he knew he deserved it. He deserved to die for what he had done to Solange. He began to cry again and Arthur held his shoulders.

'What's going to happen to the girls now?' He suddenly looked up at Arthur with fresh panic.

Arthur had been thinking about it all morning. 'I'm sure you have enough money to take care of them while all this is pending.' And there was the nurse, and a maid in the apartment. They lived extremely well at the apartment on Sutton Place.

Sam looked bleak as he stared at his friend. 'How much is all this going to cost me?' It had cost Solange her life, and now . . . Arthur had to fight his own feelings again and again. How could he have done this to her? And yet, Sam was his friend, more than that, he was almost his brother. They had survived the war side by side, Sam had carried him across the mountains, and to the medics when he was wounded near Cassino. They had liberated Paris and Rome . . . Paris . . . and the rue d'Arcole where they had first seen her. It was all so tightly interwoven, and now it wasn't just a matter of Sam and Solange, there were their daughters to think of. Hilary, Alexandra, and Megan. But Arthur tried to force his thoughts back to answer Sam's question. He wanted to know how much his defence would cost him.

'It depends on who you hire to defend you. I want to think of who to recommend. But you should have the best. This is going to be a very big trial, and there will be a lot of sympathy for Solange. You've had a lot of press with your lady friends in recent years, Sam, and that is not going to help you.'

But Sam was shaking his head with determination. 'I don't want someone else. I want you to defend me.' He looked up at Arthur and Arthur almost visibly shuddered.

'I can't do that.' His voice was a croak in the room full of echoes.

'Why not?'

'Because I'm your friend. And I'm not a criminal attorney.'

'I don't care. You're the best there is. I don't want anyone else. I want you.' His eyes filled with tears, it was all so horrible, it was beyond belief, but it was happening, it *was* real. He had made it real. He had made reality from a nightmare.

Arthur's face was suddenly covered by a thin film of perspiration. This was bad enough, but to defend him on top of it. He just couldn't. 'I don't think I can do it, Sam. I don't have the experience in this field. It would be a tremendous disadvantage to you. You can't do this . . .'

. . . to either of us . . . Oh God, please. He wanted to cry. But Sam was adamant as he looked up at him with pleading eyes.

'You have to. For me, for the girls . . . for Solange . . . please . . .' For Solange? Christ, he had killed her. But the worst of it was that Arthur knew Solange would have wanted him to do anything Sam wanted. He knew better than anyone how desperately she had loved him.

'We'll both have to think it over, but I am convinced it would be a terrible mistake. You need the *best*, Sam, not a tax attorney you drafted into this out of some misguided allegiance. I *can't* do it! I just *can't*!' It was the most emotional Sam had ever heard him, but he still wanted Arthur to defend him. 'But more importantly right now, is there anyone you want me to call for the girls?'

Sam thought about it and shook his head. There was no one they were close to, except Arthur, and the thousands of acquaintances they had had in the theatre. But Solange had had no close friends. She had been totally involved in Sam's life, his children and his career. She never had time for anyone else, nor any particular interest.

'Any family I should call?' He knew he should know that after the years they spent in Europe together, but suddenly he couldn't remember. He knew Sam's parents were dead, but he couldn't remember if there was anyone else, some remote relative he should call, but Sam only shook his head.

'No one who would be important to the girls. There's my sister in Boston, but for God's sake, don't call her.'

'Why not?'

'I haven't seen her in years, not since before Hilary was even born. She's a real tramp. Just forget her.'

But Arthur couldn't afford to forget anyone now. Maybe an aunt was just what the girls would be needing.

'What's her name? Just in case. You never know in a situation like this . . .'

'Eileen. Eileen Jones. She's married to an ex-Marine named Jack. And they live in Charlestown. But believe me, you'd hate them.' Sam stood up, and walked across the holding cell to stare out the barred window.

'I'm not planning to invite them down for the weekend, for chrissake, but right now a relative or two might come in handy.' He had three daughters, two of them practically babies, and he had no one in the world to take care of them except a nurse and a maid . . . and Arthur . . .

And then Sam turned to face Arthur again. 'Can I see them?' His eyes filled with tears at the thought . . . his little angels . . . his babies . . . how could he have done this to them? He had robbed them of their mother, a mother who would have assured them of a happy childhood and a perfect life, a mother who never failed them in any way, who was always there for them, who gave them every kiss, every hug, every bath, played every game, read every story, and whispered with them when she put them to bed at night, with giggles and tickles and cuddles, and now . . . the very thought made him shudder. He wondered if he could even take care of them himself when he got out. But there was no point thinking about it. He would have to.

But Arthur was looking at him now. 'Do you really want to see them here?'

'I guess not.' Sam's voice was the merest whisper. 'I just thought . . . I wanted to try and explain . . . to Hilary at least . . .'

'You can do that later. Right now, we have to get you out of this.'

'Do you think you can?' It was the first time Sam had asked him that, and Arthur didn't like the prospect.

'I think someone else would have a better chance of doing it for you than I would.'

'I don't care. I already told you, Arthur. I only want you to defend me.'

'I think it's going to be a tough fight . . . for anyone . . . to be honest with you, Sam.' He hated to say the words, but he owed him the truth after all. 'You'll have to plead insanity . . . crime of passion . . . you've admitted everything. It's all pretty cut-and-dried, and in the past few years you've got yourself a hell of a reputation.' It was true, they both knew that, and Arthur had always wanted to tell him what a damn fool he was, but for a different reason. He had hated him for hurting Solange, and so needlessly, but on the other hand, they were friends, and Sam's success had come so fast and hard that Arthur suspected it was difficult for him to deal with. He was only thirty-five now, and he had become a big star when he was only in his twenties. It was a lot to digest and a lot to live up to, and he had paid a price for it . . . but so had she . . . more than Sam ever knew. There was a lot about Solange he hadn't noticed, he was so wrapped up in himself and his career that in recent years he had become self-centred, and spoiled. Even his daughters seemed to know that. Alexandra had even said to Arthur recently, 'We have to make a big fuss about Daddy when he's home, or he gets very angry. Our Daddy needs a lot of attention.' It was true and Solange had explained that to them, teaching them how to stay out of his way when he was tired, or having them bring him little treats, like the chocolates he loved, or a plate of fresh fruit, and something cool to drink, or sing a little song she had taught them just for him. The entire household had been trained to revolve around Daddy.

And now they had lost both Solange and Sam. Arthur

thought about it all the way back to the office that afternoon, after he left Sam. And on his own, he decided to call their godparents and see if he could arouse any interest. With Sam in jail, and Solange gone, they had no one now except Arthur. But the godparents they had chosen had been chosen for their important names and pretty faces, well-known actors most of them, and none of them had any real interest in the children. They were much more interested in talking about the news with Arthur, why had Sam done it, had he gone crazy, had Solange done something to provoke him, what was going to happen now, when was the trial? . . . but absolutely nothing about the children, which left him right back where he started, as the only person they had to depend on, in Sam's absence. He was going to hang on to their aunt's name, just in case, but in the meantime, he was going to follow Sam's instructions and not call her.

The next thing he did was to check into Sam's bank accounts, so he could handle his affairs. And he was horrified at what he found there. The balance was infinitely less than he had expected. Sam spent everything he made, mainly on his lifestyle and his girlfriends. In fact, he had already borrowed ahead against future salary in his next play, and aside from the small amount of cash in his checking account, he was in debt up to his eyeballs. There was barely enough to pay the maid's and nurse's salaries over the next few months, until the trial was over. It was a hell of a spot to put the children in, and Arthur remembered Solange saying as much to him years before. She had always wanted Sam to think of the girls, and save some money. But instead he bought her diamond bracelets and fur coats, and God only knew what he spent on his other women. He was known to be a generous man, and he had never skimped on anything, once he could afford to. But now it left him with ten thousand dollars in the bank and ten times that in debts. It was amazing how little one knew about one's friends, and Arthur wished he had talked to him more sternly years before. He had never realized that Sam was irresponsible to this extent, and now it represented disaster for his children.

Arthur had tried to talk to Marjorie about it, bemoaning the children's fate, and hoping to stir her sympathy for them. But he was disappointed to find she only had harsh words for them, making comments about their undoubtedly being gypsies like their parents. She seemed to have no compassion whatsoever for them.

But in the next few days he barely saw his wife. He had his hands full with Sam and the girls, the press constantly badgering all of them, even the children, and he had to make the funeral arrangements for Solange. There was no one else to do it.

The funeral was set for three days after Sam had gone to jail. She lay in state for two days, and on the third day, they held the service. And it was amazing to Arthur how many people came, mostly out of respect for Sam, but there were a great many people who had known and liked her. 'She was a lovely girl . . .' he heard countless people say, '. . . absolutely beautiful . . . didn't know how lucky he was . . . should have been an actress too . . . always wanted her to model for me . . . wonderful with her kids . . . hell of a girl . . . lucky man to have a wife like that . . . she was French to her very soul . . . incredible girl . . . don't understand why he did it . . . she was crazy about him . . .' It went on and on, and Arthur sat in the front row, with the girls and their nurse, trying not to cry as they closed the lid of the coffin. Hilary sat very stiff next to him, and once she walked right up to it and stared down at Solange, and then she kissed her, and returned to her seat with a wooden look of grief, as though she were numb from the immensity of her pain, but she wouldn't let Arthur touch her. In fact, she wouldn't let anyone close to her. She only held tightly to Alexandra's hand, answering all her questions about why Mommy was sleeping in the box covered with white roses. Arthur had paid for all the flowers himself, he hadn't wanted to deplete their funds any further, even for their mother's funeral service.

Alexandra thought Solange looked just like Snow White after she had eaten the apple, and she kept asking Hilary when she was going to wake up ... and if Daddy was going to come and kiss her.

'No, she's going to go on sleeping like that, Axie.' Her voice was very quiet as the organist played the Ave Maria in church.

'Why?'

'Because she is.' She shushed her. 'Now be quiet.' She tightened her grip on her sister's hand, and her face went dead white as she watched her mother's coffin roll slowly past her. She stood silently, and then suddenly reached out and pulled two white roses from the heavy blanket of flowers that covered the casket, and handed one of them to Alexandra. Alexandra started to cry, and whispered that she wanted Mommy to wake up, and she couldn't breathe like that with the box closed. It was as though she knew her mother was dead, but none of them could face it. Even little Megan had begun to cry, as though she understood too, and the nurse had to take her outside where she could wail in the winter sunshine. It seemed incongruous to bury her on such a pretty day, but perhaps not ... everything about Solange had always been filled with light and flowers and sunshine, from her flaming red hair to the brilliant green eyes to the lithe body that was always in motion.

Arthur took the children back to the apartment in the limousine, and then went to the cemetery himself to see that everything was attended to. And then he went to see Sam at Rikers Island. He brought him one white rose from the casket, like the one Hilary had given Axie.

Arthur looked very tall and thin and pale, as he entered the holding cell in his dark suit with his Homburg in his hand. He looked like the messenger of Death, and in a way he was. Sam looked up at him and trembled.

'I thought you'd want this.' He held out the white rose, and with a trembling hand, Sam took it.

'How are the girls?'

'They're doing very well. Hilary is keeping them all intact. It's as though she's taken on Solange's role, as their mother.'

Sam dropped into a chair and put his head in his hands, still clutching the rose Arthur had brought him, but it had the smell of death, and sadness, and funerals. There was no joy left in his love for her, or his life; he felt as though everything were over. And in an important way it was. He lay in his cell day and night, and thought only of Solange. Even his daughters seemed remote now. He wondered how much they would hate him in later years, when they discovered, and fully understood, that he had murdered their mother. It would make any kind of relationship with them impossible. Everything was impossible now. And life was no longer worth living. He had already said as much to Arthur, who told him he had to think of the girls now. He owed them everything. But what did he have to give? His debts? His guilt? His bad habits? His overwhelming remorse for killing the one woman he loved . . . he was certain they would never understand.

'I've been thinking about the girls, Sam.' Arthur cleared his throat, praying that Sam wouldn't fight him. 'I'd like to sell all of Solange's jewellery so that they have a little money to fall back on, and you're going to need quite a lot for attorney's fees, particularly if I can convince you to get another attorney. In my case, all we have to do is satisfy the firm for my time. I don't want anything out of it personally or directly.' The last thing he wanted was to make money for defending Sam. But he still didn't want to do it at all. Sam had killed the only woman he had ever loved and admired, in fact almost worshipped, and no matter how close they were, or how great the bond, it was going to be almost impossible for Arthur to defend him. He had tried to explain that to him, but Sam didn't want to hear it.

'What do you think about selling the jewellery?' He looked down at Sam, who turned to him with a deathly pale face covered with beard stubble.

'Fine. If it'll help the girls, get rid of it. Do you want the keys to the safe deposit box at the bank?'

'I've already found them. Solange kept everything in remarkably good order.'

Sam only nodded, unable to answer him. It was hardly surprising that she had. She was a very remarkable woman. But they both knew that. And it didn't matter now ... she was gone ... in the box Arthur had watched them lower into the ground only hours before. The thought of it was still with him, and like the aura of sorrow around him, Sam could feel it.

'I'll take care of it this week.' He wanted as much money as possible on hand, for the girls, and Sam's defence fund.

The trial had been set for the following June, which was still months away, and Arthur wanted to be sure that there was no problem for the girls. And they were going to need money too for extensive psychiatric evaluations of

Sam. Arthur was going to plead temporary insanity, which was the only possible defence, given the circumstances and his confession.

It was an endless period of time. The nurse they had was not particularly pleasant to them. Solange had never selected her nurses with great care because she was around all the time anyway, and it was she who took care of the girls whenever possible, so the charm and skill of the nurse was never very important. Christmas itself was a ghastly day. With both parents gone, the children already seemed like little orphans.

Arthur took Alexandra and Hilary out to lunch on Christmas Day, but it was more depressing than joyful. And Alexandra saw it. Her eyes moved seriously back and forth between the two of them and then she looked up at Hilary with sorrow and confusion.

'Why are you mad at Uncle Arthur?'

'I'm not.' Hilary kept her eyes on her plate and then glared briefly at her little sister.

'Yes, you are. You took your hand away when he tried to hold it.'

'Eat your turkey, Axie.'

Hilary seemed oblivious to the Christmas songs played by the violins in the Palm Court at the Plaza. She was lost in her own thoughts, and Arthur was sorry Marjorie hadn't come with him. She was having lunch at the Colony Club instead with another woman lawyer. And he had begged her to come, but she had flatly refused.

'I'm not interested in those children, and you shouldn't be taking them out either. You're not their family, they just have to adjust to the reality of their situation.'

'At eight and five years of age? It's Christmas, for God's sake. The least we can do is . . .'

'I don't want to hear it. If you want to play Noble

Saviour, don't drag me into it.' And with that, she'd left the room so he had come alone, with Hilary and Alexandra.

In fact Marjorie's adamant stance *vis-à-vis* the girls was only an extension of her dislike for the Walkers generally, and more specifically her disapproval of his frequent lunches with Solange. It wasn't that she was jealous. It was more that she disapproved of her fawning French ways, and the fact that Sam was an actor, no matter how successful.

Sam had no contact whatsoever with the girls that Christmas. He was not allowed to call them, and wouldn't have anyway, he was too depressed to think of anyone, except Solange and why he had killed her. He couldn't even bear thinking of the children.

Arthur had tried bringing photographs of them to Sam, but he was totally withdrawn these days, talking only of Solange and the past, and chronicling his sins and mistakes and transgressions endlessly. He was like an old man, whose entire life was behind him. And Arthur was having a hard time getting him interested in the case. He seemed to have no excitement about his defence, and often said that he deserved to be punished, which was hardly encouraging for Arthur.

The rest of the winter slid by agonizingly. Hilary seemed to be running the household more than adequately, and the younger children were doing well, although Hilary had a constant look of pain and anguish around her eyes, which frightened Arthur. But she wanted no comfort from him, in fact, since her mother's death she hadn't come near him. He reminded her that he was her godfather and that he loved her very much, but she stood politely listening, and never responded. She was an odd, distant girl, unusually quiet now that Solange was gone, and she spoke of her father as though she no longer knew him, as though he had died years before her mother. It was obvious that she was deeply affected by what had happened, and it was difficult to remind oneself that she was only eight years old. She seemed so marked by tragedy and it was painful to realize how much it had aged her.

Arthur tried to have dinner with them as often as he could, and he was growing worried about paying for the help, their schools, their food, and the apartment. Little Megan had been sick several times, and there were doctor's bills, and new shoes. Most of the money from Solange's jewellery had gone to defend Sam, and what was left was barely enough to make a difference. And their meagre funds were dwindling. And there were times when he wondered if Hilary knew it. She was forcing everyone into economies, and had even learned to mend her own clothes, much to Arthur's amazement. Megan had already begun to regard Hilary as her mother.

By the spring, Sam had lost thirty pounds, and all the psychiatric evaluations had been completed. The doctors who saw him all said that he was suffering from a deep depression. They were also willing to say that he had acted, in killing Solange, under the passion of the moment, and had perhaps been insane while he did it, although they all found him sane, normal and intelligent. His only problem was his very understandable depression. Arthur almost felt as though he couldn't reach him, and Sam did nothing to help prepare his own defence. He seemed uninterested in all of Arthur's efforts, and Arthur worked all night on his defence for months, looking up similar cases in the past, searching for improper technicalities, and desperately seeking new angles.

But the trial itself was a nightmare. The prosecutor was swift and sure, and he had found every tramp, whore, and starlet whom Sam had ever slept with. There was a parade of women dragged through, testifying to the fact that he drank too much, was sometimes violent when he was drunk, and had no morals whatsoever. And the portrait of Solange painted by the prosecution was one Arthur could hardly disagree with. They described a woman of intelligence and wit and charm and almost saintly devotion to her husband, anxious to do anything possible for him, to help further his career, and keep him happy, while taking extraordinarily good care of their three daughters. She was said to have kept a lovely home, kept aloof from all the Broadway and Hollywood mischief most stars' wives seemed to get into, and it was bluntly said that despite extensive research on the subject, the prosecution had been unable to find anyone who was able to say they thought Solange had ever cheated on her husband. She was thought to have been entirely faithful to him, in fact everyone spoken to said that Solange Walker had adored her husband. The prosecution also pointed out that he had absolutely no reason whatsoever to kill her. There was no 'crime passionnel', there was no justification she had given him for becoming crazed, or temporarily insane, he had simply wantonly, carelessly, wickedly killed her. They even tried to ask for a charge of murder in the first degree, suggesting that it was premeditated, and that he wanted to be free of her to pursue all his other floozies. While Arthur, on the other hand, tried to manoeuvre a manslaughter charge, indicating that it had all been an unfortunate accident. But in the end, after less than a day's deliberation, and more than three weeks of trial, the jury convicted him of murder. Arthur felt as though a stone wall had fallen on his head, and Sam was led from the courtroom looking glassy-eyed and vague. It was obvious that he was in shock, and his depression had worsened considerably during the trial. It had been difficult to get any real feeling from him when he was on the stand, or to believe that he had actually loved his wife. But he was so far gone in his own guilt and depression that he could no longer depict any semblance of real emotion, and Arthur had feared that would hurt him terribly with the jury.

Arthur asked to see his client in the holding cell immediately after the verdict, but Sam had refused to see him, and a request from Arthur to see him in his cell had been denied. Arthur left in total despair and frustration, feeling that he had failed Sam terribly. But he had warned him, and begged him to get a criminal attorney. Arthur flailed himself all the way back to his apartment for having allowed Sam to force him into defending him. He had two stiff drinks, thought about going to see the girls, and then decided that he couldn't face it. Marjorie had left a message that she wouldn't be home for dinner. As he sat at his desk in the dark he decided it was just as well. She had never been fond of Sam anyway, and what Arthur really needed was the warm touch and unconditional love of Solange. It was what they all needed and what Sam had robbed them of. For a long moment, Arthur found himself wondering if the jury had been right, and as he shuddered at his own thoughts, the phone rang. It was the sergeant at the jail, and he said he had news for him about his client. Maybe Sam was ready to see him after all, Arthur thought as he squinted at his watch in the summer twilight. It was eight-fifteen, and he was exhausted and more than a little drunk, but for Sam, he'd go there.

'Your client committed suicide in his cell an hour ago, Mr Patterson. We just found him.'

Arthur felt his heart stop, and the bile rise. He was going to throw up, or faint, or maybe just die. 'What?' It was barely a whisper. The sergeant repeated the same words as Arthur sank into a chair with a shudder, his entire body trembling. 'My God, why didn't you watch him?' He'd been depressed for months, they should have thought of that. In fact, one of the psychiatrists had warned them. But no one had really thought . . . and now they were both gone. It was almost more than Arthur could bear . . . his only friend . . . and the only woman he had ever truly loved . . . and now he had the girls to think about. What in God's name was he going to do about them? He was going to have to discuss it seriously with Marjorie when she got home. They had no one else now. Sam and Solange were both gone, and their daughters were now truly orphans.

Chapter 6

'Are you out of your mind, Arthur?' Marjorie was staring at him in complete disbelief. She looked as though he had just taken all his clothes off in public. He had been waiting up for her when she got home. And she barely reacted when he told her about Sam's suicide. What stunned her was Arthur's suggestion that they take in Hilary, Alexandra, and Megan. It was the only possible solution he could think of. They had no money and no family, and with a bigger apartment and a live-in maid, he and Marjorie could manage easily – if she would let him do it. 'Are you crazy? What in God's name would we do with three small children? We've never even wanted children of our own, why would we turn our lives upside down for the children of strangers?'

He gulped, trying to clear his head, and wishing he had waited till morning. He had had too much to drink by the time she came home, and he was afraid that his arguments wouldn't be convincing. 'Sam Walker was my best friend. He saved my life during the war . . . those children are not strangers to us, Marjorie, even if you'd like to think so.'

'But do you have any idea of the responsibility involved in having *one* child, let alone *three*?'

'Hilary is like a mother to them. She'd make everything easy for you, Marjorie. Truly.' He felt as though he were sixteen again, begging his mother for a car, and not winning the battle either. 'And I've always wanted children. You were the one who decided you couldn't handle kids *and* a career . . .' He tried to look at her reproachfully but she seemed not to care. She had no guilt, only righteous indignation.

'I will *not* take on three children. We don't have any space, the time, the lifestyle. You're as busy as I am. And besides, raising three girls would cost a fortune. No! Just forget it, Arthur. Put them in an institution.' And the tragedy, as Arthur listened to her get ready for bed, was that she meant it.

He tried again, the next morning over breakfast, but to no avail. Her mind was made up, and he didn't have the strength, or the ingenuity, to change it.

'I don't want children of my own, why would I want someone else's? And *theirs*! My God, Arthur, I always knew you were blind but I never thought you were stupid. The man was a murderer, not to mention everything else, can you imagine what traits those children will inherit? And their mother . . .' Arthur looked ominous as she got started again, but she was too involved in her own speech to notice. 'She always looked like a French whore to me. God only knows what she did over there during the war before she caught Sam Walker.'

'That's enough, Marjorie. You don't know what you're talking about. I was there when Sam met her.'

'In a bordello?' she asked viciously and he suddenly wanted to slap her. But there was no point. She had won. He was not going to be able to take in Sam's children.

'I won't discuss brothels with you, Marjorie, and I can tell you for certain that Solange Walker was never in one. I'm just sorry you're not willing to be more compassionate about this, Marjorie. It disappoints me greatly.' But she didn't give a damn. She left for work without saying another word to Arthur.

As far as she was concerned, it was his problem. And it was. Their parents were his closest friends. He was Hilary's godfather. Those children weren't strangers to him, no matter what Marjorie wished. They were flesh and blood, and he loved them.

And Sam and Solange had loved them too. It was desperately important to Arthur that they not lose a sense of that, or feel that they were being abandoned. The idea of putting them up for adoption sounded barbaric to him, but he just didn't know what else to do with them. And things got even more complicated the following week when both the maid and the nurse announced that they were leaving. They had stayed long enough in terrible conditions. They wanted a real home with parents for the children, and a couple at home, not a murdered wife and husband who'd been in jail. They both seemed outraged by the scandal that had been foisted on *them* and had remarkably little compassion for the children. And for Arthur, it meant finding new people to care for them, which seemed even more complicated now. Finally, by the week's end, he took out the name Sam had given him, of his sister. Eileen Jones. He wondered if he would even find her in Boston. But he thought that if he did, perhaps he could induce her to take care of them for a while. Then he could let the apartment on Sutton Place go, and it would save them a great deal of money. They were almost out of funds anyway. But having them stay with their aunt would give Arthur some time to make other arrangements, or convince Marjorie that they had to take them. Either way, he needed time, and having them stay with Sam's sister would give him the breather he needed. More than anything he wanted to convince Marjorie that what he wanted was right, and not crazy, as she kept insisting. It required some adjustments, to be sure, but they were three little human beings, and well worth adjusting for, even if she didn't think so. But then what? And if they didn't take them in, who on earth would? That was what worried Arthur.

But first he had to find their aunt, and see if she would take them, even if only for the summer. She couldn't be as bad as Sam said. She was his sister after all, and blood was thicker than water. He had his secretary call Boston information, and they finally turned up a Jack and Eileen Jones in Charlestown, a suburb which boasted a naval yard, and which his secretary told him was right on the water. It sounded perfect for a little summer holiday, and Arthur called her up without preamble. She sounded stunned to hear from Arthur, and she said she had read about the trial, and her brother's subsequent suicide in the papers. She didn't sound particularly emotional about his death, and she asked Arthur bluntly if Sam had left any money.

'Not a great deal, I'm afraid, which is why I'm calling.' He decided to get right to the point and see if she would help him. He had nowhere else to turn now. 'As you may know, Sam and Solange had three little girls, Hilary, Alexandra and Megan, and for the moment, there is literally no one to take them. I want to speak to you about the possibility of . . . to see if you might be interested in giving them a home, temporarily or permanently, whichever suits you.'

There was a stunned silence at the other end. And then her sharp voice that had none of the polish of her brother's. 'Holy shit. Are you kidding, mister? Three kids? I don't even have kids of my own. Why would I want Sam's three brats?'

'Because they need you. If you just kept them for the summer, it would give me time to find another suitable home for them. But for the moment, they have nowhere to go.' He tried to appeal to her sympathies, but another thought had occurred to Eileen Jones.

'Will you pay me to take them in?'

Arthur paused, but only for a second. 'I can certainly give you enough money to pay for their needs while they're with you.'

'That isn't what I meant, but I'll take that too.'

'I see.' Arthur could see why Sam wasn't fond of her, but there was no one else for him to turn to. 'Would three hundred dollars do as a fee for you, Mrs Jones? A hundred for each child?'

'For how long?' She sounded suspicious of him. Suspicious and greedy.

'Until I find a home for them . . . a few weeks, a month, perhaps the summer.'

'No more than that. I'm not runnin' an orphanage up here, you know. And my husband won't like it.' But she knew he'd like the three hundred dollars, and she was hoping they could squeeze some more out of Arthur.

'Do you have room for them, Mrs Jones?'

'I got a spare room. Two of them can sleep in one bed, and we'll figure something out for the other one.'

'That would be Megan. She'll need a crib. She's just over a year old.' He wanted to ask if she knew how to take care of a baby. He wanted to ask a lot of things, but he didn't dare. He had no choice. He just had to trust that she'd do the best she could, for Sam's sake. And the children were so adorable, he was sure she'd fall in love with them the minute she saw them.

But it was something less than love at first sight when Arthur drove the three girls to Charlestown. He had explained to Hilary the day before that they were going to stay with Aunt Eileen for the summer. He told the maid to pack all their things, and explained quietly that she and the nurse would be free to leave after the girls left in the morning. He suggested that Hilary and Alexandra take their favourite toys. And he did not tell anyone that he would be closing the apartment and selling everything as soon as the children had left it. They would be better off with whatever meagre amount he could eke from the sale of the furniture, and not having their funds depleted by paying rent for an apartment on Sutton Place. Sam's debts were still astronomical, and there just was no money coming in from anywhere for them. He was glad to be getting rid of the apartment and the two servants.

Hilary had eyed him suspiciously when he told them about the trip to Boston. Much of her affection for him seemed to have cooled since her mother's death, but it was difficult to tell if that was just her way of expressing pain, or due to some other reason.

'Why are you sending us away?'

'Because it'll be nicer for you there than it is here. Your aunt lives near the water in Boston. It'll be cooler, if nothing else, and you can't just sit here in New York all summer, Hilary.'

'But we're coming back, right?'

'Of course you are.' He felt a wave of guilt and terror wash over him. What if she could see that he was lying?

'Then why did you tell Millie to pack all our things?'

'Because I thought you might need them. Now, don't be unreasonable, Hilary. It'll be nice for all of you to get to know your father's sister.'

Hilary was standing very quietly in the centre of the room, in a yellow organdie dress with white piqué trim, her shining black hair – like Sam's – perfectly combed into two smooth braids, her big green eyes as wise as Solange's had been, her little white anklets immaculate, and her patent leather Mary Janes shined to perfection. And she studied him, as though she knew he were hiding something from her. In a way, she frightened him, she was so knowing and so cool, and so fiercely protective of her sisters. She had taken the news of her father's suicide stoically. She had barely cried, and she had comforted Alexandra, and explained that Daddy had gone to heaven to be with Mommy. It all seemed terribly hard for Alexandra to understand, she was only five after all, but Hilary made everything easier for her, as she did for all of them. It was as though Solange had left her there to care for all of them in her absence.

'Why didn't we ever meet Aunt Eileen before? Didn't my Daddy like her?' She was perceptive just as Solange had been, and she didn't take any nonsense. The way her eyes flashed over him reminded him so much of her mother.

'I don't think they were close, Hilary, but that doesn't mean she's not a nice person.'

Hilary nodded, she was willing to suspend judgment. Temporarily. But it was easy to see what she thought when they arrived in Charlestown.

The house was a small frame house on a dark street, with shutters that had fallen off in the bitter winds of the previous winters. The paint was peeling everywhere, the yard was overgrown with weeds, and two of the front steps were broken. It was a less than auspicious welcome, as Hilary walked up the steps, holding Alexandra's hand, and Arthur carried the baby. The nurse had come with them, for the trip, but she was returning to New York with Arthur.

He rang the doorbell ineffectively, and finally realized

that it, too, was broken. And then he knocked hard on the window. He could feel Hilary's eyes on him and her silent question, asking him why they had come here. He didn't dare look at her now, he couldn't have borne to see Solange's eyes looking up at him, filled with silent reproach and unspent fury.

'Yeah?' The door opened finally, and a woman with blond stringy hair yanked the door open wearing a frayed dirty bathrobe. 'What do *you* want?' She stared at the crew on the front steps with obvious annoyance, a cigarette hanging out of the corner of her mouth, her eyes squinting shut to defend themselves from the smoke wafting up, and then she realized who they were. She smiled uncomfortably, and for a fraction of an instant, she looked like Sam, but barely. One had to be looking for the resemblance.

'Mrs Jones?' Arthur's heart was sinking slowly to his feet, and he felt no better as they walked into the living room. There was a broken couch, three battered chairs with the stuffing pouring out, a coffee table that had seen better days, and a small Formica dinner set, with a television blaring in the distance. Inside, the house looked even worse than it did outside. Eileen Jones apparently did not spend a great deal of time keeping house for her husband.

It was a Saturday afternoon and there was a baseball game blaring on the radio, at the same time as Gabby Hayes came on the TV. The noise was deafening, and the children looked stunned by it. Everyone stood awkwardly in the middle of the living room, looking at each other.

'Want a beer?' She looked at Arthur, ignoring the children. And it was difficult to believe that this was Sam Walker's sister. He had been so impeccably groomed, such a handsome man, he had had such presence and power and magnetism about him. One had felt instantly drawn to Sam, and together with Solange they had made a dazzling couple. But this woman was a parody of all that was cheap and beaten and ugly. She looked well beyond her thirty-nine years, and the ravages of booze had taken their toll on her early. She might have been attractive once, but anything pleasant in her looks was long gone. She only looked hard and bitter and ugly. Her dyed hair was thin, dirty and unkempt, cut just below her ears, and hanging limp and greasy. She had Sam's brilliant blue eyes, but there was a dullness to them, with terrible bags beneath them from excessive drinking. Her skin was sallow, and her waist was thickened by beer, while her legs looked like two little toothpicks. She was totally foreign to everything the girls had ever seen, and Arthur realized that Hilary was staring at her in shock and horror.

'This is Hilary.' He tried to encourage her forward to shake the woman's hand, but she wouldn't budge. 'And Alexandra,' who sniffed the stale beer that seemed to permeate the air, and made a face as she looked up at Hilary's obvious disapproval, 'and Megan.' He indicated the baby, who glanced at the battered blonde with wide eyes. She was the only one who didn't seem worried by her summer home or her hostess. The other two looked terrified, and Hilary had to fight back tears when she saw the room they were to be given to sleep in. Eileen Jones walked them back to it without ceremony, waved in the direction of the sagging, narrow bed that stood unmade in one corner. The room itself was a narrow cell without windows, barely big enough for the bed it held, with a crib folded against one wall that looked as though she had fished it out of someone else's garbage, which is precisely where Eileen had found it, shortly after Arthur had called her.

'We'll get the sheets on the bed later.' She smiled artificially at her oldest niece. 'Maybe you can help me.' And then, with no particular interest she glanced at Arthur. 'Got her mother's eyes though.'

Arthur looked puzzled. 'You knew Solange?' Solange had never mentioned this woman to him.

'I met her once. Sam was doing a play up here or something.'

And then suddenly Arthur remembered. Solange had hated her. But so had Sam. They had come by when he was doing summer stock in Stockbridge after the war. It seemed light years ago, but so did everything now. Arthur looked around him with a lump in his throat, hating to leave the girls there. And for a moment he hated his wife for condemning the children to this. How could she do this? But she didn't know, he reminded himself, as he fought back his own guilt and resentment. He had to force himself not to think about it and remind himself that this arrangement was only for the summer. And then ... that was the real problem. And then what? Marjorie was intransigent. And he had already put out feelers everywhere, for people who would help, people who might want to take them in, people who had large families of their own, or people with no children of their own, but who might be willing to have them. He had spoken to all of his partners at the law firm.

Hilary was still standing awkwardly in the doorway of what was to be their room, staring with dismay at their new quarters. There was no closet, no chest for their things, there wasn't even a chair or a lamp or a table. There was a bare bulb hanging from the ceiling, which dangled near the doorway.

'You got the money?' Eileen turned to him, and feeling awkward handing it over to her in front of the girls, he reached into his jacket for an envelope.

'That includes a reasonable amount for their expenses.'

Being far less genteel than Arthur, she opened the envelope and thumbed through it. He had given her a thousand dollars, including the fee, and if she played her cards right, and fed them nothing but macaroni and cheese for the next two months, she'd have plenty of money left over. She smiled happily at the girls, took a swig of her beer, and saluted Arthur as she tossed her cigarette into the sink with perfect aim. She did it often. 'That's just fine, Mr Patterson. We have any problems, I'll call you.'

'I thought I might come up to see them in a few weeks, if you and your husband don't mind, to see how they're doing.' Hilary stared at him unbelievingly. He was actually going to leave them in this place, with the filth and the beer bottles and the unmade bed ... and that awful woman. And if she had been withdrawn before, she was icy now, as he left them. 'I'll call you in a few days, Hilary, and don't be afraid to call if you need me.' All she could do was nod. She couldn't believe he was doing this to them, after everything else he'd done. For a moment, she wanted to kill him. And instead she turned to look down at Alexandra, who was crying softly.

'Don't be silly, Axie. This is going to be fun. Remember, Uncle Arthur said we could go to the ocean.'

'Yeah?' Eileen laughed raucously as they heard the car drive away. 'Where you going to do that? In the shipyard?' She laughed again. A thousand bucks was a hell of a nice price for a few months of inconvenience, and with luck they wouldn't be too bad. The baby looked like kind of a pain in the ass, and the five-year-old looked like a whiner, but the oldest one seemed to have it all in control. With luck, she'd take care of everything. Maybe she'd even cook and clean house. Eileen fell onto the couch in front of the TV with a fresh beer, and lit a cigarette. Maybe she and Jack would go out for dinner.

'Excuse me.' Hilary stood awkwardly next to the television, holding the baby. 'Where are the sheets for our bed?'

'On the back porch, I think. If you can find 'em.' She never spoke another word to them, as Hilary quietly got them organized. She found torn sheets, but at least they were clean, and she put them on the bed, but there were no pillows and no blanket. And she put a makeshift sheet in the baby's crib, propping it between her bed and the wall, for fear it would topple over if she didn't. As she had suspected, it was broken.

She washed Alexandra's face then and took her to the bathroom, changed Megan's nappy, and gave all three of them a drink of water, as they sat quietly in their new room, looking around them.

'It's so ugly here,' Axie whispered, afraid that the lady with the cigarette and the beer would hear her. 'Is she really Daddy's sister?'

Hilary nodded. It was difficult to believe, and not pleasant to think about, but she was their aunt and they were stuck with her for the summer. There was no place for them to put their toys, and the dresses the nurse had packed for them had to remain in their suitcases. It was five o'clock before Eileen saw them again, and as she had suspected, Hilary had everything in control.

'Excuse me.' She stood in front of her with her shining dark hair and big green eyes, like a miniature spokesman. 'Could you give my sisters something to eat? They're both hungry.' Eileen hadn't even thought of that. There was nothing in the house. She opened the fridge and there was nothing there except beer and some rotting lemons and stale bread. Eileen and Jack never ate at home if they could help it. All they did was drink there.

'Sure, kid. Which one are you?'

'Hilary.' There was something very distant in her eyes, as though the last nine months had left her broken. She was only nine years old and she had already had more pain and grief than most people have in a lifetime.

'Can you go to the store for me, and get yourself something to eat? A couple of cans of tuna ought to do it.'

'Tuna?' Hilary looked as though she'd never heard the word. She was used to hot meals prepared by the maid on Sutton Place, and her mother before that. Thick soups, and rich stews, and steaks cooked medium rare, and chocolate cakes with vanilla ice cream. 'Tuna fish?'

'Yeah. Here's some money.' She handed her a few dollars, as though she expected her to create an entire dinner with two dollars. Even Hilary knew that was impossible. Her nurse gave her more than that just when she went to get ice cream. 'The store's on the corner, you can't miss it. And buy me another beer too, will ya?' She was always afraid of running out, even when she had plenty.

Hilary took her sisters with her, only because she was afraid of what would happen if she didn't. And the store looked as seamy as everything else around them. Most of the houses were either crumbling brick, or wood with faded, peeling paint on them. And everything in the neighbourhood looked as though it was battered and beaten and broken. Hilary bought two cans of tuna fish, a jar of baby food, a loaf of bread, some mayonnaise, butter, half a dozen eggs, a container of milk and a can of beer for their hostess. Hilary figured she could make a halfway decent dinner out of all of it, and she could use the rest of the eggs and the bread to make breakfast the next morning. But as she came in the front door struggling to carry the package and Megan and still hold Axie's hand, Eileen asked her two questions.

'Where's my beer?'

'I have it in the bag.'

'Then get it,' she barked at Hilary, and Axie started to whimper. She hated people who shouted at her, or her sisters. Their mother never had, and even their nurse didn't shout at them, even though they didn't like her much and she said ugly things about their parents.

Hilary handed Eileen the beer as quickly as she could, and Eileen glared at her and asked the second question. 'Where's the change?'

Hilary handed her three cents, and Eileen threw it back at her, hitting the baby near the eye with one of the pennies. 'What'd you do, buy yourself a T-bone? This isn't Park Avenue, you know. Where the hell's the rest of the money?' She seemed to have forgotten the thousand dollars Arthur had given her for just this purpose.

'I had to buy them dinner,' Hilary explained. 'And there was nothing for breakfast tomorrow morning.'

'When I want you to buy breakfast, I'll tell you. You got that? And next time, don't spend so goddam much money.'

Hilary was stunned at what she was hearing, and her hands shook as she made them dinner. With expert ease, she had food in front of them in less than ten minutes. A soft-boiled egg and toast and baby food for Megan, and tuna fish sandwiches with mayonnaise for herself and Axie, and big glasses of milk for all three of them, which they drank gratefully. They were hungry and exhausted after the drive from New York and the emotional shock of Eileen and Charlestown.

Hilary did not offer her aunt anything to eat, and Eileen showed no interest in what they were doing. Hilary had them eat in their own room. The simultaneous blare of the radio and television made it impossible to talk and Eileen frightened all of them, even the baby. But just as Hilary was putting their dishes in the sink and starting to wash them, Eileen's husband came home, and Hilary was even more frightened when she saw him. He was a huge, burly man with enormous arms and powerful shoulders, and he was wearing work pants and an undershirt. The cloud of booze that surrounded him reached her all the way to the kitchen. He started to yell at Eileen almost the instant he walked in the door, but before he could hit her, she waved the envelope at him and showed him what he thought was all the money. Five hundred dollars. He broke into a big foolish grin, never suspecting that his wife had hidden an equal amount in a pile of old stockings where she kept her own money.

'Wooo . . . baby! Look at that! Ain't it purty?' Hilary watched him, long before he had seen her. 'What's that for?'

'Them.' She pointed vaguely to the back of the house and Jack suddenly spotted Hilary in the kitchen.

'Who's that?' He looked blank, and Hilary noticed that he had an incredibly stupid face, and eyes that reminded her of a pig. She hated him on sight, he was even worse than Eileen, and he looked meaner.

'Remember my brother's kids I told you about?'

'The one who snuffed his old lady?'

'Yeah. Him. Well, they came today.'

'How long we gotta keep 'em?' He looked less than pleased as he glanced over Hilary like a piece of meat. He did not seem to think of their arrival as good news, in spite of the windfall.

'A few weeks, till that lawyer finds them some place to live.'

So that was it. Hilary heard the news with a shiver. Arthur hadn't explained it to them before they left, and she suddenly wondered what would happen to their apartment.

But Eileen was smiling at her husband, as Hilary watched them. She was impervious to the children in the back room, as was he. It was as though they didn't exist, and to the Joneses they didn't. 'Hey, baby, let's go dancing tonight.' They both looked too drunk to Hilary, but Jack Jones seemed to like the idea, as Hilary watched them. He had an oily-looking face and thinning hair, and thick hands that looked like roast beef.

'Can we leave the kids?'

'Sure, why not? The older one does everything.'

'Everything?' He leered at his wife and moved closer, as Hilary sensed with a shiver that what he was suggesting was improper, but Eileen only laughed at him and pulled him closer.

'Come on, you horny old sailor . . . she's only nine years old for chrissake . . .' Eileen was laughing at him as he pressed his mouth down hard on hers, and slipped a fat hand into her bathrobe.

'And how old were you the first time?'

'Thirteen,' she said primly, but they both knew she was lying, and then with a raucous laugh she went to get herself another beer, and saw that Hilary was watching. 'What the hell are you doing here, spying on us, you little brat?'

'I was just . . . cleaning up after dinner . . . I'm sorry . . . I . . .'

'Go to your room!' she shouted, slamming the refrigerator door with a vengeance. 'Goddam kids.' She knew they were going to be a real nuisance before she got rid of them again, but as long as Jack didn't mind too much, they were good for the money.

The Joneses went out at eight o'clock that night. Megan and Alexandra were already asleep in their narrow airless room, but Hilary was lying in the dark, thinking of their mother. She would never have let something like this happen to them. Never. She would have read Eileen the riot act, taken her children home, and somewhere, somehow, she would have made a home for them, and that was just what Hilary had to do. And she knew it. She had to find a way, and a place to go ... and enough money to do it. She wasn't going to let anything happen to her little sisters. She would do anything to protect them. And in the meantime she just had to keep them away from Jack and Eileen, keep them amused, outside in the weed-choked yard, or in their room. She'd make their meals, give them their baths, take care of their clothes. She lay in bed and planned everything until she fell asleep, and she didn't wake up again until morning, when Megan woke her up at six-fifteen with a dirty nappy. She was a good-natured child with her mother's red hair, which hung in loose coppery curls, and she had her father's big blue eyes, just as Hilary herself had her father's dark hair and her mother's green eyes. But it was Alexandra who really looked like their mother, and it tore at Hilary's heart sometimes to see her looking so much like Solange, and she sounded just like her whenever she giggled.

She made the girls' breakfast before Jack and Eileen woke up, and she took them outside to play, after dressing them in matching blue gingham dresses. She wore a red dress herself with a little apron. Her mother had bought it for her before she died, and she still loved it best of all. And it comforted her to wear it now, and think of her mother.

It was noon before Eileen Jones appeared in the doorway to glare at them. She looked as though she were sick, and had they been older, they would have known she was desperately hung over.

'Can't you brats shut up? You make enough noise for a whole neighbourhood. Christ!' The screen door slammed and she went back inside, and they didn't see her again until after lunch. She stayed inside all day and watched television and drank beer, and Jack seemed to go somewhere else to do his drinking. The only change during the week was that Jack left earlier and wore work clothes. He rarely spoke to them, except once in a while, he'd make a crack at Hilary, and tell her she'd be nice-looking one day, and she never knew what to say to him. Eileen didn't speak to them at all. And it seemed aeons before they heard from Arthur. He called exactly one week after he had left them and inquired how everything was. Hilary spoke mechanically and told him they were fine, but it was obvious to anyone that they weren't. Axie had started having nightmares and Megan was waking up at night. The room was breathlessly hot and the food inadequate. Hilary did everything she could to compensate for all of it, but there was only so much she could do. She was a nine-year-old child after all, and she was slowly drowning in deep waters.

But she told none of that to Arthur.

'We're fine.' But she sounded tired and unenthusiastic.

'I'll call you again in a few days.' But he didn't. He had his hands full at the office, with a difficult case, and he was still trying to finish sorting out Sam's affairs, and find someone to take the girls, but by August, it was plainly obvious that that wasn't going to happen. And he had given up trying to convince his wife. She had finally told him it was her or the children. The die was cast. Arthur was not going to take them.

Chapter 7

By the end of the summer two of Arthur's colleagues came to him quietly, quite unexpectedly, and offered to solve his problem.

The first to do so was one of the oldest partners in the firm. George Gorham was nearing retirement age, but only the year before, he had married an extremely attractive young socialite in her early twenties. Margaret Millington had been one of the prettiest débutantes of the year when she came out, and after that she had impressed everyone by doing extremely well at Vassar. But then she had left the usual expected mould, and instead of marrying one of the young men her parents expected her to, she had become involved with George Gorham. A widower, he was forty years older than she, and perfect for her in every way. Except that he was unable to have children. He had been honest with her and she insisted that it didn't matter. But he was afraid it might some day, and he didn't want to lose her. And little Alexandra would fill the only void between them. He had discussed with Margaret adopting all of the Walker children and keeping the family intact, and although it seemed a noble deed, it seemed a little excessive to them. He didn't feel young enough to take on a child of Megan's age, and a child as old as Hilary when she was adopted could present problems. But a five-year-old sounded ideal to them, and Margaret was ecstatic.

And on the same day that George approached Arthur about adopting Alexandra, David Abrams had privately come to see Arthur. He was only thirty-four, and he and his wife Rebecca were both attorneys, although Rebecca worked for another firm with more liberal leanings. They had been married since their senior year in college and had been attempting to have a baby since their last year in law school, with no success. And they had finally been told that the situation was hopeless. Rebecca was unable to have children. It had been a tremendous blow to both of them, particularly as they had hoped to have several children, but now they found they would be grateful for one, which was really all they could afford at the moment. Like the Gorhams, they had briefly thought of adopting all three, but they felt unable to take on that large a burden. What they wanted was to adopt Megan, the baby.

Which left only Hilary. And Arthur with an enormous decision. Should he break up the family? Did he have a right to do that? But then again, Sam had murdered Solange, and in so doing, had destroyed all of their lives. Maybe all Arthur could do was save each one separately. The Gorhams were wonderful people, and both of them were enormously wealthy. There was no doubt in Arthur's mind that Alexandra would have everything she needed, and from what George had said, it was obvious that they would love her deeply. What's more, they would be near by, and Arthur could keep an eye on things, not that he needed to with George and Margaret Gorham.

And although Rebecca and David Abrams were less comfortably circumstanced than George, they were certainly two hard-working young people, with promising careers ahead of them, with families from New York, so it was unlikely they would stray far, and once again Arthur could play guardian angel to Megan.

But it was Hilary who worried him most. What would happen to her now? It was a great shame that neither the Gorhams nor the Abramses were willing to take on a second child, but when he inquired again, both of them were definite when they said they wouldn't. He mentioned it to Marjorie once again, but her answer was an adamant 'no'. And he sensed that their relationship might be in jeopardy if he persisted. He had promised her weeks before not to bring the subject up again. But that left Hilary with nowhere to go, except where she was, with the Joneses in Boston, if they would even keep her. There was going to be about ten thousand dollars in Sam's estate after everything was sold, and Arthur thought about the possibility of offering that to the Joneses for the care and feeding of Hilary for as long as it lasted. It was better than nothing, but not much, and he was unhappy with the solution as he made the final arrangements for the others. The papers were drawn up, and both couples were wildly excited. Rebecca planned to take a month off from work, and Margaret and George planned a trip to Europe in the autumn with their new daughter. George had already ravaged F A O Schwarz and Alexandra's new room looked like a toy store, whereas Rebecca had bought enough sweaters and snowsuits and underwear for quintuplets. They were two very lucky little girls and their arrivals were anticipated with breathless excitement. But it was Hilary who continued to worry Arthur.

In mid-August, he had a brief conversation with Eileen Jones, and explained the situation to her. And she bluntly said that for ten thousand dollars, she'd keep her indefinitely, but she didn't see why she had to adopt her. She could just live with them. And cook and clean, although she didn't fill in those details for Arthur. It was like having a live-in maid, she was already having her do everything,

and Hilary was so deathly afraid of her that she did whatever she told her. She had struck Alexandra once hard,
across the face, for some minor infraction she never explained, and she had hit the baby more than once, whenever she touched the television or the radio, or ventured
out of their room at all, which it was difficult not to. It
was a tiny room for the three of them, particularly a baby
who was not quite two and didn't understand that she was
being confined to her quarters.

But in any case, Eileen agreed to keep Hilary, as long as
she got the ten thousand dollars in cash. She was becoming
a very profitable little venture for Eileen. And this time
she would tell Jack about two thousand dollars and keep
eight for herself, giving him a long song and dance that
she was doing it for the memory of her brother.

'I thought you didn't like him.'

'He was still my brother . . . and it's still his kid. Besides
she's a pretty good kid, and a good worker.'

'Kids are a pain in the ass.' Jack knew at firsthand. His
last wife had had three of them, and they had driven him
crazy. 'But if you want to take care of her, she's your
problem, not mine. Just so she don't bug me.'

'If she does, just whack her.'

'Yeah.' That seemed to mollify him, and he agreed to
let Eileen keep her. And that night she locked herself in
the bathroom, checked that her other money was still
there, and figured that with the eight she got to keep from
the cheque for Hilary, she'd have close to ten thousand
dollars hidden among her suspender belt and nylons. It
gave her a good feeling, in case she ever decided to walk
out on her husband. And maybe she'd take the kid with
her, and maybe she wouldn't. Depends if she was any use
to her or not, otherwise let Jack worry about feeding her,
or let the lawyer take her back. She didn't owe the kid

anything. But the kid owed her. After all, she had agreed to keep her, hadn't she? She owed her a lot, from Eileen's point of view. And Eileen owed her nothing.

Arthur came up looking sombre with a nurse he had hired for the day, and he was startled to see Hilary looking so thin and the others so pale after their months in Boston. They looked like little waifs and he found himself hoping that they were all healthy. And he asked Hilary to come outside with him so they could talk for a while. He wanted to know how she really was, but when she went outside, she told him nothing. It was as though she had put an even greater distance between them, and he didn't even suspect how much she hated him for leaving them in this hellhole. She had spent two months trying to eke out enough sustenance for her sisters, barely able to feed them, let alone herself, on the meagre allotment Eileen gave her. She had washed, scrubbed, cooked, and baby-sat, and constantly protected them from the threatened beatings of their aunt and uncle. And at night she sang them to sleep and held them when they cried for their mother. And Arthur knew none of that as he watched Hilary's face and wondered why she was so distant.

And now, he had to tell her the news no one had prepared her for. Her sisters were leaving, and she wasn't. They would never be together again, except on visits, if their new parents would allow it, and Arthur already knew that the Abramses wouldn't. They didn't want Megan to know anything about her past life, her parents, or even her sisters. She was disappearing into a new life. Forever.

'Hilary . . .' he began awkwardly, sitting on the back steps of the Joneses house, off the laundry porch, with the weeds scratching their legs, and the flies buzzing around them. 'I . . . I thought . . . I have . . . some things to tell you.' He wished he could tell her anything but what he had to. He knew how attached she was to them, but it wasn't his fault it had come to this, he kept reminding himself. He had done his best . . . if only Marjorie had been willing to take them . . .

'Is something wrong, Uncle Arthur?' Maybe he was going to tell her now they weren't going back to their apartment, but Eileen had already told them it was gone, and she had adjusted. As long as they were together, that was all that mattered, even here. She turned her big green eyes up to him, and he felt as though Solange had reached out and touched him, but it only made him feel worse now.

'I . . . your sisters are going away for a little while.' There was no other way to tell her, except directly.

'Megan and Axie?' She looked startled and confused as she turned the familiar emerald gaze on him again.

'Why? Why are they going anywhere?'

'Because.' Oh God . . . please don't make me do this to her. There was a sob of anguish lodged in his chest. But he had to tell her. 'Because, Hilary, there's no way to keep you together anymore. Your aunt doesn't feel she can, and no one else felt they could either. Megan and Alexandra are going to two very nice families in New York, to live with them. And you're going to stay here with your aunt in Boston.' It would have been easier to run a knife through her heart, and when he saw the tears spill from her eyes he envied Sam the easy fate he had chosen, and hated him for it all at once. 'Hilary, please . . . darling, I tried, I really did . . .' He reached out to her, but she escaped him, darting through the weeds toward the front of the house again, as though they might already be gone, and shouting back at him.

'No! No! I won't let you!' She ran inside, and offering no explanation she rushed into their ugly room and pulled both girls close to her. She had left them playing on her bed, and Axie baby-sitting for Megan. She held them close to her, with tears streaming down her cheeks, feeling desperate and helpless, and knowing that there was no way to fight him. She had nowhere to go, and no money to take them with, and no one to help her, and she was only nine years old. But they couldn't do this to her . . . they couldn't . . . they were all she had . . . her mother and father had betrayed her . . . and Uncle Arthur . . . and her aunt and uncle hated her and she hated them . . . all she had in the world were Megan and Axie.

'What's the matter, Hillie?' Alexandra was staring up at her with her big blue eyes, and Megan cried when Hilary held her too tight, so she simply let her go and clung to Axie.

'I love you . . . that's all . . . I just love you . . . with all my heart. Will you always remember that, Axie?'

'Yes.' The little voice was sober, as though she knew something important was happening. They had been through a lot together, the three of them, and they had an unusual bond to each other, as though they sensed each other's moods and possible danger. 'Is something bad going to happen again, Hillie? Like Mommy and Daddy? Are you going away in a box too?'

She started to cry and Hilary was quick to shake her head. 'No, no. Don't be afraid, Axie. Uncle Arthur wants to take you and Megan on a little trip back to New York to visit friends of his.' She knew she had to make it easy for them, no matter how painful it was for her. But she could tolerate anything for them. But for Megan it would be the easiest of all. She would cry when they took her away from her sisters, but she would never remember . . . never . . . and Hilary would never forget them. She would carry them with her for the rest of her life, and one day she would find them. She swore it to herself as she held Alexandra, and a moment later, Arthur and the nurse he had hired appeared in the doorway.

'We should go soon, Hilary.'

She nodded, blinded by tears, and suddenly Alexandra began to wail. 'I don't want to leave Hillie.' She clung to her hand, and wiping away her own tears, Hilary kissed her gently.

'You have to go to help take care of Megan, otherwise she'll be scared. Okay? Will you take care of her for me?'

Alexandra nodded through her tears. No matter what they told her, she knew something terrible was going to happen, and as Hilary packed her things, she was sure of it. Eileen was staying out of their way. She was so excited about the fresh green bills Arthur had given her that all she could do was sit in the locked bathroom and count them. She was going to hide most of it from Jack, but she wanted to look at it all together first.

So Hilary was alone as she helped put Alexandra and Megan in the car. The girls sat in the back with the nurse, Megan holding her arms out to Hilary as she cried, and Alexandra sobbing uncontrollably as Arthur got behind the wheel with a last look at Hilary.

'I'll come back to see you soon.' She said nothing to him. He had betrayed her. And the cries from the back seat almost overwhelmed her as she fought to keep control, and stepped back, waving at them, shouting at the car, for as long as they could hear her.

'I love you, Axie ... I love you, Megan ... I love you ...' Her voice broke into a sob as she stood in the street, waving at the retreating car until it turned a corner and was gone, taking her whole life with it. And as the car disappeared, she sank to her knees sobbing their names, wishing that someone would kill her. She wasn't aware of anything until she felt someone shaking her, and a hard hand cracked her across the face. She looked up, blinded by her tears, to see Eileen standing over her, clutching her battered purse under her arm with a look of victory.

She spoke harshly to the child, as she always did. 'What the hell are you doing?' And then she realized that they must have gone. 'Crying won't do anything. Go inside and clean up, you little fool. People are going to think we been treating you bad.' She dragged her to her feet and shoved her into the house as Hilary sobbed uncontrollably, and another hard slap across her face did nothing to help it. She staggered inside to her room, and threw herself across the bed, which still smelled of the two children who had just left it. She could smell the powder she had used only moments ago on Megan when she changed her and the shampoo on Axie's bright red curls. The agony was more than Hilary could bear.

She lay there and sobbed for hours, until at last she fell asleep, exhausted, drained, battered by the realities of her existence. And she fell into a deep fitful sleep where she was running . . . running . . . running after a car . . . trying to find them . . . looking everywhere . . . and all she could hear in the distance was Eileen's drunken laughter.

Part III

HILARY

Chapter 8

That year, after tearing flesh from flesh, Arthur called Hilary several times, but she refused to come to the phone and talk to him, and eventually his own guilt made him call her less and less often. He knew that the other girls were all right. The Gorhams were ecstatic over Alexandra, she was a delightful little girl, and the Abramses were in love with 'their' baby. But he had no grip on Hilary now, no idea how she was, since Eileen did not keep him informed, and Hilary wouldn't speak to him on the phone.

He went to Boston to see her once, just before Thanksgiving. But Hilary sat in the living room as though numb. She had nothing to say to him, and he left with a feeling of guilt and quiet desperation. He felt as though he had destroyed the child, and yet what choice did he have, and Eileen was her aunt after all. He told himself a thousand stories to calm his conscience as he drove home again, and it was Christmas when he called again, but this time no one answered, and after that he was busy with his own life. George Gorham had died suddenly, and quite unexpectedly David Abrams had decided to move to California, which meant that a great deal more work fell to Arthur. There were, of course, several other partners in the firm, but Arthur was among the senior men there and a great many decisions fell to him, particularly about

George's estate which was very involved. He saw Margaret at the funeral of course, but she had decided not to bring Alexandra.

It was spring before Arthur saw Hilary again, and he found her even more withdrawn, with a bleak look of despair that was frightening. The house was immaculate, which was at least some relief to him, at least Eileen was making more of an effort. He had no idea that she used Hilary as a full-time maid now. At the age of ten, it fell to her to do everything, including pull the weeds outside, wash and iron her aunt's and uncle's clothes, clean, cook, and do laundry. It was remarkable that she got decent grades in school, but somehow she always did, in spite of everything. She had no friends, and no desire to make any. What did she have in common with them? The other kids in school had normal homes, they had mothers and fathers and sisters. She had an aunt and uncle who hated her and drank too much, and a thousand chores to do before finishing her homework and going to bed around midnight. And lately, Eileen wasn't feeling well. She talked about her health all the time, she was losing weight, even with all the beer she drank, and she had been to several doctors. She had overheard Jack saying something about Florida. He had friends who worked in a naval shipyard there and they thought they could get him a civilian job. He thought maybe the warm weather would be good for Eileen, and they could move down before next winter.

But Hilary never mentioned this to Arthur. It didn't matter to him. And she didn't care about him any more, or about anything. The only thing she cared about was finding Axie and Megan again, and she knew that one day she would. All she had to do was wait until she turned eighteen, and then she would find them. She dreamt about it at night, and she could still feel Axie's soft red curls on her cheek on the bed next to her and Megan's soft baby breath when she held her . . . and one day . . . one day . . . she would find them.

They moved to Jacksonville, Florida, that October, and by then Eileen was very sick. She could hardly eat or walk, and by Christmas she was bedridden, and Hilary instinctively knew that she was dying. Jack seemed to take no interest in her, and he was out constantly, drinking and carousing, and sometimes she saw him around the neighbourhood, coming out of someone's house, and kissing another woman. And it was her job to take care of Eileen, to do everything that had to be done for a dying woman. She didn't want to go to a hospital, and Jack said they couldn't afford it. So Hilary did everything, from the time she got home from school, until the next morning. Sometimes she didn't sleep at all. She just lay on the floor next to Eileen's bed, and tended her as she was needed. Jack didn't sleep in her room any more anyway. He slept on a big sleeping porch at the back of the house, and came and went as it suited him, without even seeing his wife for days sometimes. And Eileen cried and asked Hilary where he was at night, and Hilary would lie to her and say he was sleeping.

But even Eileen's illness didn't bring out any kindness in her, no gentleness, no gratitude for the impossible tasks Hilary was performing. She expected it of her, and even as weak as she was, if she thought Hilary could do more, she would threaten to beat her. It was an empty threat now, but Hilary still hated her, she had from the first day she saw her.

Eileen lived for another year and a half after they reached Florida, and when Hilary was twelve, she finally died, staring at Hilary as though she wanted to say something to her, but Hilary was sure it wouldn't have been anything kindly.

And life was simpler in some ways after that, and more complicated in others. She didn't have to provide nursing care any more. But she had to steer clear of Jack, and the women he dragged in with him. He had told her bluntly the day after Eileen died that he was willing to let her stay under his roof as long as she didn't cause any trouble. He had also told her to clear out her aunt's things, keep what she wanted, and throw out the rest. He didn't seem to want any reminders of her. She had taken her time doing it, feeling somehow that Eileen was going to come back and punish her for going through her things, but she finally got through the last of it. She gave the clothes away to a church bazaar, and threw all the cheap make-up out. She was about to throw out all her underwear when she noticed a little cloth pouch in one of the drawers and went through it just to be sure it was nothing important. There was over ten thousand dollars there, mostly in small bills, and a few fifties, as though she'd gathered it over the years, hiding it from everyone, and probably from Jack as well. Hilary sat staring at the pouch for a long time, and then silently she slipped it into a pocket, and that night she hid it among her own things. It was just what she needed to escape one day, and find Megan and Alexandra.

For the next year, Jack scarcely took any notice of her. He was too busy chasing all the neighbourhood women. By then, he had lost several jobs, but he always seemed able to find another one. He didn't care what he did, as long as he had a roof over his head, a woman in his bed at night, and a six-pack of beer in the fridge. But when Hilary turned thirteen, he suddenly became more demanding. He seemed to be complaining all the time, and asked her to do things for him. He didn't think she was keeping the house clean enough, and when he came home for dinner, which was rare, he complained that her cooking was lousy. There was suddenly no pleasing him, and he acted as though it mattered to him, whereas before he had taken no notice of her at all. Now he even criticized the way she dressed and said her clothes were too baggy and her skirts were too long. It was 1962 and mini-skirts were in, and he told her she should dress more like the girls she saw in magazines or on TV.

'Don't you want the boys to look at you? he asked boozily one afternoon. He had just come home from a softball game with some friends, most of whom were ex-Marines like him, but he was forty-five years old and three decades of drinking had taken their toll on him. He was overweight, and had a beer belly that hung way out over his blue jeans. 'Don't you like boys, Hilary?'

He kept hounding her and she was tired of it. She never had time to notice boys. She was too busy going to school and cleaning house for him. She was going into ninth grade in the autumn, a year early. And now she had ten thousand dollars hidden in her underwear drawer. She had everything she needed.

'Not particularly,' she finally answered him. 'I don't have time for boys.'

'Oh yeah? What about men? You got time for men, little Hillie?'

She didn't bother to answer him. Instead, she went to the kitchen to cook dinner, thinking about how southern he had become after only a few years. He spoke with a drawl, and a southern accent that sounded like he was born in Florida. You'd never have known he was from Boston. And thinking of it made her think back to her brief time there with them . . . she still remembered it as the place she had lost Megan and Axie. She had never heard from Arthur Patterson again, not since they'd moved to Florida, not that she cared anyway. She hated him. And it never occurred to her that the reason he hadn't called was because Jack and Eileen hadn't left an address when they moved. They had disappeared without a trace, and Arthur had no idea how to find them. He had his hands full with his own life anyway by then. Around the time the Joneses had moved to Florida, Marjorie had left him.

'What's for dinner?' Jack appeared in the kitchen with a beer-can in his hand and a cigarette. He seemed to be eyeing her with greater interest these days, and she didn't like it. It made her uncomfortable, and made her feel as though he was taking her clothes off with his eyes.

'Hamburgers.'

'That's nice.' But he was staring at her firm young breasts as he said it. She had long, shapely legs and a tiny waist, and the thick black hair she had inherited from Sam hung in a black sheet to her waist. She was a beautiful girl, and it was becoming difficult to hide it. She looked years older than she was, and her eyes held the pain of a lifetime.

Jack patted her on the behind, and brushed past her without needing to, and for the first time he stood by her side the entire time while she was making dinner for him. He made her so uncomfortable that she was unable to eat once the hamburgers were ready. She pushed the food around on her plate, and left the kitchen as quickly as she could, after washing the dishes. She heard him go out then, a little while after that, and she was asleep in her bed in her room off the kitchen long before he came home around midnight. There was a pouring tropical rain, and there had been lightning and thunder, and he staggered into the house, extremely drunk, but with the intention of doing something . . . if he could just remember what it was . . . dammit . . . it had slipped his mind . . . he was still cursing when he passed her room, and then suddenly he remembered, and gave a laugh as he stood outside her door for a long moment.

He didn't bother to knock, instead he just turned the knob and walked into her room, his wet shoes squeezing water onto the linoleum floor and his breathing heavy, from years of cigarettes, but she didn't hear him. The sheet of black hair was fanned out across her face, and one arm was tossed over her head, as she slept on top of the covers in a childish cotton nightgown.

'Purrrrtyyyy . . .' He purred to himself and coughed, which almost woke her. She stirred and turned over, revealing a graceful hip and one long leg as she slept only inches away from him. And slowly he began unbuttoning his shirt until it dropped on the floor and lay there in a wet heap. He unzipped his trousers and slipped them off with his shoes, and he stood next to her in his shorts and socks, and a moment later, they lay with the rest of his clothes next to her bed. And only the vast amount of liquor he had drunk kept him from getting a bigger erection. He came to life slowly, watching her, aching with desire, and the secret lust he had hidden for years, but now she was old enough . . . hell, he could have years of her, his very own piece right at home . . . before she grew up and moved out, and maybe after this she'd never want to. He groaned as he lay down on the bed beside her, and the cloud of boozy fumes he exhaled along with the stench of unwashed perspiration woke her.

'Hmm . . .' She opened one eye, not sure where she was and then gave a gasp and leapt out of bed. But he was quicker than that and had taken a firm grasp of her nightgown. It tore right off her tall frame as he held it, and she stood naked and trembling before him, as he lay in her bed and watched her.

'My, my . . . ain't that a purty sight, little Hillie?' She tried to cover her nakedness and she wanted to cry, or run, but she wasn't sure what to do. She just stood there, terrified. She knew that if she tried to run away, he'd catch her. 'Come on back to bed, it's not time to get up yet. First Uncle Jack's got a few things to show you.' She could see him long and hard and ominous where she'd been lying, and she was old enough to know what he intended to do to her, and she would die before she'd let him.

'Don't touch me!' she ran through the open doorway to the kitchen, and he followed her in the dark, stumbling and naked and slipping on the wet patches he had left on the floor moments earlier.

'Come on, ya little tramp . . . you know what you want. And I'm going to give it to you.' As he said it, he lunged for her arm, and tried to drag her back to her bedroom. But she fought like a cat, and scratched his face and his arm, trying to kick him as he dragged her.

'Let go of me!' She pulled herself free and almost made it to the back door before he caught her again, but for an instant, she had time to reach out for something she suddenly remembered on the draining board. She hid it carefully from him, and seeming to become docile finally, she let him lead her back to her bedroom. It was a daring thing to do, but she would rather kill him than let him rape her.

'That's a good girl . . . now you want ole Uncle Jack, don't ya, little Hillie . . .' She said nothing in answer and he didn't seem to notice as he pushed her roughly back onto her bed and prepared to mount her, but with a sudden flash of silver he felt something cold and sharp and ugly pointing at his belly.

'If you touch me, I'll cut your balls off . . . and I mean

it . . .' Everything about her tone of voice said she did, and he believed her. He backed off just a fraction of an inch, and she followed him with the knife point. 'Get out of my room.'

'Fine, fine . . . Christ . . .' he muttered as he backed out of the room and almost fell over the threshold. 'Put that thing away for chrissake, will you, dammit?'

'Not till you're out of here.' She was following him with the knife still pointed at his testicles, which seemed to worry him greatly.

'Little bitch . . . that what they teach you in school these days? In my day, the girls were a hell of a lot nicer.' She didn't answer him and he backed away, and then suddenly he had slapped the knife out of her hand and slapped her so hard across the face that she fell against the opposite wall and she wasn't sure which hurt her most, her nose bleeding profusely all over her face, or the back of her head which felt as though he had crushed it. 'There you little bitch, how does that feel?'

She grunted and struggled to her feet, still hell-bent on protecting her virtue, but he wasn't interested in it anymore, he just wanted to punish her for humiliating him. He knew he could always get the rest of her later. Hell, there was nowhere for her to go. She was his now. He practically owned her.

'Now, you gonna behave yourself for Uncle Jack next time?' He backhanded her again, his eyes glinting evilly, and this time she fell against a chair and it caught against her ribs, cutting deep into one breast, and she could feel herself bleeding there too. Her ears were ringing, and her lip was split, she thought her jaw might be broken, and she had a huge gash on one breast before it was all over and she crawled away from him. He had passed out on the couch by then, still naked, totally drunk, and pleased with his night's work. She couldn't resist him next time. He was sure of it. He had taught her a good lesson. So good, that she dragged herself, naked in the pouring rain, until she passed out cold on their neighbour's doorstep. She lay there for hours, unconscious in the rain, bleeding from her various wounds, until Mrs Archer found her there the next day when she opened her front door to get her paper.

'Oh my God! ... oh my *God*!' she screamed, backing into the house, and running to find her husband. 'My God ... Bert, there's a dead woman on our doorstep and she's naked!' He ran to the door and found her there, half in and half out of the door, still bleeding and still unconscious.

'Christ ... it's that kid from next door, the one whose aunt died ... the one you never see ... we've got to call the police.' But Mollie was already dialling. The police came almost immediately, and the ambulance was there even before that. They took her to Brewster Hospital and half an hour later she came around, and saw the Archers staring at her in the emergency room. Mrs Archer started to cry, she reminded her so much of her daughter. And it was obvious she had been beaten and raped and deposited on their doorstep. But the examination showed later on that she hadn't been raped at all, just beaten to within an inch of her life. She had stitches in various places, and the gash on her breast was bad, but the worst was the concussion he'd given her when he threw her against the wall the first time. She threw up almost as soon as she awoke and she lost consciousness several times, but the doctors assured Mrs Archer she'd be all right, and they left her there several hours later. She was unwilling to talk about who had beaten her up, but the police weren't through with their investigation.

'Who do you think would do such a thing to her?' Mrs Archer asked her husband on the way home, but it was days before the truth came to light, and Hilary didn't tell them. Jack gave it away himself the third time the police went to see him, and they brought charges against him, which Hilary begged them to drop.

'He'll kill me if you do that.' She was terrified now. He would kill her now for sure, or worse.

But the police changed everything. 'Hilary, you don't have to go back, you know. You could go to a foster home.'

'What's that?' Her eyes were wide with fear, but what could be worse than the hell she'd been living?

'It's a temporary home, even a long-term one sometimes where kids can live who don't have anywhere else to go.'

'You mean like an institution?'

The officer shook his head. 'No, like real folks who take kids like you into their homes. What do you think?'

'I think I'd like to do that.' In order to set it up, she had to be processed through the Florida courts as a homeless minor. And it turned out to be much easier than anyone had thought when she explained that she was an orphan and had never been adopted by her aunt and uncle. She went back to see him only once, and Mollie Archer came with her and stood uneasily in the doorway. Hilary had wanted to get her things and she was afraid of confronting Jack. It was the first time she'd seen him since the night he beat her, and she was terrified of what he'd do to her for setting the police on him. But he only stared at her in venomous fury and dared to say very little with Mrs Archer standing by her.

She packed her few belongings in the only suitcase she owned, and tucked the little cloth pouch carefully into the lining. She knew she had to take good care of it now, it was the only friend she had in the world . . . her escape money to find her sisters . . . her ten thousand dollars. If

Jack had known it existed and that she had it, he would surely have killed her for it.

Jack slammed the door behind her and locked it loudly, and she walked quietly across the backyard to Mrs Archer's house and waited for the juvenile authorities to pick her up again. They had a foster home for her and the people were coming for her in the morning. It was all so effortless, and for a moment, she allowed herself to think that it was going to be easy now. Smooth sailing, and then back to New York in a few years, to find Megan and Axie, and one day, they'd be living with her and she'd take care of them again. She'd be able to do that, with the windfall she'd found hidden among Eileen's nylons. It was the only nice thing her aunt had ever done for her, and even that she hadn't meant to do. But it didn't matter now. The money was in Hilary's suitcase and she intended to guard it with her life. To her, it was an absolute fortune.

The social worker came for her, as promised, in the morning, and after a brief appearance in court took her to a family in a battered-looking house in a poor suburb of Jacksonville. The woman opened the door wearing a warm smile and an apron, there were five other kids inside varying from about ten to fourteen from what Hilary could see, and the place instantly reminded her of the house Eileen and Jack had lived in in Boston. It had the same fetid smell, worn-out furniture, and battered look. But with half a dozen kids living there, it was hardly surprising.

The woman's name was Louise and she showed Hilary to her room, a room she was to share with three other girls, all of them living on narrow army cots Louise had bought from army surplus. There was a black girl sitting on one of them, she was tall and thin, with big black eyes, and she glanced over at Hilary with curiosity as she walked into the room and put down her things as the social worker introduced them.

'Hilary, this is Maida. She's been here for nine months.' The social worker smiled and disappeared, back to Louise and the mob of children in the kitchen. The house looked busy and full but wasn't welcoming somehow, and it gave Hilary the feeling that she had just been dropped off at a work camp.

'Hilary . . . what kinda name is dat?' Maida stared at her with hostility now that the social worker was gone and looked her over from the collar of her ugly dress to the cheap shoes Eileen had bought her. It was not a pretty outfit, and it was a far cry from the organdies and velvets of her childhood, forgotten luxuries by now. And with her serious green eyes, she looked at the black girl and wondered what life would be like here. 'Where you from girl?'

'New York . . . Boston . . . I've been here for two years.'

The black girl nodded, she was reed thin and Hilary could see she bit her nails to the quick. She was tall and angry and nervous. 'Yeah? So why you come here? You ma and pa in jail?' Hers were. Her mother was a prostitute and her father was a pimp and a pusher.

'My parents are dead.' Hilary's voice was dead too as she said it, and her eyes were guarded as she stood just inside the doorway.

'You got brothers and sisters?' She didn't see what difference it made and she was about to say yes, and then decided against it and merely shook her head. Maida seemed satisfied with her answer. 'You gonna work hard for Louise, sweetheart. She a bitch to work for.' It was not entirely welcome information, but somehow Hilary had suspected as she walked in the door that this was not going to be as easy as they'd told her.

'What do you have to do?'

'Clean the house, take care of her kids, the yard, the vegetable garden out back . . . laundry . . . anything she tells you to do. Kinda like slavery, except you get to sleep in the main house and she lets you eat here.' There was an evil smile in Maida's eyes and Hilary wasn't sure whether to laugh or not. 'But it still beats juvie.'

'What's that?' She was a neophyte to all this, to foster homes and juvenile halls and parents who had gone to jail, even though her own father had died there. It was difficult to absorb the changes he had wrought in her life with one night of unbridled fury. Hilary often thought late at night, when she allowed herself to think about it, that he might as well have killed her along with her mother. It would have been a great deal simpler, instead of this slow death he had condemned her to, far from home and those she loved, abandoned among strangers.

'Where you been, girl?' Maida looked annoyed. 'You know, juvie . . . juvenile hall . . .' She made a big deal of mouthing it, as Hilary nodded. 'That's jail for kids. If they don't find you a foster home, you go there, and they lock you up and treat you like shit. I'd rather work my ass off for Louise until my Ma gets out again. She'll be out soon and I can go home then.' This time she'd been caught in a drug bust with her 'husband'. 'What 'bout you? How long you think you gonna be here? You got relatives to go to?' She figured Hilary's parents had just died and maybe this was only a temporary arrangement. There was something different about Hilary, the way she spoke, the way she moved, the silent way she stared at everything, as though she didn't really belong here. But she shook her head in answer to

Maida's question, just as the social worker walked back into the doorway.

'You girls getting acquainted?' The woman smiled, as though totally unaware of the jungle she worked in. To her, these were all nice kids, and she was finding them lovely homes, and everyone was happy.

Both girls looked at her as though she were crazy, but Maida was the first to speak. 'Yeah. That's what we doin' . . . gettin' acquainted. Right, Hilary?' Hilary nodded, wondering what she was supposed to say and relieved when the social worker took her back to the kitchen. There was something about Maida that scared her.

'Maida's done very well here,' the social worker confided as they walked down a dreary hall to the kitchen.

The children had gone back outside, and Louise was waiting for them, but all signs of any food they'd been eating was gone, and Hilary felt her stomach growl as she wondered if they'd give her something to eat, or if she'd have to wait until dinner.

'Ready to get to work?' Louise asked, and Hilary nodded, having got the answer to her question. The social worker seemed to disappear, and Louise directed her outside to a shovel and some rakes. She was told to dig a trench, and promised that some of the boys would help her, but they never showed. The boys were smoking cigarettes behind the barn, and Hilary was left to wield the shovel by herself, grunting and perspiring. She had worked hard in the last four years, but never at manual labour. She had cleaned Eileen and Jack's house, done their laundry, cooked their meals, and nursed Eileen until she died, but this was harder than anything she'd done before, and there were tears of exhaustion in her eyes when Louise finally called them in out of the torrid heat and told them to come to dinner.

She found Maida there, looking victorious as she stood by the stove. To her had fallen the ladylike task of cooking dinner, if one could call it that. It was a few pieces of meat and gristle floating in a sea of watery grease, which Louise cheerfully called stew as she ladled out small portions to each of them and sat down to say grace. And despite the pangs of hunger that she felt, and the dizziness from being in the hot sun all day, Hilary was unable to make herself eat it.

'Come on, eat up, you gotta keep up your strength.' Louise grinned horribly at her, it was all like some awful fairy-tale, about a witch who was going to eat the children. Hilary remembered tales like that from her childhood, but they never seemed quite as real as this, and the witch always died and the children went back to being princesses and princes.

'I'm sorry ... I'm not very hungry ...' Hilary apologized weakly as the boys laughed at her.

'You sick?' Louise looked annoyed. 'They didn't tell me you was sick ...' She looked as though she were about to send her back to some unknown fate and Hilary remembered Maida's unpleasant description of 'juvie'. Jail for kids. That was all she needed. But she had nowhere else to go now. She couldn't go back to Jack. She knew what he'd do to her this time. So it was Louise or juvie.

'No, no, I'm not sick ... it's just the sun ... it was hot outside ...'

'Aww ...' The other kids were quick to make fun of her and Maida gave her a vicious pinch as she helped wash the dishes. It was an odd arrangement, Hilary realized again. They weren't like friends or family, Louise didn't pretend to mother them, they were just like a hired work force she'd brought in to do her work, and that was how they treated her as well. It all seemed very temporary and very distant. Louise's husband seemed to come and go. He had lost one leg in the war and the other was severely crippled. He was unable to work as a result, and Louise took these kids in to do his share of the work, and her own, and for the money it brought her. The State paid her for each child she took in, and she didn't get rich on it, but it gave her decent money. The maximum she could take in was seven, and they knew there would be another one coming soon, because with Hilary there were only six. There was a pale, blonde, fifteen-year-old girl named Georgine, as well as Maida, and three rowdy boys in their early teens. Two of them had been leering at Hilary since dinner. None of them were handsome kids, and few of them even looked healthy. It would have been hard to on the diet they were given. Louise cut all the corners she could, but Hilary was used to that from living with Eileen and Jack, although Louise seemed to have perfected the art even further.

At seven-thirty she shouted at the kids to get ready for bed. They had been sitting in their rooms, talking, complaining, exchanging stories about parents in jail, and their own experiences in juvie. It was all totally foreign to Hilary, who sat on her bed in frightened silence. The boys had their own room next door, and Georgine and Maida talked as though Hilary wasn't there. They shoved their way past her in their nightgowns eventually, and slammed the door in her face when they went to the bathroom.

I can take it, she told herself . . . it's better than Jack . . . this isn't so awful . . . She remembered the money hidden in her suitcase and prayed no one would find it. She only had to live through five more years of this . . . five years of foster homes or juvie . . . or Jack . . . she felt tears sting her eyes as she finally closed the door to the bathroom, and she sat down and sobbed silently into the torn scratchy towel Louise had given her that morning. It was impossible to believe that this was what her life had come to. And within minutes, the boys were pounding on the door, and she had to give up the bathroom, as a trail of cockroaches ran across the bathtub.

'What you doin' in there, Mama? Want a hand?' one of the black boys asked, and the others laughed at his delightful sense of humour. Hilary only brushed past them and went back to her own room, just in time for Maida to turn the light out. And a moment later, Hilary was stunned when Louise appeared in the doorway, with a ring of keys in one hand. She looked as though she were going to lock them in, but Hilary knew that was impossible, or so she thought. She could hear raucous laughter from the boys' room.

'Lock-up time,' Maida supplied the information and with that Louise slammed the door, and they could hear the key turn in the lock. The other two girls looked as though it was perfectly normal, and Hilary stared at them in the dim light from outside their windows.

'Why did she do that?'

'So we don't meet up with the boys. She likes everything nice and clean and wholesome.' And then suddenly Maida laughed as though it were a very funny joke and so did Georgine. They seemed to laugh endlessly as Hilary watched them.

'What if we have to go to the bathroom?'

'You piss in your bed,' Georgine supplied.

'But *you* clean it up tomorrow mornin',' Maida added, and then they snickered again.

'What if there's a fire?' Hilary was terrified, but Maida only laughed again.

'Then you fry, baby. Like a little potato chip with your lily-white skin turnin' all brown like mine.' In truth they could have broken the window and escaped, but Hilary didn't think of that as she felt rising waves of panic. She lay down in her bed and pulled up the sheets, trying not to think of all the terrible things that could happen. No one had ever locked her in a room before, and the experience was frightening beyond anything she'd ever thought of.

She lay silently, staring at the ceiling, her breathing shallow and quick. She felt as though someone were smothering her with a pillow, and she could hear the other two girls whispering, and then she heard sheets rustling and a series of giggles. She turned just to see what was going on and was in no way prepared for what she saw when she did so. Maida was naked in Georgine's bed, and Georgine had thrown her tattered nightgown to the floor, and they were caressing each other's bodies in the moonlight, kissing and fondling each other, as Maida moaned and rolled her eyes. Hilary wanted to turn away, but she was so horrified she didn't move and the older girl saw her and snapped at her.

'What's the matter honey, you never seen two girls making it before?' Hilary shook her head silently, and as Maida nestled her head down between Georgine's legs she laughed hoarsely and then pushed her away with another crack of laughter. 'Wait a minute.' She turned to Hilary, 'Want to try it?' Hilary shook her head again, terrified, and there was no escape from them. The door was locked, and she had to lie there listening, even if she didn't watch them. 'You might like it.'

'No . . . no . . .' In effect this was what had brought her here . . . except that it had been Jack and not two girls, and she couldn't even imagine what they would do to her, but they forgot her quickly as they went on with their nightly pleasure. They moaned and writhed and Maida screamed once, so loudly that Hilary was afraid Louise would come and beat them all, but there were no sounds in the silence except Maida's and Georgine's, the sound of hard breathing and panting and moaning, and then finally, as Hilary cried softly in her bed, they lay spent and fell asleep in each others's arms, and Hilary lay awake until morning.

The next day they worked hard again. Hilary went back to digging in the garden, and was told to scrub down the inside of the shed. The boys hassled her as they had before, and she was told to cook lunch this time. She tried to make something decent for all of them, but it was impossible with the meagre supplies Louise left out. They had thin slices of Spam and leftover frozen chips. It was barely enough to stay alive on, working in the hot summer sun, and that night she had to listen to Maida and Georgine go through their moaning and panting. This time she turned her back, pulled the covers over her head and tried to pretend she couldn't hear them. But it was two days later when Georgine slipped into her bed, and began gently stroking her back beneath her nightgown. It was the first gentle touch she had known since her mother died, but this was different, Hilary knew, and it was not welcome.

'Don't, please . . .' Hilary pulled away from her, half falling out of bed, but the girl took a strong grip on her, running an arm like steel around her waist and holding her close as she lay behind her. Hilary could feel the older girl's breasts on her back, and then her free hand stroking her nipples.

'Come on, honey, doesn't that feel nice . . . yeah . . . ain't that fine . . . Maida and I are tired of just having fun with each other, we want to share it with you too . . . you could be our friend now.' And with that the hand that had stroked Hilary's firm young breasts drifted down towards her thighs so tightly clenched in terror.

'Oh please . . . please . . . don't!' She was whimpering

and crying, in some ways this was worse than Jack. And she had no escape, no butcher's knife, nowhere to run. She couldn't escape these girls, locked into a room with them, and Georgine had a grip on her that Hilary could not pry away from, and as she held her down, her legs wrapped around Hilary's like steel snakes, Maida came stealthily from the other bed and began to stroke her, as Georgine forced her legs as far apart as Hilary's struggles would let her.

'Like this . . . you see . . .' Maida showed her things she didn't want to know, and reached into places Hilary had never touched herself as she began to scream in terror. But Georgine put one hand firmly on her mouth and let Maida do the stroking. They seemed to fondle her endlessly and softly only at first, then harder and rougher, as she sobbed and sobbed in their arms, and finally they tired of her, but when Georgine climbed out of her bed, Hilary was bleeding profusely. 'Shit, you got your period?' She looked annoyed as she saw the mess in the bed and on her legs. You could see it even in the moonlight. But Maida knew better, she had done everything she liked to do. She grinned at Georgine and down at the stricken girl.

'Nah . . . she was a virgin.'

Georgine grinned evilly. She'd come around, she knew. They always did. After the first time. And if she didn't, they'd rough her up a little, and she'd be scared not to.

The next day, Hilary washed her sheets as soon as Louise unlocked the door and apologized when she screamed at her for making a mess. The boys even laughed at her when they saw her scrubbing. It was as though all the pain and humiliation in the world was heaped on her head, as though someone somewhere wanted to destroy her. She wondered where her sisters were, and prayed that nothing like this happened to them. But she knew it wouldn't.

They were going to the homes of friends of Arthur Patterson's, and people like that didn't know about things like this . . . they didn't know of the tortures people like Eileen and Jack and Louise and Maida and Georgine could conjure, and as she washed her sheets, and dug the ditch Louise wanted deeper, Hilary prayed that her own torture would be enough, that Axie and Megan would be safe from lives like this. She promised God that He could do anything He wanted to her, as long as He kept them safe . . . please God . . . please . . . she muttered in the broiling sun as Georgine came up behind her.

'Hi baby, you talkin' to yourself?'

'I . . . no . . .' She turned away rapidly so Georgine couldn't see her blushing crimson.

'That was nice last night . . . you're gonna like it better next time.'

But Hilary wheeled on her, and although she didn't know it, she looked just like her mother. 'No! I'm not! Don't ever touch me again, you hear me?' She clutched the shovel ominously, and Georgine laughed as she walked away. She knew Hilary would have no weapons in her room that night, and of course she didn't. They did the same thing to her again, and the next day Hilary looked glazed. There was no escaping them, and when the social worker came back in a week she looked at Hilary and asked her if she was working too hard. Hilary hesitated and then shook her head. Georgine told her that if she complained she'd wind up in juvie, and everyone did it there, sometimes they even used lead pipes and soda bottles . . . 'not like me and Maida'. And Hilary believed them. Anything was possible now. Any anguish. Any torture. She only nodded and told the social worker everything was fine, and went on living her silent nightmare.

It went on for seven months, until Georgine turned

sixteen and was released as an emancipated minor, and Maida's mother was paroled from jail, and Maida went back to her, which left Hilary the only girl with three boys, while they waited for two new girls to replace the others. But for several days, Hilary was alone with the boys next door, and Louise figured one girl and three boys was not a dangerous combination, so she didn't bother locking Hilary's door, which left her no protection. The boys came stealthily one night, and Hilary lay wide awake, terrified, as she saw them enter her room and silently close the door behind them. She fought them like a cat, but she lost to their strength and they did exactly what they'd come for, and the next morning, Hilary called the social worker and asked to be transferred to juvenile hall. She offered no explanation, and Louise seemed not to care when they took her two days later. Hilary had stolen a knife and fork from the dinner table and the second time she had been well prepared for her midnight callers. One boy almost lost a hand, and they had retreated in terror. But she was still glad when she left Louise's care, and she said nothing to the social worker of what had happened.

At juvenile hall, they put her in solitary, because all she did was mope and wouldn't answer anyone's questions. It took them two weeks to decide she wasn't sick. She was rail thin, and weak from refusing to get up, but they thought that once she was put in with the other kids she might cheer up again. Her 'illness' was labelled 'teenage psychosis'.

She was assigned work in the laundry room, and put in a dorm with fifteen girls, and at night she heard the same moans and screams that she had learned from Maida. But this time no one bothered her, no one talked to her, no one touched her. And a month later they put her in another foster home with three other girls. The woman in charge was pleasant this time, not warm put polite, religious in a serious, joyless way, and talked frequently of a God who would punish them if they did not embrace Him. They tried hard to break through her shell, and they knew she was a bright girl but eventually her icy silences discouraged them. She was able to reach out to no one. And after two months, they sent her back to juvenile hall and 'exchanged' her for another girl, a friendly eleven-year-old who chatted and smiled and did all the things Hilary wouldn't.

Hilary went back to juvenile hall for good this time, and made no friends there. She went to school, did her work, and read everything she could lay her hands on. She had figured one thing out. She was going to get out, and get an education, and the harder she worked, the more she knew it would be her only salvation. She poured herself into her school work, and graduated at seventeen with honours, and the day afterwards her caseworker called her into her office.

'Congratulations, Hilary, we heard how well you did.' But no one had been there. No one had ever been there for Hilary, not in nine years, and now she knew there was never going to be. That was her destiny, and she accepted that. Except if she could find Megan and Alexandra . . . but even that hope was dim now. She still had the ten thousand dollars, hidden in the lining of her suitcase, but her hope of finding them now was slim . . . unless she went to Arthur . . . but would they even remember her? Alexandra would be twelve, and Megan only nine . . . to them, she would be a stranger. All she had left really was herself. She knew that now, as she looked at the caseworker without any trace of emotion.

'Thank you.'

'You have a choice to make now.'

'I do?' Surely nothing pleasant. Hilary had learned that

much, and she was always ready to defend herself against the miseries someone else wanted to inflict upon her. She had learned a lot since her first foster home, and her first days in juvie.

'Normally, our wards remain here until they reach eighteen, as you know, but in a case such as yours, when you graduate from high school before that date, you have the option of leaving as an emancipated minor.'

'Which means what?' Hilary gazed at her suspiciously from behind walls of steel. Her brilliant green eyes were her only peep-holes.

'It means you're free Hilary, if you want to be. Or you can stay here until you decide what you want to do after you leave here. Have you given it any thought?' Only four years' worth.

'Some.'

'And?' Talking to her was like pulling teeth but a lot of them were like that, too bruised by life to trust anyone. It was a tragedy, but there was no way to change that. 'Want to tell me your plans?'

'Do I have to in order to get out?' Like the parole she'd heard so much about. Everyone she knew in juvie had parents in jail, waiting to get out on parole. This was no different. But the caseworker shook her head.

'No, you don't, Hilary. But I'd like to help if I can.'

'I'll be all right.'

'Where do you want to go?'

'New York probably. It's where I'm from. It's what I know.' Although she had been gone from there for more than half her life, it still seemed like home to her. And, of course, there were her sisters . . .

'It's a big city. Do you have friends there?'

She shook her head. If she did, would she have spent four years in the Jacksonville juvenile hall? It was a stupid question. And at least she still had her ten thousand dollars. That was going to be her salvation. She didn't need friends. All she needed was a job and a place to stay. But one thing was for sure, she wasn't staying here. 'I guess I'll be going pretty soon. How soon can I go?' Her eyes lit up for the first time at the prospect of leaving.

'We can have your release papers in order by next week. Soon enough for you?' The caseworker smiled with regret. They had failed dismally with her. It happened that way sometimes, it was rotten luck when it did, but it was hard to say who would survive the system and who wouldn't. She stood up and held out a hand which Hilary shook cautiously. She trusted nothing and no one. 'We'll let you know as soon as you can go.'

'Thank you.' She left the room quietly and went to the single room she lived in. She no longer had to sleep in a dorm or share with anyone. She had long-term seniority, and in a few days she'd be leaving. She lay on her bed with a smile and stared up at the ceiling. It was all over, the agony, the pain, the humiliation, the horror of her life for the last nine years. She was going to be on her own now. She lay there smiling as she hadn't in years. And a week later, to the day, she was on a bus, no regrets, no sorrow, no friends to leave behind. Her eyes were cold and hard and green, dreaming of a world she did not know yet. And the past was a nightmare left behind her.

Chapter 9

The bus stopped in Savannah, Raleigh, Richmond, Washington, and Baltimore, and took two days to reach New York, as Hilary sat staring soundlessly out of the window. Other passengers had said a word or two when they stopped for lunch, or when they stretched at night, two sailors had even tried to pick her up, but she dealt with them in no uncertain terms, and after that, no one came near her. She was a solitary figure as she stepped down from the bus in New York, and in her heart she felt a terrifying trembling. She was home ... after nine years ... she had left here as a little girl, a week after her father committed suicide, to go to stay with her aunt in Boston. And it had taken all these years to come home, but she had done it.

The juvenile authorities of Florida had given her two hundred and eighty-seven dollars to start her life, and she had the ten thousand from Eileen. The first thing she did was go to a bank on Forty-second Street. The second thing she did was go to a hotel room. She took a room in a small, seedy hotel in the Thirties on the East Side, but her room was simple and spare and no one bothered her when she went in or out. She ate at a coffee shop on the corner, and read the want ads for jobs. She had taken a typing class in high school, but she had no other skills and she had no delusions about what lay ahead. She had to start at the bottom. But she had other plans as well. She wasn't going to stop there. The spectres of the women she'd seen in the past nine years had left their mark. She was never going to be like them. She was going to work and go to college at night, and do everything she had to. And one day she was going to be important, she promised herself. One day she was going to be *someone*.

On her second day in New York, she went to Alexander's Department store on Lexington Avenue and spent five hundred dollars on clothes. It seemed like a terrifying portion of her fortune, but she knew she would have to look right if she was going to get a job. She selected dark colours, simple styles, a few skirts and blouses, and patent leather pumps and a matching bag. She looked like a pretty young girl as she tried her things on in her room downtown, and no one would have suspected the horrors she had endured since her parents died.

She went on her first job interview and was told she was too young, and then three more which required shorthand skills she didn't have, and finally a job in an accountant's office where she was interviewed by a bald, obese man, perspiring profusely with a damp handkerchief clutched in one hand.

'You type?' He leered at her, as she sat watching him. She had dealt with worse than that and he didn't frighten her. And she also needed the job. She couldn't go on living forever on her dwindling funds. She had to find work pretty soon, and she would even have been willing to work for him, if he would behave himself. 'Shorthand too?' She shook her head and he didn't seem to care. 'How old are you?'

'Nineteen,' she lied. She had learned that much in the first interview. No one wanted to hire a seventeen-year-old girl. So she lied to them.

'Have you been to secretarial school?' She shook her head again and he shrugged, and then stood up, with a small stack of papers in one hand, and moved around the desk, as though to show them to her, but when he reached her side, he caressed her breast instead, and she was on her feet with lightning speed, the back of her hand across his face before she had thought of it, and they both gasped simultaneously as he stared at her.

'If you touch me again, I'll scream so loud I'll have the police up here,' she warned, her green eyes flashing at him, her whole body tense, her hands trembling as she looked at him. 'How dare you do that?' Why did they all do things like that to her? . . . her Uncle Jack . . . and the girls at the foster home . . . and the boys at Louise's place . . . it kept happening to her. She didn't understand that it was because she was beautiful. She thought of it as some kind of punishment, something she must have done as a child that she was being tortured for now. It didn't seem fair that it happened to her all the time, and she backed slowly toward the door, never taking her eyes off his face.

'Look, I'm sorry . . . no big deal . . . Miss . . . what's your name? . . . come on . . .' He waddled towards her hurriedly and she slammed the door in his face and ran down the stairs as fast as she could go. She walked all the way back to her hotel after that, feeling dirty and de-pressed, and wondering if she'd ever find a job.

But she finally did, at an employment agency, as a receptionist. They liked the way she looked, suspected she was younger than she said, but she was intelligent, neat and clean, typed halfway decently and could answer the phone, and that was enough for them. They offered her ninety-five dollars a week and it seemed like a windfall to her. She took the job and went flying back to her hotel to get ready for work the next day. She had her first job!

And it would be a quick climb up from there. She didn't know what she wanted to do yet, but she already knew where she wanted to go to school. She'd been reading all the newspaper ads, and she made some calls. She had already applied, and she was waiting to hear from them, and then she'd really be on her way.

Now there was only one thing left to do, and she decided to tackle it that afternoon. After that, she didn't know when she'd have the time, and she didn't want to call him. She wanted to see him personally. Only once. She'd get the information from him and then all she had to do was call . . . the thought of it made her tremble as she changed her clothes again. She wore a simple navy-blue dress, dark stockings, and her patent leather shoes. The dress was short, as was the style, but it was respectable. And she tied her hair in a simple knot that made her look older than she was. She washed her face, dried it on one of the hotel's little rough towels, and went downstairs again. And this time she didn't take a bus. She didn't want to waste time. She took a cab instead, and stood outside looking up when she arrived at Forty-eighth and Park Avenue. It was a glass building trimmed with chrome, and it seemed to stretch all the way to the sky as she looked up at it.

The lift shuddered as it rose to the thirty-eighth floor, and she held her breath wondering if it would get stuck. She had never been anywhere like this before, not that she remembered anyway . . . there were other things she did remember though . . . a trip with her parents to France on the *Liberté* . . . the apartment on Sutton Place . . . tea at the Plaza with Solange, with little cakes and hot chocolate with tons of whipped cream . . . and she remembered the night her mother died and the things she and Sam had said . . .

The lift doors opened easily and she found herself in a

reception area with thick green carpeting, and a young girl at a desk. She wore a pink linen suit and had short blond hair, and she had the pert look all receptionists were supposed to have. It reminded Hilary of the job she was starting the next day. But she knew she would never look like that. Her looks weren't 'cute', her hair wasn't blond, and she didn't look as though she'd bounce out of her seat if someone asked her to. Instead, Hilary looked quiet and serious as she approached, and looked straight into the girl's eyes.

'I'm here to see Mr Patterson.'

'Is he expecting you?' she beamed, and Hilary did not smile in reply. She shook her head honestly, and spoke in a restrained voice. Inwardly, she was intimidated by the surroundings, but outwardly nothing showed. She looked perfectly at ease and totally in control.

'No, he's not. But I'd like to see him now.'

'Your name?' Little Miss Smile went into high beam.

'Hilary Walker.' And then she added, as though it would make a difference, 'He's my godfather.'

'Oh. Of course,' the little blonde said, and then hit a series of buttons and picked up a phone, speaking inaudibly into it. That was another part of the job, speaking into phones so no one else could hear . . . Mr So and So is here to see you, sir . . . oh, you're out? . . . tell him what? . . . It was an art Hilary would have to perfect at the employment agency. And then the girl astonished Hilary. She looked up at her with her perfect smile and waved to a door on her right. 'You may go right in. Mr Patterson's secretary will meet you to show you to his office.' She looked impressed. It wasn't easy to get in to see Arthur Patterson, but the girl was his goddaughter after all.

Hilary stepped inside and looked down a long carpeted corridor. The firm occupied the entire floor and she could see all the way down the hall to a corner office a block away from her. It was an impressive hallway lined with leather-bound legal books, and populated by secretaries at their desks outside the attorneys' offices. She had never been there before, even as a child, and they had moved since then anyway.

'Miss Walker?' An elderly woman with short grey hair and a kindly smile stepped up to her and pointed into the distance down the hall.

'Yes.'

'Mr Patterson is waiting for you.' As though it had been planned, as though he had known she would come, as though he had been waiting for nine years. But what could he possibly know, sitting here? What could he know of lives like Eileen and Jack's, of caring for her as she died, or fighting him off with a butcher's knife, of nearly starving in their home for all those years, and the foster home in Jacksonville, and Maida and Georgine ... and juvenile hall ... and even the sweaty little man who had 'interviewed' her only days ago. What did he know of any of it? And all she knew was that he had killed her mother, as surely as if he had done it with his own hands, and her father, too, eventually. And now here he sat, and she only wanted one thing from him, and then she would leave and never see him again. She never wanted to lay eyes on him again after today.

The secretary stopped at the doorway and knocked. A discreet brass and leather sign on the door said *Arthur Patterson* and then she heard his voice. It was still familiar to her. She could still remember him lying to her eight years before ... I'm just going to take them away for a little while, Hilary ... I'll come back for you. He never did, and she didn't care, she hated him anyway. She could remember kneeling in the street after he drove off, calling her sisters' names and she had to fight back tears again, but it was almost over now . . . almost. It was almost exactly eight years since she had last seen them.

'You may come in.' The secretary smiled and stepped aside as she opened the door, and Hilary walked in quietly. She didn't see the desk at first, and then she saw it, a simple slab of glass and chrome, in front of a window offering a full view of New York, and there he sat, incongruous in the modern décor. He was fifty years old and he looked at least ten years older than that, tall, thin, balding, with sad eyes and a pale face. But he was even paler than usual now as he stood up and looked at her. It was as though he had seen a ghost, as she stood in front of him. She was beautiful and tall, with Sam's shiny black hair, but there the resemblance to him stopped . . . she had Solange's eyes . . . and the same way of moving her head . . . and she stood in front of him just as proudly now as Solange had once walked on the rue d'Arcole in Paris twenty-two years before. It was like seeing a ghost . . . if you changed the black hair to red . . . it was Solange again . . . but with angry, bitter eyes, with something fierce in her face that Solange had never had, something that said if you come near me I will kill you before I let you lay a hand on me, and Arthur instantly feared what might have happened to her, what could possibly have made her look like that? And yet she was safe and sound, obviously, and standing in front of him in his office, fully grown and very beautiful. It was a miracle, and he walked slowly towards her, holding out a hand, with dreams of recapturing the past. It was a way of having Sam and Solange back, of sharing once more in their magic. Hilary was going to bring it all back to him. But as he approached, he could sense the wall built around the girl, and she began to back away when he got close to her, and instinctively he stopped approaching.

'Hilary, are you all right?' It was a little late to ask, and she hated the weakness she saw in his eyes. She never understood till then how totally without courage he was. He had no balls, she realized now, that was why he had abandoned her, after betraying them . . . no guts . . . it was something Solange had accused him of a lifetime ago, although Hilary didn't know it.

'I'm fine.' She wasted no time with him. She had not come for a warm reunion with a family friend, she had come to ask him the only thing she cared about, the only thing she had cared about for eight years. 'I want to know where my sisters are.' Her eyes were icy hard and neither of them moved as she watched his face, not sure of what she saw, terror or grief, and she waited with bated breath for what he would say next.

But whereas he was pale before, he looked ghostly now. He realized that he could not fob her off, that she wanted nothing to do with him. She only wanted them, and he could not give them to her, no matter how much he would have wanted to do so. 'Hilary . . . why don't we sit down . . .' He waved toward a chair and she shook her head, her eyes riveted to his.

'I'm not interested in sitting down with you. You killed my parents, you destroyed my family. I have nothing to say to you. But I want to know where Alexandra and Megan are. That's all I want. When you tell me that, I'll go.' She waited patiently, the same proud tilt of her head that had made Solange so unique . . . so extraordinary . . . he stared at her, seeing someone else, but there was no escaping Hilary. She was a force to be reckoned with, and he understood that fully now. He also sensed that she knew more than he had thought so long ago, but he didn't question her now. He told her the truth, his eyes filled with regret, and damp with tears for what had been and was no more. A family had died at his hands. She was right. And he had never got over it. He had started no family of his own, and Marjorie had left him years before. The woman he loved was gone, her children cast to the winds. And he held himself responsible for what had happened to all of them, even Sam. But there was no way to explain that to this girl, or to excuse himself, least of all to her. God only knew what she had been through in the past eight years.

'I don't know where they are, Hilary. I don't even know where you've been. When I went to Boston to see you seven years ago, you were all gone . . . the Joneses had left no forwarding address with anyone. I was unable to find you . . .' His voice trailed off, filled with regret, because his own guilt had been so great, he had been secretly relieved not to have to face her again, and he suspected now she knew that about him. She had all-seeing eyes, and she looked as though she had an unforgiving heart. There was nothing warm about this girl, nothing gentle, or kind. She was entirely made of granite and barbed wire, shafts of steel and broken glass. There were ugly things inside this girl, he could see it in her eyes, and for an instant he was afraid of her as though, given the opportunity, she might harm him. And under the circumstances, he wasn't sure that he blamed her.

'You couldn't have tried very hard to find me.' Her voice sounded hard. She wasn't interested in his explanations or apologies. 'We went to Florida.'

'And then?' He needed to know what had happened to her, why she looked like that. He had to know . . . and to . . . he felt a sob catch his throat and prayed he wouldn't cry in front of her. 'What happened to you?' He wished she would sit down . . . that they could talk . . . that she would listen to him . . . he could talk to her now. He could explain about Marjorie, who was now a Superior Court judge. He could tell her why he couldn't take them to live with him . . . why nobody wanted all three of them . . . why he had done what he did. 'Are Jack and Eileen still . . . were they good to you?'

She laughed bitterly, sounding very old, and her eyes looked very green. She was thinking of Jack and that night . . . and the pathetic wraith Eileen had become before she died. 'Eileen died, and I've been a ward of the Jacksonville juvenile courts for the last four years. I've been in foster homes, and juvenile hall, and now I'm free, Mr Patterson. I don't owe anyone anything, and most of all not you. All I want now are my sisters.' Her heart was pounding as she realized he had lost them.

'Why didn't you call me when she died?' He sounded horrified. 'Surely you didn't have to go to foster homes . . . juvenile hall . . .' Those were places he never thought about, couldn't bear to think of now. 'Hilary, I'm so sorry . . .'

But her eyes flashed green fire again, and she waved a hand at him. 'Don't give me that shit. You never gave a damn about us, and you don't now. It's easy for you to sound pious and tell me how sorry you are. To tell you the truth, I don't give a damn. It doesn't change anything that happened to me. All I want from you are the addresses of where my sisters live, and don't tell me you don't know. You have to know. You took them there.' It had never occurred to her that he would lose track of them as he had of her. That was impossible. He *had* to know, and she searched his eyes now, but what she saw there was frightening. She saw remorse and guilt, and a man who was actually frightened of her.

He sat down in a chair and shook his head in despair, and then he looked up at her with sad, empty eyes.

'Alexandra went to one of my partners here in the firm. He had a lovely young wife, from a good family. And she was much younger than he. They didn't have children, and they were desperate to adopt Alexandra when I told them about her. And they did . . . they worshipped her.' He looked at Hilary as though hoping to mollify her somewhat but it was no use, her eyes were like green ice, and her hands trembled as she silently sat down in a chair and listened to what he had to say. 'They took her to Europe, they went everywhere with her . . . but six months later, George died of a heart attack. Margaret was in shock and she took Alexandra away with her. The last I heard was that they were in the south of France . . . we sent papers on the estate to her in Paris years ago . . . and I don't know anything after that. I think she stayed over there, but I'm really not sure. We've had no reason to stay in touch with her, and . . .' his voice trailed away, as two tears rolled down his cheeks.

'So you don't know where Alexandra is.' Hilary sounded numb. 'And the woman's name?'

'Gorham. Margaret Gorham. But she could have remarried by now . . . any number of things could have happened. She could be back in the States somewhere. I don't think she's back in New York, I think I'd have heard of it if she were.' He looked lamely at her.

'And Megan?'

'She was adopted by David and Rebecca Abrams, right after I . . . after she . . .' He could barely control himself, and Hilary was trembling from head to foot. '. . . after I brought her back to New York. He was not a partner of the firm, he merely worked for us, and several months later they left. She was an attorney too, and they had had an offer from a law firm in Los Angeles that wanted both of them. They were anxious to start a new life anyway, and they made a point of telling me that they did not want to stay in touch. They wanted to give Megan a new life, far away from all that had happened to her. I haven't heard from them since they left. If he's a member of the California bar, I could possibly locate him, if he's still there . . . I don't know . . .'

'You sonofabitch.' She glared at him with hatred on her face. 'You let us all drift away. You set us adrift, as though getting rid of us would rid you of your own guilt, but it didn't, did it?' She had read him perfectly. 'It destroyed your life too, and you deserve that. You deserve everything that's happened to you. May you rot in hell, Arthur Patterson. You'll live with this for the rest of your life. You killed two people, and destroyed three more lives. That's five people on your soul. Can you live with that?' She walked to where he sat and looked down on him with contempt far beyond her years. 'Can you sleep at night? I don't think you can . . . and God only knows what happened to the other two. God only knows what lives you've condemned them to. I know what mine was like. But it's not over yet. I won't let you spoil my life. I'm going to make something of myself . . . and maybe one day I'll find my sisters . . . maybe . . . But in the meantime,' – she walked slowly to the door, with tears pouring slowly down her face, she had expected so much from him, and her disappointment was so great now – 'I never want to see you again, Arthur Patterson. Never. You won't soothe your conscience with me. We won't be "friends" again, dear Godfather.' She stood and looked at him for a long, long time, before her final words, and she spoke them in a whisper that haunted him for the rest of his life. 'I will never forgive what you did to us . . . never . . . and I will hate you for the rest of my life. Remember that . . . remember what you did and how much I hate you.' And then, like the ghost of Christmas past, she closed his office door, and slipped away, and he did not have the courage to follow her. He sat slumped in his chair, like an old man, remembering Solange, and crying for what he had done to her. Hilary was right, he would not be absolved of what he had done to them all. He couldn't forgive himself, and like Hilary, he wondered now where the other two girls were.

But there were no answers to that. Hilary went from the office on Park Avenue to the Public Library and did the only thing she knew how to do. She opened the Manhattan phone book and found no George or Margaret Gorham there. She found only five in all, and when she called, none of them knew anything about Margaret or Alexandra, and it was obvious they had never heard of them. And a listing of the attorneys of the California bar was equally discouraging. There was no David Abrams listed there, which meant he had left California long before, and God only knew where he had gone. She didn't have the resources to do more than that, she couldn't hunt them down. She couldn't do anything. She had counted on Arthur to know, and he knew nothing at all. Her sisters were gone. Forever this time. And the dream that had kept her alive slipped quietly from her heart, like a rock falling to her feet. She walked slowly back to her hotel, tears streaming down her cheeks. It was as though they had died finally, as she remembered the white roses at her mother's funeral. They no longer existed in her life, hadn't for years . . . and seeing him again reminded her of that terrible day when they'd been taken from her . . . Axie, I love you! . . . she could still remember screaming the words as the car drove away, and falling to her knees in the dirt. It seemed as though she had never got up since. But she would now . . . she had to . . . she would make it alone, as she had for all these years ... but she would always remember them. Always.

She felt them slip away from her as she walked into her hotel, like people she had loved, who had finally died. She was alone, as she always had been.

Part IV

ALEXANDRA

Chapter 10

The house on the avenue Foch stood protected by a tall, impeccably trimmed hedge that shielded everything behind it from the pedestrians' view. There were gardens groomed to perfection, and a solid brick *hôtel particulier* built in the eighteenth century, with handsomely carved doors, brass knockers and knobs, beautiful shutters painted dark green, with silk and damask curtains hung at the windows.

It was a house closed off from a far more public world shielded from all publicity, a house in which perfection reigned, filled with Fabergé objects and crystal chandeliers and impeccable antiquities. It was the house of the Baron and Baroness Henri de Morigny, one of France's oldest families. His was a house of great nobility and dwindling wealth, until he married the lovely daughter of old Comte de Borne fourteen years before. The house on the avenue Foch had been a wedding present from the Count, and as a gift to Henri, Alexandra had restored his family seat for him, a handsome château in Dordogne, and a hunting box in Sologne as well. And since then they had bought a summer house in Saint-Jean-Cap-Ferrat, where they went every year with their children. It was a life of considerable luxury, and endless grace. It was the only life Alexandra de Morigny had ever known, and she played the perfect wife at all times for her husband. She ran his house, planned his dinners, entertained his friends, followed his instructions, and brought up their two daughters, Axelle and Marie-Louise, to perfection. The girls were the greatest joy in her life, and she sat at her desk with a quiet smile, thinking of them that afternoon. They would be home from school very soon, and she would walk the dogs with them in the Bois. It was a good chance to talk, to find out what was going on, who they liked, and they 'hated', who might be having trouble at school, and then they would come home for the girls to do their *devoirs*, have their bath, dine and play and go to bed. Alexandra always stayed with them until her own dinner with Henri. They were six and twelve, as different as night and day, and they were the joy and laughter in her life. Marie-Louise was serious and a great deal like Henri, but Axelle was just as she had been as a child, a little bit shy, totally trusting, and enormously affectionate. It was wonderful just being with her, stroking her pale red curls and looking into those huge blue eyes. Alexandra's heart sang just thinking of it. And she sat smiling as she stared into space, and didn't hear his step on the highly polished parquet floor as he entered the room and watched her. He was almost in front of her before she awoke from her reverie, and she looked up to see the tall, handsome man she had married. He was fifty-nine years old, and powerfuly built, with strong lines in his face, and hard eyes that bore into her, as they always did, as though he were about to ask a very important question. It was a face that was not often amused, but he was a man she could trust and depend on. And she respected him. She had fallen in love with him at nineteen, and they had been engaged for two years. Her father had wanted to be sure that she was not making a mistake or acting on an impulse. Henri was twenty-five years older than she after all, but she had been absolutely certain. She wanted someone just like her father, the old Comte de Borne. He had been sixty when she was born, or he would have been. He had adopted her when she was six years old, and he worshipped her. He had never had children of his own, and he had just lost his wife of forty years when he married her mother. He had gone to the South of France, to grieve, and instead he had met Margaret Gorham, doing precisely the same thing after the death of her husband. She was twenty-seven years old and it was a whirlwind romance — within six months they were married, and Pierre de Borne adopted Alexandra. And only he and Margaret shared the secret that she'd been adopted once before when she came to Margaret and George Gorham at the age of five in New York. It was not something anyone needed to know, and it was no longer important. She was Alexandra de Borne, and she was as dear to the Count's heart as though she had been his natural daughter. Perhaps more so. She grew up cosseted and spoiled and adored as few children are, and in return she worshipped the man she knew as her father. It was to Pierre that she turned with every woe, or wish, or dream, sharing all her secrets with him, confessing her misdeeds, of which there were few, while Margaret looked on, content in every way, filled with love for her husband and child, and full of mischief of her own. Margaret was, in effect, the child of the family, pulling pranks on both of them, hiding unexpectedly, wearing ridiculous costumes to make them laugh. She was an oversized child who loved to laugh, and enjoy every moment. And Alexandra was oddly enough like Pierre, affectionate, shy, and filled with admiration for Margaret's wild schemes and irresistible laughter.

Alexandra was protected and greatly loved and it surprised everyone when she fell in love at nineteen and said she wanted to get married. And Pierre de Borne was not pleased at the prospect of his daughter marrying Henri de Morigny, mostly because he was so much older. He also thought him far too serious, and a difficult man in the bargain. Morigny had never married before, and the old Count knew that he'd been waiting for just the right girl, with an important family, an equally important fortune, and if at all possible, a title. And Alexandra certainly had all of that to offer him. But what did he offer her, her father asked her. Was he warm enough, would he be kind to her? Pierre talked constantly of it to Margaret, and she was just as concerned as he was. But Alexandra was positive she wanted Henri and never wavered. She was married at twenty-one at the church on their country estate in Rambouillet. Seven hundred people were there, from all of Europe's finest families. And they spent their honeymoon in Tahiti, drinking exotic punches and making love on the private beach of the house Henri had rented for her. And when they returned to Paris, Alexandra loved him with even greater passion than she had before, and all she wanted was to have his babies. It took them over a year to conceive, in spite of all of Henri's most romantic efforts.

Her father lived just long enough to hold his first grandchild, two years after Alexandra's marriage. And then he died peacefully in his sleep at the age of eighty-three. Margaret was bereft and Alexandra was stunned, she couldn't imagine a life without him, couldn't imagine not having his hand to hold, his wise eyes to look into. It made her suddenly extremely dependent on Henri, whom she adored, and also a little bit frightened of him. He became suddenly all-important to her and she was obsessed by her fears of losing him too, and knew she couldn't have stood it. Alexandra had always had an irrational fear of losing the people she loved and who loved her. And it worried Margaret considerably because she thought Henri took advantage of it to control her. And in some ways he treated Alexandra like a child, someone to be scolded, and spoken to in firm tones and told what to do, as though she didn't know herself. In Margaret's eyes, he was more a father than a husband, and Alexandra did everything to please him, no matter how trivial or foolish. He had aspirations towards politics and it made him maniacal about appearances. Everything had to be perfect, constantly circumspect, Alexandra had to be impeccable at all times, the children had to be ten times more polite than any others. Margaret found it exhausting just having tea with them, and it worried her at times that Alexandra seemed to think it was all normal. Anything was all right, as long as it pleased her husband.

'That's just the way he is, Maman. He doesn't mean any harm. He's a serious man and he wants everything to be perfect.' Alexandra's own father had never been as demanding of his daughter, or his wife, and he had had a marvellous sense of humour. Margaret found Henri a dead bore, in comparison to her late husband, but she never said it in so many words. All she wanted was Alexandra's happiness, it was all Pierre had ever wanted for her too. And he left her most of his fortune when he died, leaving Margaret more than enough to amuse herself with for another forty years. She was only forty-five when he died, and in many ways she seemed far younger, mostly because she enjoyed herself so much, and she was still very attractive. She was three years younger than Alexandra's husband.

Margaret de Borne always had a good time, something amusing to say, something outrageous and entertaining to do. She was pursued by every eligible man in Europe, and she had no desire whatever to remarry. She had been happy with George years before, and she had had everything she wanted with Pierre. There was no point trying to top that, she knew she never could and didn't want to try it. But Alexandra was another story, and Margaret worried about her more than Alexandra suspected.

Henri expected so much from her. So much so that Pierre and Margaret had decided not to tell him of Alexandra's background, which she herself didn't remember. She only remembered 'Papa' as she called Pierre, although Margaret knew she had some vague other memories as well, but they were long buried. She no longer seemed to have any recollection whatsoever of George Gorham. They had told her simply that buried deep in her memory was the fact that she'd been adopted by Pierre after her father died, a man she no longer remembered, and it never occurred to her, nor did they tell her, that she had in fact been born of other parents entirely, and Margaret was not her mother at all, that she had been adopted once before, after her own parents' tragic death. Pierre had been adamant with Margaret before he died. He did not want Alexandra's husband to know anything about either of her adoptions. But he had said nothing about it to Alexandra, not wanting to stir the memories or her conscience. She was such a decent girl, she might have felt obliged to tell her husband. It was much easier if she didn't remember. Her father knew Henri well enough to know what a maniac he was about his blood-line.

And Margaret did not disagree with her husband about their son-in-law, so for Alexandra's sake, she also remained silent. And remarkably, after so many years, no one even remembered that Alexandra was adopted.

And Margaret rejoiced when Marie-Louise was born, and then mourned when Alexandra lost a baby boy a year later. And then came Axelle after an excruciating pregnancy and endless labour. And after that, her doctor urged her not to try again. He told her she couldn't have any more children without jeopardizing her life. And she was content with the two little girls they had. Only Henri was bitterly disappointed, and resentful for a long time that she had not produced a son for him. And for years after Axelle was born, he told her so whenever he was angry. And always made her feel vaguely guilty towards her husband, as though she had somehow shortchanged him, and owed him something more because of her failure.

The loss of a son was a cross Henri had to bear and having Margaret de Borne as a mother-in-law was yet another. She drove him mad with her long, American legs, her endless stride, which he declared unfeminine, her booming laugh – too loud – her ghastly accent in French, which, to him, was like fingernails on a blackboard. He hated her pranks, detested her sense of humour, and cringed almost visibly whenever she arrived, bringing water pistols in the form of lipsticks for the girls, dime store toys they adored, or at the other extreme, boxes and boxes of clothes from New York, including matching navy-blue coats with little mink muffs, which he told Alexandra were extremely vulgar. He detested everything she brought and everything she said, and was grateful Alexandra was nothing like her. He could never imagine why the old Count had married a woman like her. And he thanked God every day that Alexandra was so much more restrained than her mother. Alexandra was intelligent and kind and discreet, and still very shy, and obedient, which was one of the qualities he liked most about her.

He looked down at her as she sat at her desk, and smiled at her in a quiet, distant way. He was not a man to show his emotions, but although he expected a great deal from

Alexandra, and showed no romance, he nonetheless had deep feelings for her. He knew that without her his life would not be the same, not only financially but in subtler ways that were even more important. She ran a beautiful home for him, she had elegance and style, and her impeccable breeding showed in countless ways. Alexandra de Borne de Morigny was every inch a lady.

'You look as though you're dreaming, Alexandra.' He spoke to her quietly, with only slight reproach. He never raised his voice to her or anyone, he had no need to. People ran to obey his orders from just a single glance, as did Alexandra. He was distinguished and powerful, with dark eyes and grey hair. He had been extremely handsome and virile and athletic in his youth, and he had aged admirably. He still had a powerful frame and handsome face, and he did not look fifty-nine years old, any more than Alexandra looked thirty-four with her big innocent green eyes, and the silky strawberry-blonde hair that she usually wore up in elegant French twists and chignons.

'Have you organized everything for the dinner next week?' He handed her a checklist of things for her to go over again. She had a secretary to assist her with such things, but she preferred doing most of it herself. That way she could assure him of the perfection he expected.

'Everything's done.' She smiled up at him with respectful eyes filled with admiration, and he looked serious, as he always did, and a little distant.

'Please be sure of it.' He eyed her with a warning like that you would give a child, and she smiled at him. Sometimes he frightened her, but not very often. She knew how good-hearted he was, beneath the constant demands for perfection.

'We're dining at the Elysée tomorrow night,' he informed her.

'That's nice. Any particular reason?' She smiled at him, unimpressed. They dined there often.

'They're announcing the new Minister of Defence.' It did not sound fascinating to her, but dinners at the Elysée never were. But Henri thought they were extremely important. He was still toying with the idea of a political career when he retired from his bank, which was still a few years in the future.

'I'm having lunch at my mother's tomorrow. But I'll be home in plenty of time to get ready for the evening.' She looked away, glancing at the papers on her desk, not wanting to see the disapproval in her eyes. She hated that, always had. She had always hoped he'd come to love her mother, but she had given up in recent years, and it was an open secret that Henri disapproved of Margaret.

Almost as revenge, his voice seemed to grow cold when he spoke again. 'I'll be out for dinner tonight.' He offered no reason or excuse, and she would not have asked for one in any case. 'I suppose you'll want to dine with the children.'

She nodded, meeting his eyes again, wondering where he was going. She knew he'd had one mistress only a few years before, and hoped it was not something he was starting fresh now. It was something she accepted about him. It was hardly unusual, in France. 'I'll tell the cook.' She loved eating with the girls, as long as it didn't mean something ominous between them, and this time she wasn't quite certain. 'A business dinner, darling?' She tried to keep her voice light as she watched him.

He scowled at her disapprovingly. The question was out of place and he nodded, as his daughters bounded into the room, not expecting him to be there. There were shrieks of delight, and Marie-Louise's long, coltish legs in her short navy-blue skirt, her eyes shy and admiring as she saw Henri, and then a warm hug for her mother as he watched them. He never showed Alexandra affection in front of them. But Axelle was the image of her, she looked like a miniature as she sat happily on her mother's lap, playing with the things on the desk, and almost overturning a bottle of ink as Henri cringed in anticipation of disaster.

'Axelle!' he said sternly as she gazed up at him, unconcerned, unafraid, and with endless mischief in her eyes. At times he feared she would turn out to be like her maternal grandmother, and he was strict with her because of it. 'Be careful what you do in your mother's study.'

'I am, Papa.' She smiled up at him with her angelic blue eyes. Her mouth formed a natural pout, her cheeks were still round, and she still had the baby fat of a little girl, unlike Marie-Louise, who was long and tall and elegant, and already looked more like her father. 'They sent me out of the room today in school,' Axelle announced proudly to everyone in the room, and Alexandra laughed. She was only sorry her father wasn't alive to see them both, she knew he would have been totally in love with Axelle, and of course very proud of Marie-Louise too. They were both lovely girls, and Alexandra was very proud of them.

'That's nothing to brag about, mademoiselle. What did you do?' Henri questioned, watching them with hidden pride of his own. He loved them both, although he never said it and still regretted not having a son to bear his name. He often thought it was a shame Alexandra hadn't been able to give him that, and he thought of it as her only important failure. And she felt that.

'Can I have some gum?' Axelle whispered audibly and Alexandra blushed. It was a treat she sometimes gave the

166

girls when Henri wasn't around, because it was forbidden to them by their father. But Axelle always gave her away. Marie-Louise preferred liquorice and chocolates, but Axelle loved to blow enormous bubbles with great wads of pink goo.

'Certainly not.' Henri frowned at all three of them, reminded Alexandra of the list he had left on her desk, and went into his own study next door, firmly closing the door behind him, and then opening it just a crack, watched with a grin, as his wife handed out sweets and bubble-gum to the girls. He loved watching Axelle with the sticky stuff all over her face, but he felt it was not appropriate for him to admit it. He silently closed the door, and went to his desk with a sigh, as the girls enjoyed their time with their mother.

'Papa's home early.' Marie-Louise observed quietly as she sank gracefully into a Louis-XV *fauteuil* near her mother's desk, munching a piece of liquorice. She had large, dark soulful eyes and a natural elegance about her. She was going to be a beautiful girl in a few years, and already was in many ways. But Axelle was the more striking of the two, and her hair had her mother's natural red colour, although Alexandra used a rinse to dim the red and had worn it blond for years, because Henri preferred it. He thought red hair 'inappropriate', even though in her case it was natural. But she wore it blond, to please her husband.

'He's going out tonight,' Alexandra said matter-of-factly, handing Axelle another piece of bubble-gum, and Marie-Louise a chocolate.

'You too?' Axelle's eyes instantly filled with tears, although she was quick to take the gum from her mother's hand, and Alexandra laughed and shook her head in answer.

'No, I'm not. He's going to a business dinner, and I'm dining with you tonight.'

'Hurray!' Axelle exulted with a mouthful of gum, and Marie-Louise smiled. She loved it when her mother ate with them, particularly when their father was out. They always laughed a lot, and she told them stories about when she was a little girl, and the wonderful tricks Grandma helped her play on her father.

'Does your nanny know you're home?' she asked the girls, but she could see from Axelle's dirty hands and face that they had come to her without the governess's knowledge. The nurse always sent them in immaculately dressed and spotlessly groomed, and she preferred them like this, a little more natural, and totally relaxed in her presence.

'I think we forgot to tell Nanny we were home,' Marie-Louise confessed as Axelle blew an expert balloon with the pink gum, and the three of them laughed together.

'You'd better not let her see that.' Alexandra smiled and set Axelle back on her feet. 'You'd better tell her you're home.' The chauffeur usually brought them home from school in the Citroën, although Alexandra liked to pick them up whenever she could make it. 'I have some things to do now.' She wanted to go over Henri's list, to make sure she didn't forget anything for his dinner party the following week. She already knew who the guests would be. She had invited everyone three weeks before, on their formal *cartons*, and reminders had been sent out, formally engraved and edged in gold, letting their guests know that the Baron and Baroness de Morigny were expecting them at 14 avenue Foch, for a dinner in black tie, at eight o'clock. She already knew what she was going to wear, the flowers had been ordered, the menu set. Everything was in order, she saw, as the girls left the room, and she read carefully down the list. And she knew Henri would produce their best wines for the occasion. Probably a Château Margaux '61, or a Lafite-Rothschild '45. There would be Cristalle champagne, and Château d'Yquem afterwards, and eventually *poire* and a host of other liqueurs as the men smoked their cigars, and the ladies withdrew to another drawing-room reserved for their use while the gentlemen enjoyed their cigars and brandy and allegedly ribald stories. It was a custom few people still used, but Henri liked the old customs, and Alexandra always did things the way Henri liked them. It would never have occurred to her to suggest something different to him. She had always done things his way. Always. And to perfection.

She sat quietly in her study, after the girls left, thinking of her husband and wondering where he was going that night, and then thinking of her daughters. She heard their voices in the garden outside, and knew they were playing with the nurse. They would soon be out of school, and they would be going to Cap Ferrat as they always did for the summer. It was good for the children there, and Henri would join them in a few weeks, after settling things at his office in Paris. They would undoubtedly join friends on their yacht, and perhaps go to Italy or Greece for a few days, leaving the children alone with the nurse and the other servants. It was a golden life, the only one Alexandra had ever known, and yet sometimes, once in a great while, Alexandra allowed herself to wonder what life would have been like if she'd married a different man, someone easier, or perhaps younger. And then feeling guilty for the thought, she would force it from her mind, and realise how fortunate she was to be married to her husband.

When she saw Henri again that night, just before he went out, he looked handsome and impeccable in a beautifully tailored dark blue suit, with a perfectly starched white shirt and dark blue tie, his sapphire cufflinks glinting discreetly at his wrists, and his eyes were bright and alive. He always seemed full of energy, full of some secret reserve and strength that belied his almost sixty years, and made him seem much younger.

'You look very handsome, as usual,' she smiled at him. She had changed into a pink satin dressing-gown with matching mules, and her hair was piled on her head with a cascade of curls loosely falling from it. She looked beautiful, but it was obvious from the look in her eyes that she was totally unaware of it.

'Thank you, my dear. I won't be back late.' His words were banal, but the look in his eyes was gentle and loving. He knew she would wait up for him as she always did, in her own room, with the light on, and if he wished, he could come to see her. In most instances, he would knock softly on the door, and come in for a visit before he went to bed, in his own bedroom next door to hers. He preferred separate bedrooms. He had insisted on them since they were married. She had cried about it for weeks at first, and tried to change his mind on the subject for the first several months, if not years. But Henri was firm with her. He needed his own space, his own privacy, and assured her she would need hers in time as well. And he meant it. It was just a habit he had, like so many others. Eventually, she had grown used to it. They had connecting doors which gave easy access to the rooms, and the door between them didn't keep him from appearing in her room in his dressing-gown, late at night, with a frequency that always pleased her. And he still felt desire when he looked at her, as he did now. But there were other women who appealed to him too. He always tried to be discreet, although he suspected that occasionally she knew, by instinct if nothing else. Women had an uncanny knack for things like that. He had discovered that in his youth, and he had a great respect for it.

'Have a good time.' She kissed him lightly on the cheek, and went down to the smaller dining-room to have dinner with the girls. She heard his car pull away moments afterwards, and turned to help Axelle cut her meat, trying not to think of where he was going.

'Why does Daddy go out alone?' Axelle asked casually with a mouth full of food, and Marie-Louise frowned disapprovingly.

'That's rude to ask,' she chided, but Alexandra smiled.

'It's all right. Sometimes he has business dinners where he prefers to go alone.'

'Are they very dull?' She was interested in everything.

'Sometimes.' Alexandra laughed. 'I'd rather be here with both of you.'

'I'm glad.' Axelle grinned, and announced a loose tooth, as Marie-Louise winced in disgust at her younger sister. She was past all that, and Axelle's offer to wiggle it for them revolted her still further.

'Stop that! You make me sick!' She made a face and Alexandra smiled at them. She was never happier than when she was with her daughters. She spent a little while in Marie-Louise's room that night and discovered she had a new best friend at school, and then read stories to Axelle, and kissed them both, and said their prayers with them before retiring to her own room. It was odd. Sometimes Marie-Louise reminded her of someone else, but she was never sure whom. Henri perhaps . . . maybe that was it . . . and then she forced the thought from her mind, as she slipped off her dressing-gown, took a hot bath, and eventually climbed into bed with a new book.

It was after midnight when Henri finally came home, and she heard him in his room, before he finally came in to say good-night to her. 'Still up?' She nodded with a smile. She liked waiting up for him, sometimes he was more relaxed at night and more likely to open up to her, about his ideas, or plans, or problems.

'Did you have a nice evening?'

'It was all right.' His eyes seemed to search hers, and then he said something unusual for him, something that relieved her mind more than he could ever have imagined. Perhaps he didn't have a new mistress after all, she thought with immense relief. 'I should have taken you along. I was bored without you.' It was unlike him to pay her a compliment like that, and she smiled and patted her bed for him to sit down, and when he did she leaned over and kissed him.

'Thank you, Henri. I missed you too . . .' Her voice was gentle and her smile was the private one that always stirred him. 'I had a nice time with the girls tonight. Marie-Louise is serious and so grown up now, and Axelle is still . . . well, she's still a baby.' She laughed and he smiled. He was proud of them too, even if he didn't show it.

'They're good little girls.' He leaned over and kissed her neck. 'Just like their Maman . . . you're a good girl too, my darling.' They were tender words she loved to hear and they warmed her.

'Am I?' She smiled mischievously at him. 'What a shame . . .' She laughed then, and he lay next to her, touching her breast with one hand, and kissing her with the full measure of his desire. He hadn't intended to make love to her that night, but she looked so lovely, lying in her bed, with the pink and grey sheets, and her pink satin nightgown. And it was so hard for him to tell her how much he cared sometimes. It was easier to show her here, in the dim light of her boudoir. He loved their hours in bed, their nights side by side until he tiptoed quietly to his own room in the morning. He was deeply attached to her, and to the girls, but it was always difficult for him to show that. And he expected so much of her . . . of himself . . . he wanted her to be everything he had always dreamed of in a way, and in some ways that was why he had married her. He could never have married someone less than Alexandra. But the daughter of the Comte de Borne was of a breeding worthy of him, her upbringing suited her perfectly to become his wife, and in the past fourteen years she had proved him right. He was proud of who she was and all he had taught her. She was perfect in every way, and he could never have settled for anything less than Alexandra. He wanted her on a pedestal . . . except for these rare times . . . in his arms . . . in her bed . . . then he could allow her to be someone else, for a few moments at least. And with a contented sigh, and a last look at her afterwards, smiling happily at him, he turned over and fell asleep, totally sated.

Chapter 11

The chauffeur drove the Citroën over the Pont Alexandre III to the Left Bank, and moments later, passing the Invalides, was on the rue de Varenne. It always felt like going home to her. As beautiful as the *hôtel particulier* on the avenue Foch was, as handsomely decorated, after all these years her parents' house on the rue de Varenne still felt like home to Alexandra.

Her heart always seemed to give a happy little leap as she saw the house, and the caretaker opened the gates so they could drive into the court, and then there was still that moment of sadness, that tiny jolt, as she realized that her father would never be there again. After all these years, she still felt his absence sorely. But the prospect of seeing her mother was a comfort and a joy, and it was a homecoming each time she saw her.

Their old butler was standing smiling beside the front door, holding it open wide in welcome. And beyond, Alexandra could see the priceless artefacts her parents had collected. Beautifully inlaid pieces of furniture, Louis-XV chests covered with rich pink marbles and dripping with handsome bronzes. Urns they had bought at auction in London. And Renoirs and Degases and Turners and Van Goghs, and the Cassatts her mother was so fond of. It was a house filled with beautiful things, all of which would one day be hers, which was a prospect she didn't even like to think of, but the only one that consoled Henri for the exasperation of being related to Margaret.

'Darling, are you here?' the familiar voice called from upstairs, from the sitting-room overlooking the garden that she was so fond of. And Alexandra hurried up the marble staircase, feeling like a child again, with a happy smile, anxious to see her mother. She found her sitting on a couch, doing needlepoint with her glasses on the very end of her nose, and a glass of wine on the table next to her, and her Labrador retriever stretched out in front of the fire. Axelle and Marie-Louise loved the dog, who was old and good-natured, but Henri always cringed as she slobbered and licked and kissed and left her hair all over everyone who touched her. 'Darling!' Margaret dropped her needlepoint and stood to her full six foot, a pretty woman with blond hair and green eyes not unlike Alexandra's, in a bright pink Chanel suit with a navy-blue blouse and matching shoes, and ruby earrings the size of doorknobs. 'My God, who died?' She backed off suddenly after kissing Alexandra.

She looked at her daughter with a frown, and Alexandra grinned at her. Her mother always wore bright, striking clothes from wonderful designers – Chanel and Givenchy and Dior and de Ribes – and almost always in brilliant colours. They suited her too, but Henri preferred her in black and navy-blue and beige, and in the country in grey flannel. She had come to her mother's home in a new black dress from Dior, with a matching jacket. 'Now stop that. This is new, and Henri loves it.' Unlike her exchanges with her husband and her children, Alexandra always spoke to her mother in English, and although she spoke it well, she had a noticeable French accent.

'It looks awful. You should burn it.' Margaret de Borne sat down on her couch again, indicated to the butler to pour Alexandra a glass of wine, and went back to her needlepoint as she smiled happily at her daughter. She always loved her visits, and their private exchanges. She enjoyed going out with her too, but this was always a little more special. They both went out more than they needed to, so they didn't need each other as an excuse to go to the latest fashionable places. Instead, they preferred to eat a simple lunch of salad and cheese and fruit on trays in Margaret's sitting-room overlooking her garden. She glanced at her daughter again and shook her head in obvious dismay. 'I wish you'd stop doing your hair that colour, sweetheart. You look like one of those fading blondes from California. If I had hair your colour, I would flaunt it. I'd make it even more red!' She shook her glasses at her for emphasis before setting them down to sip her wine. She had always loved the red of Alexandra's hair before she began to rinse it blond. It seemed such a waste of one of nature's great gifts. Her own hair had to be helped considerably now twice a month at Alexandre's.

'You know Henri hates it red. It's too loud. He thinks it looks more ladylike this way.'

'Henri . . . the poor man is so afraid to be a little out of the ordinary. I'm surprised he doesn't make you wear a black wig and cover the whole thing. Seriously, darling, God gave you red hair, and you ought to enjoy it.'

'I don't mind it like this.' She smiled easily and sipped her wine. She was used to her mother's complaints about her husband. His were far worse about Margaret. And Alexandra had lived with it for fourteen years. She was only sorry they had never come to like each other, but she had given up long since. It was obvious they were never going to fall in love with each other.

'You're too good-natured. How do you like these, by the way?' She smiled happily, pointing at the new ruby earrings she was wearing. She could afford to indulge herself, partially thanks to Pierre's generosity when he died, and partially thanks to her own handsome fortune. 'I just got them.'

'I thought so.' Alexandra laughed. Her mother was always buying beautiful clothes and fabulous baubles. It was good for her, she looked well in what she bought and it made her happy, despite what Henri said about a woman spending 'that kind of money'. 'They're very pretty, and they suit you to perfection.'

'Van Cleef.' Margaret looked pleased with herself. 'And a terrific bargain.'

But at that, Alexandra laughed heartily as she set down her wineglass. 'I can just imagine.'

'No, really! They were under a hundred thousand.'

'Dollars or francs?'

'Are you kidding? Dollars of course.' Margaret grinned without a trace of guilt as Alexandra laughed at her.

'I thought so.' Alexandra smiled. It was not exactly the kind of bargain Henri would have approved of. And after thirty years in France, her mother still spoke more English than French, and calculated everything in dollars. 'What else have you been up to?'

'The usual. I had lunch with Mimi de Saint Bré yesterday.' She was another American woman who had married a titled Frenchman, and like Margaret, she had a good mind and a wild sense of humour. 'We're going to New York together next week.'

'What for?'

'Just to get our hair done and do some shopping. I haven't been in months and thought it might be fun before the summer. After that, I'm meeting friends in Rome, and I thought I might go to San Remo for a few weeks. I haven't made up my mind yet.'

'Why don't you stay with us for a few weeks afterwards?' Alexandra looked delighted at the prospect, but her mother looked cautious.

'I don't want to make your husband nervous.'

'Just don't bring the girls whoopee cushions and those hand buzzers and everything will be fine.' They both laughed at the memory. Henri had almost fainted when he sat down in the living-room with guests, and landed on one of the whoopee cushions Margaret and the children had planted.

'Do you remember how awful that was?' Margaret could hardly stop laughing at the memory, and there were tears in Alexandra's eyes when she stopped laughing. It had been awful for Henri, but in truth it was desperately funny, and they had all been banished to their rooms afterwards, including Margaret, who had taught Marie-Louise how to make apple-pie beds, which had complicated matters even further. There was no doubt in anyone's mind that she was not Henri's favourite house-guest. 'Actually, I thought I'd see what I could find for them in New York . . . nothing quite so outrageous of course . . .' But her eyes twinkled wickedly at the prospect. She used to buy silly jokes like that for her late husband, and he had always loved them. For him, being married to Margaret was like having another child. Alexandra had always been a bit more serious than that, even as a little girl, and especially after she got married.

'I'll tell Henri you're coming.'

Margaret grinned. 'Wait until you really want to annoy him.'

'Mother!' Alexandra laughed. Her mother had very few illusions. 'You make him sound so awful and he isn't!' She always defended her husband, and to Henri, she defended her mother. She was loyal to both.

'He is not awful, darling.' Margaret grinned. 'Just stuffy.'

The afternoon seemed to fly by, as it always did when they were together, and at four-thirty Alexandra looked at her watch and stretched regretfully. She was so comfortable in the cosy room, looking out at the garden, and in her mother's company. They always had such a good time together. Margaret was still her closest friend, and always had been.

'I should go . . . much as I hate to . . .' Alexandra stood up with obvious regret as Margaret watched her.

'Why? Are you giving a party tonight?'

'No, that's next week. Tonight we're dining at the Elysée, and Henri will get nervous if I don't come home early and start getting ready.'

'You ought to do something wonderful to surprise him, like wear a skintight dress covered with rhinestones, and tease your hair straight up. It would do them good at the Elysée.' She chuckled at the thought and Alexandra smiled. Her mother probably would have done something just like that, and Henri would have called his attorneys in the morning. With him, that was always the implication. Step out of line and . . . Alexandra never tested his mettle in that direction. She loved him too much to risk everything for pranks like her mother's. And besides, she wasn't like that.

'You're a lot braver than I am, Maman.'

'That's only because I'm not married to your husband. I can do exactly what I want now. And before, your father always let me get away with anything I wanted. I was very lucky.' She smiled gently at her daughter.

'Papa was lucky too. And he knew it,' Alexandra reminded her and the two women embraced and walked slowly downstairs, as the butler waited to let her out with his usual warm smile. He had been with them since she was a little girl, and he called her 'Madame Alexandra' as he helped her into her car and closed the door firmly. She waved at her mother as the driver took her home in the Citroën, and she felt the same sadness she always did when she left her mother. Life had been so simple on the rue de Varenne, living with her parents ... before ... but that wasn't fair either. She loved Henri, and of course, the children. They were the life-force of her existence. But seeing her mother always made her long for a life that was simpler, and a time when she didn't have quite so much to live up to.

She was still thinking of it as she slipped out of her dress and ran her bath, and took out a serious, well-covered black evening gown for their dinner that night at the Elysée Palace.

The girls came in to say hello to her while she was in the tub, and she heard Henri go into his study while she was getting dressed, but he didn't come in to speak to her and she didn't see him until they met in the front hall, ready to go out for the evening. Her dress had long sleeves and a high neck, and a long slender skirt with beautiful gold embroidery on it. It was exquisitely made and from an old collection of Saint-Laurent. She wore it with a short sable jacket and a pair of outstanding diamond earrings given to her by her father.

'You look lovely tonight.' His eyes were admiring, his voice restrained, and his manner impeccably formal.

'Thank you.' She turned to him with her blond good looks, her hair swept into a smooth French twist, exactly as it had been worn years before by Grace Kelly. It was a good look for Alexandra, and one that Henri approved of. 'Did you have a good day?' Her eyes looked lonely, and she suddenly wished he would kiss her, but he didn't.

'Very pleasant, thank you,' he answered. There were times when they were like two strangers, and the intimacies of the night before seemed all but forgotten in the formality of the moment. He helped her into the car, and the driver pulled away, with both of them lost in thought in separate worlds in the back seat, and two little girls in nightgowns watching from the upstairs window.

Chapter 12

The day after Hilary saw Arthur Patterson, when he had told her he didn't know how to find her sisters, Hilary felt as though the world had come to an end. She was seventeen years old and she felt as though her life was over. For years she had lived only to find Megan and Axie. And now there was no hope. They were gone forever.

She began her first job the next day with an aching void in her chest, but her face was calm, her eyes cool, and no one would have known the agony of despair she was feeling. The only thing that kept her going was her determination to survive in spite of everything, and her hatred for Arthur.

She felt like a machine as she moved through the days and nights, but she performed her job well. She improved her typing, studied shorthand from a book, and went to college at night, just as she had promised herself she would years before. She did everything she had said she would, but through it all there was not so much a sense of accomplishment but of heartless determination. She was going to succeed at all costs, but even she didn't know why she wanted to make it. There was no one to prove anything to. No one who cared. No one to love or who loved her.

She only kept the job for a year, and then she got a better one. She heard about it before anyone else, at the employment agency where she worked, and she went to the interview before anyone else even knew about it. It was as a receptionist at CBA-News. It was a fabulous job that paid almost twice what her current job did, and she had to be quick, smart, and good, and she was all three. The woman who interviewed her was very impressed with her. She got the job, and managed to stay on in school. And she got steady raises from then on. She eventually became a secretary, and then a production assistant, and within five years a producer. She was incredibly bright, and by then she had graduated from college. She was twenty-three years old and she was well on her way to a real career. She was respected by her superiors, and feared by some of her employees, most in fact, and she seemed to have few friends at work. She kept aloof and worked hard, staying late most of the time, and turning in projects deserving the praise she won. She was a remarkable girl, and when she became one of the main producers of the evening news at twenty-five, Adam Kane, the man in charge of network news, invited her out to celebrate. She hesitated and then decided it would be politically unwise to refuse him. She accepted gracefully and found herself dining at the Brussels with him, drinking champagne and talking shop, discussing how important the network was and where she hoped to go eventually. He was surprised to hear that she had long-range goals, particularly since they were more ambitious than his own plans for the future.

'Hey, hold on there . . . what is this? – staff meeting for Women's Lib?' He was an attractive man with brown hair and gentle brown eyes, and a philosophical way of looking at life. 'Why such big plans?' She was the first woman he'd ever known who had admitted her ambitions to him, and he admitted to her that he found it frightening. He and his wife had just got divorced because she didn't think she wanted to be a 'wife anymore', and it had shaken him to the core. They had two little boys and a house in Darien, and now suddenly he was living alone on the West Side, and women were talking to him about 'goals within corporate management'. He laughed softly as he looked at her. She was so beautiful and so young and so intense and yet there was something missing. 'What's happened to women who want to have babies and live in the suburbs? Is that totally out of fashion?'

She smiled at him, aware that she might have overstated her case, but she so seldom went out with men. She forgot that one had to be quiet about things, and this one was nice. She liked working for him. 'I guess that's out for some of us.' She didn't apologize for it. She knew where she wanted to go, and nothing would stop her until she got there. She was still running from the demons of the past sixteen years and knew she probably would forever. She accepted that now, though she didn't explain it to him. She never told anyone anything. She lived alone, and she went to work, and other than that, she had no interest in anything. He sensed that now, and it frightened him, for her. He knew how much more there was to life. He was thirty-eight years old and he had married at twenty-three. And now he was discovering endless new horizons.

'Don't you want a husband and kids one day?'

She shook her head. He looked as though she could be honest with him. 'That's not very important to me.' More than that, she didn't want anyone she could lose . . . least of all two little girls . . . two little children someone could take away from her . . . She knew she would never let that happen to her. She wanted to be alone, and she was, and it only hurt occasionally, like now, as she looked at this man and wondered what it woud be like to be close to him. Or was it only the champagne, she wondered.

'My children are the best thing in my life, Hilary. Don't cheat yourself of that.' She couldn't tell him that in a way, she had already had kids. She never told anyone that, and knew she never would. Ever.

'Why does everyone think you have to have kids to be complete?'

'These days they don't. Most women think like you, but they're wrong. Hilary, the women who don't have children now are going to panic in ten or fifteen years, mark my words, we're going to see a whole generation of women fighting their own biology before it's too late. But now they're all cool, they figure they've got years ahead of them. But it's a mistake to rule it out. You've never been married?' He looked into her eyes and he liked what he saw there, courage and honesty and integrity and intelligence. But he saw fear too. She was running from something and he couldn't figure out what it was that had hurt her. Maybe, maybe she'd had a bad experience with someone . . . not unlike his with Barb. He still couldn't belicve she had left him and taken his children.

Hilary shook her head in answer to his question. 'No, I've never been married.' And then she laughed. 'I'm only twenty-five. What's the big rush?'

'These days none at all. I was just curious. I was twenty-three when I got married. My wife was twenty-one. It was real important to us. But that was fifteen years ago, things have changed a hell of a lot since then. This is 1974. We got married in '59.' And then he smiled at her over the last of their champagne. 'What were you doing then? You were probably just a kid.'

Her eyes clouded over then, thinking back. 1959 . . . she'd been in Boston then, with Eileen and Jack . . . or were they in Jacksonville by then? . . . the thought of it almost made her feel ill. Axie and Megan were already gone. 'Oh, nothing much. I was living with an aunt in Boston around then.' She tried to make it sound ordinary, almost fun.

'Where were your folks?'

'They died when I was eight . . . and nine . . .'

'Separately?' She nodded, anxious to change the subject back to work again. She didn't want to talk to him about this. Not to him or anyone. 'How terrible. In accidents?' She nodded non-committally and finished her champagne at one gulp. 'Were you an only child?'

She looked him in the eye then with something cold and hard he didn't understand and nodded at him. 'Yes, I was.'

'It doesn't sound like much fun.' He felt sorry for her and she hated that too. She didn't want pity from him or from anyone. She tried to smile at him to lighten the mood, but he was looking so intensely at her, it made her nervous.

'Maybe that's why I love my work so much. It's home to me.' That seemed pathetic to him, but he didn't say so.

'Where'd you go to school?'

'NYU.' But she didn't tell him she'd gone at night, while she was working.

He nodded. 'Barb and I went to UC Berkeley.'

'That must have been fun.' She smiled and he reached out to her, not anxious to talk about his ex-wife anymore, but only about her.

'I'm glad we went out to dinner tonight. I've been wanting to talk to you for a long time. You do a hell of a job at the network.'

'I should.' She grinned, 'I've been around CBA for long enough. Years.' Six years of pushing and shoving her way up, until she was a producer. She had a right to be proud of herself and she was. It was a long, long way from the Jacksonville juvenile home, or the foster homes she'd been in, or even her life with Jack and Eileen in Boston.

'Do you think you'll stay?' he asked, and she stared at him.

'At CBA? Why would I go anywhere?'

'Because in this business people move around a lot.' He certainly had, and he wasn't unusual in their field.

She shook her head at him, with a look of determination in her eyes that startled him. 'I'm not going anywhere, my friend. I've got my eye on an office wayyyy upstairs.' And he sensed that she meant it more than she had meant anything else she'd said that night.

'Why?' That kind of ambition puzzled him. He was successful, and he liked his job, but he had never aspired to great heights, and he couldn't imagine wanting that, particularly not if you were a beautiful young girl.

'Because it's important to me.' She was being honest with him. 'It means security. And accomplishment. And it's something tangible I can take home with me at night.'

But he knew better than that. 'Until they fire you and hire someone else. Don't hang everything on your job, Hilary. You'll end up alone one day, and disappointed.'

'That doesn't frighten me.' She'd been alone all her life. She was used to it. In fact, she liked it that way, no one could hurt her or let her down, or betray her that way.

She was an odd girl, he thought, and he had never known anyone as independent as she was. He took her home that night, and hoped she would invite him upstairs but she only shook his hand with a warm smile and thanked him for the evening. And he went home so horny for her that as soon as he got upstairs, he called her. He didn't even care if he woke her up, and he doubted that she was asleep yet.

Her voice was husky when she picked up the phone, and he closed his eyes, listening to her. He was a nice guy, and he hated living alone. And she was so damn beautiful ... he knew his boys would love her too ... 'Hello?'

'Hi, Hilary ... I just wanted to tell you what a nice time I had tonight.'

She laughed softly at him, and he liked the sound of that too. 'So did I. But don't you try to distract me at work, Mr Kane. I'm not planning to lose my job over anyone. Not even you.'

'I got that. Want to have lunch sometime this week?'

'Sure. If I'm not too swamped.'

'Tomorrow sound okay?'

She laughed again, a delicious mixture of hot smoke and icy cool. 'Why don't you relax, Adam. I told you, I'm not going anywhere.'

'Good. Then let's take advantage of it. I'll pick you up in your office at twelve-fifteen. Okay?' He sounded like a little kid, and she was smiling in the dark, lying in bed, and much as she hated to admit it, even to herself, he did something to her no other man had till then. And she trusted him. Maybe it was all right ... just for a lunch or two ... what harm could that do? She hadn't allowed herself anything more since coming to New York, and oddly enough she had never wanted anyone. Other people had boyfriends, and affairs, and broken hearts. And all Hilary wanted were promotions and raises and work. That was her lover, and so far it had treated her very well. 'Twelve-fifteen?' he repeated in the face of silence from her.

'Fine.' Her voice flowed over the single word, and he felt as though he were floating when he hung up.

There was a single rose on her desk the next day, and they had lunch at the Veau d'Or and she didn't get back to her office till three o'clock.

'This is terrible, Adam. I never do things like this.' She threw the long black hair over her shoulder, and rolled up the sleeves of her shirt. It was a beautiful warm day and she didn't even feel like going back to work. 'You're a miserable influence. I just got a promotion and now you're going to get me canned.'

'Good, then will you marry me? We can move to New Jersey and have ten kids.'

'How depressing.' She looked at him with her icy green eyes, and he felt something he never had before. She became a challenge. There was a wall around her he would have done anything to climb, but he still wasn't sure how far she'd let him go. They were still circling each other carefully, but he had so much to say to her and she was such intelligent company. And he appealed to her in a way no one had before. It was a dangerous combination, and at times it frightened her, particularly when he distracted her from her work, but after all he was her boss.

He invited her to dinner on Saturday, but she declined, and she turned down his next two invitations to lunch, but he looked so unhappy about it when he stopped to talk to her that she finally relented and agreed to go out with him the following Friday night. They went to P. J. Clarke's, for a hamburger, and then a walk up Third Avenue to her new apartment on Fifty-ninth Street.

'Why do you keep such a distance between us?' He looked sincerely unhappy about it. He was crazy about her, and he was dying for her to let him get closer.

'I'm not sure it's such a good idea. It could make things awfully complicated at work. You're my boss. Adam.'

She smiled up at him, and, as attracted to him as she was, she was afraid of repercussions at the office.

And then he smiled at her regretfully. 'Not for much longer, I'm afraid, if that makes any difference to you. I'm being transferred to sales in two weeks. I just heard about it today.'

'How do you feel about that?' She was concerned for him. It was kind of a sidestep, and in his shoes she'd have been crushed, but he didn't look too disturbed as he shrugged and smiled at her.

'No big deal. I might like it better than where I am . . . except for you, of course. Will you see me more often then?' It would certainly make things easier for her, but she still wasn't sure if she should get involved with him. Life was so much easier living as a celibate.

Celibacy had become a way of life to her, and giving it up meant risking a part of herself. 'Hilary?' He was looking down at her as they walked, and he gently took her hand. He seemed very young as he smiled at her, and in some ways he still was. 'I want to be with you . . . you mean a lot to me . . .'

'Adam, you don't even know who I am . . . I could be anyone . . . *La femme aux yeux verts* . . .' The words slipped out and she laughed.

'What does that mean?'

'It's French.' She had revived her French in college, and was surprised to find it was still there, dormant but not dead, a final gift from her mother. 'It means the woman with green eyes.'

'How come you speak French?' He wanted to know everything about her, and there was so little she wanted to tell him.

'I spoke it a long time ago . . . when I was a little girl. And I picked it up again in college.'

'Did your parents speak French?' She could have told him then, could have begun to open up, could have said something about Solange, but she decided it was safer not to.

'No, I just learned it at school, I guess.' He nodded, satisfied with the answer she'd given him, and when they reached her apartment, after a moment's hesitation, she invited him upstairs. They listened to Roberta Flack on her stereo, and talked for hours over a bottle of wine, and he stood up regretfully around one o'clock and looked down at her with a wistful smile.

'I'd like to spend the night with you, Hilary, but I get the feeling you're not ready for that ... are you?' She shook her head, not sure she would ever be. People had tried to get close to her but she was not even remotely tempted. 'Are you involved with anyone?' He had meant to ask before but he had put it off. She shook her head in answer, looking at him strangely.

'No, I'm not ... I haven't been in ... a long time ...'

'For any particular reason?'

'A lot of them. Most of them too complicated to explain.' He sat on her couch and looked at her quietly.

'Why don't you try me?'

She shrugged again. She didn't want to tell him what she'd been through. That was nobody's business. She led a different life now, in another place, another world. She didn't want to drag those things with her, and yet she did, in spite of all her efforts to deny them. 'I'm sorry, Adam ... I can't ...'

'Why not?' He reached out and took her hands in his. 'Don't you trust me?'

'It's not that.' She felt her eyes fill with tears and she hated herself for it. 'I don't want to talk about it ... really ...' She stood up and walked away, her proud shoulders straightened against the world and all it had done to her. And without knowing it, she looked exactly like her mother.

'Hilary . . .' He walked up to her from behind and put his arms around her. 'Why don't you let yourself go? I know how strong you are, I've seen it at work, but this is different . . . this is us . . . this isn't a war zone.'

Her voice was tired as she spoke to him with her head bowed. 'Life is a war zone, Adam.'

'It doesn't have to be.' He was so gentle, and so innocent. She envied him his simple life. The most difficult thing that had ever happened to him was his wife's deciding she wanted to be free and no longer married. But he knew nothing of the agonies Hilary had endured. He couldn't even begin to understand them. 'Life can be so sweet . . . if you let it . . .'

'It's not as easy as that.' She sighed and looked at him. 'I don't think you understand the kind of life I've led, and I don't think I could explain it.'

'Then why not go from here? Isn't that possible, and leave the past behind you?'

'Maybe.' She wasn't sure it could be done, but she was willing to try it. He reached out and kissed her gently at first, and then suddenly with more passion. He had wanted her for weeks, months, since the first time he'd seen her, and now he couldn't hold back. He peeled her clothes from her and dropped his own, and carried her to her bed, where he began making love to her. But she lay distant and cold, and secretly frightened. Some of the things he did to her were the same things that Maida and Georgine had done . . . and some of the things reminded her of the boys who raped her the day after Maida and Georgine left. It was too much to overcome, even with a good man like Adam. And it didn't take him long to realize that she didn't want to go on. He pulled away, still throbbing with desire for her and unable to understand what had happened.

'What's wrong? . . .' His voice was hoarse, his eyes bleary with unspent passion. 'I want you so much.'

'I'm sorry . . .' She whispered the words, and turned over on her side, staring at the far wall, wondering if she would ever be normal. Perhaps she would never overcome the past. She was twenty-five years old, and she was beginning to suspect that. There were too many people left that she hated . . . Arthur Patterson . . . Jack Jones . . . the boys who had raped her . . . Maida and Georgine . . . Eileen . . . the people at juvenile hall . . . and in the far distance, even her father. It was too big a burden to carry around and still allow her to function as a woman. 'It's not you,' she tried to explain. 'I just can't.'

'Why? You have to tell me.' He was trying to sit calmly at the edge of the bed, trying to reach out and understand her. And she sat up quietly and turned around. Maybe it was better to shock him than to hurt him.

'I was raped a long time ago . . .' She didn't want to say more, and hoped that would be enough, but of course it wasn't.

'How? . . . by whom?'

'It's a long story.' And which one should she tell him? Maida and Georgine, who were the first, or the boys who had come later? Or Jack who had done his best to precede them all and then had beaten her to within an inch of her life when he didn't get what he wanted. They were all possible candidates for the role, but she couldn't even imagine Adam able to withstand any truth she might tell him.

'When was it?'

'When I was thirteen . . .' That much was true at least.

They had all happened before her fourteenth birthday. She took a gulp of air. 'And there hasn't been anyone since then. I guess I should have told you.'

'Christ.' He looked deeply shaken by what she'd said. 'It certainly would have helped. How was I supposed to know something like that?'

'I didn't think it would matter.'

'Oh really? You were raped twelve years ago, haven't had relations with anyone since, and you actually thought it wouldn't make a difference? How can you do that to yourself, and to me, for chrissake? What about counselling? Have you had a lot of that since then?' He assumed she had, of course, everyone he knew was in therapy. He'd gone right back to his own shrink as soon as his wife left him.

'No.' She spoke very calmly, and got up to put on a bathrobe. She had a long, languid body and beautiful graceful legs that made him ache with wanting her again, but he tried to force himself not to think about it.

'What do you mean "no"? You got help after the rape, no? Yes? Right?'

She smiled at him. Hardly. 'No. Wrong. I guess I didn't need it.'

'Are you crazy?'

'All right, let's say it wasn't available to me at the time.'

'Where were you? The North Pole? Where is there in the modern world that therapy isn't available?' Oh God, he understood nothing of what her life had been like. Therapy? Where? In Louise's home, or at juvie?

'I told you, Adam.' She was getting annoyed, but he was getting frantic. 'I don't want to discuss it. It's too complicated.'

'Too complicated or too painful?' She averted her eyes, so he couldn't see the pain he had already inflicted.

'Why don't we just forget it?'

'What, the relationship? Why? You're not a quitter, Hilary.' Now he was sincerely angry. She would have done anything for her job, but not for him, or the relationship they might have, if she was willing.

'Why don't we just forget the problem, Adam. It'll go away by itself eventually.'

'Really? How long's it been now? Twelve years, you said, and I wouldn't exactly say you're cured. How long would you like to wait for it to "go away"? Thirty years maybe? Or how about fifty? You ought to feel a lot better by then, and Christ you'd only be sixty-three, you could have a great sex life, Hilary, *be serious!*' He took her by the hand and pulled her down on the bed beside him, but he wanted too much from her, and Hilary already knew she couldn't give it to him. He wanted everything, heart and soul, commitment and marriage and children. She could sense that in him, he wanted everything his wife had taken back and more. And she knew for a certainty that she didn't have it in her. She had nothing left to give him. All she could do was take, or maybe extend herself for a little while, if no one asked too much, but the rest was gone. All her love had been given too long ago, and all her energies were reserved for where she was going at the network. 'I want you to go into therapy.' He sat staring at her, as though announcing he wanted her to have brain surgery, and she had no intention of obliging him. God only knew what they'd find there.

'I can't.'

'That's bullshit. Why not?'

'I don't have the time.'

'You're twenty-five years old and you have a problem.'

'It's not one I can't live with.'

'You're not living, you're existing.' But slowly, she was

getting angry too. He had no right to make judgments on how she was living, just because she didn't want to make love with him.

'Maybe it'll get better.' But she didn't sound as though she really cared and that disturbed him.

'By itself?' She nodded. 'I doubt it.'

'Give it time, Adam. This is only the first time.'

He sat silently for a long time, watching her. He saw more than she wanted. 'There's a lot you're not telling me, isn't there?'

She smiled, sphinxlike. 'It's not that important, Adam.'

'I don't believe you. I think you live your whole life behind a walled fortress.'

'I used to . . . a long time ago . . .'

'Why?'

'Because there used to be a lot of people out to hurt me.'

'And now?'

'I don't let them.'

He looked sorry for her, and leaned down to kiss her with a gentle hand on her shoulder, as they sat on the edge of her unmade bed, where their passion had been so unsuccessful. 'I won't hurt you, Hil . . . I swear . . .' There were tears in his eyes, and she wished she could feel something for him, but she couldn't. She couldn't feel anything for anyone, and she knew that now, except perhaps if he awoke some unborn passion in her, but she couldn't imagine that either. 'I love you . . .'

She had no answer to those words, and only looked at him sadly. And then he smiled at her and kissed her again. He understood, and that touched her. 'It's okay . . . you don't have to say anything . . . just let me love you . . .' He lay her back against the pillows, and gently sculpted her body with one finger, drawing it close to her centre, and then, moving it away, drifting around her breasts and all the way down her belly, and then up again, touching her with his tongue and his heart and his fingers, but with nothing else, and after hours of it, she was writhing and begging him for something more, but he wouldn't do it. Instead, he let her feel him, and touched her gently with his throbbing organ. He ran it over her like a satin hand, and she bent down and began to kiss it, and touch him gently until he was writhing as she was, and then first with his lips, and then with his fingers he touched her, and felt her grow frightened and rigid.

'It's all right, Hil . . . it's all right . . . I won't hurt you . . . I . . . please, baby . . . please let me . . . please . . . Oh God, you're so beautiful . . .' He crooned to her like a mother with a baby and slowly he entered her and soothed her until he came, but he knew that she had not joined him. But at least it was a little better. 'I'm sorry, Hil . . .' He wanted more for her, he wanted everything that he felt, but it was too much to ask for.

'Don't be. It was lovely.' She lay quietly beside him, and eventually he slept and she watched him, wondering if she would ever feel for him what he wanted, if she could ever feel it for anyone, or if her body was too filled with hatred.

He left the next morning before she dressed for work, and asked her to lunch later that morning, but she said that she was too busy. He wanted to see her that night, but she had a meeting. And in desperation he asked her to join him on Sunday with his boys. They were spending the weekend with him. She looked strangely hesitant over that, as though she were about to say no, but he looked so hurt that she accepted.

'They're great kids, you'll love them.'

'I'm sure I will.' She smiled. But she was filled with

trepidation. She had avoided children for years, and she was not anxious to get to know his, or grow too attached to them. She had had her fill of children long since. The only two she had ever loved had been taken from her.

They arranged a meeting place in Central Park, and on Sunday morning she wore jeans, and a T-shirt, and went out to meet him. He had promised to bring the baseballs and the picnic and the children. And as she spotted them beneath a tree, the littlest one on his lap, and the six-year-old sitting beside him, she felt something stir in her heart that was so long gone she almost couldn't bear it. She stopped in her tracks and wanted to run, but she couldn't do that to him. But as she approached it only grew worse. What she saw in his eyes was the kind of love she had had for Megan and Axie.

She never made it to lunch. She watched them throw baseballs for half an hour, and then she pleaded a terrible headache. She ran from the park in tears, and went all the way back to her apartment without stopping for a light or a car or a person.

She lay in bed all day and sobbed, and then forced herself to realize again that Megan and Alexandra were gone from her life forever. She had to make herself remember that. There was no point hanging on to them. No one knew where they were anyway and it would have been close to impossible to find them. There was no point torturing herself now. And they were no longer children, they were women. Alexandra would have been twenty-two by then, and Megan would be eighteen. But there was no point thinking about them anymore. They were no longer lost children, and she was never going to see them again. But she didn't want to see any other children either. She couldn't bear it.

And when the phone began ringing that evening, she

quietly took it off the hook and left it there. The next day she acted as though nothing had happened. She was pleasant and businesslike and friendly, and distant and Adam never knew what had hit him. As planned, he was transferred on to sales the following week, and he never went out with Hilary again. She saw to it that they never even ran into each other. And she never took his calls. It was as though none of it had ever happened. And what she didn't know was that he felt sorry for her. But he finally realized that he couldn't help her.

For the next several years Hilary concentrated even harder on her career. She had risen to a higher production position by then and was twenty-seven years old, and she had carefully kept away from all liaisons since her brush with Adam. She was too busy working her way up to want anything else in her life, and all of the men she met seemed to be divorced and have children. Until she met William Brock, C B A's newest anchor. Tall, blond, and handsome, he had been a major football star and had been recently hired by the network. Twice divorced, he had no children, and no desire to have them. He dated his way around the station with gusto, until he got to Hilary, and her ice-like green eyes fascinated him. He treated her with caution and respect, and sent her everything from flowers to a fur coat.

'That was cute, Bill.' She dropped it on his desk, box and all, on her way to her office one morning.

'Not your size, darling?'

'Not my style, Mr Brock. In every possible way.' She was not given to romances at the office, or anywhere else for that matter, and becoming a notch on Bill Brock's belt was the last thing she wanted. He invited her to Honolulu for a week, Jamaica for a weekend, skiing in Vermont, dinner at the Côte Basque, and anything else he could think of. But he didn't stand a chance, until one stormy night, when she couldn't get a cab home and he gave her a lift in his Ferrari. He started heading downtown from the network, and Hilary tapped him on the shoulder. 'Nice try, Bill. I live on Fifty-ninth Street.'

'I live on Fifth Avenue and Eleventh.'

'Congratulations, now take me home, or do I have to get out and walk?' She wasn't kidding and he skidded to a stop, but before she could say anything further, he kissed her.

'Your place or mine, Madam Producer, or shall we do something really crazy and go to the Plaza?' She laughed at his outrageous spirit, and demanded that he take her home, but she was no longer surprised when he stopped on the way, to take her to dinner. They stopped for a hamburger at one of his favourite hangouts, and she was surprised at how intelligent he was, beneath the playboy veneer, and the overdeveloped male body. 'And you, pretty lady? What makes you tick behind those green eyes that look like emeralds?'

'Ambition.' He was the first person she had been that honest with, but for some reason she thought he'd understand that.

'I've had a taste of that myself. It's addictive once you get started.'

'I know it.' But it was all she had to keep her going . . . getting to the top so that nothing could ever get to her again. She wouldn't feel safe till she got there. But that she didn't explain to him. 'There's nothing like it, is there? Were you sorry to give up football, Bill?'

'Sort of. It's a great game, but I got tired of having my knees kicked around and my nose broken. You can't take that kind of abuse forever.' He smiled at her in just the way that melted most women's hearts, paid the bill, and escorted her back to his Ferrari. He dropped her off at her place without a fight, and she was almost sorry as she let herself into her apartment. Somehow, she had expected a little more than that, an attempt at least, something. She was already undressed and in her nightgown, half an hour later, when the bell rang.

'Who is it?' she asked on the intercom.

'Bill. I forgot to ask you something about the show tomorrow.' She frowned and then grinned. He sounded sincere but it was probably a ploy. She decided to keep it that way, and let him stand in the snow while he talked to her.

'What is it?'

'What?'

'I said what is it?'

'I can't hear you!' He started to buzz frantically and she tried to outshout him on the intercom and then finally gave up, and buzzed him in. If it was a ruse, she would put him in his place, and quickly. She was waiting in the doorway when he came up, red-faced, smiling, and covered with the snow that was still falling. 'Something's wrong with your intercom.' He was out of breath and devastatingly handsome.

'Oh, really? Nice of you to come by. Ever heard of the telephone, Mr Brock?'

'No, ma'am, I haven't.' Without further ado, he swept her off her feet, picked her up like a rag doll, walked into her apartment and kicked the door closed behind him. She was laughing at him as he did it. It was such an incongruous scene, and there was something boyish and wonderful about him, but not so wonderful that she wanted to get involved with him, no matter how handsome he was, or how attractive. 'Where's your bedroom, Miss Walker?' He was all innocence as she laughed at him. He was like a schoolboy playing a prank on her. But he was also extremely sexy.

'In there. Why?'

'You'll see in a minute.' He deposited her on the bed, walked into the bathroom as she stared at him, and emerged five seconds later, stark naked. She was so stunned that she stood staring at him. He was the most outrageous man she had ever known, but also the most appealing. And without further ado, he began making love to her, and despite her initial resistance, his expertise melted whatever reserve she had, and she was soon moaning for him and within a very short time, he obliged her. He lay breathless in her arms, and then rolled over and smiled as she stared at him in amazement. It had aroused feelings in her she had never known existed, and before she could say anything, he began making love to her again, and she thought she would go mad as he made love to her again and again and again until morning. It was an experience she had never had before and was sure she would never have again, but it convinced her that not everything inside her was entirely dead, and maybe one day the right man might come along and find it. But in the meantime, Bill Brock had done something to her she would never forget. And when he left the next morning, she stared out the window at him wistfully as he drove off in his red Ferrari.

She knew then she would remember him for the rest of her life, but she didn't expect anything more from him. He was not looking for a relationship, or a girlfriend, or a mistress or a wife, or even a friendship. Life to him was one constant stream of pretty girls, and making love was something he did like eating and sleeping and drinking. He didn't really care who he did it with, or how often, or if he ever did it again with the same one. He just wanted to be able to do it, when and where and with whom he wanted.

When he sent Hilary a huge bouquet of roses the next day, and a diamond bracelet from Harry Winston, she gave the bracelet back, with a smile, and he didn't seem surprised. But he also didn't ask her out again. He had other fish to fry, and she was just one of a universe full of pretty women. She was disappointed but not surprised. The only surprise she got was when she went to the doctor two months later. She had had the flu for weeks, and instead of better, she was getting worse. And she was totally exhausted. All she wanted to do was sleep, the thought of food made her sick, she couldn't even stand the smell of coffee when she went into the office in the morning. So finally, after six weeks of it, she called her doctor and made an appointment. He suggested a series of blood tests, a thorough examination, and after the blood tests, he was thinking of putting her on antibiotics.

'It could be some kind of stomach virus, Miss Walker. Have you been anywhere exotic recently?'

She shook her head, depressed to be feeling so poorly. She felt two hundred years old and all she wanted to do was put her head down and sleep all day long. It was depressing to feel that lousy. But two days later she knew why. The test results came back, and the doctor did not suggest antibiotics. She was pregnant. He had done a routine pregnancy test, and a VDRL too, checking her for syphilis. When she heard the news she felt she would rather have had the latter than the former. She put the phone down in shock, staring around her office. She knew exactly whose it was. He was the only man she had slept with in two years, and she hadn't used any precautions and neither had he. It had never occurred to her, she didn't have any to use. He was only the second man she'd ever slept with in her adult life, since the tragedies of her youth. And now she was pregnant.

There was only one solution to the problem. And she called the doctor back within the hour and made the appointment. She left her office at lunchtime in a state of shock, and went home to think about the predicament she was in. Should she tell him? Should she not? Would he laugh? Would he figure it was exclusively her problem? And what about the abortion? Was it wrong? Was it a sin? A part of her wanted to be rid of it instantly, and another part of her remembered Axie as a baby, and little Megan again . . . that sweet smell of powder and the silky hair nestled in her arms at night. She remembered the little noises she made before she went to sleep at night, and suddenly Hilary thought she couldn't do it. She had already lost two children she loved, how could she kill this one? Perhaps this was God's way of making it up to her, of making it all right again, of giving her back one of the babies she had lost, of filling the empty years ahead of her with more than just work . . . and the baby would be so beautiful with a father like Bill Brock, and he need never know . . . it could be all hers . . . all hers . . . and suddenly with every ounce of her being, she wanted to protect it.

She suddenly understood why her skirts had been getting tight, even though she'd been losing weight. Her waist had been growing, and she felt a tiny bulge in her stomach. The doctor had told her, when she talked to him, that she was eight weeks pregnant. Eight weeks . . . two months . . . and inside her there was a tiny baby. She couldn't let herself kill it. Yet she had to, what kind of career could she have with a baby around her neck, who would help her? . . . but that smell . . . and the sweet cry . . . she still remembered the first time she'd seen Axie . . . but what if someone took this baby from her too, as they had Megan and Axie, what if Bill Brock found out and wanted his child. For the rest of the week, Hilary was torn by mounting panic. She had no one to talk to, nowhere to turn. She was left only with her own guilt and confusion and panic. She wanted desperately to keep the baby, but couldn't imagine how she could, but more importantly, she was terrified that one day she would lose it, that somehow, someone would take it from her, and she never wanted to love anyone that much again. It was that fear that was the deciding factor. It was too much to ask of her, the rest she could handle, but not the terrible fear of loss, she knew too well the agony it would cause her. She could never risk that again, with children of her own, or anyone else's. She would sacrifice this child in the memory of Megan and Axie. There would never be children in her life and heart again. And as she walked into the doctor's office that Friday afternoon, she thought she was going to faint as she went through the doorway.

She gave the nurse her name, and signed a form with trembling hands, and then they let her sit in the waiting room for an hour. She had taken the afternoon off from work, and she had lain awake the night before. Some part of her was shrieking at her to save the life of this baby. But the voice of the past was too important to her. It out-shouted all else and reminded her of the terrible pain of losing Megan and Alexandra. She kept thinking of the day they'd driven away, and the unbearable agony of it . . . but the agony of tearing this child from within her was no smaller.

As the nurse led her down a corridor and into a small room she felt her knees grow weak. She was instructed to take off her clothes, put on a gown and paper slippers and report to the nurse across the hall.

'Thank you,' Hilary whispered almost inaudibly,

wishing somebody would stop her before it was too late. But there was no one to do it.

The nurse across the hall looked at her as though she had committed a federal offence, and handed her a clipboard with more forms to sign. Just glancing at them made Hilary feel ill, and she sank onto a narrow wooden bench.

'You all right?' the woman asked uninterestedly.

'I'm a little dizzy.'

She nodded, unconcerned, and told her to lie on the table.

'The doctor will be here in a few minutes.' But an hour and a half later, Hilary was still waiting. She had begun to shake from head to foot well over an hour before, and she had finally thrown up out of sheer nervousness. She hadn't had anything to eat since that morning. The nurse with the clipboard finally came back, looked at her, smelt the air, and Hilary blushed.

'I'm sorry, I . . . I don't feel well.'

'It'll probably happen again afterwards,' she said matter-of-factly. 'He'll be right in. We had a little problem down the hall.' And all Hilary could think about was the baby still alive inside her, the longer they took, the longer it would live, and soon they would have to kill it. She felt desperation choke her, but there was no way out, she couldn't allow herself to love this baby, couldn't go through it ever again. A part of her tried to tell her this was different, but the rest of her knew that it wasn't. She had loved Megan and Alexandra like her own . . . and she had lost them. And one day someone would take this baby from her too. She couldn't let that happen. She had to stop it now . . . before it destroyed her.

'Ready, young lady?' The doctor blew into the room like a hurricane, in surgical garb, with a green hat to cover his hair, and a small mask hanging around his neck. She could almost sense the blood dripping from him from his last abortion.

'I . . . yes . . .' Her voice was a barely audible croak and she felt as though she was going to throw up again or start crying. 'Are you going to give me something to put me to sleep?' They had told her nothing about it.

'You don't need any of that. It'll be all over in a few minutes.' How few? How long would it take? What were they going to do to her baby?

She lay flat on the table, and the nurse forced her feet into the stirrups, they were wider than usual, and the nurse secured them with straps so that Hilary couldn't move, and she felt a sudden wave of panic.

'Why are you doing that?'

'So you don't hurt yourself.' She was about to tie down Hilary's hands too but she begged her not to.

'I promise I won't touch anything . . . I swear . . . please . . .' It was like some medieval torture, and the nurse turned to the doctor and he nodded as he put on a fresh mask.

'Just relax. It won't take long, and then you'll be rid of this.' . . . rid of this . . . she tried to be comforted by the words, but she wasn't. She told herself she was doing the right thing, but everything inside her shrieked that she was killing a baby. They had only taken Megan and Axie away, no one had killed them. It was wrong, it was a sin, it was terrible . . . she wanted . . . she felt the local anaesthetic jab into her sharply, and she wanted to cry and wanted to ask the nurse to hold her hand, but the nurse looked uninterested as she assisted the doctor. And suddenly Hilary heard a terrible machine, it sounded like it was going to eat the walls. It was the vacuum.

'What's that?' She leapt to half-sitting position, unable

to move her legs, and she still felt a sharp pain where they had put the needle in her cervix.

'Just what it sounds like. It's a vacuum. Now lie back. We'll be ready in a minute. Count to ten.' She felt an incredible pain as something sharp and metallic shoved its way inside her. No torture ever concocted by Maida and Georgine had equalled this ... not even the boys with their hard bodies pressed into hers ... this was awful, it was beyond bearing, it was ... she let out a scream, and the metal piece inside her felt as though it was tearing her apart. It was forcing her uterus to open, dilating it so that they could take out the baby. 'You're further along than we thought, Miss Walker, we're going to have to open a little wider.' The local seemed to have done nothing for her and the pain was excruciating as her legs trembled violently and the doctor gave a grunt of satisfaction. 'That's it.' He said something to the nurse as Hilary threw up all over herself, but the nurse was too busy assisting the doctor to notice or help her. And then suddenly Hilary knew this was the wrong thing ... she couldn't do it ... she had to keep the baby, and she raised her head again, trying not to vomit so she could tell him.

'No, please ... don't ... please ... Stop!' But he only spoke soothingly to her. It was much too late to stop now. They had to finish what they had started.

'It's almost over, Hilary. Just a little bit longer.'

'No ... please I can't stand it ... I don't want to ... the baby ...' She was feeling faint again, and her whole body was wracked by convulsive shaking.

'There will be lots of babies in your life ... you're a young girl, and one day it'll be the right one.' He gave another ominous grunt, which she knew now meant he was going to inflict more pain on her, and suddenly he inserted the vacuum. She felt as though every ounce of her body was being sucked out by that machine and she threw up again as it went on endlessly, and then finally there was silence.

'Now just a little scraping,' he explained, and she saw the room reel as she felt him scrape what was left out of her, but the baby was long gone ... she had lost the others, and now she had killed this one. It was all she could think of as she lay there, wanting to die like her baby. She was a murderer now, just like her father. Her father had killed his wife, and now she had killed her own baby.

'That's all now.' She heard the voice she had come to hate, and they took out all their tools, and left her lying there, still trembling and strapped to the table. She could feel something wet and warm pouring out of her, and she knew she was bleeding profusely, but she didn't care anymore what they did to her. She didn't care if she died. In fact, she hoped so. 'Just rest for a little while, Hilary.' He stared into her face, patted her shoulder, and left the room with a resounding bang, as she lay strapped to the table and sobbed in a pool of her own vomit.

They came back for her in an hour, handed her a damp cloth and a sheet of instructions. She was to call them if the bleeding seemed too heavy, and otherwise she was to stay in bed for twenty-four hours and she'd be fine. That was it. It was all over. She staggered outside once she was dressed, still trembling violently, and hailed a cab, and gave him her address. And she was shocked to realize it was six o'clock. She had been in the doctor's office for almost six hours.

'What'sa matta, lady, you sick?' She looked terrible, even to him, even in the darkness. Her eyes were suddenly dark-ringed, her face was green, and she was shaking so hard she could hardly talk. And she only nodded in answer.

'Yeah . . . I got . . . the flu . . .' Her teeth were chattering and he nodded.

'Everybody's got it.' He grinned at her then, she was probably a pretty girl when she wasn't sick. 'Just don't kiss me.' She tried to smile at him, but she couldn't. She felt as though she would never smile again, at anyone. How could she? How could she ever look herself in the eye again? She had killed a baby.

She crawled into her bed when she got home, without even getting undressed, and she slept until four o'clock on Saturday morning. The cramps she felt woke her up, but when checked, nothing seemed to be out of order. She had survived it. She had done it. And she knew she would never forget it.

On Monday, she went to work looking pale and wan, but she went, and she did her work, and she went home again, with a stack of papers. She was going to bury herself in her work, and she was going to do anything to numb herself, and she did. She worked like a machine for the next six months and for another year after that. She became the wunderkind of C B A Network. She became the kind of woman people admired and everyone feared, the kind of person no one wanted to like.

'Terrifying, isn't she?' one of the new secretaries said the day Hilary turned thirty. 'She lives and breathes nothing but this network, and God help you if you cross her. At least that's what people say. Personally, she scares me.' The other girl agreed and they went to the powder room to discuss the two new men in the newsroom. But Hilary was immune there too. She seemed to have no interest in anyone, except her work, her career, and the network.

When she was thirty-two years old, she became a vice-president, and two years after that, she got another promotion. At thirty-six, she was the most senior woman in management, and at thirty-eight she was the number three person at the network, and there was no doubt in anyone's mind that one day she would run it. And probably sooner rather than later. *The New York Times* ran a big piece about her shortly afterwards discussing her policies and her plans, and *The Wall Street Journal* did another piece on her shortly afterwards. Hilary Walker had made it.

Chapter 13

The air on Park Avenue seemed to crush him as he left his
doctor's office two hours later. He wasn't surprised. He
had expected it, and yet . . . Arthur Patterson had secretly
hoped for something different. But the pain had been so
great. The pills had barely helped him for the last month,
and yet he had tried to tell himself it was something else.
He stopped to catch his breath as he reached the corner. It
was four-thirty, and he was totally exhausted as the pain
ripped through his chest again, and he coughed pathetically. A passerby stopped to look, wondering if he
should help, but Arthur caught his breath and got back
into the car, barely speaking to the driver.

He was still thinking of his doctor's words and dire
prediction. He had no right to ask for more, reasonably.
He was almost seventy-two years old, and he had led a full
life . . . more or less . . . he had been married once . . .
Marjorie had died three years before, and he'd gone to her
funeral, surprised to discover that she had remarried only
a few years before, a retired congressman. He had
wondered as he stood there, in the dim light of St James, if
she had been satisfied with her life . . . if she had ever been
truly happy.

And now he was going to die too. It was odd that it
didn't frighten him more. He was only sorry. He had so
little to leave the world, a law practice that had slowed

down years before, although he still went to the office every day, or whenever he was well enough. He wondered if his partners would miss him when he was gone. There was certainly no one else who would notice his absence, except possibly his secretary, who would just be reassigned to one of the other lawyers.

The doorman gave him a hand as he got out of the cab, and he took the lift upstairs, making idle conversation as he always did, with the liftman on duty. They discussed the early heat, and the baseball scores, and he let himself into his apartment with a sigh of exhaustion. It was so odd to think about it now. Soon it would all be gone . . . and then as he walked into the living-room, he began to cry. For no reason he could think of, Solange had come to mind . . . Solange with her fiery red hair and her emerald eyes . . . he had loved her so much so long ago. He wondered if he would see her now, when he died, if there was an afterlife . . . a heaven and a hell, as he'd been taught as a boy . . . He closed his eyes as he sank heavily into a chair . . . Solange . . . he spoke her name in a whisper as the tears rolled down his cheeks, and as he opened his eyes again, he had a sudden feeling of desperation. He had let her down so desperately, and Sam . . . the daughters they had loved so much had been cast to the winds and totally disappeared. He had let them disappear. It had all been his fault. He could have taken them in, if only he'd had the courage. But it was too late now. Much too late. Solange had died more than thirty years before . . . and Sam . . . and yet, he knew without a doubt, what he had to do now. He had to do one last thing. He had to find them.

He sat in the same chair until the room grew dark, thinking back over the years, all the way to the trenches near Cassino, to his wound and the time Sam had saved him . . . and the liberation of Paris and the first time he'd seen her. There was no going back. No changing what had happened. And perhaps it would make no difference now. But he knew that before he died, he had to find them, to explain to them . . . to bring them together again, for one last time, and with the crushing agony of memory, he remembered that day in Charlestown when he had gone to get Megan and Alexandra, and Hilary had begged him so piteously not to take them.

He lay awake in his bed for most of the night, thinking of the little girls, wondering how he would find them, or if they could be found in time. There was only one thing he could leave them. The rest was all stocks and bonds. But perhaps the house in Connecticut would mean something to them. He had bought it years before, as a summer place, but seldom ever used it. It was a large, rambling old Victorian house, and he liked going there, but he had kept it more as a home for his sunset years. And now the sunset was coming. There would be no time for retirement, for quiet gardening, for long walks down to the seashore. For him, it was all over. The doctor said it was too late to operate. The X-rays told their own tale. The cancer had spread too far, and he was too ill now to withstand any dramatic treatment. It was difficult to estimate how much time he had. Three months, perhaps six, or less if the disease spread very quickly.

He got up at midnight to take a sleeping pill, but it was daylight before he fell asleep, sleeping fitfully and dreaming of Hilary's sobs as he drove a car away from her, clutching something to him, he wasn't sure what, and then suddenly Hilary's face became her mother's, and it was Solange crying in his arms, asking him why he had killed her.

Chapter 14

Arthur Patterson left his office at noon the next day, exhausted from his sleepless night, but determined to go back. He had conferred with one of his partners at eleven o'clock, and got the name of a man who was thought to be the best in the business. He did not explain why he needed him, and the partner did not ask any questions.

Arthur had placed the call himself, and was surprised that John Chapman was willing to see him that day, when he explained that it was urgent. But Chapman knew who he was, and it was rare that the senior partner of an important law firm called him himself, and with such obvious desperation. He said he would see him shortly after noon, although he had only an hour at his disposal. And Arthur thanked him profusely, and hurried out of his office, patting his pocket to make sure he had his pills. He couldn't afford to be without them.

'Will you be back after lunch, Mr Patterson?' his secretary inquired as he hurried past her, coughing as was now his habit.

'I don't think so,' he said barely audibly, and she shook her head as he stepped into the lift. He looked terrible and he was too old to be coming to work every day now. She wished someone would force him to retire.

It was a short cab ride from Arthur's office to Chapman's,

and he was impressed when he saw the well appointed offices Chapman kept on Fifty-seventh, off Fifth. It was a smaller building than those that housed Brokaw, Miller and Patterson, but it was respectable and well kept, and Chapman had most of a floor, with a discreet sign on the door that said only JOHN CHAPMAN. A receptionist took his name, and several other people appeared to be waiting for Chapman's associates. Most of the people in the waiting room looked like attorneys.

'Mr Chapman will see you now,' the young woman said, and ushered him inside. Chapman had an office high above Fifty-seventh street with thick carpeting and English antiques, and like his own office, it was filled with law books. It was comforting to be in surroundings that looked so familiar. He had been afraid at first that the place he was being sent to would be sleazy, and it was a relief to find that it wasn't.

The door opened to reveal a handsome blond man in a tweed jacket and grey slacks, with lively grey eyes, and the look of someone who had gone to Princeton or Harvard. In fact, he had gone to both. He had done his undergraduate work at Princeton, and had gone to law school at Harvard.

'Mr Patterson?' He came easily around the desk, and shook Arthur's hand, startled at first by how frail it seemed in his grip. He had played football in college, and even as tall as he was, Arthur was dwarfed by the young attorney who was thirty years his junior. 'Please sit down.' He indicated a chair with a warm smile, and sat down in the chair next to Arthur.

'I'm very grateful to you . . .' Arthur coughed, trying to catch his breath, '. . . for seeing me on such short notice. It's a matter of both urgency and importance, and I'm afraid I . . . don't have much time.' He meant it just the way it sounded as he coughed again, but John Chapman assumed he was referring to a deadline associated with a court case.

'I was impressed that you were handling the matter yourself, sir.'

'Thank you.'

He knew who Arthur was, and it was most unusual for the senior partner of the firm to contact an investigation service himself, no matter how illustrious the outfit was, and John Chapman's was one of the best-known in the country. It operated more like a law firm than just an investigative bureau, and his own legal background made him extremely helpful. He grabbed a pad and pen as Arthur coughed again, and prepared to jot down some notes about what Arthur wanted.

'Would you like to explain to me, Mr Patterson, so I can have an idea how we may be of service?' He was quiet and professional and had the precise diction of the upper classes, and yet he seemed oddly unassuming, easy-going almost, and Patterson found himself curious about him. Why hadn't he gone into his father's firm? His father was the head of the most important law firm in Boston, and two of his brothers were prominent attorneys in New York. And yet he had chosen this rather unorthodox career instead. It was intriguing, but Arthur didn't have the time to think about it now. He had to save his strength to tell him what he wanted.

'It's a personal . . . matter.' He wheezed, and then took a sip of water Chapman had quietly poured him while he waited. 'Of the utmost confidentiality and importance. You are not to discuss this with anyone.' Arthur flashed his eyes at him, but the effort was wasted on Chapman.

'I don't discuss my cases with anyone, Mr Patterson. Period.'

'I'd also like you to do this yourself, if it's possible. One of my associates tells me you're the best in the business. I want to hire that talent, and no one else's.'

Chapman pursed his lips, waiting to hear the rest, making no commitment to Arthur. 'That depends on what's involved. I try to stay involved in all of our cases, to as great an extent as I'm able.'

'I want you to do this yourself. And we don't have much time.' He coughed and took another sip of water. 'I'm dying.'

Chapman watched him carefully, curious now. The old man was shaking with anticipation, and clutching a file he had taken out of a briefcase. Perhaps it was an old unsolved case he was determined to tie up before he died. It was odd the things people did when they were dying.

'The doctor thinks I might have three months, maybe six, maybe less. I think three months is more like it. I want to find three young women.' Chapman looked surprised. It was an odd request from an old man, unless they were his daughters. 'They were the daughters of close friends of mine, my closest friends. Their parents died thirty years ago, and two of them were adopted shortly after, the third one was left with her aunt and uncle. They were respectively one, five, and nine years old when I lost track of them, and I have no idea where they are now. I know who adopted the two younger girls, and I know the oldest one wound up in Jacksonville, Florida, and then came to New York twenty-one years ago, but that's all I know. I've included all the information I have in this file, including clippings about their parents. Their father was a very well-known Broadway actor.'

'Did the parents die simultaneously in an accident?' It was only curiosity on his part. Thus far, it was an intriguing story.

'No.' Arthur took a painful breath and continued. 'He killed their mother, no one ever really knew why, except that they had an argument and he seems to have gone crazy. I defended him in 1958.' Arthur's face went a little greyer as Chapman watched him, surprised that he had taken a criminal case. There had to be more to the story than he was telling. 'He was convicted and committed suicide in his cell the night of his conviction. I tried to place the girls in a home together.' He seemed close to breaking down as John Chapman watched him, sorry for him, it was obviously painful for him to remember, and worse still to discuss it with this stranger. Any attorney would have felt responsible . . . but not responsible enough to go looking for the children thirty years later. Or was it that he felt guilty? 'But no one wanted to take all three. I had to place them in separate homes, and leave the older girl with the aunt and uncle.' He didn't tell him that he had considered taking them himself, but didn't do it because his then wife wouldn't let him. 'There was also a recent clipping about a young woman at C B A,' he went on, 'by the same name as the oldest girl. I think there's a possibility it might be her, but it could be just a coincidence. I included the clipping and you ought to check it out.' Chapman nodded. And Arthur remembered finding the article in *The Times* only weeks before, and praying it was the right Hilary Walker. His hand had trembled as he held the column he'd clipped out and stared at the picture. She didn't look like anyone he knew, but that didn't necessarily mean anything. Newspaper photos often didn't. 'That's it, Chapman. I want to find those three young women.' Young to him perhaps, but certainly grown-up, Chapman thought to himself. He did a quick calculation and realized they were thirty-eight, thirty-four, and thirty years old. It wasn't going to be easy to find them. And

Arthur confirmed that. 'The adoptive parents of the two younger girls moved away years ago, and I have no idea where they went . . . I just hope you can find them.'

'So do I.' Chapman took the file in his hands, and looked sombre as he questioned Arthur. 'And when I do?'

'First, I want you to locate them, and then come back to me and tell me that you've found them. Then I want you to explain to them who they are, who I am, that I am an old family friend, and that I want to reunite them with their sisters. I'd like to do it in my home in Connecticut, if that's possible. I'm afraid I can't travel anymore . . . they'll have to come here.'

'And if they refuse?' It was possible. Anything was possible. He had seen everything in the seventeen years he'd been in the business.

'You can't let them.'

'They may not even remember having sisters, two of them anyway, and it may be a tremendous shock and disruption to them.' He wondered if there was a sizeable inheritance being attached to it, but he didn't want to press Arthur on the subject.

'I owe it to them to bring them together again. It was my fault that they were separated . . . that I was never able to find a home for all of them. I want to know that they're all right, that they don't need anything . . . I owe that much to their parents.'

John was tempted to tell him that it was a little late, but he didn't want to be disrespectful. At thirty-eight and thirty-four and thirty, it couldn't matter very much to them any more why they had been taken from their sisters, if they even remembered having any in the first place. But it was not his place to question the wisdom of Arthur Patterson's final wishes. Arthur was sitting watching him with quiet desperation.

'Will you do it?' It was a barely audible whisper.

'I'll try.'

'Will you do it yourself?'

'Most of it, if that's possible. I want to read the file first, before I make a definite commitment. I may have operatives already in the field in areas we're interested in who could do the job better and more quickly than I could.' Arthur nodded, that much made sense to him. 'I'll get to the file as quickly as possible, and I'll call you with an appraisal of the situation.'

Arthur was painfully honest with him. 'There's not much there, Chapman. Not much more than I told you.'

'That's all right. Something may jump out at me.' He discreetly looked at the clock he could see over Arthur's left shoulder. It was almost one-fifteen, and he hated to keep Sasha waiting. 'I'll call you in the next day or two.' He stood up and Arthur followed suit unsteadily.

'I'm deeply grateful to you, Chapman.'

'That's all right, Mr Patterson. I hope you won't be disappointed.' Arthur nodded thoughtfully, barely able to consider that. Chapman *had* to find them. 'I should warn you as well, this could be an expensive project.' Arthur looked up at him then with a wintery smile.

'I've got nothing else to spend it on now, do I?'

Chapman smiled at him. It was a difficult question to answer, and he walked him quietly to the outer office, shook his hand, thanked him for coming, and then hurried back to his office to lock the slim file in the safe, and head out of the door at a dead run. Sasha was going to kill him.

Chapter 15

John Chapman flew out of his office building on Fifty-seventh Street, and raced the two long blocks west, glancing at his watch, and catching his reflection in shop windows. Tiffany ... I. Miller ... Henri Bendel ... it seemed to take hours to get there and he knew how she hated him to be late, but he couldn't hurry Arthur Patterson out of his office after all. The man was ancient and he was dying, and Chapman was intrigued by the case. But he also knew Sasha wouldn't understand that.

She was twenty-eight years old, sinew from head to foot, and every ounce of her was disciplined to perfection. She wore her blond hair pulled back so tight that it looked as though it were painted on her head, her green eyes had a Slavic tilt, and she wore her lips in a constant pout, which had seduced him from the first time he'd seen her. They had met at a friend's house, a ballet buff, who raved about how talented she was, and how extraordinary she'd been as a little girl. And now she was even more so as a big one. The daughter of Russian émigrés, she had studied for years at the Ballet Russe de Monte Carlo, and then gone on to Juilliard as a young girl, where she'd been a star already in her early teens. At twenty she had been invited to join the American Ballet Theatre. And at twenty-eight, she was not a prima, but she was a fine dancer with a solid career to be proud of. She indulged in the jealousies of her troupe, and it irked her not to be one of the prima ballerinas, but in truth she was too small to be more than one of the corps of dancers. She had the consolation of being very good, and she told John that every chance she got, when she wasn't complaining about her feet or the fact that he was late coming to meet her. But even though she wasn't easy to get along with, for months John Chapman had found her enchanting . . . her discipline, her intense routine, her talent coupled with her tiny face, her feet that seemed to move on butterfly wings when she danced, the huge green eyes . . . there was something very special about her.

'You're half an hour late.' She glared at him halfway through a cup of borscht, when he breathlessly reached her table at the Russian Tea Room. The atmosphere was precisely as it had been for the past fifty years, and they both loved blinis and caviar. Besides, it was close to where she rehearsed, and they met there half a dozen times a week, for lunch or after rehearsals, or even after performances, late at night, for a quick bite before they went home to his apartment. She lived with four other dancers, and it was impossible to talk, let alone make love, in the West Side walkup that was always filthy and draughty. But her green eyes were looking up at him in reproach as he apologized and sat down. 'I was thinking of leaving.' She looked like an angry child and he realized, as he always did, how much he loved her.

'I'm glad you didn't.' He gently touched her hand, and smiled at the familiar waiter. He was an old Russian who chatted with Sasha in her maternal tongue. She had been born in Paris, but still spoke Russian with her parents.

'I was hungry.' Her eyes bore into his mercilessly. 'That's the only reason why I waited.'

'I'm sorry. I had an important case. The head of a major

law firm needed some help, I couldn't shove him out of the door.' He smiled placatingly at her, wondering how long it would take him to get back in her good graces. Usually not long – her anger was hard and quick to burst into flame, but generally it abated fairly quickly. 'I'm sorry, darling.' He touched her hand again, and she looked only slightly mollified by his contrition.

'I had a very difficult morning.' She looked petulant, and more beautiful than ever.

'Something wrong?' He knew how she worried about her feet and her legs and her arms . . . it was not easy being a dancer. A pulled muscle, a torn ligament, and her life would be changed forever.

'They were trying to introduce a new choreographer, and he's impossible. He makes Balanchine look lazy by comparison. This man is mad. You cannot dance the way he asks you.'

'*You* can.' Chapman smiled proudly at her. He thought her a remarkable dancer. And this time, she smiled at him. He was almost forgiven.

'I'm trying. But I think he's trying to kill us.' She sighed and finished her borscht. She didn't want to eat too much before rehearsal that afternoon, but she was still hungry. He had just ordered blinis, and she was tempted but that was too heavy for her when she was dancing. 'Maybe I'll have a salad.' She told the waiter in Russian and he nodded and disappeared as she told John about her woes of the morning. She asked him nothing about his case. She never did. All she ever thought of was dancing.

'Are you rehearsing tonight?' he asked with eyes full of understanding. He was a kind man, and he didn't mind their life revolving around her work. He was used to that. His ex-wife had been a writer, and he had sat patiently for seven years while she churned out mysteries that had eventually become major bestsellers. He had respected her as a woman and a friend, but it hadn't been much of a marriage. Everything had come second to her work, even her husband. She had been a difficult woman. The whole world had to come to a shrieking halt when she started a book, and she expected John to protect her from any possible interruption. And he had done a fair job of it, until the loneliness of his life with her overwhelmed him. Her only friends were her characters, every plot she wrote became real to her, and she wouldn't even speak to him while she was working. She worked from eight in the morning until midnight, every day, and then went to bed, mute with exhaustion. In the morning, she'd start again, but she didn't talk to him over coffee because she was already thinking about the book. It had been lonely being married to Eloise. She wrote under the name of Eloise Wharton. And when she wasn't working on a book, she was either in a major depression because she wasn't working, or she was on tour in thirty cities in forty-five days, pushing her latest epic. He figured out before he asked her for a divorce that they spoke to each other on the average something like thirty hours a year, which was something less than what he needed for a happy marriage. They loved each other, but she loved her work more. And he wasn't even sure how much she understood when he left her. She had been deep in a book, and there had been only the vaguest of answers as he said goodbye and closed the front door behind him. It was a relief, oddly enough, and he discovered that it was less lonely being alone than being with her. He could play the stereo, sing when he liked, have friends over who made as much noise as they wanted. He went out with other women. Life was fine. And the only thing he regretted was that they had never had any children. He and Eloise had been divorced for five years, and he was only now starting to think about getting remarried. In fact, he had been thinking about it a great deal lately.

Sasha had nodded in answer to his question about rehearsal. 'We are rehearsing until eleven.' She still spoke English like someone who had learned it as a foreigner, and yet she had no clearly discernible accent.

'Can I pick you up?' His eyes filled with hope, and he told himself that he was not repeating the same pattern. He was not leading his life entirely around Sasha's dancing. Besides, she was so much more alive than Eloise had been. She was so vital, and exciting. Eloise lived in a dark room, with a single light burning over her head, haunted by imaginary people. And she hadn't changed in the last five years. She had only become more successful. She was one of the most successful mystery writers in the country. The new Agatha Christie, *The New York Times* had hailed her, and *Publishers Weekly* agreed. She was forty-one years old, and she lived in a world of fantasy. Not like Sasha . . . not at all . . .

'Thank you. I'll be at the stage door at eleven-ten.' And he knew she meant it. She had the precision of a surgeon. 'Don't be late.' She frowned and wagged a graceful finger.

He smiled at her, and touched her knee under the table. 'I won't. I'm not working tonight.' All he wanted to do was read the file Arthur Patterson had left him, and that couldn't take him more than an hour, possibly even less. In fact, that was what he was afraid of, that there wasn't anything in it of any real substance. 'I'll just look over the files on this new case.'

'Don't get too interested.' She frowned at him. He had done that before, and been an hour late after a performance. She wouldn't tolerate that from him, or anyone in fact. She didn't have to. As she pointed out to him regularly, she was a *real* artist.

'Do you want me to take you back?' He looked hopeful, like a schoolboy anxious to please her. It was something about him that had pleased every woman he'd been involved with, even Sasha, although she didn't admit it to him. She never told him how much she loved him, or how much she liked his company. It was beneath her to say those things, and he didn't need to know them.

'I'm meeting some of the others in five minutes, John. On the corner. I'll see you tonight?' She stood up, tiny and exquisitely erect, her back like a beautifully sculpted slab of marble, and one eyebrow raised over the olive-green eyes. 'On time, yes?'

'You're a tyrant.' He stood to kiss her and watched her go, as he sipped his tea, and then paid the bill. Something about her always left him feeling unnerved and excited. As though he wanted more, as though he couldn't get enough, as though she would never let him possess her. It was as though she danced away from his grasp each time he reached out for her, but in some ways he liked it. He liked chasing her. He liked everything about her. She was so much more alive than Eloise, and the endless numbers of women attorneys and ad. execs he had taken out in the five years since he'd divorced her. Sasha was entirely different.

He walked back to the office, more slowly this time, thinking of Sasha at first, and then of Arthur Patterson and the three women he wanted him to find. It was an odd story and he couldn't help wondering if there was more to it than Arthur was telling. There was a piece missing to the puzzle somehow, maybe even several of them. Why did he want to bring them back? What did it matter if they met now? They were grown women, having led separate lives, what could they possibly have in common? And why did Arthur Patterson feel so guilty? What had he done? Or what hadn't he done? And who were these women's parents? John's mind whirled over the questions as he walked along. He was good at what he did because he had an uncanny knack for seeing the pieces that were missing and then finding them, like the proverbial needle in the haystack. He had found more than a few, and had been crucial in several major cases. His most astounding work had been in the field of criminal law, and he was respected by attorneys and courts all over the country. Arthur Patterson had come to the right place. But John Chapman wondered if he could find the missing women.

He took the file home with him that night and pored over the little that was there. It was pathetic how little there was, though. Arthur had been right. There wasn't much there to help him. Only what he had said in the office. There were all the clippings of the trial, which John read first, intrigued by the unspoken elements of the story. Why had Sam Walker really killed his wife? Was it premeditated, as some thought, or a crime of passion? What had the woman done to him, and who was she? In a way, he didn't need to know those things, and yet the questions intrigued him. He read reviews of several of Walker's plays, and remembered seeing him once as a little boy. All he remembered was that it was an impressive performance and he was very handsome. But more than that he didn't remember.

There was a brief note in Arthur's trembling hand, explaining that he and Sam Walker had been buddies in the army. There was a list of the places they had been, and a description of their first meeting with Solange, which was surprisingly lyrical for a man his age, and one who had written nothing but legal documents and briefs all his life. And John wondered if therein lay some of the answers. Perhaps Arthur had been in love with her. Or perhaps it didn't matter. The facts were still the same. Sam had killed Solange for whatever reason, leaving their three children orphans.

The eldest had gone to relatives at a Charlestown, Mass., address, an Eileen and Jack Jones, and Arthur knew she had gone to Jacksonville from there, because she had told him so when she'd come to his office in 1966, seeking her sisters' addresses. Arthur had mentioned in a footnote that she had been less than cordial. He said too that she mentioned having been in juvenile hall in Jacksonville, and John wondered if she had fallen foul of the law as a young girl. If so, she might have done so again, and he might be able to find a rap sheet on her. That would make her easier to find anyway, especially if she was sitting in prison somewhere. But at least he could tell Patterson he'd found her.

The second one had gone to one of Arthur's partners, who had then died, and the widow was God knows where, remarried to God knew who. That one was a healthy project. He'd have to start with the Gorham files at the firm, and pray they'd had to contact her for something in recent years, maybe a trust or some other lingering detail of the estate Arthur knew nothing of since he was not one of Gorham's trustees . . . and then there was the baby.

The youngest child had also virtually disappeared, but not without warning. Arthur had told him that David Abrams felt strongly about Patterson's not maintaining contact with the child, that they wanted her to have a new life, totally divorced from her past, and wanted to ensure that she did so. John even found himself wondering if that had been part of their reason for moving to California, to start a new life, where no one even knew that the child was adopted.

And after that, there was nothing. There was one clipping at the back of the file, the one Arthur had mentioned, but despite the similarity of name, like Arthur, John thought it was a long shot. It was the article from *The New York Times*, about a Hilary Walker's promotion at CBA Network, and it was highly unlikely that she was the same girl. Even Arthur didn't recognize her, and it was too sweet and easy to find her within easy reach, and successful. John had been in the business of finding people for long enough that he knew a false hope when he saw one. He'd look into it of course, but he was sure she would turn out to be a different Hilary Walker.

And that was it. There was nothing else. He sat back in his chair, and thought about all three. How to find them, where to start. The wheels were already turning. And then with a sudden start, he glanced at his watch.

'Sonofabitch . . .' He muttered to himself. It was just after ten-thirty. He grabbed his jacket off the back of a chair, and hurried down the three flights of his brownstone. He had the top floor of a lovely house on East Sixty-ninth Street. And he was lucky enough to find a cab almost at once, but with post-theatre traffic, he barely made it to the stage door in time to meet Sasha.

She came out at precisely eleven-ten, as he knew she would, looking tired, wearing jeans and sneakers and carrying her dance bag.

'How was it?' There was always the tension of someone having performed major surgery, not unlike Eloise's struggles with difficult denouements in the plot. But somehow this seemed more exciting.

'It was awful.'

He knew better than to believe her, and put a protective arm around her as he took her dance-bag. 'You expect too much of yourself, little one.' She was so tiny, it always made him feel protective of her, and in any case, he was that kind of person.

'No, it was terrible. My feet were killing me. It's going to rain tonight. I can always tell.' John had learned that dancers' feet were a constant source of agony, and a constant topic of conversation.

'I'll massage them when we get home,' he promised as they climbed into a cab and headed back to East Sixty-ninth Street.

The apartment was peaceful and quiet when they arrived. There were only two other tenants in the building, one a doctor who never seemed to be there. He was younger than John, and when he wasn't on call, delivering babies at New York Hospital, he seemed to be staying with assorted women. And the other was a woman who worked for IBM and travelled eight to ten months of the year. So most of the time he was alone in the building. He had a view of the little garden outside, and the larger gardens of the town houses on Sixty-eighth Street. 'Do you want a drink?' he inquired, poking his head out of his well-ordered kitchen.

'Just some tea, thanks.' She sat down on the couch with a sigh and stretched her arms and her back and her legs. She never cooked anything in his small kitchen. It never dawned on her to do things like that for him or herself. John always did them for her.

He emerged a few minutes later, bringing her tea in a glass, the way she liked it. It was a Russian tradition he had come to like, and he had bought special glass mugs just for that purpose. He had been equally expert at preparing Eloise's snacks while she was working. But in return, she had cooked him some wonderful dinners between books. She loved to bake, and had a real flair for

French cuisine. Unlike Sasha, who thought being expected to make toast was an affront to her as an artist.

'Are you coming to the performance tomorrow?' she asked as she slowly pulled the pins from her hair, and it began to cascade in long blond sheets past her shoulders.

John looked at her with regret. He hated to remind her. He knew that whenever he did it would create a scene between them. It annoyed her when he went anywhere. She expected him to be always near. And the next afternoon he was flying to Boston.

'I'm going up to the Cape for the weekend, Sash. I said something about it a few weeks ago, but you may have forgotten. It's my mother's birthday. I tried to get out of it, but I really couldn't. It's her seventieth, and it's important.' Both of his brothers were going to be there, and their wives, and their children. It always made him feel inadequate somehow, going there without an entourage to show for his years of marriage and assorted romances. Everything they had was tangible and obvious: wives who had nice sapphires or diamonds as engagement rings and anniversary presents, kids who had skinned knees and missing teeth, and in the case of his oldest nephew, even a high school diploma. It was going to be a long weekend. But he knew it would be fun too. He was fond of his two brothers, one older, one younger. His sisters-in-law were a bit difficult, but the kids were great. And there was no way he could bring Sasha. Even at his age, his parents would have frowned on his bringing a woman with him for a family occasion. 'I'll be home Sunday.'

'Don't bother.' She straightened her back and dropped both feet to the floor gracefully. 'I have rehearsal Sunday afternoon. And I'm not interested in crumbs left over from your parents' table.' She looked so outraged that he could only laugh at her choice of words. Sometimes her English was outlandish.

'Is that what I am, Sash? A crumb?' It was more than obvious that she thought so.

'I don't understand what is so sacred about your family. You've met my parents, my aunt, my grandmother. Are your parents so much better than mine? They would disapprove because I'm a dancer?' She sounded terribly Russian and looked extremely dramatic as she paced around the room, her hair flying and her hands shoved into the back pockets of her blue jeans, her tiny little body tense with emotion.

'They're very private, that's all.' And very Bostonian. A writer had been difficult enough. A ballerina would drive his mother totally crazy. She had a healthy respect for the arts, but preferably on a stage, not in her son's bedroom. 'They don't understand relationships like ours.'

'Neither do I. Are we together or are we not?' She stood in front of him looking like an enchanting elf, but an elf who was extremely angry. She felt shut out by the family he never introduced her to, and without his ever saying so, she was aware of their disapproval.

'Of course we're together. But as far as they're concerned, you don't acknowledge those things until you're married, or at least engaged.' And she was the one who resisted that. She saw no need for a permanent statement.

'They think we're immoral?'

'Maybe. They prefer not to think about it. They don't want to have to confront this kind of thing, so they don't. And as their son, I have to respect that. They're pretty old, Sash. My mother is going to be seventy on Saturday, my father is seventy-nine. It's a little late to force them into acknowledging modern arrangements.'

'That's ridiculous.' She stormed across the room again,

and then stood glaring at him from the kitchen doorway. 'And if you were any kind of man at all, you would take me anyway, and force them to acknowledge my existence.'

'I'd rather invite them to see you dance the next time they're here. That would be a better introduction. Don't you think so?'

Sasha thought it over as she crossed the room again, only slightly mollified, and then she sat down on the couch and began to put on her sneakers. He knew it was a bad omen. She was always storming out at two in the morning and going back to her apartment.

'What are you doing?'

'I'm going home. Where I belong.' She looked at him malevolently and he sighed. He hated scenes, and she doted on them. They seemed to be part of her art form.

'Don't be silly.' He stretched out a hand and touched her shoulder. It felt like rock beneath his fingers. 'We each have things in our lives we have to do on our own. You have your work and your ballet friends and your rehearsals. I have my own work, and a few other obligations.'

'I don't want to hear it. The truth is, Mr Chapman,' she stood up and glared at him, swinging her dance-bag over her shoulder, 'that you're a snob, and you're afraid your parents won't think I'm good enough. And do you know what? I don't care. You can have your *Mayflower* and your Plymouth Rock and your Boston. I don't need to be in the social register, I will be in *Who's Who* one day. And if that's not good enough,' – she made a gesture that said it all, and stalked to the door. And for once he didn't stop her. He knew that by Sunday she'd cool off, and he couldn't appease her by not going.

'I'm sorry you feel that way, Sash.' She slammed the

234

door in answer, and he sat down with a sigh. Sometimes she was so unbelievably childish. And so self-centred. He didn't let himself think about it often, but she hadn't once asked him about his new case. The only time she noticed his life was when, for whatever reason, it enraged her.

He turned off the lights in the living-room, and went to bed without putting their glasses in the sink. The cleaning lady could do it in the morning. And as he lay in bed, he thought about her accusations . . . that he was a snob . . . and that his parents wouldn't approve of her. In some ways, she was right. His parents would not have been enchanted by Sasha Riva. They would have thought her too limited, and extremely difficult, inadequately educated and ill-informed, and yes, it would matter to them that she wasn't 'social'. It wasn't something that mattered to him a great deal, but he knew that to them, it was important. Eloise had been something else. She and his mother had never really got along, and she thought his sisters-in-law unspeakably boring. But she was from an excellent family, and had graduated from Yale *summa cum laude*. You couldn't fault Eloise's breeding, or her education. And she was intelligent and amazingly witty, none of which had made her a good wife. Far from it. Not that Sasha showed much greater promise. He thought about calling Sasha after she got home, but he was too tired to hunt her down, wake her room-mates up, and beg her forgiveness because he was going to Cape Cod to see his mother. Instead he burrowed into the pillow and fell asleep, and didn't wake up until the alarm rang the next morning.

He showered and shaved, made himself coffee and left for work, and he noticed when he read the newspaper on the subway that Eloise had a new bestseller. Good for her. It was all she had in life, and he knew how happy it made her. He envied her sometimes. He would have liked to be as fulfilled, as obsessed, as totally enthralled with what he did that it didn't matter what else happened in his life. He loved his work, but he wanted so much more than that. And so far, he hadn't found it. It was one of the reasons why he was excited about the Patterson case. There was something about it that excited him and he hadn't been this excited about his work in aeons. The first thing he wanted to do was find the oldest one, Hilary. There was something about her that haunted him. And God only knew what had happened to her after Arthur had abandoned her in Charlestown. He knew from her visit to Arthur's office in later years that she had wound up in Jacksonville, Florida. Somehow, but how or when or why, neither of them knew, and maybe it wasn't important. And what had happened to her afterwards was a mystery too. She had never contacted Arthur again. She had simply disappeared. And then there was the clipping from *The New York Times* Arthur had given him of the woman named Hilary Walker at CBA Network. But was that even the same woman? He doubted it. It seemed extremely unlikely.

Chapter 16

John got to the office before nine o'clock. He had a lot to do before leaving early for the weekend, there was something he wanted to do before he left. He wanted to try calling the Hilary Walker in Arthur's clipping. It probably wasn't the woman he wanted but it was worth a shot. It was a lead, and he couldn't afford to ignore it. She might just be at CBA, right under their noses, working near the top at a major network.

He glanced at his watch. It was nine-fifteen, and he picked up the phone himself. He called information, and then dialled the number.

'Hilary Walker, please.' His mouth felt a little dry, and he was surprised. He didn't know why he was getting to care about the Patterson case so much, except that something happened to him when he wondered what had become of the child in Charlestown.

A secretary answered, and he asked for her again.

'May I tell her who's calling?' a voice asked.

'John Chapman of Chapman Associates, she doesn't know me, and it's a matter of some urgency, if you'd be good enough to tell her that.'

'Just a moment please.' The girl at the other end gave away nothing. She had called Hilary on the intercom, and she couldn't figure out who the hell John Chapman was or why he was calling. She had a major production meeting to run at ten o'clock and she didn't have time to waste with crank callers.

'Ask him if I can call him back later,' she told the secretary and then countermanded her own orders. 'Oh never mind, I'll talk to him myself.' She pushed the button with the flashing light, and her cool, deep voice came on the line. 'Yes? This is Hilary Walker.' And for an odd moment, John was reminded of his mother's deep voice. She was the only other woman he knew with a voice as deep as that, but he got down to business with her quickly. Whether she was the right Hilary Walker or not, this one was a very busy woman.

'Thank you for taking my call, I appreciate it, and I'm going to be direct with you, in the interest of saving time. My name is John Chapman, I'm the head of Chapman Associates, I'm looking for a woman named Hilary Walker. Her father was Sam, her mother Solange, and she lived with a couple named Jack and Eileen Jones in Boston. Are you that woman?' It was fortunate that he could not see her face at the other end. She was chalk-white and shaking from head to foot as one hand clutched her desk, but her voice betrayed nothing.

'No, I'm not. What is this about?' Her first instinct had been to deny it, but she had to know why he was looking for her. Was it for the others? Not that it mattered any-more. They were long gone, and probably didn't even remember her. She had given all that up years before. All she had now was the network. And much more likely, it was Arthur. The bastard.

'This is part of an investigation for a client. He was hoping to find this Miss Walker. And he saw the articles about you in *The Times* and *The Wall Street Journal*, and hoped that you might be the right one. It was a long shot, and I'm sorry to have disturbed you.' He could hear in her

238

voice that she wasn't the right one, and he had to admit he was disappointed.

'I'm awfully sorry not to be able to help you, Mr Chapman.' Her voice was smooth and cool, but she was definitely not moved by his inquiry. It would have been much too simple if she had been the right one.

'Thank you for your time, Miss Walker.'

'Not at all.' And with that, she hung up, and he quietly hung up the phone. He had struck out. And he couldn't see the woman who sat pale and shaken at her desk across town. It was like getting a phone call from a ghost. She was sure it was Arthur looking for her, the old sonofabitch, well he'd never find her. She had no reason to reach out to him, to soothe his conscience for him. He had never done anything for her or her sisters. To hell with him. And John Chapman. And all of them. She didn't need them.

She walked into the meeting at ten o'clock and tore heads off for the rest of the day. But she was still shaken when she left the meeting and so was everyone else. She had fired three producers, and threatened everyone else in the meeting. She was merciless, but then again she was known for it. She was only slightly worse after the call from John Chapman.

Chapter 17

In his office, John Chapman sat staring into space in disappointment. The woman in the article was not the Hilary Walker they wanted . . . *he* wanted . . . He sighed deeply and put the clipping back in the file with a notation. Later, he would have to call and tell Arthur. But two of his associates were anxious to speak to him in the meantime.

Three of their biggest cases were coming to court, and they had got the goods in all three. It was very rewarding. And at noon, John looked at his watch and made a decision. He had handled pretty much everything he wanted to, the rest could wait until Monday. His parents weren't expecting him till dinnertime, and if he caught the two o'clock commuter flight out of La Guardia, he'd be in Boston at three, and he could stop in Charlestown on his way to his folks. He'd still be there in plenty of time, and he wanted to see if he could turn up anything on Hilary Walker. He had what he needed to go straight to Jacksonville on her, but he still liked to be thorough in his investigations. And a trip to Charlestown might turn something up on one of the others. It was worth a look in any case, and he was going in that direction.

He told his secretary where he'd be in case she needed him, and took a cab back to his apartment. It took him ten minutes to pack a bag. He knew exactly what he needed for a weekend in the farmhouse. And by one o'clock he was already on his way to La Guardia. He bought a seat on the commuter flight, arrived at three-ten, and rented a car at the airport. And from there it was a thirty-minute drive to Charlestown.

He checked the information in the file again and made sure he had the correct address, and cringed inwardly as he began driving down the streets of Charlestown. It was one of those areas that had been ugly forty years before, and had not improved with age. There were other sections that had been lucky in recent years, and were being restored by loving hands, but these houses were not among them. And if they had been ugly when Hilary lived there, they were worse now. They were truly awful. Filthy, broken down, with paint peeling everywhere, and many of the houses boarded up and crumbling. There were signs here and there, on houses that had been condemned by the city, and John could almost feel the rats waiting to sneak out at nightfall. It was an awful place, and the house where he stopped was one of the worst among them. He stood for a moment, looking at it from the pavement, the weeds were shoulder-high in the yard, and the smell of rubbish was heavy in the air, and the front door was almost falling off its hinges.

With trepidation, he walked up the front steps, trying to avoid the two broken ones so as not to fall through, and he knocked on the door resoundingly. The doorbell was hanging by a thread and clearly broken. And although he heard noises within, no one came to the door for a long time, and then finally a toothless old woman answered. She stared at him, confused, and then asked him what he wanted.

'I was looking for Eileen and Jack Jones. They lived here a long time ago. Did you know them?' He spoke loudly, in case she was deaf. But she did not seem so much deaf as stupid.

'Never heard of 'em. Why don't you ask Charlie across the street. He been living here since the war. Maybe he knew 'em.'

'Thank you.' A glance into the house told John that it was depressing beyond belief, and he only hoped that it had been more pleasant when Hilary and her sisters lived there. Though it was hard to imagine it ever having been much better. The street had become a slum, but it didn't look as though it had ever been pretty. 'Thank you very much.' He smiled pleasantly, and she slammed the door in his face, not because she was annoyed, but only because she didn't know there was any other way to do it.

He looked up and down the street, and thought of talking to some of the other residents. But he went first to the house she had pointed to. He wondered if anyone would be home at four o'clock on a Friday afternoon, but the old man she had called 'Charlie' was rocking on his front porch, smoking a pipe, and talking to an old mangy dog who lay beside him.

'Hi there.' He looked friendly, and smiled at John as he came up the steps.

'Hello. Are you Charlie?' John smiled pleasantly. He had been good at this, in the days when he actually did the legwork. Now he just determined it from his desk on Fifty-seventh Street, but there was a certain thrill to doing this part of it again. He had tried to explain to Sasha once how much he loved it. But she couldn't understand it. To her, there was only dancing . . . and Lincoln Center . . . and rehearsals. Nothing else mattered. Sometimes he even found himself wondering if he did.

'Yes, I'm Charlie.' The old man answered. 'Who wants to know?'

John stuck out a hand. 'My name is John Chapman. I'm looking for some people who lived here years ago. In that house.' He pointed. 'Eileen and Jack Jones. Do you remember them by any chance, sir?' He was always polite, friendly, at ease, the kind of guy everyone wanted to talk to.

'Sure, I do. Got Jack a job once. Didn't keep it long of course. Drank like a sonofabitch, and she did too. I heard it finally killed her.' John nodded as though it were something he already knew. That was part of the art form. 'I used to work in the navy yard. Damn good work too, durin' the war. I was 4-F 'cause I had rheumatic fever as a boy. Spent the whole war right here, close to home, with my wife and my kids. Sounds kinda unpatriotic now, but I was lucky.'

'You had children then, did you?' John looked at him with interest.

'They're all growed now.' He rocked back and forth and a sad look came into his eyes as he gnawed on his pipe. 'And my wife's gone. Died fourteen years ago this summer. She was a good woman.' John nodded again, letting the old man ramble on. 'My boys come to see me from time to time, when they can. Daughter lives in Chicago. Went to see her last year, Christmas, colder'n a witch's teat. Got six kids too. Her husband's a preacher.' It was an interesting history and John patted the dog as he listened.

'Do you remember three little girls who came to live with the Joneses about thirty years ago . . . right about this time of year . . . it was the summer of '58, to be precise. Three little girls. One about nine years old, one five, and the littlest one was a baby. She must've been about a year old.'

'Naw . . . can't say as I do . . . they never had any kids,

Jack and Eileen. Just as well. They weren't real nice people. Used to have some knock-down drag-out fights those two. Nearly called the cops on 'em one night. I figured he'd kill her.' It sounded like a charming home in which to leave three children.

'They were her brother's children. They were just here for the summer, but one of them stayed on afterwards . . .' He let his voice trail off, hoping to jog Charlie's memory, and suddenly the old man looked up at him with a frown, and pointed the pipe into John's face with a burst of recognition.

'Now that you say all that, I do remember . . . some terrible thing . . . he had killed his wife, and the little girls were orphans. I only seen 'em once or twice, but I remember, Ruth, that's my wife, tellin' me how cute they were and how terrible Eileen was to 'em, that it was a crime to leave those children with her. Half starved 'em, Ruth said, she took 'em some dinner once or twice, but she was sure Jack and Eileen ate it and never gave it to the children. I never knew what happened to 'em though. They left pretty soon after that. Eileen took sick, and they went somewhere. Arizona, I think . . . California . . . someplace warm seems like . . . but she died anyway. Drank herself to death if you ask me. Don't know what happened to them little girls though. I guess Jack musta kep 'em.'

'Only one of them. The rest of them left that summer. They just kept the oldest one.'

'I guess Ruth musta known that. I forget.' He leaned back in his chair, as though remembering more than Jack and Eileen, it was all so long ago, and his wife had been alive then . . . it was bittersweet to remember back that far . . . he seemed to forget John as he rocked back and forth in his rocking chair, and he had given John what he'd come for. He hadn't learned anything he desperately needed to know, but it was a little piece of the puzzle. It explained some of Arthur's guilt. He must have known how terrible they were, and yet he had left them there . . . and left Hilary to them . . . in effect abandoned her to them. He could only begin to imagine what her life had been like in the house across the street, with the kind of people Charlie had described to him. The thought of it made John shudder.

'Do you think anyone else along here would remember them?' John asked, but Charlie shook his head, still lost in his reverie, and then he looked up at John and answered.

'No one lived here that long, 'cept me. The others all been here ten, fifteen years . . . most of 'em less. They stay a year or two, then move away.' It was easy to see why. 'My eldest boy wants me to come live with him, but I like it here . . . I lived here with his ma . . . I'll die here one day.' He said it philosophically. It was all right with him. 'I ain't goin'.'

'Thanks for your time. You've been a big help to me.' He smiled down at Charlie who looked up at him with open curiosity for the first time.

'Why you want to find Eileen and Jack? Somebody leave 'em some money?' It hardly seemed likely, even to him, but it was an intriguing idea, but John was as quick to shake his head.

'No. Actually, I'm looking for the three girls. A friend of their parents wants to find them.'

'That's a hell of a long time ago to lose someone and then go looking for 'em.' John knew only too well how true that was.

'I know. That's why you've been such a help. You put the picture together with little tiny pieces of what people remember and now and then you get lucky, like I did with you. Thank you, Charlie.' He shook the old man's hand, and Charlie waved his pipe at him.

'They pay you good for a job like that? Seems like a lot of wild-goose chasin' to me.'

'Sometimes it is.' He left the previous question unanswered and waved as he stepped off the porch and walked back to his car. It was depressing just driving down the street, and it was as though he felt Hilary's eyes on him, as though he were Arthur leaving her there, and he couldn't help wondering how Arthur could have done it.

The drive to his parents' house after that took less than an hour, and his older brother was already there when he arrived, drinking a gin and tonic on the terrace with his father.

'Hi, Dad. You look great.' The old man looked more like sixty than nearly eighty. There was no tremor in his voice, he still had his hair, and he had the same long, lanky legs as John as he strode across the terrace to put an arm around his shoulders.

'Well, how's my black-sheep son?' They always teased him, but they were proud of him too. He was successful, attractive, led an interesting life. The only thing his parents regretted for him was that he had divorced Eloise, they had always hoped the two would stay together and have children. 'Keeping yourself out of trouble?'

'Not if I can help it. Hello, Charles.' He shook hands with his brother and the two men smiled. There was always a certain distance between them, and yet John was fond of him. He was a partner in an important law firm in New York and he had done well. He was forty-six years old, he was powerful in the field of international law, he had an attractive wife who was president of the Junior League, and he had three very nice children. By the standards of John's family, Charles was the major achiever. But John always felt there was something missing from Charles's life, excitement perhaps, or maybe just plain old romance.

And with that, Lesley, his wife, walked out of the house with her mother-in-law, who gave a whoop of delight when she saw John talking to his brother and father.

'The prodigal son has arrived,' she intoned in her husky voice, hugging him close to her. She was still a handsome woman at seventy, and even in her plain yellow linen dress, there was an innate elegance about her. She wore her hair in an elegant knot, a string of pearls around her neck that her husband had given on her wedding day, and the rings that had been in her family for five generations. 'Don't you look well, darling! What have you been up to?'

'A little work on the way up. I just started a new investigation.' She looked pleased. She enjoyed her sons. They were all handsome and different and intelligent, and she loved them all, but secretly she had always loved John just a little bit more than the others.

'I hear you've got involved with the ballet,' Lesley said coolly, eyeing John carefully over her Bloody Mary. There was something mean-spirited about the girl which always irked John, but he was amazed that no one else even seemed to notice. She was one of those women who had everything and should have enjoyed it – two lovely daughters, a charming son, a handsome, successful husband – and yet she seemed to begrudge everyone everything they had, particularly John. She always felt that somehow he had done better than Charles, and it annoyed her. 'I had no idea you were interested in the dance, John.'

'You never know, do you?' He smiled non-committally, amazed that she had heard about Sasha, and then he chuckled to himself inwardly, thinking that maybe she had been meeting a lover at the Russian Tea Room.

Moments later, Philip arrived, looking very tanned after his European holiday. He and his family lived in Connecticut, and he played tennis constantly. He had a son and a daughter and a wife with blond hair and blue eyes and freckles. She looked exactly like what she was, the childhood sweetheart he had married at college. He was thirty-eight years old, and so was she, and she won all the tennis tournaments in Greenwich. They were truly the perfect family, except for John who had never quite fitted into the mould, and never done what was expected.

And bringing Sasha up here would have complicated things even further. Eloise had been difficult enough. When she wanted to be sociable, she was great, and when she didn't, she would bring a typewriter, and insist on working till lunchtime, which drove Lesley nuts, and made mother worry that she wasn't having a good time. Eloise was definitely not easy. But Sasha would have really been a shock to them with her leotards and her skintight blue jeans and her fits of petulance and her scenes of defiance. The very thought of her made him grin to himself as he looked at the ocean.

'What's so funny, big brother?' Philip clapped him on the back, and John asked him all about Europe. The hardest thing of all was that they were all such nice people, and he loved them, but they bored him to death, and by Sunday afternoon it was a relief to be driving to the airport. He felt guilty for thinking it, but they all led such normal, suburban lives. By the end of a weekend, he always felt like a misfit. At least his mother had had a nice time. Each of her sons had given her something special that was important to her. John had bought her a beautiful antique diamond brooch with a matching bracelet, and it was just the kind of thing he knew his mother loved. Charles had given her stock, which John thought was an odd gift, but she seemed to be pleased with it, and Philip had given her something she had said she wanted for years, but never bought herself. A grand piano was being delivered to the house in Boston on Monday. It was just like him to do something like that, and John thought it was a terrific gift and wished he'd thought of it himself. But she seemed happy with the brooch and bracelet.

He returned the rented car at the airport, and flew back on the commuter with a mob of people returning from the weekend, and by eight o'clock he was back in his apartment making himself a sandwich for dinner, and going through Arthur Patterson's file again. He didn't know anything more than he did before, except the kind of home Hilary had been left in. And he knew exactly what he was going to do the next morning.

But Sasha was far from thrilled when he told her when she came to his apartment later that evening. 'What? You're going away *again*?' She was furious. 'What is it this time?'

John tried to pacify her as best he could, they had been on their way to bed when he mentioned it to her, which was a mistake, he recognized now, but he was still hoping to make love to her that night. It had been days, and with Sasha you had to hit it right, when she wasn't too tired, when her muscles weren't too delicate, when she didn't have a big performance the next day. It was a real feat getting her to bed at all, and he wasn't about to blow it for Arthur's investigation.

'I told you, baby, I have a big case, and I'm handling this one myself.'

'I thought you were the boss. The choreographer, as it were.' He smiled at the comparison and nodded.

'I am. But this is an exception. I agreed to do the legwork myself, if I could. It's a very important case to my client.'

'What's it about?' She looked at him suspiciously, as she stretched out again on his bed, with all her clothes on.

'I'm looking for three girls . . . three women actually. He lost track of them thirty years ago, and he has to find them quickly. He's dying.' He couldn't tell her more than that, even that was something of a violation of Arthur's confidence, but he wanted to spark Sasha's interest and her allegiance.

'Are they his daughters?' He shook his head as he unbuttoned his shirt. 'Ex-wives?' He shook his head again. 'Girlfriends?' He smiled and shook his head again. 'Then what are they?'

'They're sisters.'

'And they're in Florida?' She thought it all sounded very boring.

'One of them was a long time ago. I have to start way back. I thought I had her here in New York, but I didn't. So now we go back to the beginning.'

'How long will you be gone?'

'A few days. I should be back by Friday. We can do something nice this weekend.'

'No, we can't. I have rehearsals.' There was no denying, her schedule was not easy.

'All right, then we'll work around it.' He was used to that.

'You're sure you're not just going to Florida on holiday?'

'Hardly. I can think of a lot of places I'd much rather go, with you, my lovely.' He slid across the bed, took her by surprise and kissed her, and this time she laughed. She let him undress her, and wound her sinewy legs around his body in a way that drove him mad as they began to make love, and then suddenly she pulled away, and he was afraid he had hurt her. He looked at her through his veil of desire and whispered in a hoarse voice, 'Are you all right?'

She nodded, but she looked worried. 'Do you know what I could do to myself in positions like this?' But she seemed to forget about it as his ardour increased and along with it, her own passion. But she was always thinking about herself, her dancing, her muscles, her feet, her body.

'I love you, Sash,' he whispered as they lay in each other's arms afterwards, but she was oddly silent. Her eyes were open and she was looking at the far wall and she seemed upset as he watched her. 'What's the matter, sweetheart?'

'That sonofabitch screamed at me all afternoon today, as though I were doing something wrong . . . and I know I wasn't . . .' She was obsessed with her dancing, and for a moment it depressed him. He had been there before, only the last time it had been her goddam characters and her books, and the plot she couldn't get a grip on. Women like them were exhausting. He wanted Sasha to be different, yet he wanted her to care about him, and in the moments when he was honest with himself, he was not sure that she did. He wasn't even sure she was capable of it. She was totally engrossed in herself. And when he got up to get something to drink from the kitchen, she didn't even seem to notice his absence. He sat on the couch for a long time, in the dark, listening to the noises from the street, and wondered if he would ever find a woman who cared about him, a woman who cared about his work, his life, his friends, his needs, and enjoyed being with him.

'What are you doing in here?' She was standing in the doorway, silhouetted gracefully in the moonlight, her voice a whisper in the darkened room, and she couldn't see the sadness in his eyes as he watched her.

'Thinking.'

'What about?' She came to sit beside him and for a moment it almost seemed as though she cared and then she looked down at her feet and groaned. 'God, I should go back to the doctor.'

'Why?'

'They hurt all the time now.'

'Have you ever thought about giving up dancing, Sash?'

She stared at him as though he were crazy. 'Are you mad? I would rather die. If they told me I couldn't dance anymore, I would kill myself.' And she sounded as though she meant it.

'What about children? Don't you want kids?' He should have asked her all those things long before, but it had been hard to distract her from her dancing.

'Maybe later.' She sounded vague. Eloise used to say the same kind of thing to him. Until she was thirty-six, and decided it would interfere too much with her career, and had her tubes tied while he was away on business. And she was probably right. She was happier alone.

'Sometimes if you put it off, "later" never happens.'

'Then it was never meant to be. I don't need children to be fulfilled.' She said it proudly.

'What do you need, Sash? Do you need a husband?' Or did she only need the ballet? That was the real question.

'I've never thought I was old enough to worry about being married.' She said it honestly, looking up at him in the moonlight. But he was forty-two years old, and he was thinking of all those things, he had been for a long time now. He didn't want to be alone forever. He wanted someone to love him, and whom he could love, not just between books and ballets and rehearsals.

'You're twenty-eight. You should start to think about your future.'

'I think about it every day, with that old maniac screaming at me.'

'I don't mean your professional future, I mean your real life.'

'That *is* my real life, John.' But that was precisely what he was afraid of.

'And where do I fit into all that?' It was a night for soul-searching, and he wasn't sure if he should have started it. But it couldn't be helped. Sooner or later they'd have to talk about something other than her feet and her rehearsals.

'That's up to you. I can't offer you more than this for the moment. If it's enough, wonderful. And if it's not . . .' She shrugged. At least she was honest. And he wondered if he could change her mind, if he could induce her to marry him . . . to want a child . . . but it was crazy to do that again. He seemed to have this incredible penchant for challenges and lost causes. 'You ought to try climbing Everest sometime,' his younger brother had told him once, 'it might relieve some of the tension.' He had met Sasha twice and thought John was crazy. 'Do you want me to stay tonight?' she was asking him now. She was perfectly willing to go. She didn't mind the chaos of her apartment on the West Side with the eight million room-mates and fourteen million dance-bags.

'I'd like you to stay.' In truth, he wanted a great deal more from her. More even than she had to give, and he was only beginning to understand that.

'Then I'll go to bed now.' She got up matter-of-factly and went back to his bedroom. 'I have an early rehearsal tomorrow.' And he had to fly to Jacksonville. And more than that, he wanted to make love to her again, but she said she was too tired and her muscles were sore when he got back into bed with her and tried it.

Chapter 18

The flight to Jacksonville was brief and gave Chapman time to read some of his papers. He signed half a dozen things he had to read, but his mind always drifted back to Hilary . . . and the life she must have led with Eileen and Jack Jones, according to the description of the old man in Charlestown.

In Jacksonville, he went directly to the juvenile hall, asked for the senior administrator, and explained his investigation. It was unusual in cases like that to lay files open to anyone, but so many years had passed, and the girl would be thirty-eight years old. There could be no harm in looking back into the past now. And John assured them of his total discretion.

The signature of the judge assigned to the juvenile court had to be obtained, and John was told to come back the following morning. In the meantime, he checked into a motel downtown, and wandered the streets aimlessly. He spent some time going through the phone book and found five Jack Joneses, and then on a whim, he decided to call them. Three of them were black, and the fourth one didn't answer. But the fifth said his father had grown up in Boston and he thought he'd been married to a woman named Eileen who died before his dad married his mother. He said he was eighteen years old, and his dad had died of cirrhosis ten years before, but he'd be happy to tell him anything he could. John asked if he knew where his father used to live, say twenty-five years before, if maybe his mother knew, but the answer to that was simple.

'He's always lived in the same house. We still live here.' Chapman's interest rose sharply and he asked if he could come out and see it.

'Sure.' He gave him the address, and John was not surprised to discover that it had much the same feeling as their neighbourhood in Charlestown, the same seedy, depressing kind of area, near a naval yard, only this one was mostly black, and there were young boys on motorcycles cruising the area, which made Chapman nervous.

It was not a nice place to be, and like the Charlestown place, it looked as though it never had been.

Jack Jones Jr. was waiting for him, with a motorcycle parked in his own front yard, and he looked as though Chapman's visit made him feel important. He rattled on briefly about his dad, showed him some pictures, and invited him inside to meet his mother. Inside the house there was a terrible stench, of stale urine, old booze, and the filth of a lifetime. The house was beyond grim, and the woman Jack Jr. introduced as his mother was pathetic. She was probably only in her late forties, but already toothless, and she looked thirty years older, and it was impossible for John to determine if her infirmities were due to abuse or an illness. She smiled vaguely at him, and stared into space beyond him, while Jack Jr. made excuses for her, but she remembered nothing about a niece of Jack's previous wife. In fact, several times she seemed not to know who her own son was. Eventually, John gave up, and was on his way out, when Jack Jr. suggested he might want to talk to the neighbours. They had lived there for years, and even knew Jack Sr. when he was married to his late wife. John thanked him and knocked on the door, and an elderly woman came to the screen door with caution.

'Yeah?'

'May I speak to you for a moment, ma'am?' It had been years since he had done this himself, and he suddenly remembered how difficult it was to win people's trust. He suddenly recalled how many doors had slammed in his face in the old days.

'You a cop?' It was a familiar question.

'No, I'm not. I'm looking for a woman named Hilary Walker. She lived here a long time ago, when she was a little girl. Would you have any idea where she might be today?'

The woman shook her head and seemed to be looking John over. 'What you want with her?'

'A friend of her parents wants to find her.'

'They shouldda looked for her twenty-five years ago. Poor kid . . .' She shook her head, remembering, and John knew he'd struck pay dirt. She was still talking to him through the screen door, but slowly it swung open, and she stood there in a house dress and slippers, staring at John, but not inviting him in. 'That so-called uncle of hers beat her to within an inch of her life. She crawled out of that place in the pouring rain and damn near died on my doorstep. My husband and I, we took her to the hospital, and she almost didn't make it. They said he'd tried to rape her.'

'Did anyone bring charges against him?' Chapman stared at her, horrified. The story was getting worse. Hilary's fate had truly been a nightmare.

But she only shook her head. 'She was too scared . . . little Hilary.' She shook her head. 'I'd forgotten her all this time.'

'What happened after that?'

'She went to a couple of foster homes, and eventually I think she just stayed in juvie. We went to see her twice, I think it was, but it was like . . . well, there was somethin' missin' outta that girl, not that you could blame her. She didn't warm up to no one.' It was easy to understand that, in the face of what he was hearing.

'Thank you. Thank you very much.' So that was the reason for juvenile hall, not that she had broken the law herself. Or maybe she'd done that too eventually. Sometimes that was the way it happened.

But in her case, it hadn't. They handed the files to him the first thing the next morning. The judge had signed the order without a problem. But the file on Hilary Walker was far from exciting. She had been a model student, had given no problems to the State, had been in two foster homes, whose addresses were given, and had then spent three years in juvenile hall without event. She had been given two hundred and eighty-seven dollars upon completion of her last year of high school, and five days later, she had left, never to be heard from again. It was a slim file, and told him precious little about the girl, except that her caseworkers' reports said that she was withdrawn, had no known friends, but posed no disciplinary problem either. The caseworkers who had known her then were all long since gone, and he imagined that both foster homes had disappeared too, but just to be sure, he went to the addresses listed in her file. The first woman was, amazingly, still alive and at the same address, and she thought she remembered her although she wasn't sure.

'She was the one who was so high and mighty. Didn't stay long neither. Can't remember how she worked. She started pining, and they sent her back to the hall. That's all I remember 'bout her now.' But it was enough, the woman's harsh words about other girls, the home itself told its own tale. And the second foster home had been torn down for a development years before. No wonder the woman at CBA knew nothing about her. The girl who had been here had gone God knows where to finish her life in the same kind of misery and squalor it had started, or been condemned to at the age of eight, when her father killed her mother, and then committed suicide and their best friend had abandoned her, after taking her sisters from her. In some ways, John felt as though Arthur had led her to slaughter. And it was easy to understand why she had come to Arthur's office twenty-one years before to vent her hatred. The question was, where had she gone from there? The trail was as cold as death, and he had no idea where to go from here. Where did one begin looking for a girl who had known so much pain and misery at such an early age? He had run her rap sheet through various states and the FBI, and nothing had turned up, but that didn't mean anything. She could have changed her name, got married several times. She could have died in the past twenty-one years. She could have done a number of things. But if she was still in New York, John promised himself he would find her.

He left Jacksonville without regret, and with a sense of relief to be escaping the humidity and the squalor he had seen there. He could only imagine how Hilary felt on her way to New York to find her sisters, only to find that Arthur had not kept track of them, any more than he had of her. What a bitter disappointment it must have been for her.

He got home on Thursday night, and left a message on Sasha's answering machine. He knew it was the night of her big performance, but it was ten o'clock when he finally got home, and he was exhausted.

And the next day at the office, he reported to Arthur Patterson what he'd found, and there was a long, sad silence at the other end. John Chapman couldn't see the silent tears rolling down Arthur's cheeks as he listened.

'After she visited you, the trail's cold. I have no idea where she went from there, but I'm working on it.' He had already given one of his assistants a list of things he wanted: he wanted him to check out schools, hospitals, employment agencies, youth hostels, hotels, all the way back to 1966. It was no small task, but somewhere something would turn up, and they could go on from there. Meanwhile, he was going to start looking for Alexandra. 'I'll need to come down to your office on Monday. I want to go through the files on George Gorham's estate. I want to see if they contacted his widow recently.' Arthur nodded his head, and brushed away the tears he had shed for Hilary. John Chapman was certainly thorough.

It was a terrible thought to realize what had been Hilary's fate . . . but how could he have known . . . if only . . . he began coughing terribly as he thought of it, and eventually had to hang up the phone. And John went back to work. There was a mountain of files waiting for him on his desk, after being in Florida all week, and he stayed in the office until seven-thirty, and then stopped for a hamburger at the Auto Pub on the way home. It was nine o'clock when he got home, and the phone was ringing. It was Sasha.

'Where've you been all night long?' She sounded suspicious and angry.

'At my office. And I stopped and had something to eat on the way home. And how are you, Miss Riva?' There had been no preamble, no inquiry as to how he was, and she hadn't called him in Florida all week, even though he'd left his number on her machine, but he knew she'd been busy with rehearsals.

'I'm all right. I thought I'd done something to one of my tendons yesterday, but thank God, I hadn't.' Nothing had changed in his absence.

'I'm glad. Want to come over for a drink?' He half wanted to see her and half didn't. The week in Florida had been incredibly depressing and he needed cheering up, but on the other hand he didn't want to listen to the familiar litany about her ligaments and her tendons.

'I'm exhausted. I'm already at the apartment. But I'm free this weekend. We could do something tomorrow.'

'Why don't we go somewhere? How about the Hamptons or Fire Island?' The summer had already set in, and it was hot everywhere. It was going to be a beautiful weekend.

'Dominic Montaigne is having a birthday party on Sunday. I promised him I'd be there, and I can't let him down. I'm really sorry.' Ballet, ballerinas, dancers, rehearsals, performances. It was endless.

'That's all right. We could go for the day. I'd love to get out of town and lie on a beach somewhere.'

'So would I.' But he knew she would lie down for exactly half an hour and then she would start prancing around and flexing muscles, so nothing got stiff while she was relaxing. And there were times when it was extremely unnerving.

'I'll pick you up at nine o'clock. Okay?' She agreed, and he hung up, feeling suddenly sad, and indescribably lonely. She was never there for him when he needed her, and instead he found himself thinking about a girl he didn't know, who had been bounced between foster homes and juvenile hall more than twenty years before. It was crazy to be thinking about her now. He felt like Eloise with her imaginary characters. It made about as much sense, but she had become so real to him in the last week. Much more than he wanted.

The next day he and Sasha went to the beach. In the end they just went to Montauk, on Long Island, and it was relaxing and nice. He jogged along the beach while she exercised, and they stopped for a lobster dinner on the way home. It was eleven-thirty that night before they got back to his apartment, and fell into bed like two kids. She was in a good mood, and they made love without Sasha complaining once that his passion was going to do her great bodily harm or permanent damage. And wrapped around each other, they slept until ten o'clock the next morning, when she bounded out of bed, looked at her watch, and gave a shriek that woke him.

'What's wrong? . . . where are you? . . .' He squinted in the sunlight streaming across his room, and saw her rushing into the bathroom, and heard her turn on the shower. He threw back the sheets, and lumbered slowly in to see what she was up to. 'What are you doing in there?' The bathroom was full of steam, she had her hair tied in a knot on top of her head, and her face was turned full into the shower.

'What does it look like?'

'What are you doing up so early?'

'I promised Dominic I'd be there by eleven-thirty.'

'Oh for chrissake. What's the hurry?'

'I'm making lunch for everyone,' she announced as she turned off the shower and started to dry herself off.

'That's interesting. You never cook here.' He was annoyed. They had had such a nice day the day before, and now she was in such a hurry to leave him. He had wanted to make love to her again before she left, but she was all business.

'This is different,' she explained, looking as though what she said made sense. 'These are dancers.'

'Do they eat differently than everyone else?'

'Don't be silly.' He wasn't silly. He was just tired of the endless aggravation. 'I'll call you tonight when I get home.'

'Don't bother.' He walked out of the bathroom, picked up a cigarette on his dresser, and lit it. He rarely smoked, but when she upset him particularly it seemed to ease the tension, or added to it, he was never quite sure which, but it did something.

'John,' she smiled angelically at him as she brushed her hair with his hairbrush, 'don't be childish. I'd take you along, but they're all dancers. No one brings outsiders to these events. You know,' she smiled and for the first time he saw something vengeful in her eyes — 'kind of like when you visit your family in Boston.' So that was it. Or part of it anyway. Well, to hell with her games, and her dancers. 'Will I see you tomorrow night?' She hesitated doelike in the bedroom.

'Possibly, I have a lot of work to do on Monday.'

She walked over to him with her firm, lithe body straining against his and kissed him hard on the lips which visibly aroused him. He was standing naked in his bedroom doorway. 'I love you.' She had a way of taunting him that he half loved and half hated, and before he could say anything to her, she was gone, and he wanted to scream in frustration.

For lack of anything better to do, he called his younger brother, and spent the day in Greenwich with them, playing doubles with Pattie and Philip and their son, and swimming in the pool with their daughter. It was a relaxed, easy day, and he was always embarrassed to admit to himself, as he did on the drive home, how intensely they bored him. But they were decent people, and they were family after all, and it had been a pleasant escape from New York and the reminders of Sasha.

The phone was ringing when he got home, but he didn't answer it. He didn't want to hear about Dominic and Pascal and Pierre and André and Josef and Ivan or any of the others. He was sick to death of them all, and even a little bit of Sasha. And the next morning, he went to Arthur's law firm and went through the files of George Gorham's estate himself after Arthur gave him carte blanche, and he found exactly what he had wanted. Arthur could have found it himself, years before, if he had looked. The last contact they had had with Margaret Millington Gorham was in 1962, at which time she was already the Comtesse de Borne and living on the rue de Varenne in Paris. There had been no contact since then, but she couldn't be too hard to find. And a search of the Paris telephone directory that afternoon showed her still living at the same address, listed as Borne, P. de, and the address was the same one. Now if she was only still alive and could tell him where Alexandra was, he'd be in business.

Chapter 19

'Not again!' Sasha looked outraged, but he was unmoved this time. Business was business. 'What did you do, get a job with the airlines?' She was incensed. This was his third trip in as many weeks.

'I won't be gone long.' Things were a little cooler between them than they had been.

'Where to this time?'

He smiled. Jacksonville it wasn't. 'Paris. At least my working conditions are pleasant.' She didn't answer him at first and then she shrugged. For all she knew he was lying and flying all over with assorted girlfriends. He had certainly never done all this travelling before. It seemed odd that he was suddenly doing 'the legwork' himself, as he'd told her. 'I should be back by Friday. Monday at the latest.'

'Have you forgotten? I go out on tour next week for three weeks. I won't see you till I get back. Unless you want to fly in to see me one night.' But he knew what that was like, a whole troupe of dancers completely hysterical and on edge, and Sasha barely coherent enough to acknowledge his existence.

'That'll be all right, I'm going to be busy too.' But they wouldn't see each other for a month. A year ago that would have worried him. Now he thought it might be a relief, for him at least. Her obsession with her work was beginning to oppress him.

They slept side by side that night, without making love, and he dropped her off at her apartment the next morning on his way to the airport.

'I'll see you when you get back.' He kissed her on the mouth, and she smiled up at him, looking very innocent and pure.

'Have a good trip. I'll miss you.' Unusually kind words for her, ordinarily she would have been predicting the weather from the pain in her feet. And her sudden gentleness made him sorry to see her go. The problem with her was that she really had no idea how totally egocentric she was. To her, it seemed perfectly normal.

He waved at her from the cab, and promised to call from Paris as they rounded the corner, and a moment later, he sat lost in thought, wondering what he was going to find in Paris. Surely not a life like Hilary's if Margaret Gorham had married a French count. At least he hoped not.

At Arthur's request, he flew first class, and his flight landed in Paris at midnight, local time. He went directly to the Hotel Bristol after clearing customs, and was in bed by two o'clock, but he was too tired to sleep, and it was five in the morning before he fell asleep, and he was horrified to discover that it was eleven o'clock when he woke up again later. He instantly jumped out of bed, ordered coffee and croissants, and dialled Margaret's number, before taking his shower.

He asked for the Comtesse de Borne when the phone was answered by a male voice, speaking French, and stumbled in his limited French when the butler asked him, '*De la part de qui, monsieur?*' He gave him his name but was unable to translate the words *but she doesn't know me*. But whatever was said at her end, she was on the phone with him a moment later.

'Monsieur Chapote?' she said in French with a heavy American accent, sounding puzzled.

'Sorry.' He smiled. He liked her voice. 'John Chapman, from New York.'

'Good God. André can never get American names. Do I know you?' She was blunt and direct, and there was something in her voice that suggested quick laughter.

'No, ma'am. I'm here on a business matter I'd like to discuss with you at your earliest convenience.' He had no intention of telling her over the phone though.

'Oh.' She sounded a little startled. 'All my business matters are handled in New York.' She told him the name of the firm. 'Except my husband's, of course. Is this about an investment?'

'No.' He didn't want to frighten her, but he had to tell her something. 'Actually, it's a little more personal than that. It's about an investigation I'm conducting for a partner of your late husband's.'

'Pierre? But he didn't have any partners.' It was a very confusing conversation.

'I'm sorry. I meant Mr Gorham.'

'Oh poor George . . . but that was so long ago. He died in 1959 . . . that was almost thirty years ago, Mr . . . er . . . Chapman.'

'I understand that, and this goes back an awfully long time.'

'Was there anything wrong?' She sounded worried.

'Not at all. We were just hoping you could help us find someone. It would be a great help to us if you could. But I'd rather not go into the entire matter over the phone. If you could spare me a few moments, I would like very much to see you . . .'

'All right.' But she sounded uncertain. She wished she could ask Pierre, or someone, if they thought she should see this man. What if he were a charlatan, or a criminal of some kind . . . not that he sounded like it. 'Perhaps tomorrow, Mr Chapman? And the name of your firm in New York?'

He smiled. She was right to check him out. 'Chapman Associates on Fifty-seventh Street. My name is John Chapman. What time would you like to meet?'

'Eleven o'clock?' She wanted to get this meeting out of the way. He was beginning to make her nervous. But when she checked him out with her attorneys in New York, they knew the firm, and her attorney was even personally acquainted with John Chapman, and he assured her that he was entirely above-board. He just couldn't imagine what Chapman was doing, speaking to Margaret de Borne in Paris.

He arrived punctually the next morning, and the elderly butler let him in with a subdued bow, and then led him upstairs to wait in the countess's formal study. It was a room filled with beautiful Louis-XV furniture, and a tiny Russian chandelier with what looked like a million crystals that caught the sunlight shining into the room and cast it into a myriad of rainbows against the walls. It was the prettiest thing John had ever seen, and he didn't even hear her come in, as he stared at the beautiful lights, and the lovely garden in the distance.

'Mr Chapman?' She was tall and elegant, with a firm handshake and a strong voice, and the look in her eyes was warm and friendly. She was wearing a yellow Chanel suit, and their classic shoes, and a beautiful pair of yellow diamond earrings that had been a gift from her late husband. She smiled warmly at John and waved at one of the room's larger chairs. Most of them were extremely small and not very inviting, which always made her smile. She laughed as they both sat down. 'I'm afraid none of these pieces were designed for people of our proportions. I don't use this room very often. It was designed as a "lady's study" and I've never quite got the hang of it. My six-year-old granddaughter is the only person I know who looks comfortable here. My apologies.'

'Not at all, Countess. It's lovely.' It seemed odd to be calling her that, particularly with her easy smile and happy laughter, but he thought she might have expected the formality, and he wanted her as his ally. 'I'm afraid I'm here on a rather sensitive matter. I've been hired by Arthur Patterson.' He waited for the name to have an effect on her, but she didn't look as though she knew it. 'He was a partner of Mr Gorham's many years ago, and he was instrumental in bringing Alexandra Walker to you for adoption.' He watched her eyes, and she suddenly looked as though she were going to faint. Her face went pale as she watched him. She waited for him to go on without saying a word. But it was obvious that she now remembered Arthur.

'He is very ill now, and for whatever reasons – all of them personal, I assume – he is anxious to find all three Walker girls. Their parents were close friends of his, and he feels an obligation to know that they're all right, before he . . .' As he groped for the right word, she interrupted.

'Isn't it a little late, Mr Chapman? They're certainly no longer children.'

'I agree. But he seems to have let it go until the eleventh hour, and now he wants the reassurance that they've had a good life.'

'At whose expense?'

'I beg your pardon?'

She looked angry. And she stood up and began to pace the room, walking through the shower of rainbows. 'At whose expense does he want that reassurance? Surely those young women no longer care about Arthur Patterson, if they even knew him. And if they did, they won't remember him now. They were all very young children.' Chapman's heart sank at the look in her eyes. It was obvious that she was prepared to do anything to keep him from her daughter.'What on God's earth does it matter? They're all grown up. They don't know him. They don't even know each other.'

John Chapman sighed. In a way she was right. But he was working for Arthur. 'That is part of the reason for my investigation.' He spoke in a gentle voice, anxious to calm her down and show her that she could trust him. 'Mr Patterson wants to bring the sisters back together.'

'Oh, my God.' She sat down hard again, in one of the uncomfortable small Louis-XV chairs. And then, with intransigence, 'I won't allow it. What need is there to torture them? My daughter is thirty-four years old, God only knows how old the others are. Why would they want to discover two unknown sisters? It can only be an embarrassment to them, not to mention painful. Do you know what the circumstances of their parents' deaths were, Mr Chapman?' He nodded, and she went on, 'So do I. But my daughter does not, and there is no need for her to know it. George and I loved her very much, like our own, and the Count took her in as his own daughter. She has grown up as our child, with every advantage that could be given her, she has a happy life with a husband and children of her own. She does not need this heartache.' Not to mention how she would keep it from her husband. The very thought terrified Margaret. Not only was she adopted, but her real father had *murdered* her mother.

'I understand that, but maybe she would like to meet her sisters . . . it's possible . . . maybe she has a right to make that choice herself. Does she know she's adopted?' Margaret hesitated thoughtfully.

'Yes. And no. We told her . . . a long time ago . . . but I'm not sure she remembers. It's no longer of any importance. To anyone, Mr Chapman. I will not tell her about your visit.'

'That's not fair to her.' He spoke in a quiet voice. 'And if you force me to, I'll find her. I would prefer it if you spoke to her, and explained the reason for my visit. I think that would be a lot easier for her.'

Margaret de Borne's eyes filled with tears of anger. 'That's blackmail. You're forcing me to tell her something that will make her very unhappy.'

'If she doesn't wish to see them, she doesn't have to. She has a right to refuse to see them herself. No one can force her. But she has the right to choose. Maybe she'd like to see them.'

'Why? Why after thirty years? What kind of people are they now? What does she have in common with them? Nothing.' It was certainly true in the case of Hilary, but he didn't yet know about Megan. While Hilary was being kicked around and raped by her uncle and living in nightmarish foster homes, her sister was riding ponies in Paris. It seemed an unfair turn of fate. At least one of them had been blessed, from all appearances, but it only made him ache more for Hilary. Life had not been kind to her for a single moment.

'Countess . . . please . . . help me make it easy for her. She has a right to know. And I have an obligation to tell her.'

'Tell her what?'

'That she has two sisters somewhere in the world, and perhaps they want to see her.'

'Have you found them yet?'

He shook his head. 'No, but I think we will.' He was being optimistic, but he didn't want to share his fears with her.

'Why don't you come back when you've found them.'

'I can't afford to waste a moment. I've already told you, Mr Patterson is dying.'

'It's a shame he didn't die before he decided to ruin everyone's life.' She sounded bitter and very angry. For years, she had shielded Alexandra from the truth, and now this stranger, this man, was coming to hurt her. It made her want to kill him, and John felt sorry for her. She was a nice woman, and it was unfortunate that this was so upsetting for her.

'I'm sorry. Truly, I am.'

She looked at him long and hard. 'Perhaps you are. Can't you just tell him you couldn't find her?' John shook his head and she sighed.

'I'll have to think about this. It will come as a great shock to her, particularly if I have to tell her about her parents.' But at least, John thought to himself, she was old enough to withstand it. She wasn't a young girl, or a child. Maybe it was just as well he had waited. 'I'll be seeing her tomorrow for lunch. I'll speak to her about it then, if I find an appropriate moment.'

He nodded. He couldn't ask for much more. 'I'm at the Bristol. I would like to speak to her myself, after you've told her.'

'She may not wish to see you, Mr Chapman. In fact, I hope she doesn't.' Margaret de Borne stood to her full height and did not hold out her hand, as she rang for the butler. 'Thank you for your visit. Good day, Mr Chapman.'

'Thank you, Countess.'

He was escorted downstairs by André, who wore a

stern look of disapproval. It was obvious to him by the way the Countess had said goodbye that John Chapman was *persona non grata*, and he treated him accordingly as he closed the door resoundingly behind him.

Chapter 20

Alexandra found her mother, as usual, in the small flowery sitting-room she preferred, but she was not doing needle-point when she arrived, and most uncharacteristically, her mother was wearing a navy-blue dress and very little jewellery.

'You look very serious today, Maman. Did you have a meeting at the bank this morning?' Alexandra kissed her warmly, and Margaret smiled up at her, but the smile looked distracted and halfhearted. She had barely slept the night before, after Chapman's visit that morning.

'No, no, I'm fine,' Margaret said distractedly, and looked around the room, as though hoping for an escape. And Alexandra frowned, watching her.

'Is something wrong?' She hadn't seen her that nervous since her father died, and wondered if something had happened to upset her.

'No, just some unpleasant business meetings yesterday.' She smiled nervously. 'Nothing to worry about, darling. Ah, here's lunch.' She looked enormously relieved, and dived into her salad, giving Alexandra the latest gossip she had heard at her hairdresser's, and it was a relief to Alexandra to hear her mother laughing. But it was obvious that she was troubled about something, and as the meal drew to a close, she fell strangely silent.

'Maman.' She eyed her mother seriously. 'What's bother-

ing you? I can tell, something's wrong. Now what is it?'
She hoped it wasn't her health. She was remarkably
youthful, but nonetheless ... And then suddenly she
worried that that was why she had just gone to New York
the week before. Perhaps it was to see a doctor, and not go
shopping. She had brought back marvellous things for the
girls, and a beautiful new Galanos for Alexandra.

But Margaret only looked at her mournfully, wishing
she had never heard of John Chapman. She took a deep
breath, and waited while André poured their coffee, and
then discreetly left the room. Not that it mattered, he was
terribly deaf, and spoke no English. But nonetheless,
Margaret waited.

'I had a rather unpleasant visit yesterday. Sort of a ghost
from the past.' She looked at her daughter, and her eyes
filled with tears, and Alexandra was shocked. She had
never seen her mother look so worried.

'What kind of a ghost?'

'Ohhh ...' Margaret dragged her feet, unable to find
her footing. And she looked at her daughter and dabbed at
her eyes. 'I don't know where to begin. It's such a long
and confusing story.' She blew her nose discreetly in a lace
handkerchief she'd had tucked in her sleeve, and held out a
hand to Alexandra. Alexandra moved closer to her, and
held her mother's hand tightly in her own. It was obvious
that whatever the news from this man had been, it had
been ghastly. Margaret was looking up at her and fighting
back tears as Alexandra gently stroked her hand to reassure
her. 'Do you remember a long time ago, a very long time
ago, before I married Pierre?'

'Not really, Maman.' It was all a distant blur now. She
supposed if she tried very hard, she might remember something. 'Why? What is it that I'm supposed to remember?'

'Do you remember that I was married to someone

275

before your father? I mean before Pierre . . .' It was going to be just as difficult as she expected, and Alexandra narrowed her eyes thoughtfully, and then nodded.

'Yes . . . sort of . . . I suppose that was my real father . . . but to be honest I don't remember him. All I remember is Papa.'

Margaret nodded. That's what she had always thought. 'Well, I was married before, and that was obvious because I think you might remember that Pierre adopted you right after we got married.'

Alexandra smiled at the dim memory. She had almost forgotten, until her mother jogged her memory. But now she vaguely remembered. They had gone to a lawyer's office, and the *mairie*, and then they had all gone to lunch at Maxim's to celebrate. It had been the happiest day of her life . . . and it was odd that in a way she had forgotten. 'You know, it's funny. I think I'd almost forgotten I was adopted.' And then she blushed. 'I suppose I should have told Henri, but I never really thought it was important. And Papa said . . .' They both knew what Pierre had told her. And she had instinctively sensed that Henri would be very angry if he knew she were adopted. So she had never told him or allowed herself to remember.

'Your father thought of you that way. You were like his own flesh and blood . . . and more . . .' she added softly. And then she went on with her painful story. 'But you were adopted,' she paused as though trying to gain courage – 'not only by Pierre . . . but by my previous late husband. We adopted you when you were five years old, your parents were both dead, and a partner of George's firm came and spoke to us about you . . . and we fell in love with you the first time we saw you.' The tears were pouring copiously down her cheeks and dripping on their clasped hands, as Alexandra stared at her. What was she saying? What did she mean? Margaret was not her mother? Suddenly, her arms went around Margaret, and she held her tight, as though afraid to lose her.

'I don't remember that part at all, I thought . . . I always thought . . . that you were my mother . . .' How could she have forgotten? . . . How was it possible? . . . Not that it really changed anything. But who had her parents been, and who was really her mother?

Margaret sniffed and blew her nose again. This was even harder than she had expected. 'You were nearly four when your parents died . . . your mother anyway . . . and your father died a few months later. You were left with an aunt, I believe, on your father's side, but she didn't feel able to keep all . . . to keep you . . .' She stumbled and went on. 'So a friend of the family was looking for someone to adopt you. And you made us the happiest people in the world, and six months later George died, and we came to France, and you remember the rest after that.' She was glossing over some of it, but Alexandra was still trying to digest the fact that Margaret wasn't her mother.

'How did my parents die?' There was a long silence as their eyes met and held, and Alexandra felt a chill go up her spine. She knew deep in her heart that something terrible had happened. Margaret closed her eyes and then opened them, speaking in a gentle voice.

'There was a terrible argument no one ever understood . . . he was a famous actor on Broadway, and they said she was very beautiful . . .'

'That's not what I asked you, Maman . . .' The tears were pouring down Alexandra's cheeks as she waited. She knew, she already knew, that was the awful part, but now she needed to hear it from Margaret.

'Your father killed her.'

Alexandra spoke in a haunted whisper, looking beyond her mother at the garden. 'And my father committed suicide. They told me he had killed himself . . .' Her hand flew to her lips and a sob escaped her, as Margaret took her in her arms and let her cry. 'And I forgot . . . I forgot all of it . . . how could I forget that? . . . and my mother had red hair . . . and . . . she spoke French, didn't she? Oh my God . . . but that's all I remember.' And then she looked up at Margaret again, the pain of the memories etched on her face ravaged by the tears born of what she suddenly remembered. 'Was she French?'

Margaret spoke with obvious pain as she answered. It was terrible beyond words, and she hated John Chapman and Arthur Patterson for visiting this on them unnecessarily, so many years later. 'I think she was French . . . probably . . .' And she probably had red hair, because Alexandra did, when she wasn't rinsing it blond to please her husband. And little Axelle looked so exactly as Alexandra had at the same age. It was like seeing her again as she had the first time each time Margaret saw her.

'Why did my father kill himself? Because he killed her?' She wanted to know. It was awful, but suddenly she needed the answers to questions that were so long forgotten.

'He killed himself because he was convicted of killing her. It was a terrible, shocking story. And it left you and . . . it left you an orphan.' But she couldn't keep avoiding the rest of the story. That was the worst of it. She had to tell her. She took Alexandra's hand in her own again, and gently stroked the graceful fingers that looked nothing like her own. In fact, physically, they were very different, but Alexandra had never given it much thought. And suddenly she understood it . . . but all she could remember was the red hair, and nothing else . . . there was no face to go with it. She felt her heart was being torn from her chest, as though pain and memories long buried were rising to haunt her. 'You had . . . you had two sisters as well.' Her words struck through Alexandra like a knife, and she could feel them echo in her head like ricocheting bullets . . . two sisters . . . two sisters . . . two sisters . . . Axie, I love you . . . I love you . . . My God, how could she have forgotten? She remembered the touch, the smell . . . black, black hair, and big sad eyes . . . Hillie . . . Hillie . . . and a baby. Without thinking Alexandra pulled away from her mother and walked across the room to stare out at the garden. 'We couldn't take all three of you . . . we didn't feel . . .' Alexandra wasn't listening to the voice, the apologies, she kept hearing the same words . . . 'always remember how much I love you . . . I love you, Axie . . .' and a little girl sobbing uncontrollably. Who was that little girl? Was it her sister?

'What were their names?' She had to know now. She had to, but Margaret shook her head. She knew very little about the others.

'I don't know. I only know that one was older than you . . .'

Alexandra finished the sentence for her as though in a trance, '. . . and the other one was a baby.' She stared at Margaret as though in great pain. 'I remember them, Maman . . . I remember something now. How could I have forgotten?'

'Maybe it was all too painful for you then. Maybe it was easier to forget. You didn't do anything wrong. You had a right to a new life. We loved you very much, and we did everything we could to make you happy.' She looked so bereft, suddenly it was as though with one fell swoop she had lost her only daughter, and Alexandra went to her and put her arms around the woman she had known as her mother for thirty years.

'You *are* my mother, Maman. You always will be. None of this will ever change that.'

'Do you mean that?' She needed to hear it, and cried unashamedly as Alexandra reassured her. 'It's so awful that these people have come back to haunt you now, they have no right to do so.'

'Why have they come back?' Alexandra looked at her with eyes full of questions.

'Arthur Patterson, the man who arranged your adoption was a friend of your family . . . of your parents . . . and he wants to know now that you and your . . .' She almost choked on the word, '. . . sisters . . . are all right. And if possible he wants to bring you together.' Alexandra looked shocked.

'Do they know where the others are?'

'Not yet. But they're looking. And they found you, so I suppose they'll find the others.'

Alexandra nodded. It was a lot to absorb at once. Suddenly, in one afternoon, she had acquired two sisters, and a father who had killed a mother with red hair who was probably French, and the mother she'd loved all her life was no longer her mother, not to mention two adopted fathers she'd discovered instead of one. It was a bit much to swallow at one sitting, and she smiled weakly at Margaret and took a big swig of wine, with an apologetic look.

'I think I need it.'

'So do I.' And with that, Margaret stood up, and rang for André, and when he appeared she told him to bring her a double bourbon. 'American habits die hard, particularly in moments of crisis.' And then she turned to Alexandra, over her drink, as she slowly swirled the ice cubes with one finger.

'Do you want to see them, Alex?'

Alexandra looked up at her thoughtfully. 'I don't know. What if we all hate each other and are terribly different? Thirty years is a long time.'

'That's what I told Chapman. In truth, it's ridiculous. What can you possibly have in common?'

Alexandra agreed, and yet there was an undeniable attraction to meeting the others. But there was another problem she had to deal with first, a more pressing one. Her husband. 'What do you suppose Henri would say to all this, Maman?' She eyed her mother cautiously, but they both knew what Henri would say. He would be outraged. 'Do you really suppose it will make a difference to him?' Margaret could see that she desperately wanted reassurance. But she couldn't give it to her. The scandal would surely be too much for Alex's husband.

'It shouldn't, if he loves you. But I think it would be a shock to him. That's inevitable. And frankly, I still don't see why you should tell him. Your father and I talked about it when you married him, and we decided it wasn't important. We love you, you are our daughter in every possible way and what happened thirty years ago is no one's business. Perhaps not even your husband's.'

'But that's so dishonest, Maman. I owe it to him to tell him. Don't I?' Her eyes were still full of questions.

'Why? Why upset him needlessly?' Margaret tried to sound calm, but the whole thing was turning into a nightmare.

'Because the fact that I'm the daughter of the Comte de Borne is very important to him, Maman. He believes in all that lineage, and you know it. He's barely able to tolerate the fact that you're American, for heaven's sake, and only the fact that he knows what a fancy family you're from makes him willing to overlook it. How about telling him instead that my father was an actor, and killed my mother, origin unknown. I am the daugher of an unknown murderer and suicide, American to boot, with two unidentified sisters.' She grinned in spite of herself. It was a difficult situation. 'Frankly, I think he'd drop dead from a heart attack. And if he survived, he'd divorce me. And take my daughters if he could get away with it. But if I don't tell him, I'm being dishonest.'

'Don't be foolish, Alex. This isn't the Dark Ages. He couldn't be that unreasonable. And besides, I still don't think you should tell him.'

'You don't know my husband. If I tell him, he might leave me and the girls, but the rest of it's not so far-fetched. Particularly with his political aspirations. My God, mother, he'd die . . . And if he found out some other way . . . if I didn't tell him . . . if someone else found out.' Alexandra visibly shuddered as she paced the room, and Margaret couldn't disagree with her.

'I told you. Don't tell him.'

'And if he finds out? If there's a scandal? At least before I didn't know most of it myself. But now that I do, how can I not tell him? That's deceitful.' It was before, too, but now she was hiding a veritable mountain of information.

'Oh don't be so bloody innocent, for heaven's sake.' She took a huge sip of bourbon and looked at her daughter. 'You can't always be the perfect wife. You have to think of yourself from time to time, not that you do it very often. And it would be stupid to make a confession to Henri. What purpose would it serve except to cause you a great many problems?' And she could hardly disagree with her mother. There was so much at risk. She could lose everything. Her husband. Her marriage. Her children.

'But what if I decide I want to see the others? How do I explain that? How do I slip away to America to meet my sisters? I can't exactly say I'm coming here to lunch and then disappear for five days, can I?'

'Are you so sure you want to go?' Margaret was disappointed to hear it, but Alexandra shook her head.

'I'm not at all sure . . . but if I wanted to, I don't know what I'd tell my husband.' Margaret's solution would have been not to go at all then, but she knew it wasn't fair to say that. She had her own reasons for not wanting Alexandra to go, it was foolish but she was afraid that in some way she would lose her, to the spectre of a mother long dead, and two sisters who would help prove that blood was thicker than water. It was childish, but she wanted Alexandra to turn her back on them. But she was wise enough not to say it.

'I don't think you should say anything to him, Alexandra. Nothing at all. You would be wisest if you kept your own counsel.' She scribbled something on a piece of paper then, and handed her John Chapman's name, and the name of his hotel and phone number. 'Mr Chapman wants you to call him, so he can explain it all to you. If you want to, you can call him at the Bristol.'

'Why is he here?'

Margaret hesitated, but only for an instant. 'To see you.'

'That's why he came to Paris?' Margaret nodded in answer. 'Then I'll call him. I owe him that at least.' And as she slipped the paper with his name into her bag, she saw the time. It was after five o'clock, and she was horrified. She had to get home to Henri and the children. It had been an amazing afternoon, full of unexpected admissions. And Margaret walked her to the door, and hugged her long and hard before she left, as Alexandra looked into her eyes with tears rolling down her cheeks again. 'Maman, please know how much I love you.'

'You'll always be my little girl.' The tears began sliding down her cheeks again, and the two women held each other for a long time before Alexandra left her. It had been a shocking afternoon and she could hardly think straight on the drive home. She kept hearing a voice from the distant past . . . Axie . . . always remember how much I love you . . .

Chapter 21

Alexandra was still in shock when she got home. It was difficult to absorb everything her mother had told her. She felt as though she were moving in a dream, and she kept trying to remember things that had been gone for years . . . the woman with red hair . . . and the little girl she had called Hillie.

'You're late.' Henri was waiting in her study as she walked into the room, feeling as though she had lead weights on her shoulders.

'I'm sorry, I . . .' She jumped when she saw him, startled from her reverie. But to Henri, it made her look guilty. 'My mother had some papers I had to discuss with her . . . I didn't think it would take . . . Henri, I'm sorry.' There were tears in her eyes when she turned to him, and he was looking at her as though he didn't believe her.

'Where were you?'

'I told you . . .' Her hands trembled as she hung up the jacket to her suit. He made her feel as though she had somehow betrayed him. 'I was at my mother's.' She tried to make her voice sound calm, but she sounded nervous, even to her own ears.

'Until now? It's six o'clock.' His voice was filled with disapproval, but suddenly she turned on him, her nerves frayed beyond control. She needed time to think, to absorb what she'd been told . . . she needed time to remember.

'Look, I'm sorry I'm late. I told you, I was at my mother's.'

He backed down quietly, but he still looked angry. 'See that it doesn't happen again. I don't know why she keeps you this late. She knows you have important obligations.'

Alexandra clenched her teeth so as not to answer him. Her mother had kept her late so that she could tell her she had been adopted twice . . . and her natural father had murdered her mother . . . that she had two sisters she'd entirely forgotten about . . . little things like that. Nothing important.

She dressed hastily in a black silk dress, and sheer black stockings. She slipped into black satin pumps, washed her face, changed her make-up, re-did her hair and put her lipstick and compact in a black satin handbag. And within twenty minutes she was downstairs again, joining Henri in the front hall as they left for the evening. She barely had time to say good-night to the girls, and when she did, she almost cried. As she looked at them, she was reminded of the sisters she had all but forgotten.

'Be good to each other, you two,' she whispered as she kissed Marie-Louise good-night. 'You don't know how lucky you are to have each other.' And a life such as theirs, filled with people who loved them, safe from harm. She herself had been lucky to be adopted by Margaret and Pierre. But now suddenly, as she looked at Henri, she felt as though she had a guilty secret.

'Why doesn't your mother take her problems to her attorney or her banker?' Henri asked in a voice filled with annoyance as they drove to the restaurant where they were meeting some new acquaintances of Henri.

Alexandra looked vague as she glanced out the window. 'She thought I could help her. That's all.' He laughed, as though it were a ridiculous suggestion.

'She could at least come to me. I could be of assistance.' But she knew perfectly well that Margaret would never go to her husband. They barely tolerated each other.

They arrived at Taillevent, and Alexandra looked around the familiar décor distractedly as Henri led her to their guests and made the necessary introductions. The room was filled with *tout Paris*, men in dark suits, and beautiful, elegantly dressed women. The room was as magnificent as it always was, with the rich panelling, magnificent chandeliers, and goblets filled with fresh flowers. It was a place where only the most elite were able to get in, and even they had to wait months for a reservation.

It was Henri's favourite restaurant, and he enjoyed going there with her and their friends, and even business associates like tonight. The people he was dining with were potential backers for his political career, and Alexandra could sense that the evening was extremely important. But no matter how hard she tried, she found herself unable to concentrate, and by the end of the evening she was near tears, as Henri glared at her, and she fought desperately to stay afloat in the conversation.

'Excuse me?' she said for a least the tenth time that evening. She had totally missed what the woman said . . . had it been something about the south of France? . . . or was it something about her children? 'I'm terribly sorry . . .' Alexandra's eyes filled with tears and she dabbed at her eyes with her napkin, as though she were coughing. She felt as though the evening was never going to end, and Henri was furious with her when they left.

'How could you do that to me?' he railed on the ride home. 'Your attitude was an open insult!'

'Henri, I'm sorry . . . I wasn't feeling well . . . I couldn't concentrate . . . I . . .' But all she could think of was John

Chapman at the Bristol, and how desperately she wanted to call him.

'If you weren't well, you shouldn't have come tonight. You did more harm than good.' He was livid.

'I'm sorry . . . I tried . . . truly I did . . .' There were tears sliding down her cheeks. She hated to let him down, but there was so much on her mind now.

'You have no excuse!' he raged. But she did. And she couldn't tell him. 'I won't tolerate your behaving like that.' And then, the final blow, 'You're always impossible after you've seen your mother.' As though she were a naughty child, and he had a right to scold her.

'My mother has nothing to do with it, Henri.' Alexandra spoke in a quiet voice as she blew her nose, and he glared at her as they stopped at a light on the way home. He didn't even care if their driver heard him.

'Then where were you tonight until six o'clock?' That again. Alexandra only shook her head, and stared out the window, and then looked back at him again.

'I told you. I was at my mother's.'

'Was anyone else there?' He had never been suspicious of her before, and it hurt her deeply.

'Of course not. My God, what do you suspect me of?' She wanted to tell him that she didn't engage in the same sports as he, but she didn't want to open a Pandora's box that would cause even greater problems. She reached out and touched his hand then, but he showed no inclination to soften. 'Henri, please . . .'

'You disgraced me tonight.'

'I'm sorry. I had a terrible headache.'

He never said another word to her, but when they reached the house on the avenue Foch, he courteously opened the door to her, and then went to his own rooms, and firmly closed the door behind him.

Chapter 22

As soon as Henri had left for the office the next morning, Alexandra looked up the number of the Bristol and dialled it. She asked for John Chapman, feeling her hand tremble on the phone, and her voice cracked as she identified herself to him. It was like high espionage, and she was extremely nervous. If Henri had any idea what she was doing, or what she had learned, he would very probably divorce her.

'You've spoken to your mother?' Chapman had a calm, smooth voice, and she found him easy to talk to.

'Yesterday . . . I . . . I had forgotten everything.' Even that she was adopted. She had allowed herself to deny it to herself for all these years . . . not to mention the fact that she'd been adopted once before . . . and Hillie . . . and the woman with red hair . . . But Chapman didn't seem to condemn her.

'Maybe it was easier for you not to remember. There was no reason to.' He paused for a moment, and then spoke to her gently. 'Could we meet some time today? . . . er . . . uh . . . I'm terribly sorry, I don't know your married name. All I know is your mother's name.' He sounded very polite and well bred and well educated. She had been nervous that he might be one of those seedy investigators one saw in B-movies.

'De Morigny. Alexandra de Morigny.' She didn't bother with the title. It seemed very unimportant.

'Thank you. I was hoping we could meet. Perhaps later this morning. I'd like to show you the files I have. Perhaps you have something to add to them ... or in any case, you have a right to know as much as we do.'

'Thank you very much. I could meet you at your hotel ...' She glanced at the clock on her desk, and made a rapid calculation. She had to bathe and dress, and leave instructions for the staff. Henri was having guests for dinner. 'At eleven. Would that be all right?'

'Perfect.' And with luck, he could catch a flight to New York that night. He had a lot of work to do, and he didn't want to cool his heels in Paris forever. 'I'll meet you in the lobby. I'm six feet two, I have blond hair parted on the side, and I'll be wearing a tweed jacket, a blue shirt and grey trousers.' He sounded more like a college student than a private eye, and she smiled as she imagined the outfit. He sounded like one of her American cousins. And then she realized that he didn't know what she looked like.

'I have blond hair too. I'm one metre sixty ...' And then she laughed. 'I'm sorry. I always forget what that is in English. Five foot five, I think. And I'll be wearing a grey suit.' She had a grey silk suit in mind, one that Henri liked, not that it mattered. And when she dressed, she wore it with a pink silk blouse, and a pink Hermès scarf and the Bvlgari coins on her ears that she wore when she didn't want to wear anything flashy. She looked respectable and chic, as she walked slowly into the Bristol, feeling her heart pound as her heels clicked on the marble floor and she glanced around the lobby. She was about to go to the desk and have him paged, but she saw him instantly, sitting quietly in a chair, holding a copy of the Paris *Herald Tribune*, and he stood up and smiled at her, walking towards her on long legs, and with a smile that left her a little breathless. He had perfect teeth, and gentle eyes, and she liked him instantly. He looked as though he would have made a good friend, and she shook hands with him solemnly, trying not to look at the briefcase he carried in his other hand. She knew that within it lay the secrets of her past, and that of her sisters.

'I'm sorry I'm late.' She spoke barely above a whisper, and he sensed easily that she was frightened. 'I drove myself, and I had a terrible time finding a parking place. I finally just gave the car to the doorman.' He nodded, and they sat down in a corner, in two large red velvet chairs that seemed perfectly suited to the occasion.

'Would you like a drink? Or a cup of tea? But she was too nervous to eat or drink, and she shook her head as he pulled the file out of his briefcase. It was much thicker than it had been when Arthur Patterson first gave it to John. There was what he knew of Hilary's life in it now. And soon there would be Alexandra's.

'Thank you, I'm fine.' Her eyes looked deep into his. 'Are you close to finding the others?'

'We hope so. The last trace we have of Hilary was when she went to see Arthur Patterson about twenty years ago, to find you and your younger sister, and she was furious to discover that he hadn't kept track of any of you. I suppose she tried to find you herself, and obviously couldn't. In any case, she held him responsible for the break-up of your family, and I imagine she hates him. And that is not difficult to understand, from what we know of her early life.

'I don't know what's happened to Megan yet, but certainly compared to you, Hilary got the worst deal possible.' He told her what he knew and Alexandra's eyes filled with tears as she listened, thinking of what a terrible fate a life like that would be for anyone. She tried to imagine it happening to her own two little girls, and the very thought made her ill. No wonder Hilary was bitter. She had every right to be. Abandoned, beaten, forgotten. 'I gather that when she went to New York, she went to see Patterson, and after that we've lost her. But I have a very intense investigation going on this week, and I imagine there will be more recent information on Hilary when I get back. We already thought we'd found her once, but it was a mistake.' He was referring to the woman at CBA. But wherever she was, he would find her. 'But next time it won't be.'

'My God, what an awful life.' Alexandra discreetly wiped the tears away and he offered her the file for her own inspection. She could hardly bear what she read, and looked up at him finally with anguish on her face. 'How could she survive it?' Alexandra felt a wave of guilt wash over her as she thought of her own life in comparison to her sister's. 'Why did this happen?'

'I don't know that. The turns of fate are not always kind, Mrs de Morigny.'

'I know.' She spoke softly, but she had never seen it quite so clearly. It was like one of the kaleidoscopes she gave to her children, you turned it just a fraction, and all of the same pieces fell into a totally different pattern. One moment they were flowers, and the next moment they were demons breathing fire. It seemed so wrong to her that Hilary should have been left to the demons. With effort, she turned her thoughts back to John Chapman. 'What can I do to help you find them?'

'Nothing at the moment, unless you remember anything specific that might help us. But your knowledge would have ended a long time ago, I don't think it's of much use now. I'll call you as soon as I've found the others, and Mr Patterson would like you to come to his home in Connecticut to meet them. It's the one thing he wants to do before he dies.' It seemed a noble wish, but less so if you thought of the pain he had caused them.

'What's he like? It's odd, but I don't remember him at all.' Nor did she remember her father. She had glanced at the clippings of Sam in John Chapman's file, and had been struck by how handsome he was, and how successful. There were only two photographs of her mother, one of a smiling young woman with cascading shafts of bright red hair, and in a funny way, she looked a little bit like Alexandra's youngest daughter. And the other photograph showed the three little girls, Alexandra and Hilary, in matching white dresses and shiny black shoes, and the baby in a long ruffled gown in her mother's arms, taken after Megan was born, on the last Easter their mother was alive. It was taken outside their house on Sutton Place, but it didn't look familiar to Alexandra.

Chapman tried to answer her question. 'Mr Patterson is very old, and very sick. I don't think he'll live much longer. He's very anxious to get the three of you together before he dies. It means a great deal to him.'

'And if he dies before you find them?' Alexandra asked bluntly.

'He's made provisions to continue the investigation and bring you together. But he would like to be around to see it.' She nodded. He had thought of everything. It was only a shame he hadn't thought of it thirty years sooner. It would have made a big difference to Hilary. And she said as much to John Chapman. 'If he was so close to my parents, why didn't he take us, and keep us together?'

John Chapman shook his head. 'I don't know. He said something about his wife not feeling able to cope with it. I think he regrets it now. Sometimes we make terrible mistakes, but we only see it in hindsight.' He dared to ask her then what Arthur wanted to know. 'Are you happy,

Alexandra? Forgive me for asking . . .' But it meant a great deal to Arthur. And she smiled at John.

'I have always been very happy. I have been blessed with wonderful parents whom I have loved deeply. Pierre de Borne was a remarkable man, and I'm only grateful he lived as long as he did. He was the joy of my life,' she blushed, 'and I of his.' And then she smiled more broadly. 'And you met my mother yesterday. She's wonderful, isn't she? She's my closest friend and greatest ally. This has been very hard for her.' Alexandra's face sobered as she thought of her mother's tears the day before. 'It was terribly hard for her to remind me of the past. I don't suppose it will be easy for anyone to dredge all this up, particularly given the way it all happened.' She sighed and looked hard at him. 'Does anyone really know why he killed her?'

'Not really.' He shook his head. 'Some sort of an argument, I believe. I think he was drunk. Temporary insanity, as the defence said. Mr Patterson maintains to this day that Sam, your father, adored her.

'It's difficult to understand people giving way to that kind of violence and emotions.'

She nodded, but she was thinking about Hilary and they still hadn't found out about Megan. 'I hope Megan's all right. I hope they both are.' It was as though she knew them now, as though they had already come back to her, like her own children. 'I have two little girls of my own, Axelle and Marie-Louise. It's odd,' she mused thoughtfully, 'I think Marie-Louise looks rather like Hilary.' It was odd too that Alexandra had returned to her mother's native country.

And then Chapman asked her a difficult question. 'Have you told your husband about all this?'

Slowly, she shook her head. 'I'm afraid Henri won't

294

understand it. I think he'll be very upset that my parents didn't tell him when we got married. And until you find the others, there's no point confronting him. It will only make him unhappy.' It was a story she had been telling herself since the night before, and she was almost convinced now.

'And when we find the others?'

'Then I'll have to tell him something.' She smiled uncomfortably. 'I don't normally go off to America at the drop of a hat, Mr Chapman.'

'You did not deceive him, you didn't know all this.' He was trying to soothe her, but she knew better.

'My parents did though. He will be very angry. He believes me to be the daugher of the Comte de Borne. The bloodline means a great deal to Henri. He can trace his family back nine hundred years. I don't really think that a murderer and a French war-bride were exactly what he had in mind for the grandparents of his children.' Perhaps it was just as well they had never had a son. Then he would never forgive her. And perhaps he wouldn't as it was. Chapman felt sorry for her as he watched her face. He sensed that her husband was not an easy person.

'I think he'll adjust. You've obviously been married for a long time. And he loves you. That counts for a lot.'

'Not to everyone, Mr Chapman.' She smiled wistfully. And how could he be so sure that Henri loved her? She wasn't sure of it herself sometimes. He owned her, like a fine piece of Louis-XV furniture, or a very good painting. And if the painting turned out to be a fraud? Would he still love it enough to keep it? She knew some would, but she wasn't at all sure Henri was among them. He was obsessed with quality and veracity and perfection. And she knew now that her pedigree was badly flawed. It was not difficult to imagine Henri's reaction.

Chapman was looking at her gently as they sat quietly in a corner of his hotel, and he realized that he liked her. She was gentle and shy, and she had kind eyes, the kind of eyes he had always wanted to find in a woman. She was so graceful, and so gentle. He hoped that Arthur's investigation was not going to cause her pain. She had done nothing to deserve it.

'May I invite you to lunch, Alexandra? And will you forgive me for being so informal?' He smiled his boyish smile at her and she laughed.

'You know all the secrets of my life. I hardly expect you to call me by my husband's title.'

'Oh dear . . . is he titled too then?'

'Of course.' She laughed again, and when she did she looked so much younger. 'The Baron Henri Edouard Antoine Xavier Saint-Brumier de Morigny. Lovely name, isn't it?' She was almost giggling. It had been a very tense morning, and she needed the relief. They both did.

'Does it all fit on his driver's licence?'

She laughed at the thought. And then sobered. 'And you, Mr Chapman, what do you think of all this? You're an intelligent man. It must all seem rather shocking.'

'Nothing shocks me anymore. I think it's a shame so many lives were destroyed by one act of madness. And in some ways, I think it's a shame to disturb the embers. But it's not for me to make those judgments, and perhaps it will bring some comfort to some of you to be reunited. Are you curious about the others?' She nodded. She had to admit she was.

'I remember Hilary a little bit . . . just flashes and little bits, ever since speaking to my mother yesterday.' And then she sighed. 'It was a tremendous shock for her.'

'And for you too.' There was compassion in his eyes

and he wanted to reach out and touch her hand, but he didn't. 'I'm sorry to cause you so much trouble.'

'You haven't yet.' But he would, when he found the others.

'Can I induce you to have lunch with me, in spite of all that?' He liked her, and funnily enough, he wanted to get to know her. He told himself it was so he could report back to his client, but he knew it was more than that. The pieces of the mystery were beginning to fall into place, and she was a lovely woman, and he liked her.

She hesitated for only a fraction of an instant, calculating what harm it could do, and decided it could do none. 'I'd love it.'

'Any suggestions? I haven't been here recently, and I'm afraid I'm not very much up-to-date on the in places.'

'The best places, Mr Chapman, are the old ones.' She stood up and smiled, and he put everything back in his briefcase and locked it. For an odd moment, she wanted to ask him for the picture of her as a little girl with her sisters, but she imagined that he needed it to show to the others, when he found them. And now suddenly she understood why there were no photographs of her as a baby. She thought of it as they crossed the lobby and he insisted that she call him John, and he noticed an odd look in her eyes then.

'I just realized something I'd never really understood before. My parents have no photographs of me as a baby. And I just accepted it, as though it were normal.'

'You had no reason to doubt them. Where are we going for lunch?'

'I thought we'd have lunch at the Ritz, with all the little old ladies.' She grinned and he laughed as she took his arm and they began walking.

'It sounds delightful.'

'They make me look terribly young and attractive.'

'You are, or haven't you noticed that lately?'

'I try not to look. I only see the wrinkles.' But it was only idle talk, she didn't even look thirty, and she had exquisite skin and silky hair, which reminded him that she looked different than he had expected.

'You know, it's funny. I thought you'd have red hair.'

She smiled guiltily, and looked very feminine, and he was struck again by how pretty she was, in a subtle way. It was almost as though she were trying to hide it, with her ladylike hair-do and subdued clothes. He wondered what she would look like if she really let herself go wild. Probably a great deal like her mother.

'I do have red hair.' The smile dimmed and then faded. 'My husband doesn't like it, so I rinse it blond. Axelle, my younger daughter, has red hair too. But I haven't been a redhead in years. Henri thinks it vulgar.' She said it in a matter-of-fact way and John silently decided that Henri was clearly an idiot.

Their lunch at the Ritz was relaxed and easy and pleasant. They talked about Boston and New York, and Cape Cod and Saint-Jean-Cap-Ferrat, where they each spent their summers. They talked about sailing, and summers as a child, and how he had started his career instead of going into law, as was expected. They were like comfortable old friends, and they were both sorry when she finally left him at his hotel, and she got back into the car she had left with the doorman.

'Call me as soon as you know something, John.'

'I promise.' He touched her hand on the wheel, and then leant in to kiss her cheek. 'Take care of yourself. And I hope next time I see you, you have flaming red hair!' They both laughed, and she waved and drove into the flow of traffic, feeling as though she had made a new friend. He was handsome and charming and bright, and she wondered why he wasn't married. He had said only that he was divorced and had a penchant for difficult women and had let it go at that. But she liked him so much, she couldn't imagine why someone hadn't snatched him up the moment he'd got divorced from his first wife.

But her mind drifted quickly back to the reason he had come to Paris to see her. It was all more than a little bit amazing. And she was stunned to realize as she walked in the door that it was already four o'clock. And she was giving a dinner party that evening. She hastily checked on the flowers and the wines, saw the chef, and glanced around to make sure that everything was in order. And then she went to see her daughters, playing in the garden with a friend. They were excited that school was almost over, and they'd be leaving for Cap Ferrat soon.

At six-thirty, she went to dress, and she heard Henri in his study, but she didn't want to disturb him. Instead she ran her bath and laid out her dress, a white silk floor-length gown. She usually wore it with long diamond earrings that had belonged to Henri's late mother. And she was just taking them out of her jewellery box when the door opened and he strode into the room with a look of fury.

'Hello darling,' she stood up to greet him, but the smile froze on her face when she saw him. 'Is something wrong? I checked everything for tonight and it looked fine to me . . .' But it was obvious that something terrible had happened in the meantime.

'What exactly do you think you're doing, making a fool of me, all over Paris?'

'My God, Henri, what are you talking about?'

'I mean that you were seen today, lunching with a man at the Ritz, thinking you were hiding.'

Her face went very white, but she stood extremely still as she explained it. 'If I thought I were hiding, I would hardly go to the Ritz. It was a business lunch. He's here from New York, on some business matters for my mother.'

'I heard that yesterday, Alexandra. And you won't get away with it twice. But it certainly explains your behaviour last night. You couldn't think straight. Well, I'm not going to tolerate an outrage of this kind. You will leave for Cap Ferrat in the morning.' She was being banished, like a naughty child, and tears filled her eyes at the injustice of what he was thinking.

'Henri, I have never cheated on you. You must believe that.' She didn't dare approach him, and they stood at opposite ends of the room, she in bleak despair, and he in outrage.

'I believed that until now. But you cannot expect me to believe it in this instance.'

'It's true.'

'That's nonsense. And I have every intention of telling your mother what I think of her providing a smokescreen for you. I do not wish to see her at Cap Ferrat this summer.'

'Henri, that's not fair. She wants to see the children . . .'

'She should have thought of that before she began covering for you with your lovers.'

'I don't have any lovers!' Alexandra screamed. 'And my mother has nothing to do with this . . .'

'Aha . . . I thought this was a business matter for her.' He advanced to her slowly, victory in his eyes, and Alexandra sank into a chair, beaten and desperately unhappy.

'It is . . .'

'What kind of business matter is it?' He roughly tilted her chin up so she had to face him, but he knew she wasn't entirely telling him the truth, and she could do nothing about it. To tell him the whole truth would have been far worse. She knew that.

'I can't explain it right now. It's all confidential business matters of my parents.' She looked pale and shaken, and he stalked out of the room again, and then turned to look at her from the doorway.

'I never would have expected this of you, Alexandra. See to it that it never happens again, or you will be going back to your mother's house, *without your daughters*. Have your things packed for the Riviera by noon tomorrow.' And with that he slammed the doors to her boudoir, and she sat and sobbed in despair. She had had such a pleasant time with John, and it was all so harmless, and now Henri thought she was cheating on him. And then suddenly, she realized she had to call him. She went hastily to the phone on her desk, and called the Bristol. Fortunately, he was there, and she was able to tell him that they were leaving for Cap Ferrat several weeks early, in case he needed to reach her. She gave him the number and thanked him for lunch again, never letting on for a moment how much pain it had just caused her.

'I hope I'll be in touch with you again soon.'

'So do I.' But she was ashamed for thinking it for several reasons. He was so kind and so understanding. But he had his own life to lead, and so did she. She had enough trouble without indulging in fantasies about him.

'I'll call as soon as I hear something.'

'Thank you, John. Have a good trip back.'

'I will. I'm leaving in the morning.' He had hoped to get on a flight that night, but he had returned to the hotel so late after lunch that he was no longer in the mood to pack and run, and he decided that a last night in Paris wouldn't do any harm. He was feeling relaxed and pleased after his lunch with Alexandra, and when he'd called Sasha from the hotel she was in one of her impossible moods. He was suddenly in no hurry to get back. He was looking forward to dinner at a bistro nearby, and a pleasant stroll through the streets of Paris.

He said goodbye to Alexandra and she hung up and walked slowly into her bathroom, unable to believe that Henri so easily thought the worst of her, and wondering what the summer would be like now. But she got a taste of it that night. He spoke to her in tones of ice, and until the next morning when she and the girls left, he treated her like a pariah.

'You will do no entertaining until I arrive, is that clear? You are to stay *in* the villa, and I will call you.' He treated her like a convict who had attempted to escape and her own fury was building slowly as they said goodbye the next morning.

'May I go to the beach, or should I stay in my room wearing a ball and chain?'

'I'm sorry you feel our marriage such a burden, Alexandra. I never realized it caused you such anguish.' He had an answer to everything and for the first time she hated him as they drove away. The chauffeur and two maids were accompanying them on the trip, and they were putting the Citroën and the Peugeot station wagon on the overnight train to the Riviera.

'Why was Papa in such a bad mood?' Axelle inquired as they drove through the traffic to the station. 'Was he mad at you?'

'Just a little bit.' She smoothed the coppery curls as Hilary had done for her so long ago, and she smiled now at the distant memory of her sister. She was excited now at the prospect of seeing them again. She just hoped that Chapman would find them soon, and that she would be able to get away to see them. But Axelle didn't give her the time to ponder it as they drove through Paris.

'Papa didn't look a "little bit" mad to me. He looked *very* mad. Did you do something terrible, Maman?' Alexandra smiled and took Axelle's hand in her own. It was going to be nice to get to the Riviera, and perhaps nice too to have a few weeks' breather from her husband.

'I only did something a little bit foolish.'

'Like when you bought the hat he hated with all feathers and the veil?' Axelle had loved it, and Henri had made Alexandra send it back the same day.

'Something like that.'

'Did you buy another hat?'

'Hmm . . . yes . . . uh . . . sort of . . .'

'Was it pretty?'

'Oh yes,' Alexandra smiled at her younger child, 'very.'

Axelle smiled up at her with obvious pleasure as they reached the station.

Chapter 23

The material they had dug up on Hilary in John's absence was excellent and he was immensely pleased. They had found her enrolment in night school, her job at the employment agency, and from there they had followed her to CBA. It was perfect. They had everything they needed, and as Chapman looked through the file, he realized that they had been right the first time. It *was* the right Hilary Walker he'd spoken to when he called her at CBA, and it was equally obvious she didn't want to be found. So be it, he would wait until he found Megan, and then confront her himself. For the moment, he would let her think she had lost him.

But as he thought of her, he felt that same odd tug in his heart he felt every time he read her file. He wanted to tell her that everything was all right, that people still cared about her, that she could stop running. It was terrible to think about her angry and alone, and then he realized that there might be a lot more to her current life than he knew. He ordered his assistant to begin a fullscale investigation of Hilary Walker at CBA Network. She could be married, divorced, have six children of her own. The broken little girl he had been following from Boston to Jacksonville to New York might well be leading a happy life now. And for the most part, he hoped so. And yet, he knew that he would not feel at peace about her until he met her. It was crazy, but he was obsessed by the women in his case, their lives, and their good and bad fortunes. So much so that he called his ex-wife, and asked her to lunch, and tried to press her into explaining to him again how she felt about her characters when she was writing.

'Do you ever fall in love with them, Ellie?' He looked at her in confusion, as they sat next to the fountain at the Four Seasons. It was where all the city's publishing notables ate lunch and he knew it was her favourite place, even though he still preferred the sensual, artsy chaos of the Russian Tea Room. But Eloise was a different girl. She was tall and cool and controlled, she had masterminded a successful career and done it brilliantly, and she seemed better suited to the cool marble and discreet fountains of the Four Seasons.

'Fall in love with them? What do you mean? Are you thinking of writing a book?' She looked amused and he shook his head.

'No, I'm just working on this crazy investigation. It goes back about thirty years, and the people are so damn real to me, I can't think straight anymore. I dream about them at night . . . I think about them in the daytime . . . little girls who are practically middle-aged women now tear at my heart and I want to help them.'

'It sounds more like food poisoning than love,' she grinned, and then she reached out and patted his hand sympathetically. She still liked him. They had lunch with each other a couple of times a year, and he had even introduced her to Sasha, but Eloise had told him bluntly on the phone the next day that she thought he could do a lot better. 'You got it bad, kid. Sounds like you ought to write a book about it.'

'No one would believe the story. And besides, I can't.

That's not my bag. You know that. It's just that it's driving me crazy. How can people on paper become real?'

'Somehow they do.'

'Do they finally go away?'

'Yes, when you resolve it,' she said reassuringly, eating her salad. 'When I finish a book, the characters finally disappear. For good. But before that, it's like being haunted.'

'That's it!' He waved his fork at her. 'That's it exactly!' He was being haunted by Hilary, and when he wasn't being tormented by Hilary, he was thinking of Alexandra. He had called her as soon as he was sure that it was Hilary at the network, and she had been jubilant. Now she was waiting for news of Megan, and John had been putting pressure on all his operatives to speed it up, because Patterson seemed to be fading. 'What do I do to get rid of this thing?'

'Finish it. Wind up the case, do whatever you have to do, and then it'll go away. That's how it works for me. Is it a tough case?' Unlike Sasha, she was always interested, but then she was always looking for new stories.

'Very. But we're two-thirds there. I just have to find one more piece of the puzzle and we've got it. It's kind of an exotic tale, I'll tell you about it when the case is closed.'

'I could use a good story. I'm starting a new one next week. I rented a place on Long Island for the summer.' It was amazing. The woman worked like a fiend, but it was obvious that she loved it. And then she grinned at her ex-husband. Their relationship was more like brother and sister now that they were no longer married. 'How's your ballerina?' She said it without venom. She wished him well. She hadn't been crazy about the girl when she met her, but she knew he was.

But he shrugged as he answered. 'So-so. People involved

in ballet seem to live in their own world. She doesn't have a great grasp on reality, mine anyway.'

'Worse than writers?' Eloise smiled.

'Much worse. At least you didn't complain about your feet night and day, and worry about every muscle in your body. Just breathing is a threat to them, they might do something to themselves that could keep them from dancing.'

'Sounds exhausting.' She finished her salad, took a sip of wine, and smiled at him. He was one of the nicest people she knew, and sometimes she was sorry they hadn't stayed married. She wondered if she should have tried harder but she was also smart enough to know it wasn't in her. And it wouldn't have been right for them. She needed to be alone with her work, and she had always felt he should be married and have children. 'Somehow I don't see her as the final answer for you.'

'Neither do I. But it's taken me a while to see that. There aren't a hell of a lot of people out there who intrigue me. Most of them aren't too bright, or they're not nice, or they really don't give a damn about anyone but themselves.' Without meaning to, he realized he had just described Sasha. She had been wearing thin on him ever since he'd got back from Paris. 'What about you? Prince Charming heading toward you on the horizon?'

She shrugged with an easy smile, and waved at a publisher she knew. 'I don't have time for much of that stuff. Nothing much has changed as far as that goes. It's hard to have a career and a real life.'

'But it *can* be done,' he always pointed out to her, 'if you want to.'

'Maybe I don't.' She was always honest with him. 'Maybe I don't want more than I've got. My typewriter and my old nightgowns.'

307

'El, that's terrible. It's a hell of a waste.'

'No, it's not. I never really wanted all that other stuff. I would have hated having kids.'

'Why?' It seemed so wrong to him. People were meant to have children. He had wanted one for the past twenty years. It just hadn't worked out for him to have one.

'They're too demanding. Too distracting. I'd have to give too much of myself. That's why I was such a lousy wife to you. I wanted to save it all for my books. I guess that's crazy, but it makes me happy.' And he knew it did. They were both better off the way things were now. And then suddenly he laughed.

'You were always too damn honest. I was just going to tell you I met a great woman in this case.' Eloise raised an eyebrow with interest. 'She just happens to be married to a French baron, and not exactly available.'

'She sounds a lot better than your ballerina.'

'She is. But she's totally wrapped up in her proper life. It's a damn shame too . . . she's lovely.'

'You'll find the right one, one of these days. Just stay away from the artsy ones. They make lousy wives. Take it from me. I know!' She smiled ruefully, and leaned over to kiss his cheek as they left the table.

'Don't be so hard on yourself. We were both young.'

'And you were terrific.' She stopped to say hello to her editor-in-chief, and they walked out into the sunshine together. Then John wished her luck on her new book, hailed a cab for her, and walked back to his office on East Fifty-seventh.

And there was a windfall for him when he got back to the office. One of his assistants had found the Abramses in San Francisco.

'Are you serious?' He was jubilant. They had tried everything and turned up nothing. But they had finally

308

given up looking for David, and in doing so had found Rebecca. It turned out that they had left Los Angeles in the early sixties and gone to the deep South to march with Martin Luther King and participate in sit-ins and voter registration campaigns. They had provided free legal service to blacks in Georgia, Louisiana, and Mississippi, and had eventually set up a fullscale legal aid office in Biloxi. And eventually from there they had gone to Atlanta. It was only in 1981 they had finally gone back to California, but David had retired after extensive surgery, and Rebecca had joined an exclusively female practice in San Francisco, to defend women involved in feminist causes. For all their lives, they had been the classic liberals.

John's assistant had explained nothing to them. John had left strict orders that once Megan was located he would make contact. He had his secretary make an appointment with Rebecca Abrams, and he was set to fly out the following afternoon, which was perfect. Sasha was still on tour, and there was something he had wanted to do for days. It was something he hadn't done himself in years, but he knew now that he had to do it. It was part of what he had tried to explain to Eloise at lunch . . . part of being haunted.

He left the office just before four o'clock and took a cab to the network. He flashed a security badge and a police pass downstairs, both of which had been hard-earned and almost impossible to come by, and the network security were satisfied and instantly let him into the inner sanctum.

He took the lift upstairs, and waited inconspicuously in the reception area. He picked up a phone there and dialled her extension, and her secretary told him she was in a meeting.

'In her office, or upstairs?' He sounded like someone

who knew and the secretary was quick to give him the information.

'She's here. She's with Mr Baker.'

'Any idea what time she'll be through?'

'She said she's leaving at five-thirty.'

'Thanks.' Chapman hung up the house phone and the secretary had no idea who had phoned, but she assumed that it was someone who knew Hilary, obviously someone higher up at the network.

She came out at exactly five-fifteen, and John recognized her at once, even without the receptionist's good-night as she sped past. 'Good-night, Miss Walker.' Hilary turned to glance at her sharply and then nodded, she didn't seem to notice anyone else in the waiting area, or John as he followed her to the lifts and stepped into one beside her. He almost felt weak at the sight of her, he could see every strand of the shining black hair twisted into a knot, the graceful hands, the long neck, he could even smell the crisp scent of her perfume. She walked with a sure step, a long stride, and when he bumped into her once, she looked up at him with green eyes that pierced straight to his soul, eyes that said don't touch me, don't ever come near me. She got on a bus on Madison Avenue, instead of fighting for a cab, and she got out at Seventy-ninth Street. She walked two blocks further north, and then he realized she was going to a doctor's appointment. He waited patiently outside, and then followed her again when she took a cab and went to Elaine's where she met another woman. He sat in a booth close to theirs, and was intrigued by what might be said. The other woman was a well-known anchor from the network, and she looked upset. She started to cry once, and Hilary looked unmoved. She watched her, unhappy, but not sympathetic. And then finally John remembered as the two women shook hands outside the restaurant, that the woman who was the anchor had been fired when he was in Paris. It had created an enormous stir, and she was either pleading with Hilary for her job, or telling her side of the story. Her firing had supposedly come from higher up, but maybe she thought if she could gain Hilary's ear, she might get back in. But it was obvious from the unhappy look on Hilary's face as she walked slowly downtown alone, that she couldn't help her. She stopped to glance in shop windows once or twice, and walked with a purposeful stride, yet a feminine sway to her hips, which kept him riveted as he watched her. She turned on Seventy-second Street finally and walked all the way to the river, to an old brownstone set near a tiny park. It was a pretty place, yet everything he sensed about her told him she was lonely. She had a solitary air, and a kind of hardness and determination about her that suggested walls she had built long before and never taken down since. As he had when he read her file, he felt intensely sorry for her, and he felt sad as he walked the few blocks back to his own apartment. She lived so nearby, yet she seemed to exist in a universe of her own, a universe filled with work and little else, and yet it was not fair for him to make that judgment. Maybe she was happy after all, maybe she had a boyfriend she was deeply in love with, but everything about her present and her past suggested a solitary person with no one to love and no one who loved her. And when he walked into his apartment and turned on the light, he had an overwhelming urge to call her, to hold out a hand, to become her friend, to tell her that Alexandra still cared . . . all was not lost . . . yet . . . or maybe she wouldn't care. As he had explained to Eloise at lunch, he felt as though he were being haunted.

He tried to get some sleep, but he tossed and turned, and finally, for lack of something better to do, he turned on the light and called Sasha in Denver. She was in her room, she had just got in from the concert hall and her feet were killing her.

'I'm glad nothing's changed.' He laughed as he lay on his back, thinking of her. He wondered if he'd been too hard on her when he talked about her at lunch. She still excited him in some ways, and that night he missed her. 'Want to meet me in San Francisco?'

'When?' she sounded non-committal.

'I'm going tomorrow. I should be through in a couple of days. When do you finish in Denver?'

'Tomorrow. We go to Los Angeles. San Francisco cancelled.'

'I'll meet you in LA.'

'I don't think you should.' There was a long silence, and he frowned.

'What's up?'

'It might upset some of the other dancers,' she said vaguely and he sat up slowly in bed. He was no fool, and he had played this game before. But it was not a game he liked playing.

'Would it upset anyone in particular, Sasha?'

'Oh I don't know. It's too late to talk about it tonight.' And as she said it, he heard a male voice in the background.

'Is that Dominic, or Pierre, or Petrov?'

'It's Ivan,' she said petulantly. 'He pulled a hamstring tonight, and he was very upset.'

'Tell him I'm sorry. But tell him after you explain to me what the hell's going on. Sash, I'm too old for this kind of bullshit.'

'You don't understand the pressures of being a dancer,' she whined into the phone, and he sank back against his pillows.

'Well, I've tried for chrissake. What is it that I don't understand exactly?'

'Dancers need other dancers.'

'Ah ... now we get to the root of the problem. You mean like Ivan?'

'No, no ... well ... yes ... but it's not what you think.'

'How the hell do you know what I think, Sasha? You're so busy worrying about yourself and your feet and your ass and your tendons you wouldn't notice what anyone thought if they wrote it out in neon.'

'That's not fair!' She was suddenly crying, and for the first time in months he found he didn't care. Suddenly, in the space of one phone call, it was over. He had had it.

'It may not be fair, baby,' he spoke in his deep, gentle voice, 'but it happens to be true. I think maybe you and I had better take our bows, and step back gracefully while the curtain comes down. If I read the programme correctly, the fourth act just ended.'

'Why don't we talk when I get back?'

'About what? Your feet? ... or about how dancers need other dancers? I'm not a dancer, Sash. I'm a man. I have a very demanding job, I have a full life I want to share with a woman I love and who loves me. I even want to have children. Can you see yourself doing that?'

'No.' At least she was honest. The thought of it horrified her. She had no intention of giving up dancing for a year at any point in her life, and then fighting to get back all her muscles. 'Why is that so important?'

'Because it just is, and I'm forty-two years old. I can't waste my time with games like this anymore. I gave to the artistic community once. I made my contribution. Now I want something different.'

'That's what I mean ... you don't understand the

pressures of being a dancer. John, babies aren't important.'

'They are to me, little one. And so are a lot of other things you don't have room for. You don't need me. You don't need anyone. Be honest with yourself.' There was a long empty silence as she listened, and suddenly he wanted to get off the phone. There was nothing left to say. They had said it all, and run out of words a long time since. They just hadn't noticed. 'Goodbye, Sash . . . take it easy. I'll see you when you get back. Maybe we'll have lunch or a drink.' He knew she'd want the things she'd left in his apartment, but the truth was that he wasn't even anxious to see her.

'Are you really telling me it's over?' She sounded shocked and he could hear the male voice in the background again. He wondered if they were sharing a room, not that it really mattered.

'I guess I am.'

'Is that why you called me?'

'No. I guess it just happened. It was time.'

'Is there someone else?' He smiled at the question.

'Not really.' In a funny way there were three of them, the three women he was searching for day and night who filled his thoughts and his heart now, but not in the way Sasha had meant it.

'No one important . . . take it easy, Sash.' And with that, he quietly hung up and turned out the light. And he smiled to himself as he went back to sleep. He felt free for the first time in months, and he was glad he had called her. It was finally over.

Chapter 24

The flight to San Francisco was easy and he arrived at two in the afternoon, local time, which gave him plenty of time to get to Rebecca's office at four o'clock. When he got there, it was an old Victorian in a run-down neighbourhood. But he was surprised when he stepped inside, to find the house well maintained, pleasantly decorated, and filled with plants, and Rebecca Abrams herself was an attractive woman. She was in her early sixties and wore her grey hair in a single braid down her back. She wore clean blue jeans and a starched white shirt, red espadrilles and a red flower in her hair, and she looked like a very attractive, very intelligent, well-preserved elderly hippie. She smiled warmly at John, and ushered him into her office. She had no idea what he wanted, and didn't look perturbed when he left his suitcase in her outer office.

'You don't look like most of our clients, Mr Chapman.' She smiled warmly at him and pointed to a sunny little kitchen off her office. 'Would you like some coffee or tea? We have about a dozen different kinds of herb tea.' She smiled at him again and he shook his head. He hated to upset her, but he suspected that he was going to.

'I'm here on a personal matter, Mrs Abrams. I've been looking for you and your husband for quite some time, and I had a little trouble finding you. My last address for you was in New York, in 1957.'

Rebecca Abrams smiled again, and sat back peacefully in her chair. She had been doing yoga for years, and it showed in her tranquil manner. 'We've moved around quite a bit over the years. We spent a lot of time in the south, and then we came back here when my husband got ill. He had a quadruple bypass six and a half years ago, and we both decided that it was time for him to take it easy and enjoy life. So now I'm practising solo, or rather with a group of women I enjoy very much. But it's a different kind of practice than I had with David, although some of the concepts aren't so different. We deal with a lot of cases that involve discrimination and civil rights. We've been doing this for many years.'

'And your husband?'

'He teaches twice a week, at Boalt. He gardens. He's busy doing a thousand things he enjoys.'

'And your daughter?' Chapman held his breath.

'She's fine. She's still in Kentucky. How do you know our family, Mr Chapman?' She frowned slightly but the smile still didn't leave her eyes.

'I don't. I'm afraid I come to you rather indirectly. I'm an attorney too, and I run a firm called Chapman Associates in New York. Unlike you, I've never been terribly in love with the law, and I got hooked on investigations years ago, so that's what I do. And my client, in this case, is Arthur Patterson. I don't know if the name rings a bell, but he was instrumental in bringing Megan to you in 1958. I'm sure that now you remember.'

She nodded, the smile had faded now in earnest. 'Is something wrong? Why would Mr Patterson wish to contact us now?' She looked frightened, as though he could still take her away from them. That was what she had always been afraid of.

'Simply put, Mrs Abrams, he's dying. And he wants to

know that the girls are all right, that they're happy and well, and not in any kind of need. And he hopes to bring them together once before he dies, so that they have the benefit of knowing their sisters.'

'Now?' She looked horrified. 'After thirty years? Why would they possibly want to meet their sisters?' She looked as though she were about to throw him out of her office.

'He felt it might mean something to them, and I can appreciate your feelings. Thirty years is a long time to wait before having any contact.'

She shook her head as though in disbelief. 'We told him at the time of the adopting that we wanted no continued contact with him or the other girls. That was the main reason why we left New York and went to LA. I don't think it would be fair to Megan to drag her past out now.'

'Maybe she should make that choice. You mentioned that she is still in Kentucky.'

'She's finishing her residency there, in Appalachia. She's a doctor. She's specialized in obstetrics.' Rebecca said it with deep pride, but she looked at John with open hostility.

'May I contact her there?' To him it was a formality, but to her it was an offence and she half rose in her seat as she answered.

'No, you may not, Mr Chapman.' She sat back down again and glared at him in outrage. 'I can't believe you'd come to us after all these years and expect us to expose Megan to that pain and confusion. Are you aware of the cause of her parents' death?'

'I am. Is Megan?'

'Of course not. In fact, I will tell you very bluntly, Mr Chapman, this whole thing is totally out of the question. My daughter doesn't know she's adopted.' She looked him straight in the eye and he felt his heart stop. How could they not tell her? As liberal as they were, and as free-thinking, they had never told her she was adopted. It certainly complicated the matter for them.

'Do you have other children, Mrs Abrams?'

'No we don't. And my husband and I felt she had no need to know. She is our only child, and she came to us when she was a baby. There was absolutely no reason to tell her as she got older.'

'Would you be willing to tell her now?' He looked deep into her eyes and was frightened of what he saw there. Rebecca Abrams was not going to make this any easier for him. But at least he knew where Megan was now. If he had to, he would find her in Kentucky. It seemed a cruel thing to do, but she had a right to know about her sisters.

Rebecca hesitated for a long time. 'I don't know, Mr Chapman. Honestly, I don't think so. I'm going to have to discuss this with my husband, and with his doctor first. He's not well, and I don't want to upset him.'

'I understand. Will you get back to me in a day or two? I'm staying at the Mark Hopkins.'

'I'll get back to you when I can.' She stood up to indicate that the interview was over, and she might as well have been wearing a navy-blue pin-stripe suit. She looked as formidable as if she'd been wearing one. 'Will you be going back to New York in the meantime?'

'I'd rather wait for the answer here, in case your husband would like to see me.'

'I'll let you know.' She shook his hand, but the look in her eyes was not warm as she led him to the door and closed it behind him. And when she went back to her desk after he was gone, she put her head down on her arms and cried. It was thirty years later, but they were still going to try to take away her baby. They were going to awake a curiosity she had never had, and bonds she never knew, and introduce her to blood relatives she had never longed for. It wasn't fair after all they had done for her, and given how much they loved her.

She went to see David's doctor that afternoon, and he felt that David was strong enough to hear the news. But it took her two days to get up the courage to tell him, and when she did she sobbed in his arms, and poured out all her fears and he stroked the long grey hair and held her close and told her how much he loved her.

'No one's going to take Meg away from us, sweetheart. How could they?' He was touched by her reaction. When Megan had been a little girl, she had worried about the same things. She had wanted Megan to be theirs, and no one else's.

'All of a sudden, she'll want to know everything about her biological parents.'

'So we'll tell her.'

'But what if she feels different about us after that?'

'You know better than that, Becky. Why should she? She loves us too. In all the important senses of the word, we're her parents. She knows what that means as well as we do. But that doesn't mean she won't want to see her sisters. If someone told me tomorrow I had two sisters I'd never known, I'd want to see them too, but it wouldn't make me love you any less, or Megan.' But Rebecca was still frightened and they talked about it long into the night. Rebecca wanted to keep their pact of silence, and David felt that they owed it to Megan to tell her. It took them another full day to resolve it. And when they finally called, John felt relief sweep over him, he had been going crazy in his hotel room. But he didn't want to leave until he knew where things stood; and he didn't want to press them.

She invited him to come to their house in Tiburon that night, and the three of them talked for a long time about the difficulties of telling Megan after so many years that she was adopted, and it was obvious that Rebecca was still fearful, but David was both adamant and supportive. He told John that his only request was that they wanted to tell Megan themselves, and in person. She was due home in two weeks for a brief vacation, and they would tell her then. They would call him as soon as she knew, and he was welcome to speak to her after that and set up the meeting that Arthur Patterson wanted so badly. And John had no recourse but to accept. They had all the cards in their hands and he wanted to do the right thing for them, and for Megan.

He went home that weekend, and called Arthur Patterson at home. It was obvious that he was not doing well, and John knew he had given up going to the office. He explained that he had found the Abramses, and that they wanted to tell Megan themselves. It meant waiting two weeks, but Chapman felt there was no choice. It was the only decent thing to do, and Arthur reluctantly agreed, and hoped he would live long enough to complete his mission.

'What's left to do now?' he asked John.

'Wait to hear from them. Then I'll set up the meeting with Megan and the others. Alexandra is ready to come when I call her, and I still have to deal with Hilary. But I don't want to do that until the last minute.' He instinctively sensed that the later he did it, the more likely she might be to come to the meeting. 'That gives us another two weeks to cool our heels. I'll let you know if I hear anything sooner.'

'Thank you, John.' And then, unexpectedly. 'You've done a fine job. I'm amazed that you've found them.'

'So am I.' John smiled at his end. He had never really thought he would, and he had . . . and in a few weeks they would be back together, and his job would be over. Part of him felt bereft at the thought, and another part felt relieved and he thought of what Eloise had said when they had lunch. He would be free when it was over.

Chapter 25

The call came from the Abramses in two and a half weeks, as promised, and John could tell from the strain in David's voice that telling Megan hadn't been easy for them.

'She took it very well.' His voice broke, 'We were very proud of her . . . we always have been . . .' and then he went on, sounding stronger. 'She said she'd call you herself when she gets back to Kentucky, if you'd like to talk to her.'

'Would it be possible for me to talk to her now?' John asked carefully and David had conferred with someone at the other end and then handed the phone to someone, whose voice John recognized within moments. Without the French accent, she sounded just like Alexandra, she had the same intonations, the same voice, the same laughter.

'Mr Chapman?'

'Yes.'

'This is all something of a surprise.' She sounded matter-of-fact, and young, but very pleasant.

'I'm sorry about that. I truly am.'

'It couldn't be helped, I understand you wanted to speak to me.'

'I did. I was hoping to meet you in Kentucky briefly before I set up the meeting. When do you suppose you could come to Connecticut to meet with the others?'

'I won't know that till I get back. My schedule won't be set until the day I return. But I could call you then, if you like.'

'I'd appreciate it very much.' And she did. She called punctually the day she arrived, and John wondered if that meant she was anxious to meet the others or if she was just that kind of person.

She told him that she would be free to see him, in Kentucky, that Sunday afternoon, between one and five. And she would be able to come to Connecticut for two days three weeks later, but no sooner.

Chapman frowned as he listened to her, wondering if Arthur would live that long, and he shared his concerns with her.

'I can try and trade with one of the other docs, but it won't change things by more than a few days. We're terribly understaffed, and you'll see what we're up against when you come down here.'

'You could make it in three weeks though?'

'I could. Unless there were a major emergency, but I can never predict that.'

'I understand.' She was businesslike and very firm for a young woman of thirty, and while she had the same voice, she seemed very different from the others. She was intent on a single purpose, and she had been brought up with values and traditions much different from those of Hilary or Alexandra. She was hell-bent on helping unfortunates and fighting the war on poverty. It was something Alexandra had certainly never thought of, and Hilary had been far too busy surviving to concern herself with the more esoteric problems of the masses. It was intriguing how different they were. And John remembered something Alexandra had said to him in Paris.

The kaleidoscope had taken yet another turn and

produced a totally different image . . . this time the demons had been turned into snow-covered mountains.

He agreed to come to Kentucky the following Saturday afternoon, and would meet her at the hospital during her free time. He thanked her for spending it with him, and he confirmed the meeting with her sisters. They set it for September first, and he called Arthur as soon as he hung up. And the following morning he called Alexandra on the Riviera. They had a terrible connection but eventually the line cleared and she could hear him.

'Already?' She sounded excited. 'You've found them both?' It was amazing. 'Where was Megan?'

He smiled at her gentle voice. She already spoke of her like a sister she had never lost, who had merely been gone on a long vacation. 'She's a doctor in Kentucky.'

'Oh my God. And Hilary's all right?'

'Yes. I've seen her.'

'Has she agreed to come on the first?' She held her breath waiting for the answer, and her hopes were dashed as soon as John told her he hadn't called her.

'I don't want to give her too much time to think about it. I'll give her a call in a week or so.'

'What if she goes away?' Alexandra was worried.

'Don't worry. I'll find her.' They both laughed and a moment later they hung up, and Alexandra hurriedly called her mother. She was staying at Cap d'Antibes, at the Hôtel du Cap where she always stayed. And Henri had finally relented on her exile.

'Maman?'

'Yes, darling, is something wrong?' Alexandra sounded breathless, and suddenly very young, like one of her own daughters.

'He's found them both.'

'Both what?' She had just got up and was drinking her

coffee and reading the *Herald Tribune*. She couldn't imagine what Alexandra might have lost that someone else might have found. 'What on earth are you talking about?'

'My sisters! Chapman found them both!' She sounded ecstatic and Margaret's blood suddenly ran cold. She had somehow hoped that he wouldn't find them.

'How nice.' She tried to force herself to sound happy. 'Are they well?'

'One of them is a doctor, the younger one, and the other one, Hilary, works for a television network in New York.'

'They sound like quite an illustrious group. And you're a baroness. They ought to make a film about you.' But she was not amused, and Alexandra knew it.

'Don't worry, Maman. It's not going to change anything. Please know that.'

Margaret wished she could be sure of that. Her fears were not so different from those of Rebecca Abrams. 'When are you meeting them?'

'On the first of September. I just got the call. I'm going to Connecticut.'

'What are you going to tell Henri?'

'I haven't figured that out yet. I thought maybe I'd tell him I was going with you . . . or perhaps on business for you.'

'He won't believe that.'

'No. But I can hardly tell him the truth. I'll think of something.' They talked for a moment longer and then hung up, and five minutes later Margaret called her back, and her first words stunned Alexandra.

'I'm going with you.'

'What? . . . Maman . . . you can't . . .'

'Why not?' She had made up her mind, and thought it an excellent idea, aside from providing Alexandra with the alibi that she needed. Besides, that way she could keep an eye on things, and stay close to Alexandra. She was desperately afraid of that meeting.

'It's such a lot of trouble for you. You weren't even going back to Paris until the end of September. You told me you were going to Rome for a few weeks.'

'So? I can go to Rome in October. Or on the way back from New York. All I wanted to do was visit Marisa' — one of her oldest friends — 'and buy some decent shoes. But I'd much rather go to New York with you,' and then, almost shyly, '. . . if you'll have me.'

'Oh Mother . . .' Tears sprang to her eyes as she thought of it. She sensed how frightened Margaret was, but she didn't need to be. No one, no blood relative, no husband, no friend, could ever replace her. 'Of course I'd love you to come. It just seems like such an imposition.'

'Don't be ridiculous. I'd be a nervous wreck if I stayed here.' And then she had a totally crazy idea, but she liked it. 'Shall we take Axelle and Marie-Louise?' Alexandra's face lit up at the thought. She didn't like just leaving them at the end of the summer, even for only a few days. And Henri couldn't possibly object to a family trip like that.

'That's a wonderful idea. The three of you can stay in New York while I go to Connecticut, and then we can all have a little fun before we go back to Paris. The girls don't start school until the eleventh.'

'Marvellous, I'll call the Pierre and make the reservations today. You call the airlines. What day will we arrive?'

'Friday is the first . . . maybe we should fly on Thursday, the thirty-first of August.'

'Perfect. I'll make reservations for ten days. We can always change them if you want to come back sooner.'

'Maman . . .' There was a lump in her throat the size of

326

a fist as she thought of the only mother she had ever known. 'I love you.'

'Everything's going to be fine, darling. Just fine.' And for the first time since John Chapman had appeared at the rue de Varenne, she really thought so.

Alexandra didn't say anything to Henri for another week. And then she mentioned it casually to him one afternoon as they lay on the terrace.

'My mother wants me to go to New York with her, at the end of the summer.' She said it easily but he looked up at her angrily. He was still angry at her for her supposed transgression before they'd left Paris. They had never discussed it again, but she knew he hadn't forgiven her.

'What's that all about now?'

'Nothing. She has some business to take care of in New York. Some investments of her family's that need looking into, and she asked me to come along and bring the girls.'

'That's ridiculous. Why would you go to New York in August?' He was suspicious of both of them, and the plot they were obviously cooking up against him.

'It's actually not till the very end of August. And it might be fun for the girls to do something a little different.'

'Nonsense. You can go to New York some other time, this winter without the children.' But the harshness of his words sent a chill down her spine. He didn't know it, but nothing was going to stop her from going, or from taking her children with her.

'No, Henri. I'm going now. With my mother. *And* the children.'

He bolted to a sitting position and stared at her angrily. 'Aren't you getting rather independent suddenly, Alexandra? May I remind you that I make the decisions here, for you, as well as the children.' He had never put it quite so bluntly, but it was true, or had been until then. But slowly, things had begun to change, since John Chapman had come to Paris.

'I don't think this is worth getting excited about, Henri. It's an invitation from my mother, for myself and the girls.'

'And if I forbid you to go?' His face was red with unspent fury, and her shocking behaviour.

'I will have to go anyway. My mother has asked me to come with her.'

'Your mother is not an invalid. I'll call her myself and tell her you're not going.' But this time Alexandra stood up and faced him. She spoke in a quiet voice, but there was no mistaking the steel beneath the velvet.

'I do not wish to disobey you, but I must go to New York with my mother.'

'Why? Tell me that. Give me one valid reason.'

'It's too complicated to explain. It's all family business.'

'Alexandra, you're lying to me.' He was right, but she had no choice, the truth was too frightening to share with him.

'Please don't say that. I won't be gone long. Just a few days.'

'Why, dammit, why?' He pounded his fist on the glass table and she jumped.

'Henri, please, you're being unreasonable.' And she was frightened that he could force her to tell him. 'My mother wants to visit her family, and she wants me to come along. There's nothing wrong with that.'

'What's wrong with it is that I didn't say you could go, and I see no reason for you to do so.'

'Perhaps because I want to.'

'You don't make those kinds of decisions for yourself. You are not a single woman.'

'Nor am I a slave. You can't decide everything for me, for heaven's sake. This is the twentieth century, not the Dark Ages.'

'And you are not some sort of modern Women's Libber to do as you please. Or if that's what you wish, Alexandra, you may not do it under my roof. Please keep that in mind before you start making your own travel arrangements.'

'This is ridiculous. You act as though I've committed a crime.'

'Not at all. But it is I who decide what you'll do when. That's how it's been for fourteen years, and I see no reason to change it.'

'And if I do?' she asked ominously. For the first time in her life the way he treated her truly rankled. She knew he was a kind and decent man, but he ran her life in such a way that she was no longer happy with it. And what's more, he knew it.

'You'll have trouble with me if you try out this independence. I'm warning you now.'

'And I'm telling you, as politely as I can, that I'm going to New York with my mother on the thirty-first of August.'

'That remains to be seen. And if I let you go, you are not taking my daughters. Is that clear?' It was all a power play and she suddenly hated him for it. All he needed was a whip to complete the image he was making.

'Are they prisoners here too then?'

'Is that how you see yourself?'

'Lately, yes. Ever since you sent me down here as a punishment for a sin I didn't commit. You've treated me like a criminal all summer.'

'Perhaps it's your own guilt that makes you feel that way, my dear.'

'Not at all. And I refuse to feel guilty about a trip with my mother, or to bow and scrape and beg, I don't need to do that. I'm a grown woman, and I can certainly do something like that, if I choose to.'

'Ah, the young baroness spreads her wings. Are you telling me that you don't need my support because of the size of your own income?'

'I would never say such a thing, Henri.' She was shocked at how bitter he seemed to be. But he was furious that she wouldn't bend to his wishes.

'You don't need to, my dear. In any case, I've decided. You're not going.'

She looked at him and shook her head in despair. He didn't understand that he was choosing the wrong issue on which to take his stand. Nothing could have kept her from going. Not even her husband.

Chapter 26

When John Chapman arrived in Kentucky, it was like landing on another planet. He had to change planes twice, and a jeep met him and took him over three hours of bumpy roads into the mountains, until he was deposited at a 'motel' with a single room and an outdoor toilet. He sat huddled in his room that night, listening to the owls outside and sounds he had never heard before, and he wondered what Megan would be like when he met her the next day.

He slept fitfully, and woke early. He walked to the town's only restaurant and ate fried eggs and grits, and had a cup of truly awful coffee. And the jeep came for him again after lunchtime, with a toothless driver, who was only sixteen years old, and drove him to the hospital, high up in the mountains, under tall pine trees and surrounded by shacks where assorted families lived, most of them with a dozen children running around barefoot in what could only be called rags, followed by packs of mangy dogs hoping to find some crumbs, or leftover food the children might have forgotten. It seemed difficult to believe that this godforsaken outpost could be huddled in such beautiful country, and only hours away from places like New York, or Washington or Atlanta. The poverty John saw was staggering. Young boys who looked like bent-over old men from poor working conditions, bad health, and acute malnutrition; young women with no teeth and thin hair. Children with swollen bellies from lack of food. John wondered how she could stand working there, and walked into the hospital, not sure of what he'd find there.

He was directed to a clinic around the back, and he went there, only to find twenty or thirty women, sitting patiently on benches, surrounded by screaming kids, and obviously pregnant again with what in some cases was their eighth or ninth child even though they were only twenty. It was an amazing sight, and when he looked toward the desk, he saw a head of bright red hair, braided and in pigtails, on a pretty girl in jeans and hiking boots, and as she walked toward him, he knew without a doubt, it was Megan. She looked incredibly like Alexandra.

'Hello, Doctor.' She smiled at the greeting and led him to a small room nearby, where they could talk privately. He showed her the file he had shown Alexandra, and told her about Alexandra as well, and explained that the meeting was set for September first, as she had suggested. 'Can you still make it?' He looked worried and she reassured him with a warm smile. She had some of the mannerisms of Rebecca, but actually she looked a great deal like Alexandra.

'I can. If I can get away from them.' She waved toward the army of women waiting on the benches.

'It's an awesome sight.'

'I know.' She nodded seriously. 'That's why I came here. They need help desperately. Medical care, and food, and education. It's incredible to think that this exists right in our own country.' He nodded, unable to disagree with her, and impressed that she was doing something about it.

She looked over the file again, thoughtfully, and then asked him some questions about her parents. She wanted to know the same thing Alexandra had asked him. Why

332

had Sam killed Solange? And then, what had happened to the others? She was saddened by what she read of Hilary, and smiled after he finished talking about Alexandra.

'Her life sounds a far cry from mine, doesn't it? A French baroness. That's a long way from Kentucky, Mr Chapman.' She said it with a drawl and he laughed with her, but she still wanted to meet both her sisters. No matter how different they were. 'You know, my mother is very frightened about the meeting.'

'I sensed that when we met. Your father was trying to reassure her.'

'I think it's very threatening to any adoptive parent to have their adopted child seek out their birth family. I saw that during my residency, before I came here. But she has nothing to worry about.' She smiled up at him with ease. She knew exactly who she was, where she was going, and why she wanted to go there, not unlike the people who had formed her. David and Rebecca had lived by their beliefs too, and they were exactly the kind of parents she needed. Decent, intelligent, filled with integrity and love for the people and causes they believed in. And Megan knew it too. She had told her mother that before coming back here. 'She'll be all right. I promised to call her after it was all over. I think they'll probably visit me after that, if I know my parents.' They both laughed, and John watched her eyes. They were filled with light and life and excitement. She was a girl who loved what she was doing and felt fulfilled, and it was exciting just being near her. She was so different from girls like Sasha, who were so totally wrapped up in themselves. This girl thought of no one but the needy people around her. And halfway through the afternoon, she had to leave him to do an emergency Caesarean section. She was back in two hours and apologized for the delay.

'This is supposed to be my free afternoon. But it's always like this, that's why I don't get too far.' And then she invited him to dinner at her place. She lived in a simple shack, with simple furniture and beautiful quilts she had bought from some of her patients. She cooked up a plain pot of stew and they relaxed and talked about her youth and her parents and the people she had met. She seemed to love her parents deeply and she was grateful for all they had done for her, yet at the same time it seemed to intrigue her to think that she had once belonged to entirely different people.

She smiled once over her glass of wine, and looked very young and girlish. 'In a funny way, it's kind of exciting.' He laughed and patted her hand. In a way she seemed the least distressed, the most secure, the happiest of the three women. She was doing exactly what she wanted.

And afterwards she drove him back to where he was staying in the jeep her father had given her when she'd moved to the mountains. John wanted to sit in the moonlight and talk to her for hours, but she had to get back. She went back on duty at four-thirty the next morning.

'Will I see you in Connecticut on the first?' She asked him cautiously, as he looked down at her in the moonlight.

'I'll be there.' He smiled. 'For a while anyway. I promised Mr Patterson I'd be there to greet all of you and help get things started.'

'See you then.' She waved as she drove off and John stood looking after her for a long time, as he heard the owls hooting in the tree, and felt the mountain air soft on his cheeks, and for a moment he wished he could stay with her for ever.

Chapter 27

Alexandra had already done all her packing, and all she had left to do was organize the girls when Henri confronted her in the hallway, and grabbed her by the arm.

'I thought you understood me. I told you, you are not going to New York.'

'Henri, I have to.' She didn't want to fight with him about it. It was something she had to do, and it wasn't fair to try to stop her now. He followed her back into their bedroom where he stood glaring at her in silent fury as her suitcases lay open on the bed.

'Why are you being so obstinate about this?' He knew instinctively it had to be a man. There was no other conceivable reason.

'Because it's very important to me.'

'You've told me nothing that explains that. Why does a trip to New York with your mother mean so much to you now? Would you care to explain that?'

Her eyes filled with tears as she looked at him across the bed. He had been so unkind to her all summer, and it was so unfair of him to be difficult now. 'I really can't explain it. It has to do with something that happened a long time ago.'

'Something that involved a man?' He looked at her accusingly, and as she watched him in the harsh sunlight of the Riviera, he suddenly looked very old, and she wondered if perhaps he was frightened . . . frightened that she was involved with a younger man. It made her feel sorry for him and for a moment she let her guard down, as she shook her head.

'No, it has nothing whatsoever to do with a man. It has to do with my parents.' That was true, but she did not mean the Comte and Comtesse de Borne.

'What about them? Alexandra, I expect you to tell me what's going on.' And then suddenly, as though she could fight him no longer, she sat down in a chair, and began to cry. But he did not approach her. He offered her no comfort. From all that he knew, she still owed him an explanation, and perhaps much more.

'I didn't want to explain this to you . . . it . . . it's difficult to explain. I've only known it myself since June.' She looked up at him with deeply troubled eyes, and he suddenly realized that something was very wrong, that the transgressions he had punished her for for two months were perhaps not what he had thought them. A shiver of guilt sliced through him, but only briefly, as he waited, standing near the window, as she went on. 'My mother . . . my parents . . . there was something they should have told you . . . I should have told you, except that I had almost forgotten, and I told myself it wasn't important. But I suppose now that it was . . .' There was an inner shudder of horror as he waited and she caught her breath and continued. 'Henri, I was adopted.' He stared at her in utter amazement.

'You were? Why didn't someone tell me? Your father never said anything.' He looked horrified, but she bravely went on. She was going to tell him all of it, no matter what it cost.

'I was also adopted before that. By Margaret and her previous husband as well.' She waited for the full impact to hit him, and as it did, he sat down slowly on the bed and went pale as he stared at Alexandra.

'Are you serious? You were not the biological child of Margaret and Pierre de Borne?' It was as though someone had just told him the Renoir for which he had paid five million dollars was a fraud. His lovely wife with the impeccable breeding was not a countess by birth, but an unknown. She nodded. She knew how deeply it had shocked her when Margaret told her, and she knew how much more Henri would be stunned. 'And before that? Margaret is not even your mother?' His voice was a whisper and Alexandra nodded, ready to tell him all.

'No, she's not.'

He gave a bitter crack of laughter. 'And to think how often I've worried that you or the children were too much like her. Then who are your parents? Do you even know?' She could be anyone . . . a girl from the streets . . . from the gutter . . . of unknown parents and breeding. The thought of it almost made him ill. For ten centuries his family had married and bred with the utmost caution, and he had married a complete stranger of unknown background.

'I have known for two months. And I've wanted to spare you. That has been the secret I've been keeping from you. Nothing else.' But he was not appeased, he looked at her angrily, and strode across the room with fury, as he glanced at her over his shoulder.

'I'd have much preferred if it was a man.'

'I'm sorry to disappoint you.' She spoke with great sadness. He was letting her down. She had inwardly prayed that he would accept her . . . that it wouldn't matter to him. But she had known better than that. These things meant too much to her husband for him to be magnanimous about a surprise of this kind. And she had known it. She had only wished it might be different, but it wasn't.

'And your parents? Who are they? The real ones . . .'

She took a deep, brave breath and told him. 'My mother was a Frenchwoman, I know only that her name was Solange Bertrand, a "commoner" as you would put it. My father met her when he liberated Paris with the Allied forces. I know nothing more. My father was an actor, a well-known one, much respected, named Sam Walker. They were said to be very much in love, and they had three daughters, of which I am the second one. And then . . .' She almost choked on her words as she told him, but in an odd way it was a relief to say the words, '. . . as a result of some madness, he killed her. And when he was convicted of the crime, he committed suicide in his cell, leaving me and my sisters penniless and orphaned. We were left with an aunt for a few months, and then a friend of the family, an attorney, found homes for us, and got us adopted, two of us anyway. I was very fortunate in that I was given to Margaret and her first husband, a lawyer named George Gorham. I was five years old at the time. They say I was four when my father killed my mother, which is why I don't recall it. And I don't remember anything about the man named George Gorham. Apparently, six months later, he died, and my mother . . . Margaret, that is . . . came to France to recover, and she met my father . . . Pierre . . . and you know most of the rest. He adopted me as soon as he married my mother, which you did not know, and I suppose I had forgotten, and we lived happily ever after, and then you came along, Henri.' She tried to smile, but her face froze as she watched him.

'What a tidy little story.' Henri looked at her with unleashed fury. 'How dare you perpetrate that hoax on me for all these years? And even if you had forgotten, as you say, your mother certainly hadn't. And your "father", as you call him . . . *bande de salopards*! . . . I could sue you for divorce on the basis of fraud . . . and damages in the bargain!'

'Do you call your daughters "damages", Henri? I had no idea . . . truly . . .' The tears coursed slowly down her cheeks and onto her yellow silk blouse as she watched him, but she saw no mercy there.

'I call the entire charade disgraceful! And this trip to New York? What is that all about? To put flowers on your parents' grave?'

'The lawyer who placed us for adoption was my parents' closest friend, and he is dying. He has spent months trying to locate my sisters, and he wishes to bring us together. He feels he owes it to us for whatever pain he caused us in taking us away from each other. I was very fortunate, but at least one of us was not.'

'And what is she? A prostitute in the streets of New York? My God, it's unbelievable! In one hour I have inherited a war bride, a murderer, a suicide, and God knows what else in the bargain, and you expect me to wave my handkerchief and shed tears of joy that you are being reunited with your sisters, whom even you cannot care about after all this time. And your mother? What part has she played in this? Is she responsible for getting you back in touch with the attorney? Did she think you needed a little excitement in your life? I know how dull she thinks me, but I assure you this is not my idea of excitement.'

'Nor is it hers.' Alexandra looked at him proudly. She had told him who she was, and if he chose to reject her, it was his loss, his sin, his lack of compassion. She had done everything possible to protect him and he had demanded an answer to his questions. Now he had it. And it remained to be seen what he would do about it. 'My mother was heartbroken to have to tell me. She never wanted any of this to come out. But *I* want to see my sisters. *I* want to see who they are. And no, my sister is not a prostitute. She runs a major television network, and she has had a tragic life. My younger sister is a doctor, working in Appalachia. And I don't even know if I'll like them, or if they'll like me. But I want to see them, Henri. I want to know who they are, and who I am, other than just your wife.'

'That's no longer enough for you, is it? You had to bring this on our heads. Can you begin to imagine what this would do to my career if it got out? What would happen to my bank? To my political connections? My relatives? Can you imagine what your own children would think if they knew their grandfather murdered their grandmother. My God . . .' He sat down again, boggled at the thought. 'I can't even begin to imagine it.'

'Neither can I.' Alexandra said in a small voice. 'But I don't see why it should get out. No one is going to publicize this meeting. The children don't even know why I'm going. They just think that Grandma invited us, and we're going to New York. I'm going to spend one weekend in Connecticut, "with friends", while the girls and my mother stay in New York.'

'I don't understand why you want them with you. It makes no sense.' But it did to her . . . and to Margaret.

'Maybe I need them for emotional support.' And then she took a big step, one she hadn't imagined a moment earlier. 'You're welcome to come along. It's a little frightening going back thirty years to see people you don't know, but must have once loved.'

'I can't even begin to imagine. And no, I will not join you. In fact, Alexandra . . .' He stood up and looked at her sadly. As far as he could see, their lives had been shattered, in his eyes, beyond repair. 'I implore you not to go. I don't have any idea what, if anything, can be salvaged from our marriage, but it serves no purpose to go and see these people. They're beneath you. You must not go back there . . .' And then, in a whisper, 'Please don't.'

But this time, she could not oblige him. After fourteen years of devoted obedience to Henri de Morigny, she could not do more. She had to go to New York, for her own sake, and maybe even for that of her children. But she had to go, and face these women, reach out and touch them, maybe even love them, or not, and put to bed some old ghosts she hadn't even known existed. 'I'm sorry, Henri . . . I have to . . . I hope you can understand that. It's terribly important to me. And none of this has to hurt our marriage. I'm doing something I need to do . . . for me . . . not to hurt you.' She went to him then and gently tried to put her arms around him, but he wouldn't let her. He treated her like a stranger, which in his mind, she was now.

'I don't even know who you are any more.'

'Does my family tree make so much difference?' But she knew the answer to that, before she asked the question, and he shook his head sadly, and walked out of the room, as she blew her nose resolutely, and walked down the hall to pack for her daughters. No matter what happened to her marriage, there was no question in her mind. She had to go to New York. She *had* to. She was going.

Chapter 28

It was only three days before the scheduled meeting, when John Chapman went back to the network, flashed all his passes, and went upstairs to her office. He smiled at her secretary, and looked as though he belonged there, as he asked if Hilary was in her office.

'She's leaving in a few minutes . . .' She was about to ask him who he was, but he slipped past her and she shrugged. She couldn't keep track of everyone who went in to see Miss Walker. They were legion, and he looked all right. In fact, he looked a lot better than that. She smiled to herself, wondering if this was someone Hilary was involved with. No one ever knew anything about Hilary's private life. And as the door closed silently behind him, he stood in Hilary's office, and she looked up, startled.

'Yes?' She thought it was a delivery of some kind, a script, or urgent instructions. She was used to new faces popping in and out of her office, but not this one. And he stood staring at her quietly, as though he knew her well. It was an odd feeling as he approached her, and she was suddenly frightened as she reached for the phone to call for help. But as he smiled at her, she felt foolish. He looked intelligent and coherent and handsome, but she still couldn't figure out who in hell he was or what he was doing there as he spoke to her in a deep, gentle voice.

'Miss Walker?' But he didn't need to ask the question. He knew exactly who she was, possibly even better than she herself did. 'I'm sorry to barge in on you like this. I have to speak to you for a moment.' She stood up behind her desk, as though to take control of the situation as he approached her. The green eyes were as cold as ice, and her voice was curt.

'I'm on my way out. You'll have to see me tomorrow. What department are you from?'

It was a tough question and he wasn't sure what to answer. He didn't want her to call security and have him thrown out. Instead, he said something totally outrageous. 'I'm here because of Megan and Alexandra . . .' He waited to see the effect, and like a deep knife wound, or a gunshot, at first there was no bleeding. Her eyes were still steady green ice. '. . . They want to see you.'

'Who are you?' This time her hand was shaking as she reached for the phone, and he beat her to it, and held it in its cradle.

'Please . . . just give me five minutes. I won't hurt you. It's a long story, but I'll make it as quick as I can.' And suddenly she knew that he was the man who had called her, and he knew that she remembered.

'I don't want to see them.'

'They want to see you. Both of them. Alexandra is coming all the way from France . . . Megan from Kentucky . . .' He was stalling and she was showing signs of pain in her eyes . . . incredible sorrow . . .

'That old sonofabitch sent you, didn't he? Why now?' She stood to her full height and watched him, abandoning her grip on the phone.

'He's dying.'

'Good.'

'Maybe he wants to repent of his sins. He wants to

bring the three of you together, this weekend, at his house in Connecticut. He has spent months finding you . . .'

'Bullshit.' She cut him off. 'I know better. I went to him twenty years ago, and he had no idea and no interest where anyone was. Who found us? You did?' He nodded, not sure if she would hate him or not. He was just stirring up more pain for her. And she had long since put the past to rest. She had given up on finding her sisters after the last time she saw Arthur. After ten years, the dream had died. And now after more than twenty years, she didn't want to revive it. She didn't need them anymore. She had cut everything out of her life that might remind her of them. There were no men, no children, no love life of any kind. There was work, soothing work, and lots of it, and the people she trampled on the way up. She didn't have to feel guilty or sorry. She was heading in one direction. And she was all by herself. 'It's too late, whoever you are.'

'Chapman, John Chapman.'

'Well, tell him I'm not interested. He's twenty years too late . . . make that thirty.' She looked unspeakably bitter as she sat down. In some ways, he noticed, she looked younger than she was, and in others she looked older. She had eyes that were older and sadder than time.

'And what do I tell your sisters?'

'Tell them . . . Tell them . . .' Her voice faltered and she looked up at him sadly. 'Tell them I loved them then but . . . it's too late for me now.' He shook his head and sat down across the desk from her, praying that he could touch something still living in her heart, if anything had survived the endless pain she'd endured in her childhood.

'It's not too late, Hilary . . . it can't be . . . you were everything to them then . . .' Arthur had said so. He had once described to John how she cared for the other two

344

girls, and just talking about it had made him cry. 'You can't turn your back on them now.'

She looked into his eyes, wondering who this man was, how he had found her, and how he knew so much. 'They don't need me anymore, Chapman. They're grown up now. What are they? Secretaries? Housewives?' It was the best fate she could hope for them, as John Chapman smiled.

'One's a baroness in France, with two children, and the other's a doctor in Kentucky. They're both interesting women. I think you'd like them.' But that was beside the point, even though she was curious about them.

'Who's the doctor?' It was difficult to imagine either of those little girls as a doctor.

'Megan. She's terrific. And so is Alexandra. She's warm and compassionate and kind.'

'She was, even as a baby.' Her voice was a whisper, and then dropping her face into her hands, she shook her head. 'The thought of finding them kept me alive through ten years of hell. I stole ten thousand dollars from my aunt, and I was going to come to New York to find them.' She laughed into her hands, and Chapman could see that there were tears on her desk. 'And then he told me he hadn't kept track of them . . . he had no idea where they were . . . I couldn't find them either.' She looked up at John with empty, broken eyes. 'What's the point now, except to cause each other pain with the memories of what happened?'

'You're the only one who has those, Hilary. The others have nothing. Alexandra remembers you, and Megan knows nothing at all. All you have now is each other. What happened to your parents is no longer important. Just the three of you . . . you can't turn your back on that now.'

345

'That old bastard destroyed us. Why should I let him soothe his conscience by getting us back together now? My life won't change if I don't see them. That's all over. They're gone. Just . . . like my parents . . . like the past.'

'Your parents are gone forever . . . but your sisters aren't. They're real and alive, and they want to know you. Even if you go and you hate them, at least you can tell yourself you tried.' But she shook her head slowly and stood up again, her eyes shooting emerald fire at him.

'I won't do it. Tell Patterson how much I hate him . . . no . . . you couldn't even imagine how much I hate him.'

'Why? I know he didn't keep the three of you together, but was there more?' He had wanted to ask her that since he first read her file.

'It doesn't matter any more. He knows what he did to us. Let him live with it. For me . . . it's over . . . I have my life . . . my work . . . I don't need more than that.'

'It's a hell of an empty life, Hilary. I know, because that's all I have. Who do you talk to at night in the silence? Who holds your hand when you're sick or tired or scared? I have an ex-wife and my parents and two brothers. Who do you have? Can you afford to turn your back on those two women?'

'Get out of my office.' She walked to the door and pulled it open. She had heard enough, and she couldn't take any more. But he took a piece of paper out of his pocket. On it were the instructions of how to get to Arthur's place in Connecticut on the first of September, the phone number, the address, and he looked into her eyes as he laid it on her desk and then walked to the door.

'I've lived your life, Hilary Walker, for months now. I've cried for you. I've been to Charlestown, to Jacksonville, I've talked to the neighbour who found you near death on her doorstep, I've been to your foster homes. I

know how badly he hurt you ... I know what a rotten
deal you got,' and there were tears in his eyes as he looked
down at her and spoke, 'but please God, please don't do
this ... don't turn your back on them now. They need
you, and you need them ... Hilary ... please ... go to
the meeting. I'll be there to help you. I'll do anything I
can.' She was looking up at him in amazement, wondering
how he had known all that. 'Just be there ... please ...'
And with that he squeezed her arm gently, and left her
office, as she stood there, staring after him, all the old pain
in the past revived in her, along with a new confusion. She
didn't want to go and see them ... she didn't want to
remember Axie's bright red curls and Megan's little cries
in the night. They were gone now. Gone forever. And she
couldn't go back any more. Not even for John Chapman.

Chapter 29

'You're really going?' Henri stood looking at her across their bedroom. In Cap Ferrat they shared one bedroom, or they had, until Alexandra had confessed everything to him. He had moved into the guest room that night. And the gesture needed no explanation.

'I am.' She looked serious and firm. The girls were dressed and ready. Their bags were downstairs, and Margaret was meeting them at the airport in Nice. They had managed to book a direct flight to New York without going back to Paris.

'You won't reconsider?'

She shook her head slowly. 'I'm sorry, darling. I can't.' She walked toward him in the hope that he would let her touch him, but when she reached his side, he took a step back from her, and it cut her to the quick when he did it.

'Please don't,' he said quietly. 'Have a good trip then.'

'I'll be back no later than the tenth.' He nodded. 'And I'll be at the Pierre in New York, if you need me. I'll call you.'

'That won't be necessary. I'll be very busy.' He turned away and walked out on to the terrace, and with a last look at his back, she left and went downstairs. She didn't see him watching her as they drove away, or the tears in his eyes as he stared out at the sea and thought about her. He knew he loved her a great deal and now he felt as though he had lost her. It was incredible to him . . . all that had happened . . . he just didn't understand it. How they could have let it happen . . . in a way, he realized, she was as much the victim of circumstance as he. But to him it was so much more important, and now she was off on this wild-goose chase to meet two unknown sisters. He only wished he could have stopped her, but it was obvious that he couldn't.

Margaret had insisted they take first class on the flight, and the girls were enchanted as they ordered Shirley Temples, and blew at each other through the little red straws.

'Girls, please!' Alexandra admonished, still thinking of her husband, and Margaret told her to let them have some fun. And then as the two little girls walked down the aisles to see if they could find any children to play with, Margaret asked her how Henri had taken the news. Alexandra had told her only briefly several days before that she had told him the entire truth before leaving.

'He didn't say so in so many words,' Alexandra said solemnly to her mother, 'but I think it's over. I'm sure I'll come home to find he's contacted his attorneys.'

'But you didn't have to tell him, either. You could have just told him I was dragging you to New York.'

'He knew it was something else, Maman. I had to tell him something, so I told him the truth.' And despite the price to pay, she didn't regret it. At least she had a clear conscience.

'I think that was a great mistake.' And she didn't tell Alexandra, but she suspected that her daughter's suspicions were right. Henri would almost surely ask for a divorce. Not even ask for it, demand it, and Alexandra would never put up a fight. Margaret just prayed he left her the children. None of it was pleasant to think about, and it distracted her when Axelle and Marie-Louise came back to announce that in spite of the fact that every seat was sold, and packed, there was 'no one' on the flight.

'In other words, there are no children?' Margaret inquired with a grin and they laughed. 'Then you'll just have to put up with us.' She played Old Maid and Fish and War and taught them Gin Rummy, and they watched the movie, as Alexandra sat lost in her own thoughts. She had a great deal to think about . . . her parents . . . her sisters . . . and her husband, if she still had one when she went back to France. But she was still sure she had made the right decision, and the next morning, after a good night's sleep at the Pierre, she called the concierge and made an appointment. She went only a few blocks away to Bergdorf's, and she was very pleased with the results. When she met her mother and the girls for lunch, they were stunned. She had had the blond rinse stripped off her hair, and she was once more a redhead.

'Maman, you look just like me!' Axelle squealed in delight and Margaret laughed as Marie-Louise clapped her hands.

'What on earth brought that on?' Margaret inquired over the girls' heads.

'I've wanted to do it for a long time. Maybe it's that I am who I am now, for better or worse. But I'm not hiding any more.' And it felt good to her, as Margaret watched her.

'I love you,' Margaret whispered as she touched her daughter's hand.

They had lunch at '21', and stopped at Schwarz's for a 'little gift' from Grandma. As usual, she spoiled both the girls. And as planned, at four o'clock, Alexandra's limousine was waiting. She had explained to the girls that she was spending the weekend with some old friends in Connecticut, and they were staying in the city with their grandmother.

'I'll call you tonight,' she promised as she got into the car with one small suitcase, wearing a very chic black linen dress from Chanel.

'We're going to the movies with Grandma!' Axelle shouted.

She held her mother tight, hugged the girls, and then blew kisses to all three of them, and her eyes held her mother's for a long moment as they drove away. She was sure she could see tears on her mother's cheeks while she was waving, and tears stung Alexandra's eyes as well. It was frightening to be going back into the past, and ahead into the future, all at the same time. But it was also very exciting.

Chapter 30

The drive to Stonington on the Connecticut shore took slightly less than two hours, and Alexandra sat in the back seat, thinking of the people she had left behind her. Margaret, and the love she had lavished on her for thirty years, Axelle and Marie-Louise, so infinitely precious to her, perhaps even more so now ... and Henri, so angry at her seeming betrayal of him. She had thought of calling him that morning, before she left, but she couldn't think of what to say. In fact, there seemed to be nothing left to say at all. She knew how he felt about her trip to the States. He had forbidden her to go, and for the first time in their married life, she had disobeyed him. And suddenly, as she drove along in the back of the hired limousine, she felt oddly free, and different than she had in a long time ... almost the way she used to feel when she was a little girl, running with her father in the fields near their country house, with the wind in her hair, totally sure of herself, and completely happy. She felt as though he were with her now, as she took the journey back into the past that she felt so compelled to take. And without thinking, she ran a hand through her hair and smiled to herself. She was Alexandra de Borne again ... Alexandra Walker, she whispered in the silent car. And for the first time in fourteen years, she was once more a redhead.

There was an electronic gate when they arrived, and

they were buzzed in by an unknown voice, but other than that bit of security the property looked simple and unimpressive. There was a long winding drive up a hill, and after a sharp turn, there was a pretty Victorian house with a wide porch and widow's walk. It looked like someone's grandmother's house, or that of a great-aunt. There was a lot of wicker furniture on the porch, and an old barn behind the house. It looked cosy and inviting, and Alexandra stepped out of the limousine carefully, looking around, thinking how pretty it was, and how much her children would like it. And then she saw a familiar face watching her from the porch, and she smiled as he hurried towards her.

'Hello! . . . how was your trip?' It was John Chapman, in khaki slacks and an open blue shirt. He looked totally at ease and his eyes were warm and friendly as he shook her hand and then took her suitcase from the chauffeur.

'It was fine, thank you very much. What a nice place this is.'

'It is, isn't it? I've been poking around all afternoon. There are some wonderful old things in the barn, I guess Mr Patterson has owned this place for years. Come on in, you'll love the house.' And he walked her slowly towards it, silently admiring the shining red hair that was so different from the quiet blonde she'd been before. And then finally he decided to go ahead and say it. 'Your hair looks wonderful, if it isn't rude to say it.'

But she only laughed and shook her head. She was pleased that he liked it. 'I decided to go back to my natural colour in honour of this trip. It's going to be hard enough for us to recognize each other without complicating things any further.' She smiled and their eyes met, and she finally got up the courage to ask him what she most wanted to know. 'Have the others arrived yet?'

He knit his brows and glanced at her, trying to look

unconcerned, but he was still worried about Hilary. She had given no indication that she would come, and he was desperately afraid that she wouldn't. 'Not yet. Megan said she'd get here around six o'clock. And Hilary . . .' His voice drifted off and Alexandra looked at him long and hard and then nodded. She understood, and it saddened her. But it wasn't really surprising.

'She hasn't agreed to come, has she?'

'Not in so many words. But I told her how badly you wanted her to. I thought it was fair to say that.' She nodded in answer and silently prayed that her sister would have the courage to face them. She knew that the past was deeply painful for her, more so than for the others, and she might just decide not to do it. But Alexandra hoped that she would. Deep within, a small forgotten child desperately needed to see her. 'We'll keep our fingers crossed,' Chapman added as they walked into the front hall. There was a small sitting-room on the right, and a large parlour on the left, with a cosy fireplace, and well-kept Victorian furniture. She wondered where Arthur Patterson was, their benefactor who had brought them back together, and she asked John as much in a whisper.

'He's upstairs, resting.' He had brought two nurses with him, and when John saw him that morning, he realized that it was a miracle the man was still alive at all. It was as though he had hung on, just for this, and couldn't possibly hang on much longer. He had aged twenty years in the past four months, and it was obvious that he was in great pain all the time now. But he was coherent and alert, and anxious to see the three women he'd finally brought back together.

'Are you sure they'll come?' he'd pressed John, and Chapman had assured him, praying that Hilary wouldn't let them down. But as much as she hated Patterson, maybe

354

it wouldn't be such a bad thing after all if she didn't come. Chapman wasn't sure how well the old man would weather that kind of confrontation. And after lunch, his nurses had put him to bed, and urged John to let him rest until dinner. He was determined to come downstairs that night and dine with his guests. And the plan was for John to leave after dinner. By then the women would have settled in, he would have introduced them all to each other and the rest was up to them . . . and to Arthur.

Alexandra was peeking around the living-room, and from there, wandered into the dining-room with the long English table.

'It looks as though he spent a lot of time here,' Alexandra observed, 'the place looks well loved.' He smiled at her choice of words, and said he wasn't sure how much time Arthur had spent in Connecticut, and he didn't add that Arthur had told him he wanted to die there.

'Would you like to go upstairs?'

'Thank you.' She smiled up at him, wondering how old he was. He seemed so boyish in some ways, and yet so mature. He was serious and yet fun . . . a world away from Henri, and yet he looked childish to her compared to her husband. She was so accustomed to Henri's forceful ways, his habits of command, his way of striding into a room and taking charge, with his stern face and his powerful shoulders, and it was odd how suddenly she missed it. He made other men seem weak, and too young, and as though somehow, no matter how nice they were, they lacked something. And she couldn't help wondering if things would ever be the same again, if he'd even take her back when she returned to France . . . maybe she'd be forced to live with her mother again, or find her own house. For the time being, everything was uncertain.

John showed her to a sunny room at the corner of the

house; it was still hot from the afternoon sun, and the bedspread was sparkling white with lace trim, with a cosy rocking chair next to it, and the same Victorian furniture that seemed to fill the house. There was a love-seat and a porcelain washstand, and someone had put flowers in the room, and for some reason the room made her feel young again, as though she were a young girl coming home. And there were tears in her eyes when she turned to John and thanked him.

'It's so odd being here,' she tried to explain but she couldn't find the words, 'it's like being very young and very old . . . visiting the past . . . it's all very confusing.'

'I understand.' He left her to freshen up, and she came downstairs in a little while in a beige linen suit, her make-up fresh, her beige shoes with the familiar black toe of Chanel, and her red hair bringing it all to life. She looked elegant and in control, and she turned as she heard a stir of voices on the stairs behind her. It was Arthur coming downstairs with the assistance of the two nurses. He was bent over and frail, and he groaned with every step, but suddenly as he saw her, he stopped, and gave a startled sound, and then tears began to roll down his cheeks, as Alexandra walked halfway up the stairs to meet him.

'Hello, Mr Patterson,' she said, quietly, and as he trembled she bent down and kissed his cheek. 'Thank you for bringing me here.' But he was trembling so violently, he couldn't speak. He only took her hand and squeezed it hard, with the last of his strength, and then allowed her to assist him downstairs with the help of one nurse, and when they had settled him in a comfortable chair in the large sitting-room, he stared up at her and spoke at last in a voice hoarse from his illness.

'My God, you look so much like her. Are you Alexandra

or Megan?' He still remembered little Hilary's jet-black hair, exactly like her father's.

'I am Alexandra, sir.' She looked serious and deeply touched and he began to cry again as she spoke.

'You even have the same accent. Through all those years, she always had that lilt of French . . .' He shook his head, stunned by the resemblance between Alexandra and her mother. And it was an odd feeling for Alexandra, to be so like someone she had never known, and yet who was her mother.

'Were you very fond of her?' It was something to talk about as they waited for the others. John had appeared again and he offered her a glass of wine, which she declined. She wanted to concentrate on Arthur Patterson and wait for her sisters. She was growing more tense and excited with each passing moment.

But he nodded his head now, thinking of Alexandra's questions. 'Yes, I was very fond of her . . . she was such a lovely girl . . . so beautiful, so proud . . . so strong . . . with so much life in her . . .' With a faded smile, he told Alexandra of the first time he and Sam had seen her in Paris. 'I thought she was going to call the MPs on us, and she would have . . . except that your father was so damn handsome and charming.' He smiled, thinking back to Sam. What good friends they had been, and what good times they had had in the war years. 'He was a wonderful actor too.' He told her about some of his plays, as she listened quietly, and then suddenly there was the sound of a car outside, and John disappeared, and a moment later they heard voices.

Arthur seemed to be listening too, and unconsciously, he reached out and took Alexandra's hand and held it firmly in his own, just as the front door opened. And from where he was sitting, he could see her as she entered. She looked around, just as Alexandra had done, and then saw them watching her, and like a shy child, she walked into the room, looking suddenly like a younger double of Alexandra.

Alexandra rose slowly to her feet and instinctively walked to her with outstretched arms. It was like finding a piece of the past and looking in the mirror all at the same time. The only difference was that Alexandra's eyes were green and Megan's were blue. But otherwise, it was obvious that they were sisters. 'Megan?' she asked in a cautious voice, but it was obvious who she was. The younger girl nodded, and they went into each other's arms, with tears in their eyes, even though they had both promised themselves that they were going to control their emotions. And as Alexandra held her close, she felt for a moment as though she remembered.

'You look so much like me!' Megan laughed through her tears and hugged her again, and then pulled away to observe her with a wry smile. 'Except you don't dress as well.' She was still wearing the jeans and hiking boots and T-shirt she had worn at the hospital until she'd left that afternoon. But it was what she usually wore in any case, just like Rebecca. 'My God, you're beautiful.' She laughed, and shyly stepped back as Alexandra took her hand, and then took it upon herself to introduce her to Arthur.

'How do you do, Mr Patterson,' Megan greeted him politely, almost like a young girl, and he stared at her with satisfaction. She was almost as pretty as Solange, but not quite, and she didn't have Alexandra's sophistication, but she had something of her own that stood out, a kind of purity and intelligence that were clearly etched on her face. She looked like a lovely young woman.

'So you're the doctor, are you?'

'Yes, sir. Just about. I'm finishing my residency right now. I'll be all through by Christmas.'

He nodded again, looking from one woman to the other. There was no bitterness there, no anger, they had led good lives and it showed. He had chosen well for them . . . but not for poor Hilary. After Chapman's warning, he was afraid of what she would say to him if she came, but nonetheless he wanted to see her.

They waited until almost eight o'clock, alternately silent and then speaking all at once, nervous and uncomfortable and strange, with Arthur telling them stories of the past, and Megan and Alexandra trying to share their lives with him and each other. Alexandra had brought photographs of the girls, and Henri, and her parents. Megan had done the same, bringing photographs of Rebecca and David, the house in Tiburon, and the hospital where she worked in Kentucky. It was as though they wanted to bring each other up to date as quickly as possible. They had thirty years to account for. And it was obvious how different their lives were. The hospital in Kentucky stood out next to the photographs of the girls in front of the villa in Cap Ferrat. And Henri looked every inch the seigneur in front of his château in the Dordogne, as the photographs of Margaret and Rebecca stood side by side for a moment, the one in jeans with a flower in her hair, the other in an evening dress going to a ball in Monte Carlo the year before. And Megan mentioned it with a shy smile as they walked in to dinner with Arthur walking slowly behind them with John's assistance.

'It's funny how different our lives have been, isn't it? And yet we're still sisters . . . we still look alike . . . we still come from the same parents, and probably have similar likes and dislikes and habits we've inherited without even knowing it. And yet look at us, you grew up in all that

359

pomp and circumstance in France, and I spent half my childhood living with friends, while my parents went to jail for causes they believed in.' And yet she didn't sound unhappy. She sounded proud of them, and she was. It was all amazing to think about, and it silenced both of them as they took their seats on either side of Arthur. John's place was next to Megan, and there was an empty chair next to Alexandra, and it was becoming obvious now that Hilary was not going to join them. Alexandra felt her heart sink, and made idle chit-chat for a while, as Arthur seemed to doze, and then suddenly there was the sound of a car outside. John left the table quietly. There were angry voices outside, and then suddenly the front door flew open, as the two women watched, mesmerized, and Arthur woke up, as though he sensed that someone else was coming to see him.

'Did something happen?' he asked Alexandra, confused for an instant as he woke up and she patted his hand, never taking her eyes from the door, and then she saw her. Tall and thin and lanky as their father had been, with a long stride, and jet-black hair, and green eyes that she suddenly turned on them. She was wearing a wrinkled navy linen business suit. She had had every intention of not coming, and then suddenly after work she had decided to rent a car and come up and tell Arthur once and for all what she thought of him. And then maybe she would be free of him for the rest of her life. She didn't even care if she saw the others. They were strangers to her now. It was Arthur who interested her as she strode into the room and stood facing him, but it was impossible to ignore the two women with red hair who flanked him, and her eyes were drawn first to Megan, and then to Alexandra, as John stood carefully just behind her. He could sense the tension in the room, the anguish of the woman who stood so close to

360

him. He wanted to put his arms around her but she looked as though she might explode, and then suddenly she stopped, as her eyes met Alexandra's, and Alexandra came slowly to her feet and crossed the room like a sleepwalker and the words escaped her without rhyme or reason.

'H ... Hillie ...' She could see the face of a little girl with long black hair, and yet here was this woman ... with the same black hair ... the same green eyes ... without knowing why, she started to cry, and without wanting to, Hilary's arms went around her.

'Axie ... little Axie ...' It was the first time she'd held her since the day they'd torn her from her, and left her alone with Eileen and Jack in Charlestown, crying for the sisters she had so dearly loved, and she could barely stand the pain now of remembering it, as she held the tall, perfumed, beautifully coiffed woman from Paris ... except all she saw there was the face of the child she had once loved, and she whispered the same words over and over again as she cried ... 'I love you, Axie ...' They held each other like that for a long time, as Megan watched silently, and then suddenly Arthur began to cough, and John hurried to give him a glass of water. The housekeeper who was serving them dinner brought the pills the nurse had given her, and Megan checked the dose and gave them to John, as Hilary slowly turned towards them. 'You must be Megan.' She smiled through her tears, and held Alexandra's hand as they pulled apart from the embrace. 'You've changed quite a bit since the last time I saw you.' The three women laughed, but Hilary's eyes clouded as she saw the old man, and she held tight to Alexandra's hand as she spoke to him. 'I said I wouldn't come, and I meant it, Arthur.' He nodded, meeting her eyes with fear and pain, and he saw everything there that he had dreaded seeing. She hated him, and one could see it there like black

361

poison. But he also knew he deserved it. He knew better than anyone. 'I never wanted to see you again.'

'I'm glad you did come, Hillie,' Alexandra said in her gentle voice. 'I wanted so much to see you . . . both,' she added, smiling at Megan, but Hilary wasn't smiling now, and she dropped her sister's hand as she advanced on Arthur.

'Why did you do this to us? Bring us here after all these years, to taunt us with what we didn't have, what we missed, who we might have been if we'd stayed together?'

He choked on his own words, and clutched the table with both hands as he faced her. 'I felt I owed it to you to make up to you for what I'd done.' He could barely breathe as he spoke to her, but it didn't worry her.

'And do you think you can make it up?' She laughed bitterly and they all ached for her, but John was frightened of what she would do now. She had waited thirty years for this, and he had always sensed the full measure of her hatred for Arthur. 'Do you really think you can wipe out thirty years of loneliness and pain with one dinner?'

'Your sisters have been luckier than you, Hilary.' He spoke honestly. 'And they don't hate me as much as you do.'

'They don't know as much as I do . . . do they, Arthur . . . do they?' she shouted into the silent room, the words echoing off the walls as he trembled.

'That's all in the past. Hilary.' It was a conversation between only the two of them. Only they knew of what they were speaking, as the others wondered.

'Is it? How about you? Have you been able to live with yourself for all these years, after killing my parents?' Her green eyes blazed and Alexandra advanced to gently touch her arm, but Hilary shook her off.

'Hillie, don't . . . it doesn't matter now . . .'

362

'Doesn't it?' She wheeled on her sister. 'How do you know that? How could you possibly know, living the good life in France, while I sat on my ass in juvenile hall, after getting raped, trying to figure out how to find you. And that sonofabitch didn't even know where you were, he didn't know where any of us were. He didn't even care enough to keep track of us after he ripped you out of my arms that day, crying and sobbing . . . you don't remember that now, but I do. I've remembered it . . . I've remembered both of you . . .' She looked from Alexandra to Megan. '. . . every day of my life and I've cried for you because I never found you. And now you tell me it doesn't matter? That I shouldn't hate him for killing our parents? How can you say that?' The tears were pouring down her cheeks unashamedly.

'But he didn't kill them.' Alexandra spoke for herself and Megan. 'His only failing was in not keeping us together, or keeping track of us over the years, but perhaps he couldn't help it.' She looked benevolently at the old man, and Megan silently nodded, unable to understand why Hilary hated him so much. He had failed them, but he had not betrayed them the way Hilary said. But she was shaking her head and laughing at them through the tears.

'You don't know anything. You were babies. I was standing there the night Mama died . . . the night Daddy killed her . . . I was listening . . . I heard what they said . . .' She began to sob and John stood nearby, ready to help her if she collapsed or needed him. He was near her, as he had been for months, although she didn't know it. 'I heard her screams . . .' Hilary went on, 'when he hit her and hit her and hit her, and then strangled her into silence until she died . . .' She was gulping down the sobs and she stood right in front of Arthur now. 'And do you know why he did that?' Her eyes never left Arthur's face, she had waited a lifetime for this. 'He did it because she was having an affair with *him*, and she told Father so . . .' She was listening to the voices of the past as she spoke, and she almost looked as though she were in another world, remembering back to the night her father had killed her mother. 'He had been cheating on her, she said, with lots of different women for years . . . all his leading ladies, she said . . . and he said it wasn't true . . . he said she was crazy . . . and she said she had proof . . . she knew who he'd just taken to California . . . who he'd been with the night before . . . and she said it didn't make any difference to her any more . . . that she had someone of her own, and that if he wasn't careful, she'd leave him and take us with her. And he said he'd kill her if she did, and she laughed . . . she kept laughing at him . . . and he said she could never take away his baby girls . . . and she laughed . . . and then she told him who it was . . .' She was crying so hard she could hardly speak, but she went on, as Arthur shook more and more violently in his seat and she stood inches from him shouting down at him and crying. 'She told him, didn' she, Arthur . . . didn't she?' Hilary shouted. And then she looked at her sisters, and told them what she had always known, and they hadn't. 'She was having an affair with Arthur, Daddy's best friend . . . and he said he would kill her for it, and she only laughed, and when he told her she couldn't take us away, she told him that only two of u were his . . .' There was a stunned silence in the room, and Arthur sat back in his chair as though he'd been struck by lightning. And Hilary's voice was quiet when she spoke this time. She had done what she had come for. 'She told him that Megan was Arthur's child,' she said in a dull voice, staring down at him with contempt. 'And then Daddy killed her.' She sank into the chair next to him crying softly, as Alexandra put an arm around her shoulders and the old man whimpered softly in his chair.

'I never knew . . . she never told me . . .' He looked at Megan pathetically. 'You must believe me . . . I never knew . . . I always thought you were his, like the others . . .' He was crying openly, and Megan looked even more shocked than she had at the rest of the recital. And Arthur seemed to be making his excuses to the room in general. 'If I had known . . .' But Hilary only looked at him and shook her head.

'What would you have done differently? Kept her with you, and left the rest of us to rot? You wouldn't have done anything. You didn't stand by my mother, or your own child, you betrayed your best friend, and what you did killed them both. You have their blood on your hands . . . and ours, without you, our lives would have been very different. How could you live with yourself all these years, knowing what you'd done? How could you defend him after betraying him?'

'He begged me to, Hilary . . . I didn't want to. I begged him to let me find another attorney. But he didn't want me to. And in truth, he didn't want to live after your mother died.' His voice dropped down to a whisper. Neither did I. It ended both our lives . . . I loved her deeply from the first moment I saw her.' The tears rolled down his cheeks as Megan stared at him. He was no longer just a family friend. This was her father.

And Hilary stared at him emptily, as though seeing him for the first time. He was an old, dying man, and there was no undoing what he had done. For him, it was all over, no matter whose blood was on his hands. The blood was long since dry . . . the people all but forgotten. She stood up then, and looked down at him. 'I came here to tell you how much I hated you. And do you know something strange, Arthur, after all these years, I'm not really sure it still matters.' She felt Alexandra's hand on her shoulder and turned to look into her eyes. She was exhausted from the emotions of the evening and turned to look at both the girls. 'I loved you both a great deal a long time ago ... but maybe that's too far in the past too ...' She felt drained, spent, she had nothing left to give or take, but Alexandra wouldn't let her go, and Megan was watching her too. She was the one to speak first.

'It's a long time ago for all of us, but we still came. I didn't remember any of you. And I didn't know Mr Patterson was my father. We came to honour the past, but also to go on from here. We all have other parents now, other lives, other people we care about. We haven't lived in a void for thirty years, none of us, not even you with your anger and your hatred.' It was a quiet reproach but it was powerful and it struck home. 'You can't just come here and drop a bomb like this in our laps, and then go. You owe it to us to repair the wounds, just as we owe it to you to do the same. And that's why we all came here.' There were tears slowly running down her cheeks, as she looked at Hilary, and John Chapman silently wanted to cheer her. It would ruin everything if Hilary left now. I would destroy her life once and for all. She had to stay, in spite of Arthur, and face them.

Hilary looked at Alexandra, as though seeking confirmation and she nodded and spoke in her quiet voice. 'Please stay Hillie ... I've waited so long for this.' They had all taken such risks, paid such a high price. She had defied Henri, possibly at great expense, all for the pleasure of seeing her sisters. 'It took a lot of courage to come here. For all of us. My husband forbade me to come here ... don't even know if he will take me back now. And my mother ... the woman I know as my mother has com with me, and she is very frightened of what all this will mean. She is afraid that after all this time she will lose me.' There were tears in her eyes as she spoke to Hilary, and Megan was nodding with tears in her own eyes. Rebecca was terrified of what seeing her sisters would mean to her. They had talked for an hour on the phone the night before, and she had promised she would call as soon as possible to reassure her. 'You have lost more than any of us, Hilary . . . but you are not alone . . . we love you, even now. You cannot turn your back on us.' And then putting her arms around her again, she cried softly. 'I won't let you.' Hilary stood tall and straight for a long moment, and then her arms went around Alexandra . . . how could she know what her life had been like? But it wasn't her fault . . . or Megan's . . . or maybe even Arthur's. She hated to admit that now, but it was possible. He had been a fool and he had paid a high price for it. He looked at Hilary sorrowfully over Alexandra's shoulder.

'Can you ever forgive me, all of you?' But he was looking at the oldest of the three and she took a long time to answer.

'I don't know . . . I don't know what I feel . . .' But she held tight to Alexandra and her eyes reached out to Megan.

'I'm glad you came anyway. The three of you had a right to be together. And if I had been a different kind of man, I would have defied my wife and kept you all myself. I wanted to, but she had such strong feelings about it that I didn't dare go against her. I'm sorry now, but it's too late to make any difference.' He looked mournfully at Hilary, and then at the child he had turned away, who was his own daughter. 'I made a terrible mistake. But I've paid for it. I've been a lonely man all my life . . . ever since your mother died . . .' He couldn't go on. He only shook his head and then stood up shakily, as John Chapman and one of the nurses came to help him. 'I'm going upstairs now. We all have a lot to think about.' Hilary's revelation had shocked them all, particularly Megan and Arthur. In a strange way, Megan now wondered if she was responsible for her mother's death . . . if she hadn't been born, would Sam have killed Solange? But it was too late to think about that, too late to cry over what had happened thirty years before. It was time to move on, as best they could. And he turned to them again before he left the room. 'I want you all to stay for as long as you can . . . for as long as you want to. This will be your home one day; I am leaving it to all of you, so you have a place to come, a home together finally, and a place to bring your families and your children. I'll stay out of your way while you're here, but I want you to stay here and get to know each other.' Alexandra and Megan thanked him quietly, and Megan rose quickly to help him upstairs, as Hilary watched, saying nothing. And when he was gone, she turned to Alexandra and shook her head.

'I don't know if I'll ever stop hating him, Axie.' It was still so easy to call her that, even after all these years, and the younger of the two smiled.

'You will. You have to. There's nothing left to hate any more. He's almost gone.' Hilary nodded. It was clear that the man wouldn't live much longer. 'I'm only grateful that he brought us together in time. That he still cared enough to do that.' They walked slowly upstairs arm in arm, and Hilary walked into Alexandra's bedroom, thinking suddenly of the room they had shared in Jack and Eileen's house, and three of them in one bed, as she tried to keep the baby from crying so Eileen wouldn't beat them.

'What are your children like?' She sat down in the rocking chair. It was a comfortable room, but she hadn't decided yet to spend the night. She just wanted to sit and talk for a while with Axie.

Alexandra smiled at the question. 'Marie-Louise looks a lot like you. She has your eyes . . . and Axelle looks a lot like photographs of me as a little girl. She's six . . . and Marie-Louise is twelve. I lost a little boy in between them.' And with a slice of pain, Hilary remembered her own abortion for the first time in years. She had been so careful after that to avoid any contact with children, and now suddenly had two nieces. 'Do you still remember your French?'

'Some.' Hilary smiled. 'Not much, I guess.'

'Marie-Louise and Axelle speak English anyway, thanks to my mother.'

'What's your husband like?' Hilary was curious about so many things about her . . . her husband . . . her parents . . . her life . . . her children . . . her habits . . . She wanted to know if they were alike. If after all these years, they had anything in common. And marriage was certainly not one of them. Hilary had assiduously avoided it.

Alexandra sighed, feeling very honest. 'He's difficult. And intelligent. And demanding. He wants to run everything, from the house to the office and back again. And he expects nothing less than perfection.'

'Don't you mind that?' She looked intrigued, her green eyes watching Alexandra as she shrugged and smiled.

'Not really. I'm used to it. And underneath his gruff exterior, I know he loves us . . . or he did.' She sighed. 'I don't know what's going to happen now. He was shocked when I told him our story . . . I mean about our parents . . .'

'It's not very pretty, is it?'

'Especially for Megan,' Alexandra added softly, just as she came down the hall. Megan had put Arthur to bed. He

369

had been in terrible pain, and he was crying. And she had given him an injection to sedate him.

'He's not going to live much longer.' She spoke quietly as she walked into the room, and Hilary noticed as John had, how much she sounded like Alexandra. 'I suspect he's got metastases everywhere. But he's still very alert.'

'The old bastard.' Hilary spoke in an undertone and Megan turned on her with flashing eyes.

'Don't talk about him like that. He's repented for his sins . . . he brought us here. What more do you want from him?'

'Something he can't give us,' Hilary shot back at her. 'The past . . . something decent we could have shared, instead of the heartbreak of tearing us apart.'

'We survived in spite of that . . . even you, Hilary. Look at you, you're a big success. You have a fantastic job, a nice life.' But it was an empty one, as only she knew, and Alexandra suspected. There was no one she cared about, and no one who cared about her, no one she was aware of anyway. And as they talked, John Chapman appeared in the doorway. He had disappeared discreetly for a while, and he suspected they would be talking late into the night. They had a lot of things to resolve, and a lot to learn about each other. And his job was finally over.

'Will we see you again, John?' Alexandra was the first to ask, and he shook his head, with a bittersweet smile.

'Not unless you want to look for someone else some-time, and I hope you never have to. My job's all done.' And then in a soft voice, he added, 'I'm going to miss you.' He had been living with each of them for months, hunting them down, seeking them out, getting to know them. And it suddenly came to him that he would miss Hilary most of all. He had ached so much for her past, and he had been too late to help her. 'Good luck to all of you.'

'Thank you.' They each stood up and shook hands with him, and Megan kissed him gently on the cheek with a shy smile. She had really liked him.

'If you ever get to Kentucky, call me.'

'Will you be there long?' he asked, hating to leave them, and she smiled at him, with the red hair that was exactly her mother's, and Alexandra's.

'I'll be through with my residency in December, but I'm pretty sure I'll stay on. I haven't told my parents yet,' she shrugged with an easy laugh and she looked very young again, 'but I think they already kind of expect it. My Dad does anyway. He knows how crazy I am.' They exchanged a long warm smile, and then Alexandra hugged him.

'Take care of yourself.' She mothered everyone, and it touched him as she patted his shoulder afterwards. 'Thank you for everything.'

'Don't let anyone talk you into dyeing your hair again ... you look beautiful ...'

'Thank you,' she blushed and he smiled and Hilary held out a hand and gruffly thanked him.

'I'm sorry I gave you such a hard time in my office ... I was fighting all this ...' And then with great effort in a low voice. 'But I'm glad I came.' She looked at both of her sisters, and her eyes filled with tears again, and then she looked back at him and without invitation he gently pulled her into his arms and she nestled there as he held her, wishing he could keep her there forever. There was still so much life owed her.

'You're going to be all right now, Hilary ... it's going to be just fine ...' His voice touched a place in her that had been closed for a long time, and she was sorry when she pulled away and looked up into his eyes with a shy smile.

'Come and see me sometime at the network.'

'I'll do that. Maybe we can have lunch sometime.'

She nodded, unable to say anything, she had to turn away as the tears coursed down her face. After so many years of isolation, she was surrounded by people she cared about deeply, and who seemed to love her.

It was Alexandra who put her arms around her this time, and smoothed back her hair as they walked John Chapman downstairs and waved as he drove away. And she and Hilary walked back upstairs again to Hilary's room. She had been given a room adjoining Alexandra's and Hilary changed into her nightgown and came back to chat, as Megan and Alexandra talked about Paris and Kentucky and the south of France, and whether or not Megan ever wanted to have children. She wasn't sure if it would interfere with her career or not, but Alexandra was telling her it was her greatest joy, as Hilary sat down in the rocking chair and shook her head in amazement. It was extraordinary being back together after all these years, and talking as though they had always been there.

'I never wanted kids, and I never regretted it,' Hilary lied, thinking back for a flash of a moment to the abortion. 'Well, I don't know . . . maybe I did when I was younger. It's too late now anyway.'

'How old are you?' Megan frowned. She had momentarily forgotten. She was thirty, and Hilary was . . . almost eight years older.

'Thirty-eight.'

'These days most women don't even have their first child till then. In this part of the world at least.' She smiled. 'Where I work, I see them having their first babies at twelve and thirteen, younger than that even sometimes. It's amazing.' It was a whole other world from this comfortable old house in Connecticut, and the lives her sisters led in the places where they lived. And then suddenly she laughed. 'Isn't it amazing how different we all are, and yet how similar? I live in the hills of Kentucky,' she said, looking at Alexandra then, '. . . and you live in a fancy house in Paris, and a château somewhere else, and a villa in the south of France in the summer,' and then she turned to Hilary, 'and you practically run a television network. Isn't it amazing?'

'It would have been more so,' Hilary said quietly, 'if we could have seen each other twenty-five years ago. My life wasn't so pleasant then.'

'What was it like?' Megan finally asked what they both wanted to know, and little by little, over the next two hours, with tears streaming down her face, she told them. All of it. The uglier and the ugliest, and the tragic and the brutal. But it helped to share it with them, and whereas she had once been the one who protected them, they comforted her now, and Alexandra held her hand, as Megan told her story, of sit-ins in Mississippi, and the time her father had been shot on a rainy night in east Georgia, of what decent people they were, and how totally they believed in their causes, and how much she loved them. And then Alexandra told them about Margaret, and Pierre before he died, and her life with Henri, and how she was afraid that now he would divorce her.

'He'd be a damn fool if he did.' Hilary spoke up, as she flung her long black hair over her shoulder, in a gesture that struck a chord of memory for Alexandra as she watched her.

'He is so obsessed with his lineage, and you have to admit, ours is a bit exotic for someone like my husband.' The three of them laughed and the sun came up as they talked. They went to bed amidst yawns and kisses and hugs and promises to meet again in the morning. They all slept until noon, and Alexandra was the first one to get up. She called her mother and the children at the hotel, but they were out, and she left a message that all was well and she would be home on Sunday night. And then she thought about calling Henri, but she didn't know what to say, so she went back upstairs and showered and dressed, and when she came back downstairs again, Megan was wearing a clean pair of jeans and a white blouse with a ribbon in her hair. And she looked more like a little girl than a doctor, and Alexandra said so. The two of them chatted over coffee and hot biscuits, and one of Arthur's nurses informed them that he had had a difficult night, so Megan went upstairs to check on him, just as Hilary came downstairs in shorts and a silk shirt, her black hair pulled severely into a bun, and her feet bare as she came to breakfast. She looked somehow much younger than she had the night before, and Alexandra realized that they all did. They were travelling back in time, and burdens that had aged them were falling from their shoulders. In her case it was the fear of what Henri would do to her, and that no one would love her any more if he divorced her. If he did, she still had Margaret, and the girls, and now she had these two women to support her. It didn't seem so terrifying any more. In fact, she felt good, and for the first time in a long time, she didn't feel frightened.

'Late night, last night, wasn't it?' Hilary smiled lazily over her coffee. 'What'll we do today? We could talk ourselves to death by tomorrow night, if we don't watch out.' She and Alexandra both laughed, and Alexandra looked at her thoughtfully. 'You're going back tomorrow night too?' The message she had left at the hotel said she would. She didn't want to abandon her mother and the girls for too long. She had promised to spend a week with

374

them in New York, and she knew her daughters would wear her mother out eventually.

'I have to,' Hilary answered. 'I have some important meetings scheduled for Monday morning.' So what else was new? When didn't she? She grinned. 'When are you going back?'

'To New York, tomorrow night. I left my mother at the Pierre with Axelle and Marie-Louise. I think by tomorrow night she'll have reached her breaking point, even though she's very good with them. But they're a handful.' Alexandra paused, thinking of Margaret and how worried she had been about this meeting. 'I also feel like I should get back to reassure her. I think she was afraid I would stop loving her when I met my sisters, as though she wouldn't really be my family any more. I owe her a little reassurance.'

Hilary nodded and smiled. 'I could drive you in, if you like. We could go out to dinner this week . . . or lunch . . .' She looked at her hopefully, like a shy child with a new best friend, and Alexandra's eyes lit up in answer.

'I would love it. And you could meet the girls! We're going to be here for a week. And then,' she said triumphantly, Henri de Morigny be damned, 'you could come to visit us in Paris!'

'That's a great idea!' Hilary laughed, as Megan joined them.

'What are you two cooking up today?' She was smiling but her eyes were serious.

'Just a little mischief in New York,' Hilary smiled at her. She still thought of her as 'the baby'. 'Care to join us? You could stay at my place with me.'

'Or at the Pierre with us,' Alexandra offered, but Megan had already made another decision.

'I'd love to, and I'll come and visit both of you as soon

375

as I can. But I'm going to stay here for a few days. He seems much worse today.' Her eyes indicated Arthur upstairs. 'I'd like to be here if anything happens.' And it was obvious that it was going to very soon. It was the only thing she could do for him now, her first and last gift to him as his daughter, to be with him when he died. She tried to explain her feelings about it later to Alexandra, as they strolled in the garden. 'He seems so pathetic . . . and so frail . . . as though he's already gone. I know Hilary hates his guts, but I have no axe to grind with him. I had a good life. I love the only parents I've known . . . he's kind of like a late gift in life. Someone who might have meant something to me once, but it's too late now. It's too late to do anything but say goodbye and help him go. And if I can help him do that, it would make me happy.'

'Then that's what you should do, Megan.' Alexandra smiled at her. In an odd way, she reminded her of her daughters.

They had a quiet dinner that night. The housekeeper was extremely discreet and left them alone most of the time, and eventually they began talking about John Chapman.

'I thought he was going to attack me when he forced his way into my office.' Hilary laughed, and Alexandra smiled, and blushed as she often did.

'The first time I saw him I thought he was very handsome.'

'So did I,' Megan confessed, and the three women laughed like three young girls and speculated about his wife.

'I think he said he was divorced.' Alexandra frowned, trying to remember, but Hilary shrugged. She hadn't opened her heart to anyone in years, and it was enough to have done so to two sisters. It had been an exhausting twenty-four hours. But it was like coming home, to the warm, comfortable country house, their ship finally safe in the harbour.

Chapter 31

The next day, they sat on the porch and talked for a long time. They promised to visit, and to write, and all three of them cried as Hilary and Alexandra got in the car, and drove away, waving to Megan until they could no longer see her. She had promised to stop and have dinner with both of them in New York that week, before she flew back to Kentucky. And Alexandra had tiptoed into Arthur's room to say goodbye to him, but Megan had just given him a shot and he was sleeping. He had opened one eye, and smiled at her, as though seeing someone else, and then drifted off again, as Hilary stood and watched from the doorway. She had nothing more to say to him, and she looked at him for a long moment, before she turned and walked downstairs, and got in the car to leave with Alexandra.

'Do you think he will die soon?' Alexandra asked, as they drove back to New York. She was sorry for him. He was so alone and so lonely, and she was glad Megan had decided to stay with him.

'Probably. He'd done what he wanted to do.' Her voice held no tenderness for him, but at least it no longer held anger.

They got to the hotel just before dinner-time, and Alexandra insisted that she come upstairs and meet the girls and Margaret, and finally after some protest that she wasn't dressed properly, it was late . . . when in truth, she was scared to meet Alexandra's family, what if they hated her? . . . she finally went upstairs with her. They looked like two girls returning from camp, slightly dishevelled, but relaxed and happy, and Alexandra opened the door of the suite with her key, and heard Hilary gasp as Axelle ran towards her.

'Hi, sweetheart . . . look who I brought! . . .' She acted as though Santa Claus had come home with her, and Axelle stopped in her tracks and stared at the tall, dark-haired woman who was openly crying.

'Who is she?'

'She's my sister,' Alexandra said as she began to cry too, and reached out for Hilary's hand. 'We haven't seen each other for a long, long time. And we have another sister named Megan . . . but she couldn't come tonight. This is your Aunt Hilary.' She spoke in a gentle voice and Axelle went to her cautiously as Hilary opened her arms and began to sob. All she could do was whisper the words of long ago . . . 'Oh, Axie . . .'

Marie-Louise came next and kissed her solemnly, and even Hilary could see how much they resembled each other. It was like having a daughter of her own, and they held hands as Alexandra introduced her to her mother.

'Maman, this is Hilary . . . Hilary, this is my mother. Margaret de Borne . . .' And suddenly all three of them were crying, and Margaret took Hilary in her arms, like another daughter.

'How are you? Are you both all right? I've been so worried about you!'

Alexandra smiled and wiped her eyes, and Hilary did the same, and looked down at the girls with a grin. 'Aren't we a mess? But I haven't seen your Mommy in a long, long time . . .'

'Why?' It was all a little confusing for the girls, and Alexandra sat down with Axelle on her lap as she looked from her to Marie-Louise to Hilary and her mother.

'A lot of very sad things happened to us a long time ago, and we never saw each other again after I was five years old, just a little younger than Axelle. And Hilary grew up in a lot of very sad places. And we missed each other very much, and we just couldn't get together till now.'

'Oh,' Axelle said, as though it all made sense to her now, and Marie-Louise nodded. And then Axelle added something important of her own. 'We went to the Bronx Zoo yesterday, and then we saw the Rockettes at Radio City Music Hall!' And everyone laughed, as Margaret ordered champagne for all of them. And when Alexandra put the girls to bed, Margaret told Hilary quietly how relieved she was that the meeting had gone well for them. She admitted that she had been very worried.

'Alexandra loves you very much.' Hilary comforted her, surprised by how much she liked her. She was a woman with warmth and courage and style, and a wonderful sense of humour. 'She told us all about you and her father. Nothing will ever change what she feels for you, and what you did for her. In her heart, you will always be her parents.'

Tears rolled down Margaret's cheeks at the words, and she patted Hilary's hand gratefully and then asked her a question. 'And Henri? Did she mention him?' Hilary nodded. 'He hasn't called since we left. He took all of this very badly. It was a great shock to him, and I think she was wrong to have told him.'

'She wants to be accepted as she is, I think. That's very important to her. And I can't disagree. He'll have to adjust. Just as we have.' She sounded matter-of-fact.

Margaret smiled ruefully at her. 'You don't know her husband.'

'What's all this about?' Alexandra had just come back from putting the girls to bed, in spite of their protests that they wanted to stay up with their aunt, but she had promised them that they would see her the next day. 'The girls want to have lunch with you tomorrow, by the way. Are you free?'

'For you? Hell, yes!' Hilary grinned. She could hardly wait to show the girls around the network, take them out to lunch, and to '21' for dinner. She was suddenly an aunt, and amazed at how much she liked it.

They made their plans for the following day, and Margaret smiled as she listened to them, and kissed Hilary as she would her own daughter when she left. And then she looked deep into Alexandra's eyes.

'You're happier, aren't you, sweetheart?'

Alexandra nodded. 'Yes, I am. It meant a lot to me to meet the two of them ... even more than I thought it would. I'm so glad we came.' She threw her arms around Margaret and held her tight. 'And I'm so glad you came with me.'

'So am I.' The older woman had to fight back tears again. They had all cried a lot in the past few days. And then Alexandra told her about Megan. 'What a shock for Mr Patterson.' She looked horrified.

'It was. I thought it might kill him. Megan's staying with him for a few days. She doesn't think he'll live more than that.' It was sad to think about, but maybe Hilary was right. He had done what he had wanted to do, and now he could go in peace, holding the hand of his daughter.

Chapter 32

Their lunch with the girls the next day was great fun, and Margaret insisted on leaving them alone with the children. She said she had some errands to do on her own, and she wanted some time to herself, and Hilary and Alexandra had a marvellous time with the girls. After some major juggling, Hilary even managed to take the afternoon off, and they went to the park, and then to the Plaza for tea. And over the girls' heads, as they munched on *petits fours*, Hilary and Alexandra mused about what it would have been like if their parents hadn't died, and they had gone on living the good life in New York, living on Sutton Place, their father a star, and doing things like taking them to have tea at the Plaza.

'I guess we'll never know, will we, Axie? But this isn't so bad.' Hilary smiled as they strolled outside and crossed the street to the Pierre where Alexandra and the girls were staying. She had dinner with them that night, and when she went back to her apartment she was exhausted. She was not used to children, and as delightful as they were, they were much more tiring than a day at the office.

The phone was ringing when she got inside her front door and she was surprised to realize that it was John Chapman. Megan had called him an hour before. Arthur had died peacefully in his sleep, and the funeral was in two

381

days in Connecticut. Megan was staying for that and then going back to Kentucky.

'I thought you'd like to know. I'd be happy to drive you out.' She thought about it for a long moment and then shook her head in the quiet apartment.

'I don't think so, John. I don't think it's my place to be there.' Although she had a suspicion Alexandra would go, but that was different, because Alexandra herself was very different.

'Are you still angry?'

'Maybe not. I'm not sure yet. And in any case it's over now. I just don't think I need to be there.' It was honest in any case, and John was embarrassed at how grateful he was for a reason to call her, even this one.

'How was the weekend?'

'The happiest in my life. It was wonderful. I spent the whole afternoon with my nieces today. They're terrific, and so is Alexandra. So is Megan . . .' And then with embarrassment, 'Thank you for everything you did to bring us together, John.' She was much more grateful to him than to Arthur.

'Mr Patterson made it possible. All I did was find you.' . . . and think about you day and night . . . and worry about you and your sisters . . . and spend sleepless nights . . . 'I was wondering if . . . if you'd like to have lunch sometime? Like maybe later this week, after I get back from Connecticut . . .' He felt like a fifteen-year-old kid and he laughed. 'This probably sounds crazy, but I miss you . . .' His voice trailed off and what he had said had touched her. She seemed so open suddenly to tenderness and pain and other people's feelings. And she sensed something very powerful and warm coming from him, and it aroused a host of new feelings in her. The weekend had given her something she'd never had before, not in thirty years. Love. And she was like a flower that had just been watered.

'I used to worry about you a lot.' It was easier saying things to her on the phone than it would have been in person.

'Why?' She sounded surprised. 'You didn't even know me.'

'Yes, I did ... in a lot of ways ... I knew you better than most people know their own children.' And he told himself he was crazy for telling her those things, but suddenly he couldn't stop now. 'You must think I'm nuts.'

'Sort of.' She laughed. 'But nice nuts. Sounds like you take your job to heart.'

'Not always ... but this time ... When can I see you for lunch?' He felt more than ever like a schoolboy, but at her end she was smiling. 'Is Thursday all right?'

'Sounds fine.' And if it wasn't, she'd cancel anything else she had, maybe even Alexandra. 'You know where my office is.' They both laughed.

'I'll pick you up at twelve-fifteen. And if I'm late, just relax. Sometimes I have a hell of a time getting out of the office.' But unlike Sasha, she understood that only too well. She frequently had the same problem.

'Don't worry. We'll both be lucky if I'm not stuck in a meeting. I'll do my best to get free by twelve, even if that means firing fewer people.' She laughed and he smiled to himself as they hung up. He could hardly wait to see her.

Chapter 33

As Hilary had suspected she would, Alexandra had gone to Arthur's funeral, mainly to be with Megan. And afterwards, she and Megan and John had driven back to New York in the limousine, and that night the three sisters had dinner together for the last time. Megan was flying back to Kentucky at midnight. She met Margaret, and the girls, and they had another pleasant evening, although Megan was a little subdued. It had been a strange week for her, discovering a father that she had never known and then watching him die in her arms only a few days later. But the greatest gift of all was that of the two sisters he had left her.

They talked about the house Arthur had left them, and what they would do with it. The housekeeper was going to stay on until everything was settled, and Arthur had left ample funds to care for it, and the remains of his estate were to be divided between the three women. He had no other relatives of his own. And Alexandra wanted all three of them to plan on spending some time there the following summer.

'We could do it every year! Make it a tradition!' She smiled at them, and Megan grinned.

'Can I bring some of my hillbillies when I come?'

'Why not?' Hilary added with a mysterious look. She was looking forward to lunch with John Chapman the next day, but she hadn't said anything to either of her sisters. It was a little embarrassing, and she was afraid they would suspect how much she liked him.

They drove Megan to the airport at eleven o'clock, and then Hilary and Alexandra drove back to town together. Hilary dropped her younger sister off at the hotel, and then went home. They were both exhausted. It had been an emotional week for all of them. And Alexandra was looking forward to her bed and an early evening.

The lights in her room were on. The door was closed, and Margaret had apparently gone to bed, but Alexandra could hear someone stirring in her room as she stood outside the door, and then someone pulled it open, and she found herself staring at her husband. He had just arrived a little while before. And Margaret had wisely retired, after greeting him. He offered no explanation as to why he had come, and acted almost as though his visit had been planned and he was expected.

'Henri?' Alexandra stared at him as though she'd seen a ghost.

'You were expecting someone else?' But this time it was not an accusation. He was smiling at her, and she stared at him in amazement. 'I certainly hope not. The children are well?'

'Very, thank you. We've had a lovely time.'

'So your mother told me. I saw her when I arrived.'

And then Alexandra could not stand the charade any longer. Why had he come? Why was he there? What threat was he going to make now? But it was odd, she was not nearly as frightened of him as she had been before. She stood eyeing him curiously from across the room, as he sat down and sipped a glass of champagne he had ordered while he waited for her. 'Would you care for some?' He was very nonchalant as he held out his glass to her, and Alexandra could not understand it.

'No, thank you. Henri, why did you come here?' she said coolly.

'I came to see you . . . and the children . . .' He spoke cautiously as though he wasn't quite sure what to say. 'I thought we needed to talk.' He looked at her with troubled eyes.

'You could have called me.' Her eyes were cold but she was protecting herself from the pain she knew he could cause her.

'Would you have preferred that?' He looked so sad, it tore at her heart, even though she was resisting the impulse to reach out to him. She was still afraid of possible rejection. Maybe he had come to tell her he was going to divorce her. And she wanted to know now.

'I just don't understand why you came here.'

He stood up and set down his glass, and then slowly walked toward her. 'To see you, *ma chérie*. Difficult as it may be to believe sometimes, I love you very much . . . no matter who you are . . .' He added carefully, '. . . Or who you've become.' He smiled almost shyly at her. 'I see you're a redhead again. It's not quite as loud as I remembered it.' He was watching her, looking into her eyes for something he hoped was still there, if he hadn't broken it this time forever. 'It was a great shock to me when you told me about . . . about your family. I think it might have been for anyone . . . and I can't come here now and tell you I've reformed, that I won't be demanding any more, that I'll stop dragging you to the Elysée for dinner . . . but I accept who you are . . . if you will accept who I am . . .' There were tears in his eyes as Alexandra looked up at him in astonishment. This was the man she thought hated her . . . and here he was, telling her he loved her. 'I love you very much. And I want you to come home . . . in a few days . . . and if you'd like, I will stay with you here . . .' He pulled her firmly into his arms and she knew with total certainty that he would never change, but he had come to her with open arms and she owed him a great deal for that. She owed him her life. And she turned her lips up to his with a gentle smile as he laughed softly.

'You know, I love your hair . . .' He ran his hands through the silky strands of red and they both laughed. Maybe things had changed just enough . . . perhaps . . . and if not, she had lived with him for fourteen years . . . for better or worse . . . and she had no intention of doing anything different for the rest of it.

He pushed the door closed and took his wife in his arms with a smile of expectation and pleasure. He was glad he had made the trip and as he felt her gentle hands on him, he was even more so.

Chapter 34

Their last night in New York was happy and sad and emotional. They had dinner at the Côte Basque, and Henri and Alexandra brought the girls, Margaret came, at Alexandra's insistence, and Hilary had said something about bringing a friend, which Alexandra thought was a little unusual, but she didn't dare question her sister. But she was secretly thrilled when the friend turned out to be John Chapman. She had always liked him, and she could tell Henri approved of John, looking very handsome in a dark suit, with his quiet ways, and obvious intelligence and good breeding. The group got on famously. Margaret entertained them all and Henri even let the girls drink champagne at dinner. It was a perfect culmination of the trip, and everyone hugged and kissed goodnight as though they might never see each other again. Although Hilary and John had insisted on coming to the airport the next day when the others left for Paris.

It was a classic scene with Axelle carrying an enormous doll under each arm and Marie-Louise clutching her new magic kit, from her Aunt Hilary of course. Alexandra's trophies from Bergdorf and Bendel's seemed virtually limitless, and Margaret's stack of Louis Vuitton seemed to have grown considerably in a mere ten days as Henri attempted to keep track of it all, hold the tickets, and rescue the passports from Axelle's busy little hands. And meanwhile Hilary and Alexandra were talk-ing a mile a minute, promising to meet again as soon as possible. Hilary was thinking of spending Christmas with them in Saint Moritz, unless Megan came to New York, in which case she'd come in the spring instead, but in spite of all the words and the frantic talk, the final moment came anyway. Margaret shepherded the girls on to the plane, waving at Hilary every inch of the way, and Henri left the two women alone, standing apart from his wife, chatting with John, and suddenly Hilary looked into her sister's eyes and began to cry as she reached out to her.

'Axie, I can't leave you again . . .' She choked on the words, and Alexandra held her tight.

'I know . . . promise me you'll be all right.' They were crying again, and Hilary thought she would never let go this time. It was too much like the past, the red curls in her arms, the little girl she had loved. '. . . Axie . . . I love you . . . Axie, I . . .' The echoes of the past rang out in her ears as Alexandra held her tight. 'I'll see you soon and I'll call you all the time from Paris.' Henri was beckoning her towards the plane and she knew she had to go. They would be closing the door in a moment, but she couldn't let her go, couldn't leave her alone. And then John walked quietly up to them, and gently took Hilary from her, holding her in his powerful arms as she stood there with tears streaming down her cheeks.

'Have a good trip, Alexandra. We'll see you soon,' John said in his quiet voice. Alexandra slowly pulled away, her eyes blinded by tears as she looked at Hilary, her eyes huge, her face deathly pale, as John quietly held her. Alexandra waved for a last time with a tearful smile, and as Hilary stared after her and whispered the familiar words, 'Goodbye, Axie,' she waved and then smiled slowly through her own tears and Alexandra disappeared into the plane with her husband.

'It's all right, sweetheart . . .' John whispered to Hilary as he held her tight, and suddenly for the first time in her life, she felt safe. She looked up at him, and he smiled. 'It's all right, Hillie . . .' He held her tightly in his arms and she knew that he was telling the truth. 'Everything's going to be all right now.'